Kay Stephens was b[...]
She spent the first [...]ing life as
a librarian, and since then has written several short
stories and novels, including *West Riding*, *North
Riding*, *Pennine Vintage* and *Stones of Calder Dale*,
all set in the Yorkshire she knows so well.

The Soaring Fells

Kay Stephens

HEADLINE

First published in 1992
by Random Century Group

First published in paperback in 1993
by HEADLINE BOOK PUBLISHING PLC

10 9 8 7 6 5 4 3 2 1

ISBN 0 7472 4042 6

Printed and bound in Great Britain by
HarperCollins Manufacturing, Glasgow

HEADLINE BOOK PUBLISHING PLC
Headline House
79 Great Titchfield Street
London W1P 7FN

In memory of Helen Macgregor

1

Lashing rain was increasing the gloom of blacked-out London roads. Almost too late, Irene noticed the driver ahead braking at level-crossing gates. Stopping an inch from his bumper, she shuddered, realizing how narrowly she'd escaped an impact. The threat to her safety created an instinctive flutter inside her which gradually steadied. Grimly, she recognized how little surviving mattered.

The ceaseless downpour had sealed petrol fumes in the suburban streets, aggravating the constriction gripping her chest. She switched off the engine. It was thrusting out more pollution, intensifying the pounding in her head.

The train was approaching, a rhythmic pulsing, another echo of the throbbing in her skull. 'You don't belong, you don't belong, you don't belong,' its wheels taunted. She raised both hands to cover her ears; still the taunt persisted. She swallowed, hard.

Carriages, their windows darkened for the war, slowed towards the platform. People prepared to alight, their faces peered through the night, staring faces . . . staring straight at her. They couldn't − surely, they couldn't all *know*?

Irene closed her eyes and breathed deeply, time and again, battling for self-control. She mustn't start weeping here.

Two sharp blasts of a car horn, right behind her, jolted her back to awareness and made her reach for the ignition. When had the barrier moved, when had that car in front driven off into the void unrelieved by street lighting? Why wasn't it darker still − to preclude the curious looks of all these other drivers reflected in her mirror? Desperate to avoid being trapped, she hurtled forward, her wheels thudding across the tracks. 'You're useless now, useless now, useless . . . '

Irene drove on, heedlessly, uncaring. She didn't know where she was going. Away from here somewhere, away from London, away from today.

The day that John had left she'd believed nothing could be worse. She couldn't bear to dwell on it, but clawing through her subconscious came the memory of the agony that dreadful morning; the breakfast they could not eat, the goodbye neither of them would say . . . And then watching him, broad-shouldered, his fair hair stirred by the breeze, as he walked away down the road strewn with debris from a recent flying bomb.

And yet, somehow, she had survived, with an effort of will that had taken her round to unlock the surgery, and then had compelled her to sit behind her desk, glaring at its tooled-leather top to keep back the tears. Inexorably, patients had filed in from her crowded waiting room, offering their pains, their tragedies and losses. And she had been thankful, then and in the unreal days that followed. Resolutely, she had examined, prescribed, listened – had been needed . . .

Today, she had listened again, wretched and struggling not to be soured, while her life was taken just as surely as if Hitler's air raids extinguished her. No one had recognized the love that she and John had shared. Nor had they cared that she was devastated – too utterly wrecked to return to her North London home, or to her surgery.

It was totally dark now. Out beyond the rows of houses and shops, where even the bomb damage was more sparse, she was isolated in the thin glow from shrouded headlamps slanting through heavy rain. The road was vaguely familiar, if she had tried she'd have remembered where it led. There'd been a signpost once, before they were removed, had it said St Albans? It didn't matter. There was a wall somewhere, a long, high wall that encircled a country estate long since commandeered for some ministry.

John had gone to the country, but miles away from London, wangling a transfer to another Boots branch needing a dispenser. A branch close to his wife's Land

2

Army work. It was best, he had decided, would give him and Vera a fresh start, well away from all that had happened, away from *her*. He'd even made it sound as though he were being fairest to Irene herself, leaving her free to continue with the practice. Only now there'd be no continuing.

It wasn't that she had thought being struck off couldn't happen, perhaps rather that it wouldn't, to her. There seemed now no possible reasoning to account for the supposition that her career would be safe. And yet, until today, she had believed that the worst she would receive would be a reprimand.

Doctors were needed so desperately, to patch up men for returning to the front, to bolster and repair civilians needed to work on munitions or in other vital industries.

Irene shuddered, shocked, feeling dreadfully alone. The very need to get away from everyone and everything reminding her had produced the solitude fast growing unendurable.

Briefly, the doctor who had watched others for signs of breakdown saw the snagging nerves, the overstretched senses. 'Stop thinking,' she murmured between taut lips, 'you know you can. Concentrate on driving.'

Faster, she sped, tyres swishing over the puddled road, steering unresponsive as she cornered abruptly. No need for fuel economy now, with no work ahead, no use for her neat little car. Being careless of her own safety generated a strange freedom; momentarily, she revelled in the thrum of the engine, the thrust, the power beneath her pedals and in the wheel held in long-fingered hands.

A surgeon's hands, someone had said, in thirty-nine as she finished training. Once, she'd thought of devoting them to that, after a time in general practice. *Once*.

Stop thinking. She swallowed, tasted the salt of tears which, so far, were contained. Stop thinking – if only there was some way . . . some kind of a wall to keep out thought.

Over Central London sirens wailed, distant aircraft droned, Irene felt curiously detached. Everything was dead to her.

The windscreen wipers, worn like everything else, were failing to clear the screen. Or was it tears, had she finally weakened? She could hardly see. And the road appeared to end, suddenly, beyond the range of dim headlights. Irene stamped on her brake pedal, and remembered. This was the estate she'd passed before; the road snaked for some distance around its perimeter. She was going far too quickly for the bends.

Instinctively, she changed gear, clumsily, neglecting to double declutch, then kept her speed down, meandering with the road. Constructing the boundary of this place, the owner must have followed the line of existing fields, creating a zigzag wall and a road obliged to parallel its course. Or was the road made before the wall? Which had come first?

Thinking, for even a few seconds, about something else was a relief but required enormous effort. Better not to think at all. But how not to? And how not to feel . . . especially so *alone*?

The road continued on for a quarter of a mile, then turned acutely, with the high wall. Irene pictured the wall before she reached the turning, knew precisely where it was.

Down went her foot on the accelerator, harder, harder, faster, faster. It's all right, no one's coming. No one will. She closed her eyes. Instinctively, she bent her head.

With the terrifying impact, metal scrunched, rain-borne shards of glass scattered over her, a tree branch tore at her ear. The steering wheel rammed into her, savagely, went on ramming, until everything was obliterated.

'She's conscious, at last . . . ' The dark-skinned man wearing a white coat spoke, then nodded to a nurse.

Conscious? So she hadn't . . . ? Oh, God!

The group split into twos and threes, moving away, except for the fair-haired nurse who came towards her. As she felt fingers on her pulse, Irene inhaled deeply, trying to clear her head; she must catch what they were saying. They were almost out of earshot now, somewhere beyond the curtains closed around the bed. Irene forced her attention towards the murmur continuing out in the ward.

'... lucky to be alive. She was going too fast, suicidal ...' His tone told her what the situation was. They didn't suspect – not for one moment did they suspect it had been a real suicide attempt.

How readily she might pretend . . . that the car had skidded. That she *hadn't* ached for oblivion.

Irene sighed. She could only blame herself. She ought to have known better. She shouldn't have risked a means that she could so easily bungle. The cool, calm, medical practitioner who, aeons ago, had been Dr Irene Hainsworth should have thought it through, in the quiet of her surgery, and used one of the irreversible methods available there.

How despair had changed her, already. The emptiness when John left had been harrowing, but now . . . She seemed unable to work anything out coherently. She'd lost all that good Yorkshire practicality. Nothing made sense, there wasn't one single thing to interest her, no one to care for. No reason to think ahead, to plan, to prepare.

Enduring the horrendous exhaustion of the blitz had been wasted effort. All the years of studying, standing through an interminable succession of operations, taking examinations, had been for five short years. Five years, that was all, then it had been tossed away. No – *given*.

'Comfy, dear?' The nurse jerked her back to reality; a reality she was sure she could never face.

Irene nodded, whispered her thanks – may as well pretend. If only they would leave her alone.

But was that what she wanted? She'd tried despairingly to escape being isolated.

Irene hadn't managed to clarify her thoughts by morning when Martin Fyson walked in, his brown eyes concerned, his face pale above the clerical collar. She braced herself for the lecture, then remembered that no one knew the truth, yet.

Martin sat on the edge of the bed, cleared his throat. 'I'm so sorry . . . it was a dreadful accident, Irene.'

5

She frowned, then confronted his clear eyes. The awkwardness in her own gaze must have told him.

'You skidded, Irene, and hit that wretched tree,' he prompted hastily, willing her not to contradict.

Wordlessly, she shook her head. She took a deep breath. 'No, Martin. The tree got in the way. I hadn't seen it. I was driving straight at the wall.'

For too long he did not speak. Slowly, his brown eyes sought her face. 'I'm sorry,' he repeated. 'You were going through hell . . . we, *I* should have prevented this.'

Her smile was twisted. 'What? My surviving?'

It was Martin's turn to frown. And hitting out at him had been unjustified, cheap. Irene apologized. 'No one could have helped.'

'Not even . . . ?'

'Least of all the Church. You forget what I'd done – "thou shalt not . . . " And I had.'

'The war's put too much pressure on lots of people, creating too many situations where they're in desperate need, sometimes just for one other person. And we exist for those who're sorry.'

'But I'm not, Martin. I love John – I can't regret anything that happened between us.'

'Even . . . '

'Even now.'

He sighed. 'If only . . . ' he began, and paused.

Irene raised an eyebrow. 'If only what? If I hadn't made the mistake of sleeping with a patient – one who belonged to someone else? Or if only he and I hadn't been found out? Or – or if only I hadn't been struck off.' The lump in her throat overcame words. She closed her eyes.

She sensed Martin shaking his head. 'If only I knew what to say!' He was smiling ruefully when she looked at him.

Despite the ache in her throat, she smiled back, just a little. It was so like him, trying to be worldly, often seeming rather out of his depth. Martin was best at practical goodness: hauling the injured out of the rubble that yesterday was a home, tending old folk who'd lost everyone, shielding youngsters bereaved of their mum.

6

Maybe he'd understand she needed him more as a friend than to represent a Church that rarely seemed sufficiently relevant, for her.

'How on earth did you learn I was here?'

'Finding no one in your home, the police came to me.'

She nodded, gnawed her lip. 'Have you heard from . . . ?' It was the one question she'd been keeping firmly withheld for endless days. Had all self-discipline been drained along with her strength?

'From John and Vera?' He shook his head. And they would be okay; well away from London, together.

Irene wished he hadn't emphasized 'and Vera', but it was inevitable. Martin, who tied matrimonial knots, couldn't be expected to sympathize entirely with entanglements. Was that all it seemed to everyone else – their brief spell of genuine happiness? A sordid entanglement.

She sighed. It didn't matter. It was all irrelevant now; even John's 'Nobody's ever made me this happy' must be forgotten. It belonged to a different life. A life with a future which, even when she'd believed it would be endured alone, would have had some purpose.

'What will you do?' Martin's anxiety prevented her shrugging aside the question. 'I do care, you know,' he continued when she didn't reply. 'Two dear friends . . . ' She looked surprised and he nodded. 'Yes – friends, not just parishioners, have reached a crisis. Have made decisions, difficult ones. You've had decisions made for you – even more difficult.'

He did understand. Warmth, fragile as a candle flame, touched the ice compacted within her chest. By coming here, caring, Martin had become far more than the helpful neighbour he'd always seemed. Was his the hand that might haul her out of her personal blitz?

'I'm appalled, Irene, more than I can say, that they took such a hard line.'

'I knew the rules, I must accept the consequences – now it seems I'm not to evade them.' She sounded far more ready to combat it than she felt. And she might have

7

believed she would have sacrificed everything for John, but she hadn't known then how massive this loss would feel.

Martin didn't comment. If he had it might have stopped her thinking. 'God, what a bloody mess!'

He let her weep; when she eventually ceased, he was still sitting there. Irene reached towards the locker and he forestalled her with a crisp white handkerchief.

'Here.' Then he added, disarmingly frank: 'About all I can offer. I can't see clearly enough to advise, not yet. Only read their decision last night, in the paper.'

With the rest of London, Irene thought. Homeward bound in trains like the one she'd seen, in the Underground, sitting by firesides smoky with the nutty slack that masqueraded as coal. They'd all have read it. NORTH LONDON DOCTOR . . . She imagined the headline. Had her father, himself a doctor, seen it?

'Was it in the nationals as well?'

'Haven't opened mine yet today.' There never seemed enough time, these days. So many of his people were being ground by sheer exhaustion into the ruins of their parish. His only prayer now was that they'd endure that bit longer. Earlier in this March of 1945 Cologne had fallen to the Allies. The other day Montgomery's carefully prepared crossing of the Rhine had proved successful.

Irene had withdrawn into her own distress. It was a fact – the notoriety which she'd been unable to face. And a hundred times worse now she had failed to escape both that and a pointless future.

'Will – will this get in the papers too?'

'That you had a motor accident?'

Irene stared at his collar. 'You should stick to the truth.'

'Are *you* sure what the truth is?'

'I'd braked once, Martin, when I almost ran out of road. This was a calculated attempt at . . .'

' . . . Making someone notice you need help? You're a doctor, Irene – if you'd meant it to be final, you had the means.'

'I wish I could believe you.'

Martin went away shortly afterwards, but came again – and again. He was the one person who didn't criticize or condemn.

'It's made me think,' he confided, when she was over the effects of concussion and her abrasions were healing, 'a doctor forbidden to practise . . . That's how I would feel if I wasn't allowed to continue as a vicar.'

Irene wished fervently that everyone would try to relate like that. She'd anticipated the hospital's scant sympathy with a suicide attempt, especially when casualties of the war were justifiably taking so much of their time. But when the fact that the car crash had *not* been accidental didn't come to light, there'd been no feeling of relief. The news of her being struck off had circulated, and she'd felt that she had destroyed all respect from her old colleagues. And she dreaded the visits of friends, the embarrassment, perhaps even disgust in their guarded eyes.

No one seemed to recognize any injustice in there remaining certain professions which – even during today's stresses – demanded an impeccable image.

She was becoming adept at sidestepping discussion of arrangements beyond her discharge date. But that day came, and she was collected in Martin Fyson's aged Austin Seven.

'I've got to get away,' Irene said, despite all her determination, as she led the way indoors. No matter how positive she'd been that she wouldn't weaken until she was alone, she couldn't prevent the words rushing off her tongue.

Martin set down her suitcase and turned, frowning. 'You've only just come home . . . ' She'd have asserted that anyone else must be allowed time to adjust, why was she so harsh on herself?

Irene sighed. Giving up this place would tear out her heart. Her control was yet again on the verge of snapping. Abruptly, she escaped to the kitchen. It didn't help. Everything looked so nice – and sane, ordinary. She could not believe that she wouldn't be getting up early in the morning, going round to the surgery. She loved her work;

9

even being on call one hundred and twenty hours a week seemed a fair price. She clutched the edge of the gas cooker, swallowing again and again.

When Irene gathered sufficient composure to return to Martin he was holding out a glass. '*My* prescription.'

'Have one yourself.'

He poured whisky, then crossed to the sofa. Irene removed her coat and sat in the fireside chair. She sipped her drink. Martin seemed pensive.

'If you're serious about getting away, there's something you could try . . . '

She was too dispirited to even pretend to enthuse. 'Go on . . . '

'It needn't be permanent, you wouldn't have to decide about this place yet.'

Irene checked her gaze before it travelled completely around the room. 'How far away is it?' Until the question was out, she hadn't understood how desperately that mattered.

He smiled slightly. 'Far enough, I think – near Skipton.'

She stilled her tongue just before she blurted out, 'But that's Yorkshire!' Skipton certainly was far enough away for there to be little interest in news of this trouble, but was it far enough from her own roots? She sensed Martin's keen brown eyes noting her hesitance, and couldn't for the life of her recall how much he knew of her background. Suddenly, though, her mind's eye sketched in the market town with its castle and the surrounding Dales. And all she experienced was a massive longing for the freedom which would feel all the wider for good fresh country air.

'Couldn't be better,' she told him at last.

His smile faded. 'Surely you want to know what kind of work . . . ?' It was so unlike her to be this uninterested. He'd seen people face loss before, but had never been so moved by their despair. If he'd been a demonstrative man, he'd have put an arm round her. Unhappily, he was not.

Irene gave a tiny shrug, and he smiled again, encouragingly. 'Could be more interesting than you think – it'd use your knowledge of medicine.'

'I'm not permitted,' she said very quickly. He couldn't have forgotten? 'You know that's . . .'

'Only unofficially,' he interrupted swiftly. 'But it might be better than . . .'

' . . . Nothing?' Irene finished for him. 'Fire away, I'll listen.'

Martin settled more comfortably on the sofa and was thankful when she sank back into her armchair again.

'I heard about Richard Hughes through a friend who's his family doctor. It's not a pretty story. A solicitor, attractive, quick-witted with a wide range of interests, he was forty when he suffered a stroke. He's almost completely paralysed, unable to speak.'

'What a sentence!'

Martin nodded gravely. 'I imagine he must have felt very much as you have, Irene – that there's no future. So far as I know, he's never tried . . .' He checked, cursing himself for being tactless.

' . . . the easy way out?'

He frowned again, but made no comment. Irene might be no more than a neighbour who also had become a friend, but he knew her well enough to understand that if she *had* opted for suicide the decision would have been as difficult as choosing to survive.

'What Richard needs most of all, initially, is somebody there constantly, a sort of – companion. He can pay well.'

'As if that mattered.'

'You still need to eat.' And surely this would be preferable to wasting her expertise by going into some munitions factory?

'Suppose you're right – haven't really thought.' Irene weighed the proposition. It wasn't only the need to remain unidentified, undiscovered now; there were deeper anxieties. Raising a fair eyebrow, she challenged his very direct eyes. 'Aren't you taking a risk suggesting me? In no time at all we'd have a suicide pact.'

'Would you?' Martin's gaze, steadily holding her own, confirmed that he knew the answer long before she shook her head.

11

Irene smiled slightly. 'Thanks. I need somebody to have confidence in me again. And in an odd kind of way crashing the car brought me to my senses. If I am to live, I'd like to be useful.'

'It sounds depressing, I know . . .'

'What's the medical prognosis?'

'According to Giles, hopeful – given time, patience, and persistence.'

Irene still felt doubtful, especially about her ability to cope. Draining her glass, she looked at him again.

'Martin, be honest with me – do you think I'm the right person?'

'You're a compassionate woman, Irene.'

Her own laugh sounded strange. 'A great many patients wouldn't agree. "A hard-faced so-and-so" would be their verdict.'

'Some people need firm handling.'

'And is Richard Hughes in that category?'

'I've no idea. Up to you to find out.'

'If I decide to go, he'll get tough treatment. Frankly, I don't feel fit for human company.'

'But you'll think about it?'

She could scarcely avoid doing so, now. 'At least it's miles away.' From *here*, if not from confrontations which she wished to avoid. 'Need he know – about me?'

Less than a week later, Irene was in the train, watching the countryside, but through a haze because she was so pensive. She still was not really sure why she was taking the job, or even if she'd be permitted to remain should she be able to settle. Since the early stages of this conflict with Germany and the Axis powers, being a doctor in London had rendered her exempt from direction of labour. Now she was becoming a sort of companion, she suspected some official somewhere might have other plans for her.

Reminding herself that all she wanted was to be of use, she resolved she would not let that matter if it should arise. All she was doing now was severing all connections with the past. She had been very thorough. Martin alone knew where she was going. She had let the house for a month with a possible extension of the lease, to a family who had lost their home in the last severe bombing of the capital. The car had been a write-off and, in any case, even to herself she'd be unable to justify using petrol now.

In a way, she relished this freedom from possessions and glanced up approvingly at her one suitcase on the rack. The train was unheated, of course, but crammed with the customary assortment of uniformed men and women and a disturbing number of wounded. And although the obligatory March wind swept across ploughed fields as they passed, to sway the skeletal trees surrounding them, the sun blazed through the glass beside her head. At any other time this would have been soporific, but her mind was far too active. There'd been so much needing attention before leaving London that she'd hardly studied the significance of what she was tackling. And she knew little more about Richard Hughes than Martin had told her. The man's sister had telephoned, pleased that Irene would be joining them, but that was all.

Irene changed trains. As the hills and grey industrial towns began forcing her to acknowledge they were travelling deeper into her native Yorkshire, she felt she was nearing her objective long before she was ready.

God, help me to cope. Let it be better than I expect, I can't take too much gloom. Almost a prayer, it surprised her. Although she attended church, she'd never considered herself religious since leaving her parents' home in Halifax. In recent years churchgoing had been, in a way, an extension of the job – the 'right' thing for the local doctor. Reflecting, that seemed like hypocrisy. But it had drawn her closer into her community. She supposed constant brushings with the realities of life and death had subtracted the awe from them – and the wonder. And since coming round in hospital she hadn't permitted herself to analyse the ethical, much less religious, implications of trying to kill herself.

Grimly, Irene smiled. Richard Hughes wasn't getting much in the deal to acquire company. The more she

13

contemplated the person she'd become, the less she liked that person. Despite feeling warm, she drew her coat around her. She felt very alone again. Being robbed of her work had destroyed all faith in herself. *Hope to goodness I get it back . . .* She supposed that was another prayer.

The train was lurching along, stopping at a succession of familiar stations. They were into the heart of the West Riding. Tall forbidding mills, rows of blackened back -to-back houses, and the occasional glimpse of a glinting canal all combined to induce a strange conflict of emotions. She could so easily get off at the next station and take the bus over the green of the distant hills and visit her own folk. Even as the compulsion rose through her, though, she knew she'd not bring herself to face them.

As they chugged along the last stretch of line towards Skipton, Irene took out her mirror. Even with the windows closed, smuts from the engine always permeated, and she'd no desire to arrive looking a mess. Carefully she renewed the lipstick which she'd hoarded for special occasions, then tidied her silver-fair hair. She wore it long, but swept up on to the top of her head in the style she'd modified only slightly since 1939. Although practical, it seemed to reveal too much of her face. But at least every last cut and bruise had disappeared, and she was thankful. She had enough inhibitions at present, without trying to field questions about damaged features.

The blue eyes gazing back so solemnly were cold and lacklustre. In a patient she would have diagnosed trouble – exhaustion, anxiety or excess tension. Maybe the flying bombs terrorizing London would seem a likely explanation of her condition.

They'd run out of the sunlight amid the industrial towns of the West Riding. When Irene stepped on to the platform at Skipton it had begun snowing; flurries of flakes, settling on her blonde eyelashes and on the fur of her collar, an old bit of fox donated by a grateful patient. Smiling rather ruefully, she looked around for the man who'd arranged to meet her.

Tall, middle-aged, stooping slightly, he hurried forward as Irene handed in her ticket at the barrier. 'Miss Hainsworth?' he inquired, raising his grey trilby hat.

Irene flinched; would losing her profession always hurt this much?

She nodded, made her smile more agreeable. 'That's right.'

'Giles Holroyd.' His grasp was firm, reassuring. Irene flicked an assessing glance towards his calm features and steady grey eyes.

'Richard's looking forward to meeting you.'

This coloured her attitude, was probably intended to. 'The case' became a person before she even met him.

An immediate rapport between Irene and this quietly spoken doctor eased the first few minutes of their acquaintance, and made her feel that she needn't necessarily fear that losing her right to practise medicine automatically denied her the joy of having colleagues.

They drove out of Skipton along the road which she was fairly sure headed towards Gargrave and eventually Settle. Once they were past the last straggle of houses, her companion turned off up a steep country road, little more than a lane, with hills to all sides of them. Irene had always felt her entire person lifting whenever she returned to the Yorkshire skyline of moors that nudged each other for miles as they radiated from meadows and the woodland embracing towns.

Giles Holroyd soon make it plain that he considered her a vital link in the chain, instrumental in restoring his patient's health. Though she didn't know it, the hope venturing inside her wasn't only for Richard Hughes. To this doctor alone had Martin revealed her recent background, and evidently he chose not to dwell on it. Irene gave a sigh of relief, began breathing more easily. Maybe it wouldn't hurt either to have one person who understood.

Dr Holroyd laughed when, rather awkwardly, she asked if Richard Hughes knew anything about her. 'He has little patience with the medical profession, just as well you decided to keep it dark!'

Irene managed a smile. They had stopped for a herd of cows being driven along the narrow lane, their udders heavy with the urgency of another milking. Giles glanced sideways at her.

'Wait till you see his attitude to me. Expert supervision, without the attendant irritations – what could be better?'

And then he outlined the extent of his patient's incapacity. Evidently, his only means of communication was a nod, or a slight shake of the head, and by the sound of it he wasn't particularly interested in maintaining that.

Irene frowned. 'How on earth does he occupy the time?'

'He doesn't, just lies there, staring into space, sleeping – or feigning sleep.'

'Not exactly promising.'

'That's why you're here.'

She smiled ruefully. 'Or as an escape?'

'If that was all, you'd have chosen something more congenial.'

'Because I've nothing to lose then? Literally nothing.' Was it because this doctor was so likeable that she needed to be totally honest with him; or to prepare him for accepting less than her utmost? When he remained unperturbed Irene's confidence received another boost.

Once they were past the dairy farm and climbing again the last flurry of snow ceased and the sun emerged briefly to glint on distant white-clad fells. Patches of snow had gathered beside drystone walls which were paler here, of limestone which spattered the slopes among their tough Yorkshire sheep. And now Giles Holroyd slowed the car to negotiate the curving drive of a large stone house before turning to her again.

'In that case, let's hope you both have the sense to make something out of nothing,' he retorted, with a grin that crinkled the lightly tanned skin around his grey eyes.

Irene felt startled, yet couldn't resent his response to her earlier remarks. And he was parking near the front door now, which already was opening.

Daphne Hughes welcomed them into an exquisite hall, its pale green walls contrasting with dark woodwork, and

16

a beautifully kept parquet floor. Dr Holroyd made the necessary introductions, and the slender, attractive woman smiled, then took Irene's coat.

She looked younger than Irene had expected, roughly her own age, thirty-two. Or was that merely the effect of living in such glorious surroundings, far removed from potent reminders of the war ravaging the rest of Europe? Sleek dark hair framed an oval face, and her eyes were sensational – green, with very long black lashes. Irene wondered why such a lovely young woman was tied to her brother. His illness was quite recent, so couldn't have precluded marriage and having her own home. It could, of course, have resulted in Daphne's withdrawing from war work.

While she was thinking about Miss Hughes, Irene sensed that she herself was undergoing guarded scrutiny. And she didn't like the narrowing of green eyes which suggested aversion. Had she come up against one of these tiresome people who imagined no one was good enough to cope with their relative?

She wasn't allowed the time to even guess at the reason behind the woman's disturbing glance, nor to prepare herself for the next encounter. Daphne Hughes crossed rapidly towards a door near the foot of the stairs, gave a perfunctory knock, and led the way inside. Irene scarcely noticed furnishings that continued the good taste of the hall.

'Here they are, Rich.'

Irene's gaze followed hers. She swallowed down a dismayed gasp. She had believed her training and five years in general practice had inured her to incapacity. She'd never felt physical pain when confronted with it, but here it was now – searing through her. He looked so young to have been stricken so cruelly.

2

Irene caught her breath, stammered 'How do you do?' or something equally inane, then forced herself to regain composure. Never let the patient see how depressing the prospect is, she silently reminded her wayward self. Maybe it didn't quite fit the situation, but it would serve while she found the necessary positive approach.

Immobility can have a certain grace, bordering on tranquillity – his spelled utter loss of hope. Richard Hughes seemed lifeless until, moving nearer, Irene was confronted by his brown eyes, very dark, full of sadness, alarm and resignation. His face was pale, the few lines etched by suffering, not age. The hands, inert on the bedspread, were long-fingered, an artist's. Remembering they were useless *hurt*. He was caught, as she herself had been, by unjust fate.

Irene was not really aware that Giles Holroyd was talking about her until she heard her own name. Mr Hughes gave a slight nod, his only acknowledgement of her. There was some conversation, Irene murmured the odd response, but she was preoccupied, trying to recall how she'd begun to emerge from a similar state. She was relieved when the doctor glanced at the clock and moved towards the door. But as she began following something checked her. She returned to the bed.

She recognized his feelings, must help to change them. 'I'll see you again this evening,' she said, quelling the urge to bolt. It made no difference, anyway, he didn't nod or smile – maybe he couldn't.

Irene panicked when Dr Holroyd headed immediately for the front door.

'Just a minute . . . ' She followed him out on to the icy steps. 'God, how awful!'

He sighed. 'Yes. Well, do what you can.' When he reached his car he glanced back. 'You see how he needs you.'

The sun had gone behind a cloud. Beyond the garden the steep-sided fells seemed suddenly to be walling her in with this massive dismay.

Daphne Hughes was waiting in the hall and showed Irene upstairs to her room. She was too upset to pay much attention to her surroundings and was aware only that it was bright, though not large, and overlooked the garden at the side of the house. The wind appeared to have carried the light snowfall across one of the paths which a man was clearing.

'Shaun O'Connor,' Richard's sister explained. 'His mother cleans here a few hours most days. Shaun's a writer, happy to supplement his income with odd jobs – and helping Richard bath and all that. He's set up a desk in one of our guest rooms so he can write, yet be around if Rich needs him.'

Irene wondered idly how O'Connor was avoiding conscription, but wasn't sufficiently concerned to inquire. She was more interested in the scope provided by the large garden here.

'Your brother can sit out there in summer,' she observed, nodding towards the lawn.

Daphne made a face. 'You don't know Richard!'

'But why ever not? It's quiet, seems secluded . . . '

The answer was a shrug. 'You're an optimist!'

'But you can't just give up because . . . '

Daphne Hughes had reached the door and turned, her green eyes blazing.

'You try it! I've coaxed, pleaded, shouted, nothing gets through to him.' She paused, swallowed. 'And it isn't that he doesn't understand. I *know* Rich, he simply does not care. Don't get on at me, please. Believe me, I have tried, but there are limits to anyone's persistence.'

'Sorry.'

Daphne gave a tired smile. 'Forget it. I'm just . . . ready for a break. I'll be thankful if he takes to you, then I can think of going out to work again.'

'What's your job?'

Again, Irene sensed some reservation building between them. Daphne contemplated her for a moment, frowning, then sighed. 'It's a long story. Any old job will serve, now.'

Irene wasn't sorry to be left with her thoughts. She had had only minutes with Richard Hughes, yet already felt she'd been trampled on. She had seen enough severe illness in the past, had treated disgustingly sickening complaints, but this was worse, far worse. She was emotionally involved, she cared – not as a doctor for a patient, but as one rather lost human being for another.

Irene hadn't joked, telling Martin Fyson what her patients had thought of her. She had been the expert, her task forcing them to observe her instructions, to the letter. She stood no nonsense, refused to mollycoddle; they knew and, in the main, accepted that. She had intended adopting similar tactics here. The man was uncooperative, reluctant to make the best of things . . .

She sighed, unpacked a few things and washed her hands and face. Looking in the mirror, she was startled. Even the contours of her face seemed to have softened, and her blue eyes were troubled. But there was an expression she hadn't seen in ages – tenderness. And this wasn't her – not as she needed to be now. Self-contained, composed, was how she planned it. She possessed a skill, that skill was healing. And that was all.

After that somewhat uneasy conversation with Daphne Hughes, Irene trod warily while they ate dinner together. She consequently learned nothing to help in coping with her new employer, and the two women established a cool neutrality. Irene was disappointed – she'd always set great store by the contribution of relatives in a person's recovery. But she had wanted more of Daphne than an ally, she'd unconsciously counted on her as a friend in a strange locality.

This might be a part of her home county, but North Fell House was still in an area that she hardly knew, and it felt vastly different from the West Riding mill town where she'd grown up.

Feeling that she'd failed to use their initial contact to any effect, she lingered after the meal, helping to clear the dishes into the kitchen. They were silently finishing off the washing-up together while she was trying to adopt the right frame of mind for another encounter with Richard when his sister spoke.

'Did you say you were looking in on Rich?'

'That's right.'

Daphne smiled. 'Good, that lets me out.'

When Irene eventually headed towards the door, Daphne detained her. 'He's not really as difficult as I make out. But it's been a strain.'

Irene nodded sympathetically. 'I'm sure it has.'

Crossing the lovely hall to his room, she took a deep breath. Knocking when he couldn't answer seemed pointless, but she did so nevertheless.

Shadows cast by the one dim light emphasized the weariness of his expression. Irene sat in the bedside chair; she was going to make herself comfortable and stick this out. Once and for all, she would conquer the urge to desert which had engulfed her the moment she saw him. She had been trained to help people in precisely this situation. No one must stop her using her knowledge.

She angled the chair so Richard Hughes could see her without turning his head, then began talking.

'I've no idea when you like to sleep, you must indicate if I'm disturbing you.'

He shook his head.

Irene smiled slightly. 'Too much time for sleeping anyway?'

Maybe her old intuition remained; it had aided many a diagnosis, she only hoped it would accelerate communication with her new employer. He was nodding agreement – promising. Two responses in as many minutes. And there had been no hesitation, which was far more encouraging than she had anticipated. From what she'd been told, she had believed he was suffering dysphasia, and unable to

21

fully comprehend what was being said. Now she wondered if it could be otherwise – his sister had stressed how readily he understood.

Seeking something to trigger some train of thought, she noticed shelf after shelf of books. 'Do you still read?'

He shook his head, then closed his eyes. But, again, he'd answered immediately.

'Too much of a strain, eh?'

Richard looked at her again, but gave no sign whether she was right or wrong. And this was something she would need to know. All too often, a stroke impaired the ability to make sense of the printed word.

'I'll read to you sometimes, if you like.'

He sighed and glanced away.

'Please yourself.' She wasn't grovelling for tasks. And she felt sure already that it wasn't that he would be unable to follow what was being read. His refusal to show interest was more alarming than any disability, and more tragic. But suddenly he turned towards her again.

Irene sat forward earnestly in the chair. 'I need an interest as well as you. I can't stand doing nothing. I'm here because I need something to keep me occupied.'

The first glimmer of curiosity showed in his dark eyes. Encouraged, she continued. 'My life was in rather a mess, so I chose a new beginning. Are you going to ensure that it's interesting?'

Richard appeared astounded. Irene was compelled to smile. He raised a dark eyebrow. How different he looked! If animation returned to his thin features, he'd be strikingly attractive.

'That's enough about me,' she said hastily, before he became *too* curious. Glancing again around the pleasant but heavily masculine room, she spotted a record player.

'Are you fond of music as well?' Her own fondness didn't extend beyond the occasional orchestral concert, but she'd welcome any alternative to this non-conversation.

Richard nodded.

'Do you often listen to records?'

He shook his head.

22

'Why ever not?'

Again, he sighed.

'You could, at least, try to make the best of things!'
This was more her, she thought ruefully, impatience. Then
she remembered the last few weeks; how hopelessness
makes anyone totally uninterested. And how feeling so
desperately alone seemed to diminish the ability, as well
as the desire, to respond to anybody. She swallowed,
hard. And then she leaned forward again, and touched his
arm.

Before she said anything he gazed at her hand as if it
shouldn't be there, but Irene didn't move it. She looked
him straight in the eyes.

'I know what you think – that it's all pointless. I'll show
you you're wrong.'

She changed the subject then, to surer ground. 'Can you
move at all?'

He lifted one hand a few inches above the cover and
let it drop. Irene took the hand. 'We'll make this more
use . . . '

Richard turned away his head, would have withdrawn
from her grasp if he'd been able. Anger soared inside her.
If he didn't want to make an effort . . .

She sat on the edge of the bed, raised a hand to his
face, and none too gently made him look at her. Immediately, she regretted it.

She had seen the expression before, when trying to
release a small dog caught in a trap. The hurt, the bewil-
derment, of being captive.

Miserably, Irene bit her lip. She had made an unfortunate beginning, and didn't know how to rectify that. In
the surgery, she'd have fallen back on detailing treatment,
restoring the balance, showing the patient who was in
authority. But in the surgery she'd never felt this depth
of compassion, welling up from the source of all feeling.
And she could no longer retreat to a professional standing.

Somehow, she managed an awkward smile. 'I haven't
made a very good start, have I? In case you haven't
guessed, the situation's new to me – give me time.

Tomorrow's another day – do I get a second chance? I do want to help.'

Richard was actually smiling, as if amused as well as pleased. She'd never felt more thankful.

Irene grinned at him. 'Didn't know you could smile.' Slowly, she stood up. 'I'm afraid I really am very tired, it's been quite a day. Until tomorrow then . . . '

He nodded. Irene was about to walk away when he raised that left hand, just a few inches. She took it in both of hers and smiled down at him. 'You won't believe me, but things could be worse, I've come here because I'm sure we can improve them.'

When Irene eventually went to bed, in the room now strange but soon to become so familiar, she could still feel that cool, limp hand in hers. It seemed vitally important, their only real contact; Richard's way of keeping in touch with life. And her sole connection with the rest of the human race.

Although deeply conscious of the quiet of the countryside and of a curiously substantial certainty that they wouldn't be disturbed by overnight raids, Irene seemed unable to simply let go and sleep. In her overtired mind thoughts churned back and forth. And still awareness of that slender hand predominated. It was something he could use, she must find a way of forcing him to do so. Together, they must discover what else he could manage, and continue on from there, improving . . .

It must have been after one o'clock when the idea came to her. And then Irene slept with, for the first time in weeks, a smile on her lips.

Around the black-lined curtains a narrow chink of sun-light had appeared. Irene stretched, yawned and then, remembering the idea conceived before sleeping, she smiled.

When she had dressed after bathing in the statutory five inches of water in the large, chilly bathroom, she located Daphne Hughes setting a tray in the kitchen.

'Find everything all right?' Daphne inquired.

'Yes, thank you.' The question had merely been polite, and Irene didn't wish to talk, her mind was so busy finalizing her plan that any diversion seemed unwelcome. But later this exquisite woman would have a part in Richard's recovery, would be included in what was going on.

'Rich eats in his room. I – see to that for him, then have mine. Do you mind waiting?'

'Of course not.' She eyed the tray that had been prepared. 'Why not let me – I wouldn't object.' Despite initial misgivings about Richard's sister, Irene could see he always came first with her.

Daphne gave a fleeting, humourless smile. 'You may not – he would. Let him get used to you first.'

'Sorry, I didn't think.' Or only as a doctor who tried to make people live with reality. Viewed from this aspect, incapacity seemed very different, most unappealing. She sighed.

'It's taken me ages to,' his sister admitted. 'It's the little things, you see. Like – well, thinking you make a mess of eating a meal.' With that, she went, leaving Irene feeling rather inept. But she was warming to Daphne, whose understanding of her brother's feelings showed great insight.

She came back in a very short time, grimacing over how little Richard had eaten. 'Now you see what you're up against.'

While they sat at the kitchen table having breakfast, Irene began questioning her about dealing with Richard's condition. The green eyes regarded her curiously and Irene wondered what she was thinking. But the long black lashes lowered, and Daphne concentrated hard on her portion of the scrambled eggs which well disguised their powdered origin. She might have been stiffening herself to remain hostile.

'You're the expert,' she observed at last, then stopped abruptly.

Irene froze. Surely Giles Holroyd hadn't broken his promise to keep silent? How much did this woman know about her?

'You wouldn't be here if you weren't experienced in coping with illness,' Daphne said quite calmly.

Irene accepted that. 'And that's why I'll have a go at anything.' If necessary, she would hammer away at Daphne Hughes until she penetrated those reservations and they established some sort of bond.

She felt pleased when Daphne smiled. 'I'll put it to him soon. I'll be only too glad to miss out on some of the routine. Much as I love my brother, he can be an impatient devil, now.'

'Well, the offer's there, Miss Hughes, and to relieve you in any way I can.' There must have been enormous stress in caring for him.

'Thanks. And you'd better make it Daphne, hadn't you? We can't have all this formality while you're living here. If you *can* put up with us . . .'

Immediately after breakfast Irene hurried towards Richard's room. Now that she had something positive to try, she was eager to begin.

He looked up when she went in after a brief knock. She found herself smiling.

'Good morning. How did you sleep? Or don't we ask?'

His lips curved slightly. She couldn't tell whether in amusement or what. But, again, his comprehension had been instant. And now he'd caught sight of the large sheet of paper she was carrying. He seemed interested, so without preamble Irene explained.

'I'm not a brilliant conversationalist, you'll have to help me out.'

She sat on the bed to show how she'd set out the alphabet in a semicircle. 'You've one hand you can use, you're jolly well going to!'

Richard was astounded; it was quite some time since anyone had given him an order. But if her intentions were what he supposed, he was the last person to argue over who took charge.

'It'll be slow at first, but you'll be able to spell out words.' At least, she hoped he would. Spelling could elude someone following a stroke.

He was nodding enthusiastically before she'd finished explaining. Irene was trying to think of a simple question as a beginning but, incredibly, he was spelling out something already. She waited.

THANK YOU.

She smiled again. 'Surprised nobody else thought of it, it's not that original. And it'll be a lot easier for me than one-sided conversations. Well, you've soon grasped what it's about, let's practise . . . '

Richard nodded, but her lips twitched and she indicated the paper.

YES PLEASE, he agreed. Irene grinned.

They spent an hour on questions and answers; halfway through she made it harder by helping him to use a pencil as a pointer. Richard persevered until she could see he was exhausted.

'You've had enough for the first session,' Irene began, about to move the paper.

He shook his head, spelling out slowly, for he was indeed very tired. NOT BEFORE I SAY HOW GRATEFUL I AM.

Irene smiled again. 'Glad you're pleased, Mr Hughes.'

He returned to the alphabet. RICHARD.

'Now you must rest, I'll leave you in peace for a bit.'

Emphatically shaking his head, Richard looked pointedly at the bedside chair. Irene went to it.

'I'll stay if you wish, but you must relax.' Impulsively, she took hold of his hand. 'You'll know I haven't sloped off, so close your eyes.'

He didn't do so at once but gazed at her instead, appearing unable to fully comprehend what had brought her here.

Irene started talking, quietly – about the previous day's journey, the home she'd left in London, and how fortunate she was that it had survived amid so much devastation – anything to make him forget himself. Presently his eyelids lowered and she watched the tension ebbing. Sure he wasn't asleep, she continued speaking. She remarked on the snow, and the beautiful Yorkshire countryside. 'We'll have you out and about before the spring's over.'

Richard's eyes jerked open, but she forestalled him. 'And don't go worrying over *how* that'll happen, we'll find a way.'

He shrugged disbelievingly.

'Will you shut your eyes and stop raising obstacles, or am I going to my room?' Irene demanded, and grinned when he nodded.

'I've agreed it *looks* hopeless, but you can only improve – I'll ensure that you do.' How often would she have to repeat that?

She dropped the subject of his illness, chatting about how little the area seemed to have suffered in the war or anything that came to mind, until Daphne appeared with coffee. Daphne had been holding the cup for Richard when the telephone rang and she went to answer it.

It seemed natural to take over from her, and he didn't protest.

'You cope very well,' Irene remarked when Richard paused for breath. He looked incredulous.

'I mean it – you should see the state some people get into just because they can't hold the cup themselves. Nothing to it really, is there?'

His knowing glance revealed that he suspected her of flattery, but for the present he would accept it.

Returning, Daphne appeared surprised the cup was empty, but the look she exchanged with Irene was her only acknowledgement.

Somehow, Irene kept talking for the rest of the morning, dredging up subjects which she hoped might interest him. After lunching with Daphne she found Richard sleeping, and silently admitted to being relieved to have a respite. She wanted to renew acquaintance with Skipton and was pleased when Daphne told her there was a convenient bus.

She had been wandering round the shops for only a few minutes when she bumped into Giles Holroyd, who naturally asked how things were going. The alphabet idea delighted him, but he nodded understandingly about his patient's lack of interest in other directions.

Irene sighed. 'He wasn't keen when I suggested reading to him.'

'Then don't just talk about it. He'll find it's better than nothing. Meanwhile, the fact that you're there is worth a great deal. Boredom's his strongest enemy.'

This was better. During these first few days, she need only reawaken Richard's interest. The rest, his desire to improve his condition, would spring – she hoped – from that.

She was about to turn away when Giles Holroyd caught her arm. 'What do you think, as a doctor?' he asked seriously.

This was no time to split hairs over her standing. Something was puzzling her. 'Richard seems . . . don't know how to put it – worse than he should.'

Dr Holroyd nodded at once. 'The extent of paralysis? With the massive haemorrhage that would have brought this on he'd have . . . '

' . . . Been dead?'

'Exactly.'

'And the facial muscles are unimpaired.'

'They recovered almost immediately.' He appeared very thoughtful. 'Time for a quick cup of tea?' He nodded towards a cafe across the road. 'I can't spare more than a few minutes, but we have to talk this through, preferably well away from my patient.'

Irene smiled. 'I'll be glad to get out of this icy wind. Seems far colder than London.'

The cafe was unheated and was offering only the limited menu permissible, reminding Irene that restrictions were nationwide; but the tea was hot. Giles continued as soon as she had poured.

'Confirm something, will you – when Richard's asleep. Raise the limbs in turn, comparing one side against the other. I think you'll agree those on the left don't fall so suddenly or helplessly as those on the right.'

'You mean . . . ?'

'Could be shock, or any manner of things; the hospital were puzzled, as I am.'

'Then why on earth didn't they investigate further?'

'That requires the patient's consent. As with any brain haemorrhage, Richard had a dreadful fright. Once out of

29

danger, though, he appeared to give up. As if his own body
... disgusted him. When the drip feed was removed, although he'd started taking liquids, he refused them. Somehow he convinced his sister he must go home. She begged
the hospital to agree. I think she – they both – thought it'd
only be a matter of time. When it proved otherwise nothing
would induce him to return to that ward.'

Irene swallowed, recognizing the dismay of realizing that
you were trapped in a situation that seemed intolerable.
And yet, if this had been the attitude of one of her own
patients . . .

'But couldn't you have . . . ?'

' . . . Done what? Talked to him? I have, but there are
only so many hours in a day. We've had several large local
houses commandeered as military hospitals, you know. As
well as having existing facilities stretched to accommodate
men from the forces who need to recuperate where they're
less likely to be blasted out of their beds.'

'And all doctors remaining in civvy street are working
a twenty-five-hour day!'

He grinned. 'Something like that, aye. Now *you* have
the time.'

'To make him determined to live?' She understood for
the first time the extent of Richard's despair, but also the
greater degree of hope which existed.

Giles nodded.

Irene smiled. 'I began to wonder when I realized Richard
could understand everything we said. His brain is hardly
affected, is it?' She told Giles how he'd had no difficulty
spelling out words.

'Good. Whatever the initial brain damage, there's no
doubting the steady improvement, possibly due to re-
absorption of the blood that had been effused.' He smiled
at her. 'Richard Hughes possesses considerable strength of
will, it's up to you to get him to employ it.'

Saying goodbye to Giles Holroyd outside the cafe, Irene
was feeling elated. Perhaps Richard wasn't too devastatingly paralysed. If she could convince him of this, and that
they could overcome the illness together . . .

30

'Thought it was you!' a voice exclaimed just behind her, and Irene turned to see who had followed them out of the cafe.

'Mrs Bradshaw!' she cried, looking into the keen brown eyes of her parents' near neighbour.

'Hallo, love – Ted said as how it couldn't be you, but I knew I weren't mistaken.'

They were joined by Dorothy Bradshaw's husband, who gave Irene a nod and a sharp glance before continuing to check the change he'd been given.

'Your mum and dad didn't say you were coming up to Yorkshire,' Mrs Bradshaw went on after her husband had shaken Irene by the hand. 'Having a few days' break from them awful doodlebugs, are you?'

'Well, no, as a matter of fact I'm working just outside Skipton,' Irene managed, though all the while her pulse was pounding. However would she explain if they asked where her new practice was?

'Fancy that, and your father never mentioned a word!' Ted Bradshaw exclaimed. 'Were it a sudden decision then to move back up here?'

Irene swallowed. Instead of replying she asked if they were in Skipton for the day. Anything to give herself more time for finding an answer for this, and any potential, questions.

Mrs Bradshaw beamed. 'Don't let on to more nor a dozen, but we're having a bit of a holiday. Pity it's so cold, but we're enjoying ourselves. Ted has a cousin who's taken a farm near Gargrave. Sheep, so we're not short of a nice chop or two.' She gave Irene a nudge and winked. 'Ted's on the panel, hurt his back at work.'

Irene began commiserating but Ted interrupted rather awkwardly. 'Nay, it's not so bad now, lass. Only needed a bit of a rest. Strain, you know.'

Irene knew. She also recalled that, although an old friend of her father, Ted Bradshaw had always been his opposite, and given to coddling himself.

Apparently embarrassed by her husband's making light of his incapacity, Dorothy Bradshaw glanced at her watch

31

and remembered an errand to be completed before returning to the farm. Irene was thankful to avoid further questioning. Her relief soon expired.

'We're going home tomorrow,' Ted assured her. 'Any messages for your mum and dad?'

'No – no, thank you. Just give them my love, tell them I'll be seeing them soon.'

If she hadn't only so recently emerged from that cafe, she'd have hurried inside immediately to sit with a cup of tea and try to recover. She could hardly believe that she'd had the misfortune to bump into Mr and Mrs Bradshaw so soon after her arrival here. And she didn't for one moment doubt that they would tell her parents about the encounter.

She'd already been afraid that her family would have learned by now that she had been struck off. And she hadn't known how to begin to give them an explanation. Part of her own distress had been because of the knowledge that they would be as upset as she herself about the dismal end to her career.

How they would react in their disappointment she'd been unable to predict, maybe this was one reason that she'd delayed contacting them. And now they would be doubly hurt because she was in Yorkshire and hadn't been near. No matter how committed she was to ensuring that Richard Hughes began to improve, she must find the time for considering how best to placate her family.

When she returned to the house Richard seemed apathetic. After what she and Giles had agreed about his condition, this made her feel deflated. Or was this the influence of her own problems created by seeing the Bradshaws? Certainly being confronted by them had erased all the warmth generated by Giles Holroyd's respect for her professional opinion. She couldn't eradicate that wretched meeting, she would have to discipline herself to forget it until she could do something constructive to put matters right. And as for life here, she'd have to accept that living with Richard would be to live with his despair – to experience and surmount it, with him.

Tentatively, she began now to tell him where she had been. She soon sensed how bored he was. It struck her then that tricky legal issues must provide infinite mental stimulus for a solicitor. What a contrast this must be – isolated from the active, outside world. With only her to evoke a reaction. *Only* her? She'd got to stop thinking this way.

Where had her vitality gone – the drive carrying her through endless years of training, the presence that had made patients trust a young doctor? Happen this was why she'd had misgivings. She needed all her resources far sooner than she believed she could summon them.

'Getting you down, is it?' Daphne asked, sensing Irene's preoccupation during their meal that evening.

'Not yet. Just thinking – seeking something fresh to keep him going.'

'You'll need to be a genius.'

Irene laughed. 'He's had it then!' But she didn't mean it: somehow she would win Richard's cooperation, satisfy him that the effort could be worth while.

Tired again, she intended popping into his room for only half an hour, but something indefinable in his expression convinced her that he might be more receptive. She couldn't leave. She turned on the radio, but he didn't enthuse about the *Carroll Levis Show* and the play on the Home Service was all but over. And then the nine o'clock news began with an account of the appalling conditions found by the Allies when they liberated the prison camp at Belsen. No matter how important the facts, they made harrowing listening and soon were switched off.

But now Irene remembered Giles Holroyd's advice and crossed to the bookshelves. No title meant a thing to her, so she selected at random a book of short stories.

When she had been reading for about a quarter of an hour, Richard drew her attention to the alphabet. THANK YOU VERY MUCH.

His gratitude touched her, she'd to steady her voice to continue. Before the end of the first story his even breathing told her he was asleep. Turning out the light, she went quietly through to the hall.

In the kitchen Daphne was pouring hot milk into cups. Irene smiled as she joined her. 'If there's one for Richard, I don't think he needs it.'

'You don't mean he's actually gone off without sleeping tablets!'

His sister's delighted astonishment was almost as rewarding as Richard's gratitude had been.

Irene laughed. 'Think I've bored him into it!'

During those first few weeks Richard was no more bored than she was. Imperceptibly, they were establishing an easy companionship. And being immersed in something that blotted out so much of the past did her the world of good. The sheer hard work ensured that she slept every night, through exhaustion. Best of all, the nature of the work meant she was not, as she had feared, frustrated by the inability to practise medicine. And her training was invaluable in assessing how much Richard could take. Knowing the danger signals, she could drive him as far as possible, then enforce a break.

The only distraction was the knowledge that if she wished to avoid antagonizing her parents she must visit her old home. Being so busy meant that she was able to consign the prospect to the back of her mind. But it also meant that when she finally set out she felt ominously ill prepared.

3

The day was pure June transplanted into April. All the way in the bus Irene had been gazing about her, thrilling despite herself to the glorious expanse of hills. She'd never relished more all the differing greens, from the mauve-tinged rim of distant moors to nearby meadows and woods. Then suddenly they were descending the final hill towards Halifax. Her spirits plunged again, returning her to the gnawing reluctance with which she'd started out from Skipton.

Even on a Saturday smoke lingered over the grey stone centre of the town, making her realize how the industry once bringing Halifax prosperity had continued and diversified, producing munitions and other wartime essentials. She knew about the changes here, and wished with all her heart that she could believe her own family might have altered.

Ever since that encounter in Skipton when Dorothy and Ted Bradshaw had promised to tell her parents about seeing her, Irene had known she was compelled to visit them. And she still wasn't ready. Needing to sort her thoughts, she began walking the rest of the way uphill from the bus terminus to her father's surgery in Parkinson Lane.

She was wearing her winter coat which was proving far too heavy for the weather. But then she'd always associated Halifax with the remembered chill of biting winds. Today's unseasonable warmth felt as unreal as her own situation.

Nothing was quite as she recalled. King Cross Street was quieter, its traffic limited by shortage of fuel and the weekend absence of motorists whose business interests alone kept them on the roads. After days spent in the tranquil countryside where she'd been acutely conscious of being far removed from the war, these reminders plummeted her into anxiety for the safety of her old home town and its folk.

I'm being irrational, she silently reminded herself; her own eyes were steadily providing evidence that the one stray bomb of which she'd been told ages ago had been the only source of damage. And every bulletin indicated that the war in Europe was all but over. In any case, if she were honest, until seeing her parents' neighbours she'd been ready enough to pretend the place no longer existed.

Walking past the People's Park, she felt drawn towards its grass and terraces which even the bare-branched trees failed to endow with anything less than this strangely summery atmosphere. If she heard strains of brass instruments wafting from the bandstand she'd be in no way surprised, even though she felt certain that such concerts were unlikely now, unless to raise funds and enthusiasm for some aspect of the war effort.

Memories of family Sunday afternoon walks accompanied her as she turned into Parkinson Lane and continued uphill. Soon Irene was passing the infants' and junior schools which she'd attended. Despite unfamiliar signs pointing to their air-raid shelters, she would recognize every classroom, and knew that she'd come home. Even if the welcome awaiting her proved to be no better than she feared, a part of her was embedded in this town, and always would be.

The front door of the large soot-darkened house stood open for Dr Donald Hainsworth's patients now congregating in the austere waiting room to the left of the entrance. Allowing her no more time, her father himself, tall and erect and his grey hair much thinner than she recalled, was descending the last few stairs. He saw her just as he turned, about to cross to the room where he held his surgery.

'Irene.'

If he hadn't been wearing his professional smile, reading his reaction might have been easier. As it was, every line of his body as well as of his face seemed to register guarded distaste.

He'd never been a demonstrative man, but she'd have been glad of a handclasp.

'Your mother's in the kitchen, I believe,' he announced over the top of her own greeting.

Feeling dismissed and trying not to mind so keenly, Irene continued past the surgery door and on towards the domestic regions.

Elsie Hainsworth had heard her husband's words, was shaken by Irene simply turning up without first telephoning. Waiting now, she was willing herself *not* to rush to her oldest child and smother her with unwanted sentiment.

'You've condescended to visit your family, at last then,' she said sharply. 'Taken you long enough.'

Determinedly not apologizing, Irene crossed to hug her mother, tried not to wince when she felt the angularity of big bones now possessing too little cushioning. The war had hit home.

A part of her brain was urging her to admit that she'd had difficulty assessing what her welcome might be. But that would open the way to having her worst fears confirmed.

'I am working,' she said calmly instead. 'When I was obliged to – to give up the old life I was offered a position just outside Skipton.'

'That's where Ted and Dorothy spotted you,' her mother said needlessly, and sniffed.

Was she concealing emotion, wondered Irene, but a glance showed only that Elsie Hainsworth had veiled her eyes.

'*Would* you have come here otherwise?'

'Of course, Mother.'

'When you'd cooked up an explanation. We heard, naturally. One of your father's colleagues told him on a hospital day.' Hearing that way had almost been as bad as the news itself. Elsie couldn't understand how her daughter could look so composed.

'There's no explanation good enough, is there,' said Irene wearily. She found a hook for the coat that she'd carried the last half mile, and sank on to a chair. 'I don't expect you to understand, or to condone. But I do love John.'

'Didn't you know he was married?' her mother demanded, her back to Irene as she filled the kettle.

'Not until – until we were too deeply involved.'

'But he's gone back to her now.'

As though that made everything better, thought Irene grimly.

After lighting the gas, Elsie faced her again. 'We are sorry, you know; that you've been upset. I just wish you'd stopped to think. Happen you would have if you could have seen how shattered your father was.' She loved all her family, but couldn't bear Donald being hurt.

Briefly, Irene contemplated revealing where her own distress had driven her. But they'd suffered enough. And on her behalf, an' all; sharing her loss was making them feel all the worse.

'How are you both, anyway? And the others . . . ?'

'Your dad and me's surviving. He's tired out, but it's only to be expected, the hours he's putting in. Happen it won't be so much longer now, any road, the way things are shaping over yonder.'

Irene nodded, managed a smile. 'Yes, I think it should only be a matter of weeks before we're through.'

'Aye. That should ease things a bit. Though there's still them Japanese.'

Her mother's hatred flared through the simple words, reminding Irene that this dislike of the Japanese was intensified by Aunt Maureen's husband having died out there. The conditions in their prison camps were reputed to be brutal.

'Have you heard anything of our Norman yet?' Irene asked anxiously.

'Heard about him? You don't know, do you – he's at home. Been here for t'past week or two. He was shot down, like they thought. It was the French got him out, eventually.'

'I'd no idea. How bad . . . ?'

'I did write to let you know.'

'I've been in hospital for a while, before I took the new job.'

'Summat else you didn't bother to tell us.'

Irene sighed, swallowed. 'I – had an accident, in the car. It was nothing, I was over it in a few days. But what about Norman . . . ?'

'He can tell you himself. He always gets up for his dinner.'

Long before her brother came downstairs Irene and her mother had achieved a kind of neutrality. Nothing more was said about her being struck off, nor about her failure to keep them informed. And when she began telling Elsie details of her present position, she saw in the softening of the brown eyes that her sympathy was aroused.

'Poor chap, he must have felt fair hamstrung by being confined to his bed so sudden like, and him so young. No more nor forty, you say? Poor fellow! And is he going to get better?'

'Too soon to say, yet. I'm only just getting to know what he can manage. Though I suppose I'd not be there if the situation was hopeless.'

'Not much of a job for you though, is it, not when there's thousands of wounded men needing doctors.'

The remark was her father's, from the kitchen doorway. Between patients, he'd given in to the urge to speak to his elder daughter.

'Hallo, Dad. It's better than doing nothing,' she responded softly.

'Aye, I daresay.' His collar felt too tight for him, he eased a finger inside it. Ever since he'd heard, he'd been determined to give her what-for. Letting him down like that – chucking everything away to sleep with a chap that wasn't hers. Now she was here, though, all he saw was this favourite lass of his, not looking much different except for the sadness in those lovely blue eyes. 'See you later on,' he murmured, and strode away towards his surgery.

'He'll not forgive what I've done, not if he lives to be a hundred.'

39

'Ay, I don't know,' her mother sighed. 'You might be surprised.'

They paused, hearing Norman coming slowly down the stairs, and then along the hall to the kitchen.

'Well, I'll go to heck!' he exclaimed, seeing Irene. 'Never thought you'd show your face here so soon.'

'Had to, hadn't she,' Elsie observed. 'Ted and Dorothy had given her away.'

I was planning to come, Irene insisted, but only inwardly. Protesting too much would make her sound like a guilty schoolgirl. And wouldn't make one iota of difference to her mother's opinion.

'You made it back home all right then,' she said to her brother as he flopped on to the nearest chair. 'Must have been hair-raising.' He certainly looked as if he'd had a gruelling time of it.

'Could have been worse. The Resistance folk were very good.'

'He's supposed to be going into hospital,' their mother explained. 'Find out why he's losing all this weight still. Seems a long wait.'

'Hospitals everywhere are crammed with limbless soldiers and others needing radical surgery,' Irene remarked.

'Pity you didn't reflect on that before doing summat you knew you'd get chucked out for then,' Norman snapped. 'You're not that daft that you can't have understood you were needed.' Before he learned of her disgrace he'd been that proud, telling all his mates he'd a sister who was a doctor. It still wasn't a profession where the numbers of females even approached the quantity of trained men.

'I agree they can use every available pair of hands, specially down London where there's air raid victims needing treatment as well. As a matter of fact, I was astonished that they didn't think better of getting rid of someone qualified, as things are.'

'Is that what made you take the risk . . . ?' He still couldn't credit that the sister he'd idolized could have been that desperate for sex.

40

'Norman . . .' Elsie began warningly. She'd not have such outspoken talk in their house.

Briefly, Irene was thankful. But she knew her brother: if he didn't get an answer now, he'd persist until he did receive one. 'If you ever fall in love, you'll happen realize that it's not a state of mind where you weigh all the pros and cons.'

Norman grinned. 'I'm twenty-seven, you know. It'd be a poor do if I hadn't had a bit of experience by now. You should have had more sense, like me – and kept to them that were single.'

No doubt his RAF uniform and sergeant's stripes had drawn the lasses to him. Irene smiled. If she had to learn to live with the fact of her indiscretion, she might as well look cheerful about it. 'Next time, I'll come to you for advice,' she told him dryly.

Their mother was peeling potatoes at the sink. Irene went to stand beside the scrubbed wooden draining board.

'Can I do that for you?'

'It's all right thanks, love.' Elsie was better occupied with everyday tasks. While her hands were busy she could somehow cope with this lass of hers who'd broken her old heart by getting herself into such a mess. 'If you want to make yoursen useful you could take a look at your brother – see why you think he's still that thin. I've done my best to feed him up.'

'What good'll that do?' Norman objected hastily. 'Dad's poked around at me oft' enough.'

'And what did he say?' Irene asked.

'About as much as them I'd seen already – that there's nowt they can find. I'm tired out, that's all. Who wouldn't be?'

'Another opinion can't hurt,' Elsie continued. 'And our Irene's here, doing nowt.'

That's it, Mother, rub it in, she thought. But her brother was shaking his head anyway.

'Thanks, but no thanks.'

Irene caught herself gnawing her lip, and forced a smile on to her face instead. At the back of her mind she could see North Fell House near Skipton and longed to be trans-

41

ported there. To some kind of peace. She'd had enough of her family now, yet knew she'd be obliged to stay at least until she'd had a meal with them. Trying to feel worthy of their love was such a strain. She returned to her chair.

'What time does our Mavis come in?'

'Depends on her shift. This week she finishes at two, that's why we're having dinner so late.'

'And so we can sit down together when I've done with surgery,' Donald Hainsworth added, joining them again. He was drying his hands on a towel brought through with him.

'How did it go, Dad?' Irene asked, longing for contact with patients, needing the warm feeling that only came from identifying and helping to cure their ills. And yearning to win back his support.

'Not so badly. There weren't so many, being Saturday. Them that aren't really poorly have summat better to do.' He stuffed his pipe with that evening's ration of tobacco, reminded himself he'd not have to care later on when he ran short. It was now that he needed summat to take his mind off what had happened.

He wished she hadn't asked that, about the surgery. Hadn't he always dreamed of a day when their Irene might be here like this, only working alongside him, happen preparing to take over when the practice got too much for him? Hadn't he cherished pictures in his mind of how they'd discuss difficult cases, combine her fresh ideas with his experience? And now there'd be nowt of that sort. 'What is it exactly that you're doing then?' he asked, drawing on his pipe.

Ay, I have upset him, thought Irene. He cares that much about me it's turning this awkward. 'I'm sorry it had to happen, but I want you to understand I'm not wasting more than I can help. I'm acting as a – sort of companion. To a man who's paralysed by a stroke.'

'Aye, and he's a lot younger nor you and me, poor chap,' Elsie put in.

'It happens,' said her husband gravely. But he smiled at Irene.

42

She jumped to her feet again. 'I'll lay the table for you, Mum.'

'Nay, you won't,' Norman contradicted. 'That's my job for t'present.'

Irene could see that there wasn't much he'd be able to manage yet. If he'd been a prisoner of war he couldn't look much more emaciated. She just wished she wasn't so unaccustomed to sitting idle.

'Ted Bradshaw said he was recuperating from back trouble. Is he over it now?' she asked.

Her father snorted. 'I'm saying nowt, Ted's all right and he's not my patient.'

Thank God? Irene wondered, but her father was as loyal to friends as he was fair to other practitioners.

Her mother was less constrained. 'I'm surprised Dorothy's put up wi' all his aches and pains all these years. Most on it's in the head, you know. I'd have given him a talking to . . . '

Irene found her brother's amused blue glance seeking hers, was warmed by the momentary reminder of old confidential looks, of opinions shared covertly. Happen something remained in her old home still. And she was beginning to think and talk like the rest of them.

'Ted's right enough,' Donald asserted, and was interrupted by the outer door opening. He beamed as his younger daughter trudged in and discarded her coat in a heap by the door.

'Hallo, Mavis,' Irene said, smiling.

'Oh, it's you.' She sounded utterly gob-smacked.

Irene had been afraid that there wasn't one of her family who would have crossed the road to help her if she'd dropped in the street. She'd been wrong about Mum and Dad, though, they were *too* concerned. But her sister would never trouble to disguise her distaste. They'd never really got on since the day she began training to be a doctor. Mavis had claimed Irene was getting above herself, and talking swanky.

'What're you after then – a bed?' she asked now over her shoulder as she scrubbed her hands at the sink.

She was wearing a boiler suit and her hair was pinned up inside a grey turban. Both were smeared with black oil and she removed neither before sitting beside Irene at the table. She had put on weight and Irene edged her chair along to make more room.

'That's it,' Mavis snarled. 'Mind you don't get contaminated – I know I smell. It's the oil. They use a lot round machines . . .'

'Now, love . . .' Elsie began.

'I wasn't – I didn't mean . . .' said Irene. 'You're doing a good job, I'd be the last to . . .'

' . . . Turn up your nose?' Mavis snorted. 'I daresay you'll admit it's a damn sight more use nor handing out library books in Boots.' She'd always resented her older sister for insisting she ought to do better than that. And now who'd distressed Mum and Dad? Irene – who was the clever one.

'What has brought you here then, Miss Glitter-knickers?' she asked.

'Mavis, watch your . . .'

' . . . Language!' Mavis finished amiably for their mother. 'Sorry,' she said to Irene. 'But you did used to be the smarty-pants around here.'

Irene had quelled the urge to rise and walk away from the table. 'And look where it's got me,' she said, and managed to smile. These were her folk, after all, she should have been ready for all their faults, should have minded less that they'd all been embarrassed by hers. Years ago, at school and then at medical school, she'd believed all her rough corners had been erased. One way or another. She hadn't suspected that was to be a continuing process.

She glanced at her watch. 'I'll have to be going soon. But I'm glad I've been, that we've begun to clear the air.'

'I want a word with you when you've had your dinner,' her father told her. 'I hope you won't rush off too fast.'

'No. All right,' she said, but absently.

She had been studying Mavis, noticing that despite the ugly boiler suit she was showing signs of pregnancy. And working in that engineering factory, what a start for her first bairn!

'How's Ralph?' she inquired.

Mavis's answering smile was more tentative than it should have been. Her husband's father was a colonel in the army, a regular. Ralph had spent the war at a desk job in Whitehall, relatively safe. Irene wasn't the only one convinced that it had been wangled for him.

'He was all right last time he came home. He can't get away so often, though, too many folk rely on him.'

Irene nodded, suddenly afraid for her sister. 'Shouldn't be long before the war in Europe's won, any road.'

'Oh, but Ralph will still be kept in London long after the hostilities are at an end, even wi' Japan.'

And who is being conditioned . . . ? Irene wondered again, hoping she was wrong.

'Have you got anywhere in mind – for living in, I mean?'

Mavis shook her head. 'Ralph says it's best if I stop where I am, till he's free to make plans at after.'

Being led aside towards the surgery by her father broke into her concern for Mavis, but she couldn't let go without inquiring after her. 'Is she going to be all right, Dad? Ralph will do the decent thing, and behave like a married man, won't he?'

'Ay, bless you, love, if I could tell you that I'd be a darned sight easier in my mind. You know there's a youngster on the way?'

Irene nodded.

'Since her condition were brought into the open he's been here once. And that were no more than twenty-four hours. You can't tell me that Ralph Parkin couldn't get away for longer if he had a mind.'

'Ay, dear. And our Norman – is it everything he's been through that's made him look like a skeleton?' And given him horrified eyes!

'Well, he did have a bad time, I gather. Hiding out in barns and suchlike, and the dread of being caught. But I expected him to start filling out again by now. I shall see he gets proper attention. I've already had a word in the right quarters. I shan't see my own lad neglected.' He paused and smiled, quite gently. 'You shouldn't be taxing yourself with other folk's problems, you know, lass. You've more than your share yoursen.'

'And have burdened you with them an' all. I am sorry, Father. I honestly never thought for one moment that they'd strike me off.'

'Aye, well . . . It'd be that much more of a blow to you then. That's what I wanted to say. We're your family, after all, we're here when any of you is in trouble. Now think on – and don't ever feel that awkward about owt that you hesitate to walk through that door.'

Although she didn't feel inclined to repeat this visit in the near future, Irene was surprised. She crossed the small space between them and hugged him. She was surprised again when her father's arms came tightly around her and she felt his lips in her hair.

Pleased though she was that he'd seemed so understanding, coming here had been an ordeal. She felt drained, physically as well as emotionally. When she'd said goodbye to the others and was kissing her mother Donald Hainsworth opened the outer kitchen door.

'Come on, love, I'll see you on to your bus.'

She didn't protest that he shouldn't be wasting his ration of petrol. Much as she welcomed the lift into town, she soon began to appreciate equally the insight it gave her into her father. The day had continued sunny and the streets were full of people. In the main, their good Saturday clothes failed to disguise that money was tight. Lots of the women wore their years of anxiety for absent menfolk on resolute lined faces. But many of them knew that car, and weary eyes lit as they waved or nodded to the doctor who cherished their families. He's always been one of them, Irene realized, a knowledgeable man whom these working-class folk have literally taken to their hearts.

Donald asked for her telephone number before she got out of the car. 'Now think on – you'll always have a home in Halifax.'

Home or not, she wasn't sorry as the bus carried her through the rest of the town, past clusters of mills and rows of back-to-back houses, out into the countryside. She needed space for thinking, and for recovery from the confrontation with too many truths. No matter how strong her own reasons for loving John, the repercussions had hit other people. And they had enough difficulties. She'd never get over the shock of seeing Mavis so worn and dirty, and pregnant. *Mavis*, who'd always fancied herself. Even worse though was finding her brother so weak that she wondered if he'd ever get better. And she'd grown so distanced from them that she hadn't even known.

By the time she was leaving Skipton for the last few miles towards the fells, Irene's mood was changing. Instead of being a relief to her troubled soul, the open landscape appeared suddenly too lovely, invoking sentiments that were too *easy*. At first, when leaving London, she'd relished the absence of air raid warnings and flying bombs. Since then her subconscious seemed to be missing the earnestness of conflict, and the indomitable spirit rising from ruins.

Today again, returning to the industrial heart of Yorkshire, where being removed from the blitz had *not* withdrawn folk from the ravaging of war, she'd felt in touch with reality. Was this job she'd taken too soft to be satisfying, and in surroundings that were too pastoral to provide something she could get to grips with?

Irene resolved that for a time she would simply get on with her work and give herself a rest from questioning the direction she was taking. And once she settled down from the disturbance of going home, she began to find some of the satisfaction she was seeking.

Within a month Richard was gradually regaining the use of his left hand. He himself seemed unaware of any improvement until she remarked on it. He'd been slogging away, spelling out answers to her questions.

He didn't know, but she spent hours away from him concocting them, in order to avoid too much time lag. And he seemed eager to question her, these days, keeping her talking. His interest in her was a new experience for Irene in recent years. Doctors grew accustomed to patients being riveted by their own welfare and, with the exception of John, she'd had no time for other one-to-one relationships.

But Richard's frustration often made her swallow hard. His mind was always miles ahead of his hand. Today, he eventually lost patience and flung the pencil across the room.

Halfway to a laughing rebuke, Irene stopped. 'Do you know, Richard Hughes, you couldn't have done that a month ago!'

He gazed incredulously at her.

'Well, could you?'

He grinned, rather awkwardly, and shook his head.

'I told you – you will get better.'

Irene began massaging his hand. 'We'll get this right, then start on the other. It's going to take one hell of a time, but I'll see you through. If that suits you . . .'

She needn't have asked. It was all there in his dark eyes – and a plea for something better. She prayed that she and Giles Holroyd were justified in believing only a part of Richard's paralysis was due to the stroke. If the rest were psychosomatic that allowed more chance of recovery.

Throughout that day Richard appeared pensive. After dinner he was alert with curiosity. Only too thankful for his awakened eagerness, Irene handed him the alphabet. She sat on the bed, watching while he began the long sentence. She was frowning, horrified, long before he reached the end.

YOU SEEM TO KNOW A LOT ABOUT MEDICAL MATTERS, ARE YOU A DOCTOR?

She inhaled deeply. She could only tell him the truth. 'No.'

THEN HOW DO YOU KNOW SO MUCH?

Irene panicked. She couldn't tell him any more, couldn't talk about it to anyone. 'I'm not, I'm not,' she heard herself saying, gripped by agitation, fear and despair. Being able to inter the past had been so good, would this end her brief peace of mind?

Richard hadn't been deterred. He coughed, one means of attracting her attention. He was as close as possible to laughter, so very certain he'd uncovered an interesting fact. YOU MUST BE! COULDN'T YOU TAKE THE PACE AS A FAMILY DOCTOR?

She closed her eyes against threatening tears. 'There's only one thing I can't take,' she answered savagely. 'People who have to be so bloody inquisitive.'

This was how she'd felt before on that appalling day – that everybody knew, was staring, curious ... And now Richard ... Would his determination to find out cost her this job which she was beginning to love? Where would she go now? Would it be like this for ever? People wanting to know too much so that she had to move on. Never allowed to settle anywhere, to put down roots again, to feel she belonged ...

Irene couldn't look at Richard, but she felt his gaze on her. Was he reproaching her, judging – as even her own family had done? Was he like all her friends who wanted the truth, then found avoiding her less embarrassing? Her silence could well have answered all his questions. She daren't look up to learn the effect.

Something touched her hand. The pencil sliding to the floor as Richard relaxed his grip. Thankfully, blinking back tears, Irene knelt on the carpet and started to search. She retrieved the pencil but remained where she was, wishing there was some escape, yet knowing already that she would not take it.

Richard tugged at her hair, forcing her to heed him. WHATEVER THE TRUTH, FORGET I ASKED. IT MAKES NO DIFFERENCE.

That did it. Irene wept, more than she had that other time when Martin Fyson had proved so understanding. But Martin was more than a neighbour and a friend – a priest whose blitzed parish brought him far worse problems than her own. Here, who would even want to understand all these hang-ups? Thoughts scurried through her brain – maybe London was the place for her: with so much happening there, what she'd done would have been a nine days' wonder. She still had a home there, hadn't even offered it on extended lease . . .

But how could she walk out on Richard now? How accept never learning how thoroughly he would recover?

Eventually, feeling a wreck but having wept out all her distress, she stood up, drying her eyes. 'Good night,' she mumbled.

Shaking his head vehemently, Richard was smiling at her. She sighed, made herself wait to see what he would say.

HOWEVER ACQUIRED, YOUR KNOWLEDGE MEANS ONLY THAT YOU ARE BETTER EQUIPPED TO CURE ME.

That nearly triggered off the tears again. Richard nodded towards the edge of the bed and Irene sat down.

'Oh, Richard,' she admitted ruefully. 'I was going to turn and run.'

LET'S MAKE A PACT. WE'LL NEITHER OF US DO THAT NOW. BUT YOU MIGHT LET ME RECIPROCATE THE UNDERSTANDING.

I wish I could let you, she thought, and brushed his cheek with the back of her fingers. 'When I'm sure you won't despise me.'

Richard frowned. Why on earth did she expect he'd be so unjust? I WAS A SOLICITOR, REMEMBER. TRAINED TO LOOK FOR THE REASON BEHIND EVERYTHING THAT HAPPENS.

And if you don't like that reason? she thought dismally, afraid of having him turn against her.

MEANWHILE I PROVIDE YOUR ESCAPE, EH? SOMETHING TO THINK ABOUT.

'Everyone needs some purpose.'

Briefly, Richard was motionless, digesting that, and then: BUT WHY ME?

'You were a long way away and . . . *then*, I thought, more in need of a bit of help than I was myself.' It takes some adjusting when you're accustomed to always . . . prescribing. 'None of that seems so important now.'

He grinned. WELL, I NEVER BELIEVED BEING HELPLESS COULD BE OF USE TO ANYONE. It was the first glimmer of humour in his attitude to the incapacity.

'As of now, it isn't. And I haven't even started on you yet. Just remember I don't usually give up on a challenge!'

I CAN BELIEVE THAT!

Daphne interrupted, bringing in two steaming cups. Irene hurried to the curtained window, away from the light. She sensed Daphne was looking towards her, and with more concern than curiosity. When she glanced towards the bed Richard was nodding from his cup to her, his meaning plain.

'Fine,' Daphne approved, smiling in Irene's direction. 'Then I'll say good night.'

When she had gone Irene returned to Richard. For the past week he had attempted holding the cup himself, with her fingers curled round his own, and clearly was pleased by this promise of some independence.

After Irene had shaken up his pillows, straightened the bedcovers, and gone to her own room, Richard still seemed to feel her fingers covering his. Whether or not you're a doctor, he thought, whatever your reasons for being here instead of in a practice, I can't stop you getting through to me. If only it had been that way before – with Margaret. If only there'd been just *something* to prevent her accepting that he was telling her to keep away.

If, God forbid, the situation had been reversed, he'd never have deserted. Wasn't that what love was all about? If Margaret had been landed with this, he'd have fought and gone on fighting, until there was no way that she would accept what had happened to her.

4

Irene awakened the following morning feeling charged with energy. She had slept more soundly than during recent nights when the stillness had been beginning to prove almost as disturbing as frequent sirens. And since Richard now had some inkling of her medical background she'd decided to exercise it to the full.

As she reached the foot of the staircase, a door slammed in the normally quiet house. Shaun O'Connor was coming towards her, a rueful smile lighting his blue eyes. She liked what she knew of Shaun, if despite both working with Richard they'd little time for talking.

Shaun's expression connected with the sound of a slamming door, and she smiled to herself. At least it seemed Richard was showing spirit.

Because of sleeping quite badly, he generally insisted on starting each day at an early hour. And Shaun, after seeing to bathing, shaving him and so on, was only too eager to disappear to his desk, enabling him to write whilst remaining on call. She had learned that he was epileptic, as unfit for working with machinery as for serving in the forces. His current book was non-fiction, begun as a protest against epilepsy being treated as a grave disability. She looked forward to his promise of a sight of the final version.

Shaun grinned now and ran a hand through his sandy hair as he reached Irene's side.

'You'll have to watch it today. The boss is more than a little abrasive. If he could speak, he'd have given me a right swearing at just now. As it is, my ears are smarting from the curses I imagined!'

Irene smiled. 'Oh, dear. What have you done?'

'Ay, I don't know. It's not so much that as my total inability to be any use at all. Richard's misplaced some of his classical records. I thought finding them would just be a matter of working methodically through all t'cupboards in his room . . . '

'But . . . ?'

'In certain moods, he doesn't give you a chance, does he? I made a big mistake, beginning with the cupboard near the bed. Unfortunately, he could reach me from there. I don't go much on searching for summat while somebody's literally prodding me along.'

Irene laughed. 'Are you telling me it's my task to continue the search?'

'Up to you. But happen it'll be the only thing that'll make him bearable. I walked out afore I blew a gasket!'

She smiled. 'Okay then. Thanks for warning me, any road, Shaun. Forearmed, and all that.'

She didn't believe Richard could have heard their hushed conversation, but he was having the grace to appear somewhat shamefaced when she went into his room.

'Good morning, Richard,' she said brightly. And waited for his usual acknowledging smile.

'I gather from Shaun that some of the records from your collection have gone missing.'

He nodded, his expression guarded. What else had she learned?

'Do you want me to look? It'd maybe save your temper.'

Richard drew the alphabet sheet towards him. PLEASE.

'Where do I start, how far had Shaun got?'

Wryly, he smiled. NOT VERY FAR, I'M AFRAID. He indicated the cupboard at the other side of the bed, one of a series which occupied most of that particular wall. Just having her here was cheering him.

Irene opened the doors and knelt between the cupboard and the bed. One section was fitted with shelves and most of these were piled high with books, there was no sign of any records. But she did come across a boxed chess set and board. 'Hey – I didn't know you played chess.'

Richard shrugged.

'That's no sort of answer, can't you do better?'

He sighed and then, as if humouring her, reached again for the alphabet. I USED TO. And maybe challenging her would be interesting.

Irene smiled. 'So did I. We'll have a game later on.'

DO I HAVE NO CHOICE? he teased, but wouldn't miss this bit of fun.

Sitting back on her heels, she continued to face him, still smiling. 'I wouldn't like to attempt making you do anything against your will. Well, shall I leave this out?'

Containing a smile, he nodded. Chess was something he might win.

Having failed to find the records, Irene was about to close the cupboard door and move on to the next when she noticed in its other half a folded wheelchair.

It occurred to her at once that she'd never even considered how Shaun got Richard to and from the bathroom. That wasn't part of her involvement in life here, and there was quite sufficient that *was* to keep her occupied. Now, though, finding the chair tucked away like this told her how Richard must hate his dependence upon the object. And she ought to utilize it to introduce more variety into his life. Without a word she took out the chair and unfolded it.

Richard, scowling, was emphatically shaking his head. She didn't need to watch to know what he was spelling out. NO.

'Richard, listen . . .'

His dark eyes misted. The seesaw of his emotions dipped again.

Irene willed her own eyes not to fill, reminded herself that one aftermath of a brain haemorrhage was the inability to control the emotions. This meant far less than seeing a healthy man so moved. But knowing what she had to do made it all the harder.

She smiled sympathetically. 'Yes, I daresay you must detest it.' Her tone hardened. 'Master it then – don't let an inanimate object like that master you.'

STOP THIS, IRENE. And yet he sensed how right she was. That she could even be providing the opportunity to prove he wasn't finished.

'We can have breakfast in the kitchen, for once. There's only me around, you'll have to stop minding. I don't matter. Remember what you learned last night. I've seen hundreds of folk far worse nor you, and lots that were better. Think about it – am I likely to think less of you because you can't get around under your own steam?'

Richard was thinking. Staring down at the eiderdown, avoiding her very direct blue eyes, he was trying to consider what *she* thought. Of him. That he was a coward perhaps, that he funked using that infernal chair, because it unmanned him? No – that wouldn't be it; Irene was too understanding for that. Too understanding altogether, that was the trouble. With no more than a glance, a gesture, he could reveal far more, to her, than ever he intended. And by locking that damned thing away out of sight . . . Had he led her to guess how he felt – how he really felt, outside this room?

How, elsewhere about the house – the bits of it that he could reach – he was reminded unbearably of how different everything was now. How different it had to be. That this was his home, but he could never again be at ease here. He couldn't just let go and be himself, because that self was hopelessly inadequate. Whatever he did, no matter how he struggled, he could not restore dignity, nor pride. Well – pride, maybe . . . a little. By not letting her think him too cowardly to try.

He glanced at the clock, met her gaze challengingly with his own. ONE HOUR, WE'LL TRY FOR AN HOUR.

She was toying with a strand of the exquisite hair that gleamed midway between gold and silver. *Nervously* toying. She was too young, he thought, too young to have to cope. Yet those hands were capable, sensitive but capable.

The smile lit her entire face. 'Right then.' Her voice was extremely brisk.

Irene was glad of her expertise that soon had him into a dressing gown and transferred to the chair. Richard also

55

was glad of it; when people fumbled what was necessary it prolonged the need to discipline the urge to scream — at them, and to have the power to see to things himself.

As it was, they were almost out of the room before he remembered and snatched the alphabet from the bed. He would have some say in the next hour.

In the kitchen Irene positioned his chair by the work surface where the toaster stood, then cut some bread and handed it to him. Astonished, Richard raised an eyebrow.

'Any toast you burn is yours,' she told him with a mischievous smile. 'Bacon, scrambled egg . . . ?'

BACON PLEASE. He hated that reconstituted dried egg and it worsened as it grew cold. When they were lucky enough to have fresh eggs they were messy for him to manage.

Keeping one eye on the toaster (he meant to do one thing right) Richard watched her cooking bacon. She looked surprisingly at home here, he'd never thought her the domesticated type yet somehow she seemed to belong. He caught himself wondering what else he might have missed by resolutely remaining in his room. After all, she only spent a proportion of her time in there.

Suddenly, Irene turned, glanced towards the toaster.

Richard checked her reminder with a look.

She chuckled. 'Okay. I'll concentrate on the bacon, or I'll be burning that!'

Richard smiled to himself.

Eating was no better and no worse than in his own room. And at least there were distractions. It was a bright morning and when Irene had tossed out bacon rind for the birds they'd come flocking, and now were working their way over the lawn, devouring insects. There were blackbirds, countless thrushes, and the inevitable sparrows. He watched for some of the rarer species that he used to see in the garden, wondered if it was the wrong time of year, and realized how out of touch he was. Today it seemed to matter more, yet curiously not to hurt as much. That didn't make much sense, but what did, these days?

'More tea?'

His hand over the rim of the cup, he shook his head. Irene wasn't so pedantic now about forcing him to reply by utilizing the alphabet. And that made sense, it was laborious, a nod or a gesture was quicker. All the same . . .

'Can you see that robin?'

NO. WHERE?

'He was in the apple tree. Can't see him now.'

She crossed to open the door. Before he realized, she was pushing the chair out into the garden. Was she out of her mind? The house wasn't called North Fell for nothing. And the mild spell a few days ago hadn't lasted. Frost still lay thick in the crevices of the rockery. Despite the sun, the breeze was icy.

'There he is . . . you see? On that low wall.'

Smiling, Richard nodded. The bird was perched on a stump of the iron railings taken away for the war effort.

'We never saw many birds in London. Not as many as this, any road.'

The robin took off, hastily, as a cat appeared, stalking.

'He's not yours, is he?'

He shook his head.

'Next door's?'

Irene swooped quickly, scooped the cat in her arms, then suddenly plonked the animal on Richard's lap.

'Here – better hang on to him. Then we'll see if the robin returns.'

Richard's eyes narrowed. The poor thing was terribly cold, must have been out half the night. He stroked the chilly fur. The cat purred appreciatively. He smiled. They'd had an amicable truce, the cat and he, as much as any gardener would with a visiting feline. It had been understood between them that he'd a right to vent his anger if too many precious bulbs were disturbed. And the cat had a right to spit back – from a distance.

The garden wasn't looking too bad, considering the recent cold snap and . . . things. Shaun didn't neglect it, but maybe he needed a bit of supervision, someone who'd be more imaginative. Once the war ended, vegetables could come out of that flowerbed over there. Several of the rose bushes needed replacing; were they available any longer? But then roses would have to go in fresh ground.

Yes, it was time he gave some thought to it, and a bit of direct advice. Another week or two and that warmer weather should return for good, he could spend some time out here. It wouldn't hurt to show who still kept a hand on the reins.

'Looks like the robin's taken himself off. You can let the cat go.'

The cat seemed content where he was, but Irene came and transferred him to the ground. He wouldn't go away but turned, placed two paws on the footrest and rubbed himself against Richard's ankle. Irene and he exchanged a smiling glance.

And then she turned away, rather quickly, and gazed up at the snow-topped fells.

Here and there an outcrop of limestone emerged from the white covering, on the lower slopes the young grass threw into focus the stark outline of occasional bare-branched trees. Below it all, between the garden trees, glistened the silver of the rocky stream.

'Lord, how beautiful it is!' she exclaimed softly. 'Don't you love it, Richard?'

He could not respond. She was wearing a high-necked dress and a jacket that matched. They were the red of the few remaining berries still clinging to the nearby holly. She glowed with warmth. Out here, each thread of her hair glinted. Even if one could speak, words sometimes were inadequate.

Irene looked away from him again, trying to stop her eyes blurring as she turned towards the fells. Did one love anything, could one, when everything seemed spoiled? She'd seen patients turn bitter, soured by what fate had done to their bodies. That must not happen here.

'Are you cold?' She tested his cheek with a hand.

He wasn't warm, and maybe he'd endured enough. She turned his chair and eased it up over the kitchen doorstep.

It was blessedly warm indoors, but she was glad they had been outside, and hoped he was glad. Not knowing, never being sure, sometimes played on her nerves.

At the table he made her stop, and pulled the alphabet sheet towards him across its pine surface.

IRENE, I HAVE GOT TO SPEAK AGAIN.

She swallowed hard, then drew up a kitchen chair, smiled as she sat at his side.

'I've heard all about that – Shaun said you'd have sworn at him if you could!'

Amusement lighting his brown eyes, Richard smiled back. But he shook his head. THERE IS SO MUCH I WANT TO SAY TO YOU.

Richard Hughes, she thought, much more of this and I shall go all emotional. And there'd been enough of that last night.

But wasn't this precisely what she had ached for? The first concrete evidence that he was improving, that he wanted to improve further.

They went into the cool sitting room to the telephone. Irene found Giles Holroyd's number in the book. When he answered she discovered she was smiling yet again.

'Do you know of a speech therapist, one who'd come to the house?'

There was a moment's pause while Giles digested every implication of what she had asked.

'I'll make damned sure I find one! It may take a little time, Irene, to locate someone who'll visit North Fell repeatedly, but I'll ring you back when I have something arranged. Tell Richard . . .'

'You can tell him yourself,' she said swiftly, and handed the receiver across, checking to see if he needed assistance holding it to his ear. He coped.

Richard seemed pensive as he hung up afterwards.

'What did he say?'

He hesitated before replying. 'CONGRATULATIONS.' BUT I RATHER THINK THAT WAS MEANT FOR YOU, IRENE.

'Nonsense.'

THEN IT SHOULD HAVE BEEN. YOU'RE A CRAFTY LADY, AREN'T YOU?

'Are you sorry?'

Smiling a little, he shook his head. He glanced towards the piano. DO YOU PLAY?

Irene grinned. 'Badly!'

He nodded to the piano. GO ON . . .

She wanted to refuse, she'd never been very good, and yet . . . it was rare that Richard asked for anything, she couldn't say no.

For what felt like a long time she sat at the keyboard, her mind blank, almost afraid to disturb the stillness of the exquisite room. The walls were peach-toned, the sofa and chairs cream coloured; how could anybody bear to possess such a place, and ignore it? How keep away?

Suddenly she was playing something half remembered from the days when she had struggled to master the piano, Liszt's *Liebestraum*. She was deeply aware that Richard was watching her, his expression inscrutable. He glanced, briefly, down at his hands. So – he used to play. Perhaps, one day, this might be a good exercise. Meanwhile, she'd put him through quite a bit for one morning.

'Are you going back to bed?' she asked as the final bars died.

He looked at the clock on the white marble fireplace, then back again to her. It was almost exactly an hour since he had left his room. Irene crossed the thick, pale carpet towards him, holding her breath while she waited for an answer. Instead, he took her hand, pressed it for several seconds against his cheek. When he let it go she caught the tangy scent of his aftershave.

'Or would you take charge of a game of chess more forcefully from the chair?' This beautiful antique table was just the right height to accommodate the board and pieces.

Richard smiled wryly again. DEFINITELY A CRAFTY LADY!

And are you going to resist, she wondered, going back to your own room, if only to prove whose will is the stronger?

60

The chessboard won, but the game soon proved more tiring than Richard had anticipated and he was compelled to rest. But they left the pieces in place on the chessboard to be continued.

Giles Holroyd called that evening. Daphne was out with Peggy, one of her friends with whom she was enjoying the return of some liberty. At first when she heard the bell Irene thought Daphne had come home early and must have mislaid her key. But then she opened the door and Giles was there, smiling, his grey eyes brilliant.

'I've got it fixed,' he announced after a hurried greeting. 'I had to come over and tell you instead of telephoning.'

Irene smiled up at him. 'Richard's the one you must tell, come on . . . '

Before they moved away from behind the front door, though, Giles detained her with a firm hand.

'One moment – I want you to know first that you have my sincere admiration, as a fellow professional. You've succeeded where I failed. I shall want to know later how you did it.'

'Not sure myself. It seemed a natural progression of events.'

'Really?' Giles grinned. He began heading towards Richard's room.

Irene smiled. 'Actually, he's in the sitting room.' Except for a short rest on his bed, Richard had spent the remainder of the day in his wheelchair.

Now Giles really was astonished. Irene watched his grey eyes crinkle with delight. He grasped her shoulder, squeezing it quite hard.

'Well, I've said it already, Irene, but I didn't understand how fully justified it was. Had quite a busy day, haven't you?'

She said nothing, emotion was constricting her throat. They were approaching the sitting room. Within seconds Giles was settled in an armchair, telling Richard about the speech therapy he'd arranged.

Richard was elated, later that evening he told Irene that he wanted her in on the sessions. She was reluctant, but silently admitted that she might be more use if she learned the methods employed by the therapist.

She soon was loathing every moment of those agonizing early lessons, and frequently had to steel herself not to turn from Richard's struggle to master speech again.

For some time she couldn't understand why he wanted her there, an embarrassed onlooker, especially since Daphne was allowed no part of it. Richard insisted that the fact that he was having this therapy be kept from his sister. He claimed he wanted, one day, to give her a pleasant surprise. Seeing the effort entailed, Irene suspected it went far deeper than that.

Concealing things from Daphne was becoming easy, however, as she was now working part time, as a clerk at a military hospital. The outside interest seemed to make her more relaxed. But Irene still wondered about Daphne's career, what it had been – and why she had been evasive about her old job.

The telephone call came one Saturday morning. Mavis was on the line, so perturbed that initially Irene couldn't grasp what was troubling her.

'I'm telling you . . . ! What's up – can't you take it in?' her sister snapped. 'It's our Norman. He's had a heart attack or summat. Even Dad panicked, but he's got him into hospital.'

'How serious is it? I'll try and come over.'

'I hope you will, an' all. Norman's that agitated he won't listen to anybody, says he's not having any tests.'

Although she doubted that Norman would take any more notice of her than when she last saw him, Irene quickly explained first to Richard then to Daphne. They both sympathized, and Daphne checked out times of buses while Irene gathered things together for an overnight stay.

Despite the weeks that had passed since her previous visit to Halifax the weather was unseasonably cooler, and a miserable drizzle fell from skies as dismal as the surrounding mills.

When Irene arrived at the house nobody was there, and she cursed herself for not thinking to ask which hospital Norman was in. Praying that either Dorothy or Ted Bradshaw would be at home, she hurried round the corner to their house.

Dorothy answered the door, and her smile faded to concern. 'They haven't come back from the hospital, love. I do hope it isn't too bad. Your father's pinned a note on t'door cancelling surgery.'

'Thank you, Mrs Bradshaw. Can you tell me which hospital it is?'

'Aye, love, of course. He's in the Infirmary.'

'Thanks. I'll see you later. I shall be stopping over the weekend.'

Curbing the urge to run, for the Infirmary was about a mile away and she couldn't hurry for that distance, Irene continued along the street and into Fenton Road. She turned left, hastening downhill until St Paul's church was facing her, then down again to King Cross. There seemed more traffic today, and instead of waiting Irene turned left again until a break in the stream of cars allowed her to cross.

A network of streets confounded her for a moment, but then their layout came back to her and she was pressing on again, through Haugh Shaw Road and Emscote until at last she emerged in Savile Park Road. The Royal Infirmary was nearly in sight now, and down the hill. Once she reached Free School Lane, Irene began a weary jog.

The first person she saw before she inquired at the porter's window was her father. He looked so haggard and distressed that, anxious though she'd been to get here, she feared the worst and hardly dared approach him.

Donald Hainsworth had spotted her as well, though, and all but hurled himself on her in a massive hug.

'Ay, Irene, Irene!' he exclaimed. 'Thank God you're here, lass.'

'What's happened?' she demanded. 'Don't say our Norman's gone . . . '

'No, love – no. It's not as bad as that. I'll take you in to see him in a minute. It's just . . . ' He paused, drawing away from her. She saw his eyes fill. 'We can't fathom what's wrong. He passed out at home, as you've probably gathered. When I sounded his heart, I detected a definite murmur . . . '

'Oh, no!' Irene exclaimed, scarcely able to believe it.

'His heart rate was well over a hundred and thirty. They've given him summat for that, of course.'

'But he can't have a wonky heart, he passed all the medicals.'

'I know. And I can't get a straight tale out of anybody here yet.'

Irene still couldn't credit that Norman had had a heart attack, despite how ill he'd looked. She said so to their father as they hastened along corridors with the all-too-familiar antiseptic reek.

'Aye, I'd be inclined to agree with you, if he weren't showing all the symptoms of heart failure. You should see his feet and ankles, all puffed up wi' fluid. There's some in his lungs, an' all. And from what he says he's all but blacked out afore.'

'That doesn't have to be heart.'

Donald gave her a look. Was he merely questioning another medical opinion, or was he querying her right to express one . . . ?

'And how does Norman seem now?'

Their father sighed. 'Hard to say. Alarmed – understandably.'

Irene soon saw how true this was. She immediately felt sorry for her mother who was sitting stoically beside the bed where Norman, his eyes starting out of his head, was plucking urgently at the covers.

'What's all this then?' she asked him briskly. 'Was it the only way you could get yourself admitted quickly?'

'What've you come for?' he asked gracelessly, though his restless hands stilled. 'It were only a bit of a faint I had.'

'We'll have to see, shan't we?' she said far more calmly than she felt, then kissed both Norman and her mother.

Elsie plainly was at a loss, and near the end of her tether. 'They can't tell us what's up,' she whispered.

'Why don't you and Dad try and find a cup of tea,' Irene suggested. 'He must know somebody here who'll provide one.'

Her being alone with Norman seemed to quiet him, though she noticed as he reached towards his locker that his fingers trembled.

'You've not had bother with your heart before, have you?' she asked. And wondered if she was willing him to confirm that she needn't be picturing him in a similar condition to Richard.

'Course I have, pounding ever since I came down across t'Channel. Only I kept telling mysen it were just because of the fright I'd had.'

'Happen it was, love,' Irene said, and wished for some reason to substantiate that theory. It was true that Norman was looking better now than she'd expected, but she'd no cause to doubt their father's diagnosis, nor the conclusions of the staff here.

'It wasn't only the scare I had being shot down, you know,' he began suddenly. 'That would have been over once I was relatively safe with t'folk belonging the French Resistance. It was losing my plane. It went up in flames, soon as we'd baled out.'

Irene gazed sympathetically into his eyes, saw the tears and how staring his pupils were.

'Now, love . . . ' she started, but Norman interrupted.

'Sounds daft, I know, but – like a death, that's what it was, watching that plane blazing.'

'That's it!' she exclaimed.

Norman scowled at her for sounding triumphant. 'What is?'

'I'd better not say, not till I've had a word with somebody. But I don't think it's your heart that's at the bottom of all this.'

'Oh, aye? What're you saying – that I'm going batty?'

Irene grinned. 'No more nor usual. And if I'm right you'll happen only need regular medication to keep you on an even keel.'

'You do think I'm mental, don't you! I'm not shell-shocked.'

'I know that, love. But you're in the right place for getting tests done. And if they proved it wasn't your heart, that'd be a load off your mind, wouldn't it?'

'You're not kidding! Just wish I could believe that were possible. These past few weeks have been diabolical. Knowing that something serious was wrong with me, because I can't even go upstairs without gasping. Today, when Dad detected that heart murmur – well, I felt there was no point in anything, that I were as good as finished.'

'Aye, well – we'll have to see what they find. Afraid you'll have to try and be patient, and not to worry . . .'

'Ah – sounds like somebody's talking sense,' a voice behind her approved, and Irene turned to look into steady dark eyes.

Irene's slight smile began in her own eyes. Before she could speak, though, her brother was saying plenty to the white-coated stranger: 'It's easy for her to talk. To her, this is summat that happens every day. She was a doctor *once*. Till she was struck off.'

The young houseman was less perturbed than Irene herself. 'You must be Dr Hainsworth's eldest then. Norman's sister.'

She nodded, willing herself not to react to realizing that this young man knew all about her, which probably meant that the rest of the staff knew.

'We've been stumped, so far, I'm afraid. There's so much about Mr Hainsworth's case that doesn't add up.'

'Aye, I thought there might be,' said Irene, then remembered that her opinion would no longer carry much weight. 'I gather from my father that he's leaning towards its being thyrotoxicosis.'

'Is he now? He never said.'

'No, well – I daresay it was only a few minutes since that he reached that conclusion.'

'This certainly puts a different complexion on it. I'll have a word with my colleague,' the houseman said, and turned from them.

He moved on to a patient several beds away, but Irene's humiliation grew no less. Each man in every bed had been riveted – she hadn't felt that so many people were staring at her since that dreadful night before she crashed the car. And this time their curiosity was no illusion. She could have told Norman that he might have spared her, but that would only increase the interest of the entire ward.

'Where's our Mavis?' she inquired softly. 'At work . . . ?' She didn't want to leave her brother alone, yet she must talk to Father.

'Don't think so. She were in here earlier on, wi' Mum and Dad.' Norman was puzzled by Irene's refusal to retaliate. *He* would have, in her place. But then, she had always been one on her own. And he had seen that look. She'd seemed so composed that other time, he knew now how much losing her job hurt her. But what about his own job?

'I were going to be a pilot at after. This is a right bastard.'

'Happen we shouldn't expect life to be fair – look at some of these chaps. Is it fair if folk are crocked up fighting for their country? But you shouldn't be so gloomy, not till we know what's wrong.'

'It's not only that, old girl. Afraid my nerve's gone or summat.'

'You'd probably have got bored, any road, piloting civil aircraft.'

'I'd have liked to have given it a try.'

'What will you do, have you thought yet?'

'Course I've thought. Nowt else to do but think, have I? I allus liked being an overlooker down yonder. Reckon I'll go back to that, *if* I end up with a ticker that can stand doing a man's job.'

Irene tried not to show her concern. Father had always been disappointed that his only son had no aspirations beyond working in a mill. She could only hope he'd keep such reservations to himself now.

Norman seemed to read her thoughts. 'Keeping them looms running properly was quite a demanding job, you know. After t'war there'll be lots of firms investing in new equipment. As technology advances, there'll be more and more refinements – it'll be challenging work.'

She met their parents returning down the ward. They were arm in arm, but it was difficult to tell who was supporting whom. Behind them Mavis staggered awkwardly on high heeled shoes, saved from before rationing and shortages. There was something gallant about her efforts to look smart, but the bulge in what had once been a good tweed costume destroyed the effect. Why couldn't she have made herself a nice maternity smock, Irene wondered.

'So you think it's over-active thyroid,' Donald Hainsworth said. 'You might be right, an' all – even if you've given me the credit.'

'Hallo,' Mavis interrupted. 'What have you done to your hair?'

Irene put an exploratory hand to her head. 'I'd forgotten it was raining all the way here. You know my hair's as straight as a yard of pump water.' The drizzle had taken what curl there was out of the sides and had encouraged the rest to escape from the hairpins securing it on top. 'I'd better go and tidy up a bit.' She asked the way to the ladies cloakroom when their father went seeking the consultant.

Mavis came with her, clattering along on her ridiculous heels.

'You want to wear something a bit more sensible, don't you?' Irene suggested. 'You can't be doing either yourself or the baby much good tottering on those.'

'How do you know?' Mavis asked, wishing her older sister didn't have to think she knew best every time. 'You've never had one.'

'No, but . . . ' Irene began, checked, and clamped her lips together. She couldn't stop thinking like a doctor. And every time she opened her mouth the remarks she invited from other folk struck right through her.

Mavis surprised her, though, with a sudden turn of understanding. 'You'll never be any different, will you?'

she said, sympathetic tears filling her eyes. 'You're a doctor through and through, no matter what folk do to you.'

'Aye, I suppose I am,' she said grimly.

They were standing side by side in front of the mirrors now. Mavis's reflection grinned. 'Then happen we'd best smarten you up a bit. Where's your comb?'

'Ay, I don't know. I bet I've left it in my overnight bag, beside our Norman's bed. I wasn't thinking.'

'Never mind, love. We'll use mine.'

Mavis produced a far from clean comb from the depths of a cluttered handbag.

All at once Irene didn't care about the tangle of her sister's loose hairs still adhering to the comb, and cared less than before about the problems creating such a struggle these past few months. Whatever their differences – and they were many – the Hainsworths were a good family. Just having their Mavis care enough to take her hair in hand, was cheering. A reminder that she wasn't alone.

'I was only trying these shoes out today,' Mavis admitted around the hairpins held in her teeth. 'Ralph is coming next weekend and I wanted to brighten mysen up for him.'

'Don't blame you,' Irene said, watching in the mirror while Mavis drew her hair up on top of her head and trying not to flinch as the comb encountered tangles. 'You must get sick of wearing drab overalls and such for work.'

Mavis laughed. 'Sometimes, I quite like it. None of the other lasses look any better, and it's rather a relief not to have to bother. Maybe there's a lot of slob in me!'

Irene willed neither her face nor any murmur to betray that she agreed.

Again, Mavis laughed. 'There's the difference in us! I'd have said what I were thinking.' She grew more serious again. 'About these shoes – am I daft wearing 'em now I'm expecting?'

'It's a risk I wouldn't take. Supposing you fell, love – think what that might do to the baby . . . '

69

Mavis swallowed, finished pinning her sister's hair in place. 'I'm not quite potty, you know, except about Ralph maybe. I will be more careful.'

'You could buy a new pair that were a bit more sensible. I'll let you have the coupons.'

'Are you sure?'

'Aye, go on.' In London she'd been too busy to worry about what she wore and had gone easy on coupons. The clothes she had were good and would last, at least until the war ended.

Mavis hugged her. But it was Irene who was feeling better, warmed by affection. It might not be evident, most of the time, that there was more than diverging opinion between them all. Somehow, though, the fact that all their idiosyncrasies didn't vanish made being part of their family feel all the more enduring.

5

Even though Donald Hainsworth was as well respected as he was well known at the Infirmary, the ward sister soon protested about there being four people round Norman's bed.

'I'll stay with him for a while,' Irene suggested. She'd seen how shattered their father and mother looked. 'You've had your turn.'

Neither of them seemed inclined to argue; Irene could imagine they'd had enough, even though the consultant had agreed that Norman's condition might be due to nothing worse than his thyroid overacting. Shock and bereavement were two classic causes, and he'd had his share of both these past few months.

Mavis stayed as well, and suddenly seemed irrepressible as she recounted recent incidents in the engineering works. Evidently, the jobs undertaken by Mavis and the other lasses were so monotonous that they enlivened the day with practical jokes.

'We got the foreman t'other day,' she exclaimed. 'Had him going round all morning with a notice on his bum saying "Explosive device – keep clear".'

Although the works' humour sounded juvenile to Irene she was thankful that it soon had Norman laughing.

'About time,' Mavis told him. 'If you're on the sick list much longer, I'll get you fixed up wi' a job down yonder. There's some work where folk sit at benches, you could manage that.'

'Better nor you, happen. You'll have to grow longer arms to reach round yon lump if you get much bigger.'

Mavis grinned. 'By the time I'm that big, we'll not be making any more munitions. I'm not having my bairn born in wartime.'

Norman chuckled. 'What're you planning on doing then – bunging a cork in to hold it there till t'duration?'

'If our Mavis knows how to time a baby to arrive to suit her, she'd best let on about her secret,' Irene put in. 'Sounds like we could make a fortune . . . '

'*You* don't need to, should think you've been earning far more than ever I have,' Norman told her sharply. Just before the war when Irene was newly qualified, he'd been staggered by what she was paid.

Irene could have retorted that whatever she'd earned as a doctor had been justified by the years of training, but she let it go. Now Norman was much more cheerful, she'd make that sufficient. And there were so many reminders about her being a doctor that each one she endured felt like a small, private victory. If only over her own emotions.

'You shouldn't have said that,' Mavis reproved him nevertheless.

When they were eventually sitting in the bus, Irene thanked her.

'You stuck up for me back there as if you didn't just think that I've let you all down, made you ashamed of me.'

Mavis raised an eyebrow. 'Ay, lass – I could see last time that you've been harder hit by this than any one of us suspected. What's the point in letting folk keep reminding you?'

Before Irene could respond a strident voice called across the bus to them. 'How's your Norman getting on?' the middle-aged lady inquired. 'I were right sorry to hear Doctor Hainsworth had had to get him taken in. My hubby were in t'chemists getting his bottle made up when somebody came in with the news.'

'Norman seemed not too bad by the time we left just now, thanks.'

'Thank goodness for that. I'll tell them in t'street an' all. They'll all be wanting to know.'

'Who is she?' Irene asked when the woman got off the bus at the stop before their own.

Mavis shrugged. 'I don't know. One of Dad's patients, I suppose. They all seem to think they own all t'family of us.'

Her sister had said that as though it were a fault. To Irene, it seemed to emphasize how successful Donald Hainsworth had been in demolishing any barriers.

Rested, both parents appeared brighter by the time she and Mavis walked into the house.

'Was he any better?' Elsie asked immediately.

'I think so,' Irene confirmed. 'Our Mavis had him laughing, at least that was an improvement on when I got there.'

'You should have seen him earlier. When your dad said he thought he'd had a heart attack, the poor lad seemed suicidal. I suppose you'll find that hard to understand . . .'

Will I? thought Irene. You don't know one half of it. And it was as well that they didn't. They certainly didn't need to be concerned about what her state of mind had been; they'd enough on their plates just now.

They were having a late high tea when somebody knocked on the front door. Thinking to save her father if it was a patient seeking him outside surgery hours, Irene went to answer it.

The woman on the step was perhaps slightly younger than herself, personable despite her shabby macintosh, and smiling rather awkwardly.

'Is it Father you want?'

'Well – yes, in a way. You don't remember me, do you?'

'I'm afraid not – I've been away a long time . . .'

'Aye. Well, we were at Parkinson Lane School together, though you were in the class above me. I've really come to see how your Norman is now . . .'

Donald Hainsworth had followed his daughter through the hall and was beside her, smiling.

'Come on in, come in,' he invited. 'Good on you to call round like this. He didn't seem as bad by the time our Irene, here, left him.'

'Oh, that is good news. And was it his heart?'

'Early days to be sure yet. And there are one or two other theories, they'll be doing tests.'

'I was wondering,' she began, 'about how they did so much for me, finding the right tablets to keep me going, and that. I thought – if you'd like me to, I'd go in during visiting tomorrow, talk to your Norman about it. It might set him thinking that things aren't so bad . . . '

'Aye, it might at that!' Donald exclaimed, wondering how he could restrain her until they located the cause of Norman's collapse. 'It's right decent of you to think of going . . . but perhaps if you hung on for a day or two, just till we know a bit more.'

'I'd do anything I could to help any on you,' the woman confided as Irene walked her to the wooden gate that replaced the wrought-iron one taken for salvage. 'Dr Hainsworth's always been a brick to my mother. And I'll never forget the way he got the consultant to see me when I was discharged from the ATS.'

When she went back indoors Irene learned that the poor woman hadn't been allowed to return after sick leave. She had suffered minor injuries to her right arm, when the searchlight they were manning near the perimeter of an airfield had received a direct hit by a flying bomb. Hospitalization had brought routine tests which had found a defective heart valve, missed during her original medical.

'So, our Norman could have had something similar without it being detected when he joined the RAF,' said Mavis.

Donald nodded, but he was smiling just the same. 'He could – but I'm growing increasingly convinced that our Irene's right. All that losing weight points to that, and his tiredness.'

It seemed by the following afternoon that this opinion was endorsed by the doctors at the hospital. Confirmation, though, would take time; the necessary blood tests would be prolonged. Meanwhile, however, Norman himself was banking on thyrotoxicosis being diagnosed, and questioned both Irene and his father about treatment.

'Medication is the first option, and will begin right away,' Donald told him.

'And if that doesn't do the trick?'

'They might have to operate. You've heard of having a goitre removed? But don't go worrying about it, happen it won't come to that. You've no swelling of the area, which is a good sign.'

Irene's relief to be getting away again was almost as strong as that which she felt about her brother's more hopeful condition. Although beginning to be more at ease with her family, she still found their company exhausting, and meeting old acquaintances made her wonder how much they knew about her. If anybody had told her that so many, even innocuous, remarks would trigger emotions about her lost position, she'd not have believed them. And there was the special place which her father had earned within the local community. That, more than anything, made her pine for the chance to have folk feel as affectionately towards her.

Pining, however, never did anybody any good. She was resolved to really leave the past where it was. If she gave her mind to it, she could make an interesting future for herself, no matter how different from her original ambitions.

I'VE MISSED YOU, Richard greeted her frankly when she went into his room. And although Daphne was sitting there and clearly had been getting him to use the alphabet as they conversed, Irene couldn't help feeling delighted.

HOW WAS YOUR BROTHER?

'Yes, how was he?' Daphne added, rising.

'Well, before I left he seemed a lot better, thank you.' She went on to tell them how the situation might be less serious than they had feared.

And the next news she received was that Norman appeared to be responding to medication. He was less agitated, and his pulse rate had slowed considerably. The following telephone call revealed that tests had proved him thyrotoxic. By this time he was back at home, though easily tired, and had gained only a few pounds.

'They still might have to operate in the end,' her father added.

'But at least he should be able to go back to work once this lot's over.'

'Does that mean he won't return to the RAF?'

Although the war in Europe had ended with nationwide V-E Day celebrations, there was still the Far East conflict and there seemed no prospect yet of the forces being demobilized.

'Oh, gracious – yes. Or so we hope. Whether he'll go into a desk job there depends on them. It's a great pity this had to crop up.' They were still waiting for confirmation that the RAF wanted Norman back, let alone would want him to fly again. And Donald couldn't rid himself of wishing his son might pilot civil aircraft. There would be a massive upsurge in airline travel once the war ended.

Although away from her family now, Irene found it less easy to forget them. Seeing how highly regarded her father was in the locality had given her such a lasting insight into his qualities as a doctor who communicated better than many with his patients. And she hadn't missed the closeness which existed between her mum and dad, a mutual support and understanding that she'd always taken for granted. These days, it seemed to her that it was rare.

And there was Mavis; although they weren't a bit alike, Irene was compelled to admire her sister's spirit. Despite her husband's absence, whenever she was away from the munitions factory she appeared to make the best of life. Irene pictured her now, showing off her new wedge-heeled shoes, her legs covered in liquid sun tan and a carefully drawn line of eyebrow pencil faking each stocking seam.

Her own lisle stockings felt heavy and looked frumpy, yet even here in the country she'd be reluctant to go around bare-legged, and her precious silk pairs were for special occasions. Another hangover from the old life, she supposed. At least that didn't depress her. In fact, apart from the speech therapy which she found distressing, Irene was cheered by Richard's progress.

A marked improvement in his left hand had given him more incentive, and now he rarely spent an entire day in his room. They played records, talked as best they could using the alphabet sheet, and Irene read aloud. Now that the newspapers were carrying more optimistic news, she

76

went through them with him, and was told that he had resented being deprived of the facts even before the hope of peace had grown so realistic.

They also often played chess, although she had learned very quickly that she wasn't in Richard's class.

In the few hours she took off, Irene was getting to know the surrounding countryside and loving it. Once out of doors, she often walked for miles up into the lower slopes of the green fells where she revelled in air fresher than any that she remembered. Years ago, long before her training, she had enjoyed visits to the Dales, now she deeply appreciated living where she only need pause to admire the splendour of their hills.

Sometimes she told Richard about her walks or mentioned some hamlet of stone-built houses, but never knew for sure if this was good. Maybe his own life, by comparison, seemed more restricted.

Daphne had left for work one Friday in August when Irene went into Richard's room. She had heard laughter coming from there, earlier while Shaun was helping with the morning routine, and now Richard looked very bright. Fleetingly she wondered why, but then remembered she hadn't seen the newspaper and turned back to the door to go and get it. News was coming through of a second atom bomb attack on Japan. Although lots of folk were distressed by hearing of the devastation over there, everyone hoped it heralded the Japanese surrender.

'Irene . . . '

She couldn't believe her ears. After what had felt like an eternity of barely discernible sounds, there her name was – quite plain. She swung round, eager for confirmation of what she'd heard, and needed only Richard's smile.

Irene rushed to hug him. An instinctive gesture that she couldn't have checked. 'Oh, Richard, how good that sounded!'

He smiled again, and reached for the alphabet.

SORRY I CAN'T MANAGE MORE THAN THAT – YET. GIVE ME TIME. AT LEAST I CAN BRING YOU TO HEEL NOW.

'And learn to answer me back!'

For a long while Irene sat on the edge of the bed, gazing at him, not really knowing what to say. There had never been a moment, from the beginning of her career, when she'd felt better rewarded. No matter what they'd done to her, she still seemed to have the ability to encourage someone to make the most of what was there. And she was glad that person was Richard.

On the following Tuesday the news on the wireless was all about the final surrender by Emperor Hirohito.

'At last,' said Richard.

Irene saw those two simple words as recognition that his own victory would come. As they drank a toast with Daphne that evening and listened to radio accounts of the celebrations in London and other major centres, she felt as though the first hurdle of her new existence here might have been cleared.

From that day, Richard delighted in calling her – about the house, or whenever she entered his room, and she began thinking she could tire of the sound of her own name. But he was working harder than ever now, increasing his vocabulary at a rate which indicated that he must spend most of his solitary hours practising. It wasn't long before he managed a whole sentence. When she finished congratulating him, Irene sat beside him.

'You're winning, aren't you. This fight back . . .'

'*We* are,' he corrected.

She reached for the now dog-eared alphabet. 'You won't want this any more.'

Richard snatched it from her. 'That's mine.' He'd never part with it.

Irene nodded. 'The first glimmer of hope – chance to . . . communicate again?' She understood as never before how vital that had been.

Richard gradually found conversation easier, but it was some time before he explained why she'd been included in the speech therapy. 'You hated it, didn't you? Sorry. At first I had to have you around, you've become my lucky mascot.'

Briefly, she was amused, picturing herself along with goats and more unusual animals adopted by famous regiments. But some time afterwards when Richard finally was able to enlarge on this she was too moved to think of laughing.

'I wanted you to see, Irene, that I was determined – that no matter how hard or awful it was I'd keep at it. Because you'd convinced me that particular disability was something I'd got to overcome.'

By this time she was seeking every possible way of exercising Richard's vocal chords which seemed hitherto to have been frozen. By chance, they'd discovered a mutual interest in crossword puzzles. This soon proved an ideal means of keeping his mind alert as well. Irene read out the clues and had Richard tell her the solutions.

Most of the time this worked very well, giving them both some fun and satisfaction; but occasionally getting his tongue round some of the less common words frustrated him. Irene wondered if she was being unnecessarily cruel, but Richard laughed the day she put this to him.

'Somebody has to keep me at it.'

'I'm not driving you too hard?'

'Irene, I'm only sorry that you get let in for all the rotten tasks.'

'Don't let that worry you. I wouldn't have believed I'd find so much satisfaction again in any job.'

He raised a dark eyebrow. 'Is that all this is to you – another job?'

She avoided his straightforward gaze. 'How could it be only that when it's been my salvation? There was nothing . . .'

'So, even I am better than nothing,' he interrupted.

'Richard . . . ?' Irene was frowning. His bitter tone hurt. He glanced up, and shrugged.

So, that was it. *She'd* hurt him, something which she certainly hadn't intended.

'Richard,' she continued, disturbed into being absolutely frank. 'Whatever else, you've shown me that I cannot exist in a vacuum, avoiding all feeling in case it becomes painful.

This isn't just another treatment of another patient. I've done what I can because you matter to me.'

It was his turn to look away. She had answered as he had hoped, but it made everything worse, not better. He had wanted her to feel something, perhaps to prove he wasn't a . . . vegetable. She'd become so important to him during these past few weeks that it seemed already that she had been at North Fell House for ever. But what could he give, or do, in return?

He would never explain, therefore she'd never understand.

'I know,' Irene said quietly, going across to his chair by the sitting room window. 'I'm the same, an' all – always want to contribute something. And if you think there's not much . . .'

'Think!' he flared. 'Think? Do you believe I'm not everlastingly aware of how useless I am?'

'Richard.' Earnestly, she knelt by the chair, took him by the shoulders and made him face her. 'That isn't so, and if it were it wouldn't matter now, because you're improving all the time . . .'

'Ha.'

'Oh, if you're taking that attitude . . . ' She was all set to lose her temper, until she noticed him slowly shaking his head. Sensing his despair, Irene slid a hand to the back of his head, holding him to her, hoping her arms would convey the comfort she somehow couldn't voice.

All at once she had begun to see that, to Richard, even these weeks when he was gradually improving must have felt interminable. He had been confined for such an age within these four walls. Whilst she had been distracted by living with her own difficulties, to say nothing of concern for her folk in Halifax.

She didn't know how long they remained like that, she was determined not to move.

At last Richard gave a great sigh. 'Sorry.' If only everything altered when your body deteriorates, he thought, so you no longer had the same emotions. Wanting to win affection.

'I was being childish,' he said briskly. 'Wanting too much.'

'To be liked?' she suggested, shattering him by coming so near the mark. 'I'd never have stayed this long if I didn't like you. You may have provided my escape, but I'm not such a coward that I'd hide here for ever!'

'Is that a warning?'

Getting to her feet, she smiled affectionately. 'No – just a reminder that nobody can measure the use they are, just be being around.'

Again, Richard raised an eyebrow. 'It was very different when I was working, I was able to repay anything I considered extra in the way of service. Every so often I'd arrange an outing for my staff, even in wartime that is possible.'

Irene grinned. 'A model boss, eh?'

'I'm serious . . . '

'Too much so at times. With us, none of this matters.'

'To me, it does. And I've been thinking – you don't get a real change of scenery often enough. Use my car, Irene, take yourself off somewhere. Think of that petrol allowance doing nothing.'

She shook her head. But he had crystalized her own half-formed ideas.

'Thanks for the offer, Richard, but not yet. When you're up to coming with me.'

'Bit of a pipe dream, isn't it?'

'You know really how much you're improving. You could widen your horizons a little.'

He snorted scornfully.

But this was her opportunity. And if he snarled back she could take it.

'Richard – how long is it since you came out of hospital?'

He shrugged.

'And why haven't you pestered the life out of Giles Holroyd to get something done about this paralysis?'

Again, that shrug.

'Is it – is it because you don't want to learn the truth?'

Richard smiled ruefully, then inhaled deeply. 'Tell me . . . '

'Not sure I'm the one, ask Giles . . . '

'Forget the medical etiquette. You know as much, if not more, about me.'

'Well then – but remember I've no authority to say this – I believe you'll make a reasonable recovery.'

'Reasonable?'

'Walk again, get about, eventually.'

'Seems like a million years away.'

'Could well feel like it.' Suddenly, she was aware that she would stay here with him, however long it took. Even if . . . But John wouldn't come back to her. And that no longer hurt quite so much. 'The position's this, my dear, Giles and I both suspect a percentage of your paralysis isn't directly caused by the stroke.'

Richard was nodding. 'It'd have finished me off; or impaired other faculties.'

'So you've worked that out. Why the hell didn't you demand treatment?'

'What point was there? I couldn't even speak. Now, well . . .' His dark eyes delved into her skull. 'Irene, how do I go about it?'

Smiling, she swallowed her sigh of relief. 'By letting me contact your doctor. Each day you're immobilized counts against you. If you were my patient, I'd have had you along to physiotherapy long before this. And don't quote me on that to Giles Holroyd!'

So, you were a doctor, thought Richard, glad to have his suppositions confirmed. 'I quit stalling then, next time he brings that up, eh?'

He was actually grinning. She could have shaken him. Or hugged him again.

'You're not going to wait around till he raises the subject! He told me you didn't cooperate, now I know I have to believe him. Richard, why – why prevaricate over something this vital?'

He half turned from her to stare towards the garden trees. He didn't need to tell her; she knew that, dreary as his life here had been, it seemed safe.

'Most physiotherapists I've known have been quite tame. And, usually, attractive young women,' she said.

82

'The kind I'd have chatted up, once upon a time?'

'I wouldn't know, I've no idea what type you go for.'

'Too late for that, anyway.' He'd stopped smiling again.

'Who says?'

'Oh, come on, Irene – don't pull that one. I just might walk again, but more than that – no.'

'For someone with no medical knowledge you've remarkably fixed opinions!' Something else occurred to her. 'Have you thought what you'll do in the future?'

'Didn't know I had one.'

'That's up to you. I believe you've just decided you have. And it isn't as if yours is a fiercely active profession.'

Richard was looking pointedly at his right hand. Irene gave him the newspaper and a pen.

'You've plenty of time to practise with your left. Just finish that crossword we've begun.'

He was about to protest, but she forced herself to let him get on with it alone.

'I didn't know you were lazy!' she exclaimed as she went out of the room.

For the first time in Irene's working life, though, there soon were entire days when there seemed nothing she could do for anybody. If she even extended a hand in Richard's direction he was likely to brush it aside. 'I can manage – I'm not a child.' And he kept reproving her for fussing.

She went home to Halifax for a weekend, hoping the excitement there would take her mind off the situation at North Fell, and restore her sense of proportion.

Mavis had produced a baby girl and Irene had been waiting eagerly for the opportunity to admire her niece. As soon as she opened the door and heard a very new infant crying she experienced a powerful urge to run in and pick it up.

Mother and baby were occupying the sitting room, with the proud grandmother in attendance. Both Mavis and Elsie beamed when they saw who had arrived.

'Ay, Irene – just come and have a look,' her mother urged, while Mavis, still smiling, beckoned.

'She's awake,' she announced, as if her sister were deaf. 'You're lucky to catch her with her eyes open.'

'And her mouth!' exclaimed Irene, grinning. But her feelings were anything but flippant. And now she was close enough to see properly she found the tiny girl was adorable.

Deep violet-blue eyes vied for attention with a quantity of extremely dark hair.

'Mavis, she's gorgeous! What are you going to call her?'

'We haven't rightly decided as yet. I want it to be Heather, but we haven't had chance to talk it over.'

'Heather would be nice. And look at all that hair . . .'

'Ralph is very dark,' said Mavis, in the tone of voice that suggested he'd selected his colouring himself.

'Well, you've certainly produced a beauty, old love,' Irene remarked. And the little one had stopped crying now.

Delighted though she was with her first grandchild, Elsie wasn't best pleased with the reminders that the baby resembled her father. 'That hair'll all disappear, of course,' she observed. 'There's no knowing what colour she'll end up with.'

'And how are you feeling, Mavis, did you have a bad time?' inquired Irene, sitting beside her sister's nursing chair.

'I'm all right now, thanks. Yesterday was my first day up, though I'd said from the start that stopping in bed for a fortnight were proper daft.'

'And the actual birth?'

Mavis shrugged. 'Not so bad, I suppose.'

She tried to shelve the memory of the pain and how scared she'd been, and failed. Ever since that awful night and the day that followed she'd been unable to shut her eyes without living again through some part of that nightmarish labour.

Nothing had been like she'd imagined. Having a father who was a doctor, she'd felt reassured that he would know what to do. Only, perhaps through a subconscious wish for it to be otherwise, she'd somehow overlooked the fact that he didn't treat his own family.

As soon as her pains began gaining pace, the midwife had been sent for. And when Dad was called out to a sick patient, Mavis could have sworn he seemed relieved. The cramp-like agony might have been more endurable if her husband had been there, holding her hand, reassuring her. But Ralph was miles away in London, unable to get leave.

She had kept telling herself that she only had to keep going until morning – by the time it was daylight she would be a mother. But that had been wishful thinking. It was early evening before the baby finally decided to appear. To Mavis it had seemed that for hour after hour she was being stretched and torn. And in her tormented mind she'd begun to fear it would all be for nothing.

Now that this tiny scrap who depended so much on her was here, though, she could forgive her the pain she'd caused. Even if she didn't feel like other mothers who said they'd forgotten it already.

'I'll bet Ralph's highly delighted with her, what did he say?' Irene began, and felt her mother's warning look.

Mavis's smile was tight. 'Didn't I say? He couldn't be spared just for the moment. They're all planning towards demobilization, you know.'

'Oh, I see. Well, he'll be thrilled when he does get chance to see her, any road.' She herself had never been more entranced with an infant. And had never experienced such a powerful urge to start a family of her own.

'You can hold her for a minute,' said Mavis and handed across the shawl-enveloped bundle.

The baby was warm through the layers of crochet and knitting, and smelt of milk and soap as well. From appearances, Mavis lavished more time and attention on bathing her than ever she had on herself. Despite her interest in appearing glamorous, her own daily preparations had always been slapdash, hurried because of the need to get on with something more exciting.

Irene reflected on how her sister might adapt to motherhood once the novelty had expired. And experienced a protectiveness so fierce that if the child had been less fragile she'd have hugged her tightly.

Watching her, Elsie wondered why on earth her elder daughter had been so *senseless*. Why did she have to go and fall for a married chap when the outcome could only be a deal of heartache?

'Don't you wish you'd got wed, and had a bairn like her?' she asked, her troubled eyes revealing her longing to see Irene happy.

'I certainly would love this one if she were mine!' Irene said, smiling. And wondered if her family would ever stop reminding her about John. Grimly, she kept the smile glued on to her face; no one would learn how deeply she suddenly was yearning for a kiddie.

Soon the baby would cry again, or stir fitfully, and Mavis would reclaim her. Savouring the nearness of the child and relishing the perfection of those beautiful eyes would have to end. And she herself would have to learn to live with yet another longing that seemed to have no prospect of being satisfied.

'How's our Norman going on?' she asked. 'Have you heard lately?'

At long last he'd responded well enough to medication to be allowed away from his own doctors, and was convalescing at Grange-over-Sands.

'We had a postcard t'other day,' Elsie informed her. 'It's on the mantelpiece there. Let me have the bairn, then you can have a look.'

Surrendering the baby wasn't what she wanted, but happen it was for the best. Holding her like that was increasing these ridiculous fantasies which were all the more powerful for being unpredicted.

Norman's card was as brief as she'd expected, merely confirming his safe arrival and that the meals were awful.

'No doubt you'll feed him up again once you get him home,' she said. He mustn't be permitted to lose the bit of weight he'd regained since the thyroid was stabilized.

Their mother smiled. 'I'm not waiting till then! I've got your dad to say he'll run me over there on Sunday. And I shan't be going empty-handed.'

'You can take him some sweet coupons,' Mavis offered. She was determined to get her figure back. Ralph had always liked her narrow waist and said she had the tightest little bottom he'd ever seen.

'I could have let you have some an' all, only I've left my coupons at North Fell.'

'You could post some coupons on to him, Irene. He'd be glad of a few sweets to help pass the time.'

The weekend went by pleasantly enough, although when their parents set off for Grange leaving her and Mavis together Irene soon gathered that her sister wasn't happy about her husband's attitude.

'I did think he'd have been wanting to see her by now,' she confided, her large grey eyes filling. 'It's all right for men, in't it? They don't have to go into labour and all that. And they aren't wakened in the night for feeds. Not that I'm grumbling – she is a lovely little thing, isn't she?'

Irene wished she'd had the opportunity for a quiet word with one or other of their parents about Mavis's husband. It seemed most unnatural to her that he hadn't been near to see his daughter. But most of the time Mavis was putting on a brave front. When Irene gave her a last hug and tenderly kissed the sleeping baby, she left the house full of admiration for her sister's pluck.

When Irene next had a letter from Halifax she learned that Ralph Parkin had finally visited his wife and infant. And Norman was home again from Grange-over-Sands. According to their mother he still tired easily, but he seemed to have accepted that, and was more cheerful. He was reporting back to the RAF, joining the rest of a large number of forces now complaining about how long demobilization was taking.

A month had flown since the Japanese surrender, yet once victory celebrations were over it seemed to Irene and Richard that the news continued to be war-related. There was a certain satisfaction in hearing from Oslo that Quisling had been condemned to death for treason, and knowing the commandant of Belsen and guards from there and

Auschwitz would be tried for their atrocities was some consolation. But our men returning emaciated, and many of them mentally shattered, were bringing home the full extent of the horror.

Already appalled by pictures of conditions in the German camps, they both shuddered now at tales of folk condemned to working literally as slaves, constructing the Siam to Burma railway. Irene was particularly angered by the Japanese withholding vital medicines from prisoners. Despite thousands of years of civilization, men seemed to be growing more barbaric.

'Will we ever recover from this lot, will we ever get everything sorted out to folks' satisfaction?' she demanded. Today there'd been news that the Congress Party in India was calling for their country's freedom from colonial rule. Was that going to cause another upset?

Richard sighed. 'Let's hope the repercussions will only serve to reinforce everyone's resolution that wars solve nothing, and differences must be sorted by peaceable means.'

'Aye, but we've heard that before, haven't we? "The war to end wars", wasn't that what they said about the last lot? I was nobbut a year old in 1914, but by the time the Armistice came I could understand that the grown-ups in our family were optimistic – counting on having won the right to a better future.'

'Let's hope we've all matured a bit, and that there'll be rational methods now for easing tensions.'

'I certainly hope there will.'

The problems seemed unending, though, and anyone who cared at all was compelled to admit they might be overwhelming. So many people who had come through the past six years or more of suffering appeared to have lost everything except their lives. What was going to happen about the Jews, Irene wondered. The government had referred the issue of Jewish immigration into Palestine to the United Nations. Where would all that lead?

Amid continuing international difficulties her own seemed small by comparison and made her feel ashamed. But they were increasing, and real enough to her.

These days, fond though she'd grown of Richard, they flared at each other too frequently. And always over some aspect of the same situation. One Tuesday evening in that September of 1945 she caught herself arguing with him over something and nothing – who should fill in the crossword puzzle. Horrified by her own attitude, she realized beyond doubt that there must be some kind of reappraisal.

She knew she was wrong to oppose anything that was helping Richard to progress. Was she subconsciously clinging to a state of affairs which had made her happy? It had been agreeable doing things together, getting him to struggle to become more active. And she did prefer being in charge, she supposed she always had.

Irene went for a walk. She climbed the lower slopes of the fells that led straight up from the garden, and sat on a great wodge of limestone, trying to analyse why she was like this, what she really needed.

As she sat staring out across towards Fountains Fell, some of Richard's words came back to her. 'I'm not a child . . .' Had he, albeit unwittingly, come very near the truth? Had she channelled into caring for him not only her doctor's skills, but her mothering instincts? She'd been eager enough to supply every need. He never would recover completely, though, if she held him back by preserving this relationship. He must be helped to help himself, no matter the cost to her feelings.

There was a certain chill in the air, more than a touch of autumn in the breeze catching her skirt, some of the leaves were bronzing. The back end, as Yorkshire folk called it, often brought this feeling that shortening days implied that opportunities too were diminishing.

Irene returned to the house very tired, and feeling raw. She looked around the door of Richard's room to say good night.

Waving the newspaper, he grinned at her. 'I've finished it – every single clue.'

'Jolly good, show me . . .'

She eventually went up to her own room feeling shattered. If her new role was offering praise and encouragement, and no practical assistance, she didn't think much of it. Was it perhaps time she looked for a more demanding job? There seemed little here but reminders that she was no longer entirely happy with the way she couldn't show the depth of her feelings for Richard.

While she lay in bed, unable to settle, she again became almost overwhelmed with the longing for a different life, for a home that was her own, for children. She pictured them dark-haired – and realized with a jolt that their colouring had no connection whatever with her having admired baby Heather's.

6

By October, as the first of the men who'd been imprisoned by the Japanese were returning to Britain, Irene was regularly driving Richard to hospital for treatment. Encouraged by the prospect of greater freedom, he increasingly used the wheelchair for getting about the ground floor of North Fell House and also the garden.

He didn't say very much, but his changed attitude to life was very apparent. Irene was delighted for him and found renewed interest in ensuring that he improved further. She was pleased that Giles Holroyd confirmed the hospital reports were favourable, in line with their own conclusions. There was no reason why Richard shouldn't in time lead a far more active life.

It was good having him around, sharing meals with Daphne and herself, as he did except when Daphne had friends in. He then retreated to his room. It wasn't healthy, but understandable, and since she still hadn't got to know Daphne as well as she'd have liked, Irene always left her to her friends and joined Richard.

There was a lot about Daphne that puzzled her, even since hostility towards herself had eased. There had to be more to Richard's sister than was evident on the surface. Now he was so much better, Irene couldn't help noticing how attractive he was, but Daphne was stunning.

One evening, sitting with Richard, Irene tried to learn the truth. 'This job of Daphne's, is it the sort of thing she's always done?'

'More or less, it was clerical work before. Why?'

'I just wondered. I thought she might still be single because of dedication to a career.'

'Oh.' Suddenly he sounded wary. Irene couldn't imagine why. Richard sighed. 'She hasn't told you then?'

'Told me what?' Irene only wished Daphne did confide in her.

'How I've messed things up for her.'

Richard certainly was disturbed. Irene silently cursed herself for probing. Now she'd begun, though, the damage was done. She might as well get to the bottom of this. And in any case it was a mistake to always overprotect someone purely because they'd been ill.

'Surely, these days, she could continue with whatever it is.'

'It's not that simple. It isn't feeling that she must stick around as a kind of watchdog. That need ended with your arrival.' He paused. This was difficult. Yet beyond the unpleasantness of what had to be said was a glimmer of light – the relief which would come with talking this through with Irene.

She smiled. 'Forget it – it doesn't matter. Nothing to do with me, any road.' There'd be other ways of really getting to know Daphne.

Richard swung his wheelchair around and moved to the window, then patted the window seat. 'Come and sit here.'

When she had done so, he gazed intently at her for a moment. He felt strangely sure that she would understand.

'I've never discussed this with anyone, it's her business more than mine. But you'll keep it to yourself. Irene – I've done the most awful thing to Daphne, and there's nothing in the world I can do to rectify it.'

He looked deeply distressed. Irene felt sickened, a frown narrowed her blue eyes. What on earth could he mean?

'She was a strange little thing, even as a child. I'd been more serious minded than lots of youngsters, I know. But there was something . . . otherworldly about Daphne. As you'll have seen, there's quite a difference in our ages, she was born when Mother was in her forties. A difficult birth, Mother died a year later. Father was a professor, of theology and philosophy. Daphne idolized him. The sort of relationship they had made me jealous. Don't get me wrong – he was scrupulously fair, you can't help natural preferences.

'He and I had some grand old arguments – he labelled me too materialistic. I don't honestly believe I was, but he didn't always understand my analytical approach, although he respected it.' Richard hesitated. 'Am I boring you?'

'No. I've always wanted to know a bit more about you.'

He was surprised. When he'd time to think about it, he'd be pleased. But he must get this lot said. 'Well, this was really to put you in the picture about young Daphne. You see, she took to all his ideas and beliefs, whereas I offered the logical difference of opinion. Hers was the trusting, unwavering faith that I dismissed as "Sunday schoolish". Know what I mean?'

Irene nodded. Happen nobody knew better.

'A couple of years ago we learned how much it all meant to her. Father was still alive and the two of them spent hours talking things over. One day she told me. She was convinced she had a vocation to become a nun. She'd already contacted the Anglican Order at Horbury. Once the war ended, she would throw everything up and enter the convent. Even when the old man died so suddenly, that didn't deter her. "I'm glad he knew what I want to do," she said, "now I'll never change my mind." '

'But you talk as if she has changed it . . .'

His gesture embraced the wheelchair and his legs, and he was scowling. 'Because of this.'

'You said yourself she doesn't have to stop here now.'

'You don't see it, do you? Nor did I for long enough. I'd got it all worked out. Once over the initial shock of finding myself a crock, I decided no one was making sacrifices on my behalf. I got Giles to fix up a daily nurse and to arrange for someone to look after me and the house. Then he explained to Daphne that she could either go then, or as soon as the war was over.'

'I'd been that wrapped up in myself I hadn't seen how she'd changed. I didn't believe her when she told me. Didn't want to.'

93

Irene could guess what was coming, and couldn't bear that he should be hurt any more by dwelling on it. But Richard ploughed on again before she could stop him.

'Yes, it had all gone. She stood in this room, looking too upset to weep. "You can cancel all that, Rich. I don't want to any longer. If there is a God, I can't serve him, not now." ' Yet again, he paused. 'I hoped that, given time, she'd recover her faith. But . . . ' He shook his head, was silent.

Irene touched his arm. 'I am sorry, Richard.'

'Yes, it's tough on her.'

'I don't mean that. I mean for you.'

'Me?' He was astounded. 'Nonsense. I took away the only thing she had — what mattered most to her.'

'It wasn't in any way your fault.'

'Does that help her?'

Despite the gravity of his expression, Irene smiled slightly. 'Ay, lad! I think your father was right, you see things too coldly. They aren't purely black and white.'

'Philosophizing now, are we? What's coming next — the search for truth, and all that jazz? I have tried it, you know. Used to read all those knowledgeable authors who're supposed to have all the answers . . . ' He was staring unseeingly beyond her, towards a past irretrievably gone. 'Spent hours talking it all out, M . . . er — this friend and I.'

Irene sensed that Richard would confide no further and this friend, whoever he or she was, had meant a lot to him. And had since been excluded. It was time they changed the topic.

'Come on,' she suggested, 'let's sort out some records.'

Richard smiled wryly. 'Take his mind off it — that your antidote?'

Irene laughed. 'You know my methods too well!'

He grinned. 'Some of them do pay off.'

They were listening to Chopin, a polonaise, when Richard said out of the blue: 'It's helped enormously, telling you. As if I'd been allowed to explain. You know, Irene, I'd never consciously hurt anyone, nor destroy anything for them.'

94

'I'm sure you wouldn't.'

'Yet I seem destined to bring trouble to everyone I care about.'

'You don't to me.'

It was out before she weighed counting herself in that category. 'Oh.' It wasn't embarrassment she felt, so much as dread of having him remind her she was only employed here.

Richard laughed good-naturedly at her exclamation, and relief warmed her.

'Go ahead, include yourself,' he said. 'I was, anyway. Couldn't do otherwise – my constant companion.' Quite suddenly he wasn't laughing at all. 'It's good to learn that's how you feel. It has meant one hell of a lot, you know – having you here. Not only because you ensure that I don't neglect any possible progress, but you've always given me something to look forward to . . . '

'M'm?'

'When things were really bad especially – knowing that, no matter what, through sleepless nights or whatever, the moment would come when you'd walk through that door. And I wouldn't be shut up inside my own head, with the difficulties chasing each other around there. There would be a let-up, you'd give me something else to think about, a fresh challenge or two.' And, he thought, a hope to which he'd clung.

Richard's honesty that evening did Irene the world of good. She was sure now that, at last, she was over losing John and all the repercussions of the affair. She was actually happy.

For a time everything was fine. Richard was making progress with the physiotherapist's help, he could stand unaided, and she herself kept him to the exercises at home. He was relaxing increasingly so that they enjoyed most of the hours spent together.

The first peacetime Christmas came, and was celebrated quietly at North Fell House. Irene had decided to remain with Richard and his sister rather than going home. Her father was on duty for much of the holiday, and with

Norman and Mavis and the baby around, her parents would hardly be lonely.

Some weeks afterwards Irene was driving Richard home from treatment when she felt him glancing repeatedly towards her.

'What is it?' she inquired.

He smiled, but his dark eyes were too anxious to lighten.

'Do I get to drive again? I often wonder, especially these days when there's hope petrol won't always be rationed.'

Irene frowned. 'Sorry, love, I can't tell you that. You'll have to ask the hospital people.'

'Is that a kind way of saying it's impossible?'

'No. Truthfully, Richard, I simply can't be sure. But I have known folk with a similar history who've driven at after.'

'I see.' He sighed ruefully. 'You know how I love asking the experts back there what they think. Still, could be worth while.'

'And whatever their verdict you'll make yourself live with it.'

He laughed. 'Flatterer!'

'I think I know you pretty well by now.'

'Or have shaped me into the person I ought to be?'

'God, that's hysterical! I wouldn't back my will against yours, ever.'

Richard smiled. 'If you lack anything in willpower, my dear, it certainly is compensated by being crafty.'

'Are you grumbling again?'

'You know damned well I'm not. Somehow, you always find a way to prove how right you are. But now I'm being angelic about physiotherapy I'm trying to be patient – waiting for some kind of reward for good conduct . . . '

'You're getting better, isn't that sufficient?'

He laughed again. 'You're slow today, Irene, I mean a real treat. Like an outing somewhere, simply to enjoy ourselves.'

'About time! You've kept me waiting long enough.'

Irene carefully planned every detail of their first day out. Because neither of them could delay until summer, they took thick sweaters and drove just a mile or two to where she could draw the car off the road at a spot where a gap between trees offered a view across Malham Tarn.

The weather cooperated fully; although it was only March it proved warm enough to justify spreading car rugs on the grass for the picnic they had intended eating in the car.

'The best limestone scenery in Britain,' Richard informed her, already relishing getting away from the house. He'd brought binoculars for observing any birdlife congregating about the tarn, but first was training them on Fountains Fell, renewing acquaintance with medieval sheep walks. And with evidence of the tiny folds and fields once used by Celtic herdsmen. His sigh of sheer delight told Irene how well this outing was chosen.

A few feet away squirrels descended from a pair of trees and amused them as, enticed by scraps, they grew venturesome. While they were watching the darting creatures a car stopped farther along the road and a mother and toddler hurried towards them, fascinated by the squirrels. The little lad demanded a share of their crumbs and Richard obliged, solemnly passing them across by the handful, then teasing the youngster when chubby fingers failed to disperse the bait accurately.

The boy's mother began talking, telling them that they lived in the house just visible a mile or more away in a fold of the hill.

'I know,' said Richard quickly. 'I've represented you, haven't I?'

The woman smiled. 'Thought perhaps you'd have forgotten. Yes, you saw me through the divorce.'

He nodded towards the boy. 'You remarried then.'

'Oh, yes. And never cease to be thankful that you talked me into extricating myself from a man who used wartime partings to excuse his liaisons.' She smiled again, and beckoned the child. 'Beginning afresh can prove infinitely more rewarding than any of our earlier enthusiasms.'

'I'm sure.'

As mother and son left, Irene felt Richard's gaze resting on her.

Neither of them had much to say while they felt the quiet and the expanse of wild countryside soaking into them, renewing a sense of proportion. When it grew chill and they were obliged to think of returning home Irene began collecting together their picnic things.

She helped Richard the short distance to the car. But when she opened the door he checked her. 'In a minute . . .'

Irene went back for the rugs and, kneeling, glanced towards him. He was standing very erect, absorbing the tarn, the fells beyond, the breeze rippling the water. How tall he was, she noticed and – smiling – how extremely attractive.

When Irene returned to him again, Richard looked down at her. She felt his arm about her shoulders and, briefly, he held her close against his side.

Their affinity that day ought to have made Irene more contented, yet as weeks passed she became increasingly troubled. Richard, steadily overcoming the paralysis, was naturally eager to extend his independence. She was delighted for him, but her dread that she soon wouldn't be needed here kept returning. She awakened one morning feeling particularly uneasy. When she went downstairs she found an envelope with a London postmark had arrived for her. The writing was Martin Fyson's and she itched to open it immediately, his letters generally cheered her. But there was no time for that, this was Richard's hospital day.

Waiting in the car outside Physiotherapy, she opened Martin's letter. Only the news wasn't good – or not for her. Vera, John's wife, had had a son. Irene didn't like admitting it hurt, but it did. She was cross with herself for being irrational: she wanted no further contact with John, would be annoyed if she happened to meet him again. But she could have done without this information. Suddenly, she felt as badly alone as ever. And, Lord, but she couldn't bear the thought of never having children.

She'd been shaken by her emotions while holding Mavis's baby, she hadn't needed another reminder that, with each year that passed, motherhood for herself grew less likely. Had John killed that hope? She could hear him now: 'Irene, there's only one thing to do. Vera needs me. I love you – maybe love you both in different ways. But she is my wife, is having difficulty coping with this Land Army job she's doing, and hasn't your ability to survive alone.'

Memory was interrupted when Richard emerged from the hospital, laughing and talking with the accompanying nurse, as he skilfully steered his chair down the ramp. He always was cheerful on hospital days. He looked utterly carefree, all agog at some pretty young thing's attention. While she hung around, alone, waiting till he spared her a glance.

Waving cheerily to the nurse, he headed towards the car. Like an automaton, Irene helped him into the passenger seat, then folded and stowed the chair. As she drove off she felt his glance that told her she'd omitted something. But she was too choked to speak, desperately afraid of breaking down. And this time there was no way that she could explain her distress. Richard made one or two attempts at conversation but Irene didn't take them up. Passing near a place where a gap in the wall gave them a clear view of the river running alongside, he spoke again.

'All right, stop the car – just here.'

'Why?'

'Because I want you to.'

Irene shrugged and parked. The engine died to an ominous silence. But he'd wanted this, he'd better get on with it.

'What the hell have I done wrong?'

Shaken by his sharp tone, Irene blinked then shook her head.

Richard sighed, tried again, this time quietly. 'Irene, what have I done?'

'Nothing.' Again they sat in silence. She reached towards the ignition.

'No.' His voice was very firm. 'We'll have this out.'

'But it's nothing to do with you.'

'Then why this treatment?' He forestalled her protest: 'Don't pretend with me. I don't go much on hypocrisy.'

'It's not your fault – at least . . .' Irene bit her lip. 'You're not going to like me for it . . .'

'Let's get it over with then.'

'It's proper daft really, something that's built up over the past few weeks . . .' She hesitated. 'Don't get me wrong, I'm delighted you're making such good progress . . .' Put into words, it seemed more as if she were trying to hold him back to boost her own self-esteem. But she must set the record straight. 'I – well, now you're so much better, I'm beginning to feel rather superfluous.'

'I guessed as much. Afraid I'm not remaining an invalid to justify your existence.' Richard succeeded in making it sound even worse. 'If you must have someone helpless, you'll have to look elsewhere.'

It was all true. Irene couldn't think of a thing to say. Awkwardness, tangible as a fence, filled the space between them in the car.

'You'd better decide whether you want to move on,' he said eventually, still angry and disappointed. He had been relying on her to be here, to see him through. 'Maybe your coming to me has served its purpose, for you . . .'

'And – and for you?' she ventured.

He merely shrugged. Whatever happened, whatever his needs, he'd never attempt to hold her against her wishes. Nor against what was best for her.

Irene gazed across the glistening river, wondering if he was right, no longer sure what she wanted. Except – she remembered about Vera's baby and that adorable infant of her sister's. Her eyes filled with tears. Surreptitiously, she wiped them away.

'It can't be that you're frightened of losing this job.' Slightly mocking, Richard's voice was gentle now.

She couldn't hold back any longer. 'If you must know, there was this man – John. I've just heard he is now a father.'

Richard felt his throat constricting. That was a shock – and not really because there'd been someone that she'd lost, and certainly not because this chap was capable of fathering a child.

But what of all the times when they had seemed so close, times like sitting near the tarn the other week, had they meant nothing to her? And what of the things she had said – that *he* mattered to her, had they been no more than a few empty words?

'Nothing very extraordinary in that, is there?' he said. After another uncomfortable pause, he continued: 'That locks you out, doesn't it?' He couldn't let her go on eating her heart out for this fellow who plainly did not give a damn.

'You needn't be so brutal.'

'I'm not apologizing. Sounds like it's high time you were convinced that episode is over. If this is the only way, I'm glad it's happened.'

'Glad! Can't you see how upset I am?'

'You'll get over it, *if* you want to.'

Again, Irene reached for the ignition key, this time Richard didn't stop her. They drove home in a silence which was maintained during luncheon. He shrugged when asked if he needed her that afternoon, so Irene made herself scarce.

Throughout that day she tried to analyse her feelings. Was he right – did she wish to leave now his independence was increasing? Would she be happier with somebody who needed her more? Would she be better in work that didn't make her so isolated, where there might be a chance of living a more normal life, of meeting someone who would eventually want the home and family which suddenly seemed important to her?

She tried to imagine the kind of place she would go to – and couldn't. All she could see, even when she eventually closed her eyes that night, was Richard – smiling, as he did when he mastered some new feat.

Lying sleepless in bed, Irene realized that other factors had contributed to her dissatisfaction. She didn't go out much, but she read newspapers and listened to the wireless. And everywhere folk were planning what they would do now the war was over. Nearer at home, Mavis was always on about setting up home with Ralph and the baby. Norman had visited his old firm while he was on sick leave, had made sure the job they were obliged to give him would mean carrying on from where his RAF service had interrupted. And *she* had no plans.

By the time daylight came next morning, she was thoroughly wretched. Drawing back her curtains, she looked out at the fells. A few traces of mist were drifting away now, but there was no sun breaking through, and their steep sides appeared grim. Everything about them seemed daunting, much like her own life. She had struggled and struggled to overcome all that hopelessness, to take this job, to compel Richard to begin fighting to get his health back, and now where was she . . . ? She felt as if she'd battled to carry some great burden up these slopes, only to find she had to start all over again right from the bottom.

Happen part of today's burden was of her own making, though. She might have spent hours wondering what Richard really wanted her to do, but she had realized among it all that she owed him an almighty apology. Even if the worst happened and they both decided that she might as well leave, she couldn't have him believing she would ever try to hold him back.

When she eventually went downstairs and Richard wasn't in his room, Irene felt more disturbed than ever. Was he continuing to avoid her?

On the threshold of the kitchen, she halted, surprised. Despite her low spirits, she smiled. Richard's chair was parked alongside the work surface; beside the toaster he'd placed slices of bread. It was the first occasion, since the morning she'd never forget, that he'd attempted to help prepare breakfast. She had assumed Richard was very much the kind of man who kept out of the kitchen as much as possible anyway. And so long as he'd continued to be as active as he could she hadn't cared.

Today she couldn't fathom what his motives were. Was he perhaps demonstrating that even when his sister had gone off to work he was capable of managing on his own?

'Good morning,' he greeted her, his smile wry.

Irene realized that she had simply been standing there, staring, wondering. 'Good morning,' she responded, but warily. He sounded bright enough. Until yesterday, she'd thought she knew him sufficiently well by now to predict most of his reactions. But he'd bewildered and upset her, she was no longer so sure of him that she could behave as though nothing had happened. And there was still that apology which had to be said . . .

'Toast?' he inquired genially.

'Please, Richard.' Again, Irene looked at him. He appeared perfectly relaxed. She wished she was! Yet was there some tension in the angle of his head, were his brown eyes just that bit guarded? Would she be wiser if she kept off references to the previous day?

Instead of popping bread into the toaster, Richard returned to studying the newspaper. 'There's something here should interest you,' he began, without glancing up.

Irene smiled. It really sounded as though things were back to normal. She started crossing towards the cooker.

'Yes,' he continued, 'they want help at a new home for disabled soldiers, over at . . . '

Frowning, Irene faced him again. His expression was inscrutable.

' . . . Somebody who's willing to work with the chronically sick.'

Her heart plummeted. So he had no use for her now. He wanted to prove that he could cope. She would have to go.

'I'm not interested in owt o' that sort,' she said, reverting to her local vernacular without even noticing. Suddenly, she was too distressed to even pretend that she only cared about what was best for him.

'It's just up your street . . . '

He beckoned, and she crossed reluctantly and snatched the paper. She was so disturbed it took her a few minutes to read the heading.

Houses for Sale.

Irene stared blankly at him. Slowly, Richard smiled. And then he laughed.

'Sorry. A rotten trick. But it told me all I wanted to know.'

'M'm?' She was utterly confused, too upset to think.

'At least, you're not after the first job getting you away from me!'

'You daft bat! Playing a trick like that.'

Just as swiftly, Richard had grown serious. 'Irene, come and sit down. I want to talk to you.'

'I've something to say an' all – how sorry . . .'

'That can wait – this isn't going to.' He reached out towards the nearest chair and dragged it close to his own. 'Sit down.'

This firm line made her give him a look. She smiled, and complied.

'I've done a lot of thinking since yesterday,' Richard told her. 'I believe I'm beginning to understand what it must be like for you. You've obviously had medical training. You've spent the whole of your working life doing things for others. Trying to make people well, coaxing, cajoling, chiding them into doing your way – because it was the only way they'd recover. You're not my doctor – perhaps as well, I'm a lousy patient. But you are still pretty important. I tried to tell you – the one who's made me want to go on living . . .'

'Don't say any more, please.' This lump in her throat was choking her. If she began weeping, relief would ensure that tears flowed without any restraint.

'You won't stop me now, Irene. I was desolate when you came. I shall be sorry if you don't wish to stay on and take your share of the easier times ahead.' And he would miss her as he'd only ever missed one person in his life before.

'But I might have been holding you back, that was wicked.'

'Yes – you're a tyrant of a woman!' Richard was laughing now, and she felt infinitely better already. But then a shadow fell across his expressive features. 'There is something else, though . . .'

'Go on . . .' she prompted.

'I was brutal about John. I'm sorry.'

'Happen you were right, though, an' all.'

Richard raised an eyebrow, but said no more. Pensively, he gazed at her. Yesterday, when he'd have let her go, he'd been less than honest even to himself about his real feelings, about his needs. He must learn where he stood. Once, he'd have managed alone to tackle whatever lay ahead. Limitations made that more difficult; he'd realized during the slow night hours that he was past sacrificing what he most needed to a bit of pride.

'Irene – just how tied are you to this kind of work, to this pseudo-nursing?'

'Don't know really, never tried anything but medicine.' She wondered what was coming next, but already was eager with anticipation.

'Would you consider a post as – say, personal assistant, cum chauffeuse, cum confidante . . . '

'Depends who the boss was,' she interrupted. And couldn't keep the sheer thankfulness out of her voice.

Her obvious satisfaction warmed more truth from Richard than he'd intended.

'Oh, some old chap who, much as he mightn't like admitting it, knows in his heart of hearts that he'll never go back to life as it was.' He looked her straight in the eyes. 'Used to pride myself on being a lone wolf, now – well, Irene, I wouldn't admit to needing anyone else.'

'Working with you sounds very tempting. But, Richard – and I mean this – it'd be on one condition.'

'Which is?'

'If you catch me trying to make you depend on me too much, order me to cut it out.'

He nodded, smiling, then leaned across and astonished her by kissing her cheek. 'Glad we've settled our differences.'

Guiltily, Irene recalled something. 'How did you get on yesterday? I'm afraid I was too bitchy to ask.'

Amused, Richard smiled. 'Yes – what did give you that face like thunder?'

'Sounds ridiculous, but . . . it – it was the way you and that young nurse were laughing together.'

Richard laughed then, heartily. 'Now I've heard the lot! A crock like me giving somebody pangs of jealousy.'

'Afraid it's all part of being possessive and . . .'

' . . . And hating to feel excluded. Like John and his wife; and Richard and . . . whatever that kid's name is?'

Irene couldn't meet his gaze. But with his good hand he made her face him. His brown eyes were very serious. 'My dear, sometimes it's good for all of us to learn somebody's sufficiently interested to care if it isn't always with them that we share . . . what little there is.'

Irene nodded, swallowing hard, containing the impulse to put her arms round him. She tried to sound brisk. 'Well, you still haven't told me about physiotherapy. What did you manage?'

'Three.'

'Three what?'

'Unaided steps, you idiot, what do you think?'

'Richard! That's magnificent. But you never said.'

'No. Well, there were reasons.'

'My fault. I'm ever so sorry. Any road, Daphne would be thrilled. What did she say?'

'Daphne was out. Have you forgotten?'

'Oh. So . . .' She was beginning to feel dreadful about her resentment which had been so needless.

'So, I had a huff! Didn't do much for me, and you see – you missed out on something I was only too eager to share with you. Still, it did force me to consider where we go from here, about working again. And that was your influence originally.'

Irene smiled. 'It'll be great! Where will you open up an office?'

'Probably here at the house. It'll simplify matters, initially, and property is likely to be in short supply, in any case.'

'I think you'll be ready before the summer's over. You need only wait until you're walking better, then there won't be too much to overcome all at once.'

7

The whole family would be together. Irene had arrived that morning, after leaving North Fell House just as the autumn sky was lightening over the fells. And Mavis was absolutely elated because Ralph had promised to travel up from London on the same train as her brother.

They were celebrating Norman's demobilization. He was due at Halifax station in the early afternoon. There'd been quite a discussion about who should meet him; they couldn't all cram into Donald Hainsworth's car. In the end, Irene had suggested that their mother ought to be there, and Mavis. After all, her husband would be arriving at the same time.

'I'll look after Heather if you like,' she volunteered, she could hardly wait to get hold of her. 'I'll have the kettle on an' all.'

'I'd be glad if you would keep an eye on her,' Mavis responded. 'She should be having a nap, so you might be lucky and she won't be yelling her head off.'

Heather tended to be a restless baby, who rarely slept for long periods and seemed bored with the idea of lying in her pram or cot.

Irene was unperturbed by the prospect of her niece being wakeful. The station was only down the bottom end of the town, they wouldn't be away that long. And she didn't see enough of the little one.

Developing quickly, Heather seemed interested in everything that was going on. The one thing she didn't like was being ignored. When a tentative wail set up from the pram parked in the hall, Irene smiled to herself and rushed to lift her out. She was certainly gaining weight, was far less fragile; there was no cause to feel nervous about holding her. Today, she ceased crying the instant Irene touched her.

'You wanted company, is that it?' she suggested, smiling into the dark eyes now changed from violet to brown.

Heather kicked chubby legs and wriggled in her arms.

'I think we'd better sit down.' Irene went through to find an easy chair. She was going to enjoy these few minutes. And who would know that she couldn't help picturing herself at North Fell with an infant?

Two large tables had been pushed together at one end of the room, and both were covered with crockery and plate upon plate of sandwiches, homemade sausage rolls and cakes. Their mother must have been busy for weeks, never mind days, preparing this spread. Mavis claimed to have helped with the baking, but Irene knew her sister. Mavis had never been particularly domesticated, now she had the excuse of a baby needing attention she wasn't likely to have changed.

Still, the lass did seem to always be tired, even though she hadn't gone out to work again since Heather was born. Irene only hoped that Ralph would buck her up by proving more amenable during this visit. She herself had never taken to him, but happen that had a lot to do with the way he'd been on the day they were introduced.

She wouldn't forget in a hurry how Mavis had brought him across Commercial Street to her in the blackout. Irene had been home for the weekend at the time, snatching a few hours away from the blitz because their parents had complained for weeks that they hardly ever saw her.

The previous night in London a bomb had dropped in the next street to her surgery. She had been tending casualties as they were hauled out of the ruins of their homes until daylight sent the last of the Luftwaffe home. In a daze, she had still worked on, identifying and certifying the people who hadn't survived.

The following night could well be as bad and even though she was supposed to be off duty she might be needed. Irene had tried to telephone through to Halifax to cancel their arrangements. Not surprisingly, the lines were down. At one time she might have sent Mum and Dad a telegram; in wartime everyone knew what alarm its arrival would cause.

She had caught the train, but only because it was running late. As ever, the corridors were crammed already, there wasn't a hope of finding a seat. Wedged between a couple of gum-chewing Yanks and a badly wounded airman who was moaning constantly, she'd begun the laborious journey. Soon after they drew out of the station, she had explained she was a doctor and asked if there was anything she could do for the man who was so evidently in considerable pain.

He had shaken his head. Before the first hour had passed, he'd collapsed all over them. The Yanks were very good, insisting that someone in the nearest compartment surrendered their seat, and helping as she struggled to get the barely conscious airman into it.

In too much agony to speak, he answered her question about his injuries by pointing downwards with a heavily bandaged hand. Gently, Irene drew up his trouser leg.

Blood was seeping from thick dressings. Even through the layers covering it, she could tell from the shape of the leg that the front of his shin had been destroyed. His other leg, when she inspected it, looked even worse.

'There's not much I can do. I'm sorry. I don't carry that amount of dressings.'

She gave him something to deaden the pain, and spent the rest of his journey with her attention riveted on his face, terrified that he was going to die on her.

The airman was taken off to a waiting ambulance at Doncaster, but by then she was feeling the effects of her stressful night as well and yearning for sleep.

She had met Mavis in the centre of Halifax while the long trudge uphill from the station was making her light-headed. Her sister's yell had startled her. And then there she was striding across the road with a khaki-clad officer in tow, and looking like an excited little girl who'd been given the Christmas fairy.

'This is Ralph,' Mavis had enthused breathily. 'He's here for t'weekend.' After introducing Irene to him, she'd added: 'He's in your old room. Mum didn't want to put him in with all our Norman's clutter. She knew you wouldn't mind.'

Irene had minded, not because of her brother's untidy room, but for the longing she harboured just to let go in somewhere where she belonged.

Ralph Parkin had a wide smile revealing immaculate teeth and the knowledge of his attractiveness to women. 'If there's anything you wish to retrieve from your domain, you must feel free, any time.'

Irene had felt Mavis tensing, and experienced an urge to laugh. Her sister needn't bother, *she'd* never be tempted into tête-à-tête situations with him. 'Thanks, but I daresay I'll manage without. If there's owt worth having in there, it's that long since I've lived here that I've forgotten where it is.'

'You're based in London, as well, I gather. Where the life is,' he'd said genially.

And death, Irene had thought though she'd kept the words back. But she had sensed him studying her weary face and dishevelled hair. 'There was a raid in our area last night, a bad one.'

'Can be trying,' Ralph had said glibly. 'Fortunately, they consider us worth protecting. Shelters are well equipped too.'

And there's no ordinary folk there, she'd thought, making a mess by getting crushed or blown to bits. But somehow she had contained the reflection while Mavis and he had gabbled on, clearly besotted with themselves and with each other.

Happen she'd been unfair, she wondered now, judging him for all time on that first impression, which had been on a bad day for her. She would soon know, she supposed, would discover whether Ralph lived up to the image conveyed since of a chap who didn't care deeply enough about his young wife.

She heard the car while she was still sitting hugging the baby, smiled to herself over her neglected promise of having the kettle boiling. When she went into the hall

Mavis burst through the front door, exhilarated, and giggling about sitting on Ralph's lap in the car. He was following their parents in, and apparently trying to impress Norman with his army officer swank.

'Has she been a nuisance?' Mavis inquired, but off-handedly. Now Ralph was here she didn't need to be all over Heather.

'She's fine,' Irene responded warmly as she prepared to hand her over.

Ralph interrupted, rushing the last few paces along the hall and stretching out his well-kept hands. And then he checked, as if too awed to handle the babe. 'Wow!' he exclaimed, and pressed a finger and thumb towards his closed eyes. Opening them again, he grinned at Irene, shrugged self-consciously.

Seeing the moisture on his lashes, she smiled back. 'Go on, take hold of her, Ralph. If Mavis entrusts her to me, I'm sure you'll do no worse. And she really is quite substantial now.'

'Certainly feels it, thank goodness.' Previously, he hadn't known what to do with such a tiny scrap. And had been made to feel inadequate because he could see no resemblance to either Mavis or himself. 'Hallo, Heather,' he murmured, and was halted by the catch in his voice.

Mavis was beside them, beaming. 'I knew you'd think she's adorable now, she's getting really interesting. And look at those eyes, aren't they just the colour of yours – and the same long lashes.'

'Sweetheart, she's perfect. I just can't take in that she's real.'

'Oh, you will – wait till she's yelling in the night, that's real enough. You'll wish you were back in London.'

'That I'll not! I'm crazy about her already, can't you see? No kidding!'

To Irene's relief and astonishment, Ralph certainly seemed totally enraptured by his child. Later that evening he insisted on going upstairs with Mavis to see Heather prepared for bed. And when they reappeared the couple were hand in hand.

111

'I've just witnessed the most beautiful experience,' he told his mother-in-law softly. 'My wife feeding our baby.'

Although a little taken aback by such an admission from him, Elsie smiled. 'Aye, well – it's giving t'little lass the best start she can have. And saves on baby food,' she added, with true Yorkshire thrift.

'Economy's not going to come into it,' Ralph assured them. 'Not with my family, ever. Mavis and Heather will have the best that money can buy, from the minute the shops begin being fully stocked again.'

'And Ralph wants us to go back to London with him until he's demobbed,' Mavis said, smiling.

'Oh, aye,' Donald Hainsworth remarked, trying to be glad that his younger daughter would be happier, and not to mind that she wouldn't be around.

'Is that where you mean to settle then?' asked Norman, wiping the foam from his lips as he savoured a pint of Webster's bitter.

'Shouldn't think so,' Ralph replied. 'My paternal grand-father's about to retire from the blanket works. It's on the cards that I'll be offered a directorship.'

And what do you know about blanket mills? Irene wondered, but was growing adept at containing her thoughts.

'Glad to hear you'll be coming back to Yorkshire one day,' Elsie said. London still seemed unsafe to her, even though the end of hostilities naturally meant that bombing wouldn't return.

She was disappointed that she would be losing Mavis and the bairn for a while, and just as she'd been thinking it would be like old times having their Norman at home again. But this was *his* celebration, she reminded herself. And bustled across the room to make sure he'd tried her cheese and onion pasties.

'You want plenty to eat wi' that beer, you know, love,' she insisted.

'Oh, aye? You're not afraid I can't hold my drink, I hope?' he said lightly.

Their mother laughed. 'Nay, lad – I daresay you've had plenty of practice this past few years. But there's going to be no skipping meals and not eating proper food, think on!' Now that his medicine had got him stabilized, she was going to feed him up right.

'Your mother'll never stop fussing over you,' Donald warned him, and grinned. He himself couldn't have been more relieved than when Norman started putting on a bit of weight again. 'They do reckon as how a pint or two fills you out, though. Happen it won't hurt to keep her happy that way!'

'Donald Hainsworth, I'm surprised at you!' his wife exclaimed. 'You a doctor – and conniving with him already. You're supposed to know what's best for folk.'

'And maybe I do – after that there war, there's a lot of men and women need nowt more than a means of letting down their hair.'

Norman chuckled. 'There was plenty of that afore I was demobbed. The past few weeks was a succession of farewell dos.' Not that it had all been so cheery: he'd made good pals in the RAF, couldn't imagine this different life without them. And without flying. Even though he'd been grounded ever since coming down over France and the aftermath of that, he still dreamed of being in the air again.

'You'd see there was a letter from your old firm?' Donald checked. 'Are they wanting a word with you straight away?'

'Aye, soon as I'm ready. I'll have to wear my suit!' he added, and laughed.

'They'll have a fit if they see you in one!' Irene exclaimed.

Norman groaned. 'Does nobody tell you owt? We've all been issued with a new set of clothes. Best you can say about mine is it fits where it touches.' He swallowed another mouthful from his tankard, set it down and turned towards the door. 'And it doesn't touch much! I'll show you what I mean.'

'Ay, he does look a lot better, bless him,' Elsie remarked as they heard Norman running upstairs. Seeing him a

113

healthier colour and with none of that dreadful breathlessness was like having him restored as good as new.

When Norman returned, however, he was scarcely recognizable. The suit hung grotesquely, too long in sleeve and leg. And the trilby hat, so over-large that it touched one eyebrow and concealed the other, made him look like a gangster. Ralph gave him a wink.

'Yes, well – that dark brown's serviceable enough,' said Elsie seriously. 'They'll stand you in good stead for years . . . '

The rest of them were laughing unrestrainedly.

'You daft lot,' she reproached them. 'How do you think he's going to go out in them now?'

'With a row of pin tucks in the sleeves and in them legs?' Irene suggested mischievously. 'And maybe a good downpour would shrink that hat.' She laughed as Ralph snatched the trilby and tried it on.

'Will you be getting a suit like that?' Mavis asked her husband.

Ralph was discarding all dignity. 'I sincerely hope so – I'd like to give my people one good laugh. The old man tends to take the family image rather solemnly.' He tilted the hat backwards.

'Well, happen you don't want for a decent suit, Ralph,' Elsie persisted. 'But our Norman does. There'll be nowt wrong with this, once I've done a bit of altering.'

Their amusement over Norman's new outfit became a focal point of the weekend, though. In quiet moments one person's lips would begin to twitch, then someone else would beg him to try on the suit again.

'Nay, that's t'last time you'll see me got up like that,' he retorted, but feeling glad that from now on he could wear what he wanted. Ralph had understood, agreeing civvies would feel great.

Returning to North Fell House, Irene thought what a tonic the weekend had been. And not least for the hilarity which seemed to confirm that all their fears for her brother had been unfounded. He appeared full of life again, in the right frame of mind for making a go of his old job. And he wasn't the only one about whom she felt much easier. Mavis's Ralph had astonished her by having become so patently enthusiastic about fatherhood. And being so pally with their Norman.

When she arrived in Skipton the pavements shone with recently fallen rain, reflecting back the gas lamps outside the Georgian town hall. With all its shops closed and the market stalls absent, the place seemed strangely subdued; its castle guarding a town that felt dead. But then the bus came rattling along the setts, and when Irene climbed aboard she was warmed by the conductress's grin.

'Looks like you managed to miss the downpour, love,' she exclaimed as she issued a ticket.

'Aye – I was in the other bus when it began,' Irene replied, sitting down with a jolt as they moved off. Other passengers turned from their scrutiny of her and re-started their conversations.

'Been far, have you?' an elderly countrywoman asked from across the aisle.

'Only to Halifax, for the weekend.'

'That's far enough! I've been there twice, as I recall. Didn't think much of it – all them 'ills!'

Irene laughed. 'Happen they are a bit daunting if you're not brought up with 'em.'

'What're you doing round here then, love?'

'I've got a job up the dale, not far from Malham.'

'You'll not beat the scenery round there, that's if they give you time off to look at it . . . '

'Oh, yes. My employer's very good.'

After she had left the bus, however, and begun the climb towards North Fell, Irene noticed that the unnatural stillness which she'd sensed in Skipton remained with her. And when she thought ahead to being inside the house she recognized that Richard's home *was* too quiet, and maybe too ordered. What he needed was a family like hers, even though she'd returned to Yorkshire with such a dread of meeting them. She wished there was some way she could share them with him.

Irene soon dismissed thoughts of there being anything lacking at North Fell. Richard had spent the weekend thinking about the solicitor's practice which he would reopen. They soon were filling whole days with plans and preparations for organizing the office. When the weather was good they talked out of doors while Richard increased the amount of walking he could tackle.

And when rain drove down from the fells and they retreated indoors Irene occasionally insisted that they relaxed, listening to records, reading, or playing chess. Often enough her ability as an opponent became the target of Richard's sometimes astringent wit. But so long as she gave him an interesting game she didn't care. Or thought that she didn't.

One night they were both laughing at the checkmate which he'd achieved and she should have averted when she felt suddenly and absurdly hurt. Irene continued laughing, but somehow Richard knew.

'You do everything else much better than I do,' he exclaimed. 'Thanks for letting me win.'

He was being gallant. She could develop rather a liking for that, and wasn't sorry that he now knew her so well.

This easy companionship, often needing few words to nourish it, combined with anticipation of the day when he would work again. Irene was lulled into feeling all was well for both of them. Given time, life would become most satisfying, with a great deal of purpose. And if it was all channelled into making *Richard* successful? She quelled her slight resentment. After all, she had no ambitions beyond helping him overcome everything the stroke had done.

One Saturday the sun streaming through the curtains wakened her, and she smiled contentedly, while she relished the absence of blackout materials which for so long had prevented homes being flooded with early morning light. She was looking forward to today. They would have a leisurely breakfast then she would make sandwiches. Richard had suggested that they visit Burnsall and picnic near the river.

When she had dressed, Irene ran lightly downstairs.

Daphne was pacing the hall, her expression anxious.

'What is it?' Irene demanded, her heart already racing agitatedly.

'God knows! I took in Richard's cup of tea, and I thought it was odd – he didn't answer my good morning. And he was awake. He didn't reply when I asked what was wrong either. When I persisted, he just said "nothing" and turned his face to the wall. You know – like he used to.' She paused. 'Oh, Irene, I'm so worried . . . '

Irene was past her in a moment and, with a brief knock, hurried into Richard's room.

She sat on the edge of the bed, trying to make him face her. She said his name. He didn't respond.

'Do you feel ill? Sick? A headache?' Still he said nothing. Again, she tried to make him turn towards her, this time she succeeded. He was pale, otherwise he appeared normal. Just in case, she checked his pulse, then went for her thermometer. Both temperature and heart rate were as they should be.

'Richard, I want an answer – are you ill?'

He shook his head, and turned away again. Frowning, Irene went to telephone Giles Holroyd. He arrived very quickly, gave Richard a thorough checking over, and was smiling as he emerged from the room.

'He's perfectly all right, no need to worry.'

'But I am worried.'

'We both are,' Daphne added.

The doctor nodded. 'Naturally. But I assure you it's nothing physical. There is no regression.'

'But what can we do?' Irene persisted. Generally, she liked Giles Holroyd, had infinite confidence in him. Today, she could have shaken him until he showed greater concern. There was something desperately wrong with Richard. Didn't he care?

Giles sighed. 'There you have me – don't know what to advise. He's not had a bit of bad news? Something that's disturbed him?'

Irene shrugged. 'He's said nowt to me.'

Daphne was shaking her head. 'Not to my knowledge.'

'Oh, well – happen it's just another bout of depression.'
Evidently in a hurry, Giles fastened the catch of his bag.

'But he's been such a lot better,' Irene insisted, still
perturbed.

'I know. This is disappointing. But I'm sure it won't
last. Sorry I can't be more help, but there's a difficult
confinement pending. Should you need me later – though
I'm sure you won't – my wife knows where to find me.'

Irene followed him out on to the steps. Briefly, she
recalled doing likewise on the day she had arrived here.
She had suspected then that she already cared too deeply
about Richard Hughes. Now she was so anxious that she
felt literally sick.

'Irene, I really do have to go,' Giles said firmly. His
grey eyes seemed to chill with unconcern. 'You know no
doctor can devote all his time to one patient.'

'*All* his time?' she snapped, worry unbridling her annoyance. 'You've hardly looked at Richard, how can you
be so sure there's nowt wrong with him?'

Smiling a little, he sighed. 'I've carried out all the
routine checks, but you know what they are. I shan't be
offended if you repeat them. You've taken his pulse and
temperature already. Don't you trust yourself?'

'You're his doctor, Giles.'

Gently, he took her by both arms as they stood beside
his car.

'There is nothing I can do, Irene. It's not a doctor
Richard needs.'

'You can't know that.'

'I'd stake my practice on it,' he said seriously, his grey
eyes levelling with her gaze. 'And, even if I were mistaken,
there's no cause for alarm, because *you* are here. You're
very fond of Richard, aren't you?'

Irene glanced down at her hands and did not reply. But
Giles took her answer for granted. He smiled.

'That's good. I've known for a long time that he's
receiving very capable professional attention.' His fingers
tightened over her arms. 'You don't forget the knowledge
you've acquired over the years, lass.'

'But . . .'

'Since you also have such genuine regard for each other, I've every confidence you'll cope. You shouldn't doubt your own medical ability, love, it's still on tap. But that is *not* the skill you'll be wanting today.'

When Irene walked slowly back indoors, Daphne glanced towards her. 'Dr Holroyd doesn't seem particularly perturbed. I suppose we ought to be thankful.'

Irene nodded. 'But it looks like that puts paid to our day out.' And she was realizing now how much she'd looked forward to going somewhere with Rich. Even if her anxiety was easing, she felt dejected.

'And to mine,' Daphne murmured.

'Ay, I'd forgotten. You were going out as well, weren't you.'

'Only with Peggy. I'll give her a ring.'

'Is there any point – what can you do here? What can either of us do for that matter?' She felt apprehension stirring again. How on earth would she discover what was wrong?

Daphne shrugged. 'It doesn't matter. Peggy and I were only going shopping, then I was having lunch with her and her husband.'

Irene smiled sympathetically. Daphne couldn't have a very interesting life, compared with what she'd once intended. She deserved a break.

'Why not go, all the same? If you leave their number on the pad, I'll ring you up at dinnertime.'

Daphne smiled warmly, making Irene wish she'd had time for getting to know her better.

'Sure you don't mind being landed, Irene?'

She grinned. 'It is supposed to be my job.'

After Daphne had left, Irene looked in on Richard again. She offered him breakfast, coffee, the papers to read. He refused them all. She decided that was his privilege. He was neither a child nor, these days, an invalid. Happen he needed to be left alone.

She went upstairs and tidied her room. And could not stop thinking about him, aching to know what was wrong.

She picked up a book and returned to Richard. His eyes were closed but she knew he wasn't sleeping. When he remained silent Irene kept quiet as well.

Several hours later she took pains over preparing lunch, making the tray as attractive as she could. She might have saved herself the trouble; he wouldn't look at it. Hoping the smell of food would arouse interest, she decided to eat in his room. It didn't – and the atmosphere coupled with worry gave her indigestion.

Being Saturday Mrs O'Connor wasn't there, and Shaun had never appeared at weekends since Richard mastered walking again. The entire house seemed uncannily still. In the kitchen washing the dishes, Irene was straining her ears for the slightest sound from Richard's room. She was more than a little annoyed with him by now. He was not only spoiling the day for them both, but doing his health no good.

She spent a wretched afternoon, unable to cease wandering between Richard's room and her own, unable to settle to anything. She had told Daphne over the telephone that sacrificing her day out would serve no purpose, now she prepared to face a long vigil.

Compelling herself to sit still, Irene began writing letters beside Richard's bed. When making tea she offered him a cup. His 'No, thanks – I couldn't' was firm, and dauntingly cold. She ran her mind back over the past few days, seeking anything that she might have done or said to offend him. Recalling nothing proved even more disturbing. She was getting desperate for some explanation of Richard's sudden refusal to cooperate.

Determined to waste no more food, she asked at seven o'clock what he wanted for dinner.

'Nothing, thanks.'

She sat on the bed. 'This nonsense has to stop, Richard. You must eat something.'

'Why must I?'

'You're not that stupid. You can see this won't do you any good.'

'So?'

'Look, I'm having plaice, and there are some new potatoes. And for pudding I thought . . .'

'You can think away, I am *not* hungry.'

Irene flung out of the room, slamming the door. She'd never felt more ineffectual. If she'd been a doctor still, she might have been able to compel him to heed her. As it was, she felt as though she would never get him to listen to her again. Whatever might be wrong with him, *she'd* soon be weeping with frustration.

Daphne came in while Irene was in the dining room. 'Any improvement?' she asked, instantly halving the anxiety again.

Irene shook her head. 'Afraid not. I feel rather a failure.'

Briefly, Daphne smiled. 'It's nothing you can help.' She sounded genuinely concerned that Irene shouldn't feel ineffectual.

'You know something, don't you?'

Daphne nodded. 'Was the local paper in Richard's room?'

'Didn't notice, why?'

'I was glancing through it over at Peggy and Don's. If he's seen that, it'll explain . . .'

Irene crossed towards the hall. 'I'll look.'

Richard was feigning sleep. Without saying anything, she located the paper and took it to his sister.

Daphne soon found what she was after. 'Yes, it's in this edition as well.' She gazed into space. 'Poor old thing . . .' All her affection for her brother showed in her brimming green eyes. Then, as if remembering Irene, she continued: 'It's Margaret Stewart, she got married on Thursday. She . . . well, I suppose she and Richard once had a sort of understanding. She's years younger than he is, used to work in his office. Peggy's heard more than it says here. It's some chappie from London, they met on holiday only very recently. I don't blame Margaret, she got short shrift here after Rich had the stroke. He wouldn't see her.'

Irene nodded, torn now between relief that Richard's distress had a cause, and her own disquiet created by

121

learning there was some woman in his life. A woman who had meant a great deal – hadn't she herself realized how few people he related to?

'I see,' she said finally. 'What do we do?'

'I don't know, Irene. What do you think?'

'Stick around – see him through . . .' She couldn't do otherwise.

Daphne was frowning. When she spoke her voice was tart. 'I'm just surprised Margaret didn't let us know. I'd have told Richard if she couldn't face him. I know they'd lost touch, but something he'd mentioned made me think he might have heard from her again.'

'What did you say the name was?'

'Margaret. Margaret Stewart.'

'I thought it rang a bell. You know he intends opening up an office again, here . . .'

'No,' Daphne interrupted, sounding annoyed because he didn't always tell her everything these days. But then she shrugged, and grinned. 'I don't suppose that matters, so long as he talks to somebody. There's just been the two of us for ages – you ought to remind me how glad I've been to share the anxiety and the responsibility with you! And to rely on your knowledge. Go on, though – what were you saying?'

'I'm sure it was someone called Margaret that he'd said would most likely return to do clerical work for him.'

Daphne sighed. 'Oh, well – too late now. So, he's lost a secretary too. But I doubt if that's the aspect worrying him.'

They sat silently, both busy with similar thoughts, and then Daphne stood up. 'I only popped in to see how he was, and to tell you what I'd discovered. Although, if you like . . .'

Irene smiled. 'If you've somewhere to go tonight, you may as well. No sense in two of us hanging around like spare parts.'

As Daphne drove off Irene waved, thinking how good it was that they confided in each other now. She'd admired Daphne ever since learning to what lengths she'd go for her beliefs. Returning to Richard's room, however, she still didn't know what to say or do. Would avoiding the subject be most effective? Determined to end the silence, she turned on the radio; that might evoke some reaction.

It did, the moment it was clear *Saturday Night Theatre* was a comedy: 'Do you have to?' Richard demanded with a withering glance.

Irene switched off and picked up her book once more. But she was unable to read. She went back over the same paragraph repeatedly without taking in more than the occasional word. And she couldn't analyse why she still felt so disturbed. She knew now why Richard was in a foul mood, couldn't she simply leave him to accept what had happened? But knowing seemed to make the problem more real.

Just after eleven o'clock Daphne opened the door.

'You're not going to sit there all night?' she asked with a smile when Irene joined her in the hall.

'Depends how long it takes to get through to him.' At the present rate or progress, that would be weeks!

'You're mad, you really are,' Daphne exclaimed, yet her beautiful eyes gleamed with appreciation. And she gave Irene a hug.

Reminded that the day had created a bond between the two of them, Irene immediately felt better. She grinned and returned to Richard. But she had decided he'd had long enough pondering the situation.

Sitting on the bed again, she grasped his shoulder. 'I am sorry about Margaret.'

'Time Daphne kept her mouth shut.'

'You want to be glad you've a caring sister. Richard, look at me.'

Slowly, reluctantly, he raised himself on an elbow and turned towards her. 'Well?'

'I mean it – I am sorry.'

'Where's the rest – "You'll get over it, *if* you want to." It's what I said to you.'

'It was true, for me.' She sighed. 'But I wasn't recovering from an illness. The kicks come all the harder when you're already down.'

He nodded slowly. 'I can't argue with that.'

His tone was quite even but the dark eyes had clouded. Irene's hand tightened on his shoulder.

Richard inhaled deeply then suddenly, leaning forward, rested his head against her. She was relieved he had said something at last; now they could begin facing facts.

As he raised his head again he smiled ruefully. 'No secrets from you now, eh? You've really seen me in the depths.'

'Not to worry. I've had a grounding in this kind of thing, remember. I've seen my share of folk who've had enough. Most of them survived to tell the tale.'

'There's one who wouldn't have – but for being almost out of sleeping tablets,' he announced. And wondered why she wasn't looking shaken.

8

Irene was remembering what she had attempted, ages ago – or so it seemed. Yet again she'd nearly forgotten the trouble bringing her to North Fell House. But the great swell of gratitude for being made to forget was replaced immediately by the ache to help. No one better understood this feeling of hopelessness. And how imperative it was that it should be superseded by something constructive.

Richard was searching her expression. 'Aren't you horrified?'

Smiling slightly, Irene shook her head. 'Ay, Richard love, I'm the last person to be shocked by contemplating suicide.'

'How do you mean?' He hadn't a clue, had never considered that she would do anything but despise him for such appalling weakness.

'What do you think?'

'No.' He shook his head disbelievingly. 'Not you . . . ' As well as astounded, he felt perturbed. Perturbed by past emptiness which could so easily have continued. There was so much that he might have missed.

Briefly, Irene closed her eyes. His astonishment ought to have pleased her, it proved she'd concealed such a lot. Instead, she was conscious that she'd never quite forgive herself for what she'd done. But that episode was in the past, and must be kept there. Tonight, Richard didn't need any more gloom.

She managed another smile. 'It was a remarkably inept attempt.'

'Thank God!' His voice was hushed.

She met his glance, and held on. And found herself telling him: 'Thank you,' she said huskily. 'I'd never felt

125

so alone – it was the day the Medical Council struck me off. I was in the car, and I felt as if everybody knew and was staring. And there was no one to talk to about how hopeless the future seemed. Pointless. I just drove on and on, eventually I simply had to stop thinking. I . . . put my head down and drove straight at the wall.'

'Put your head down? Surely, that was self-preservation?'

Irene glanced up at him. 'Don't be too nice about it – I might weep all over you again.'

'Woman's privilege.'

'M'm. Unfairly so, perhaps. Nothing like a good howl for restoring a sense of proportion. Any road – we weren't supposed to be going on about me this time. Though I'm glad you know it all now.'

'Certainly brought me up sharp.'

'How do you mean?'

'You spoke of feeling alone, and I haven't been, have I? Not recently. Except from choice, by excluding you.' He swallowed. This wasn't easy, yet saying it was a strange sort of relief. Maybe even an acceptable alternative to this daft longing to be held by her. 'It'll do me good, won't it – to contemplate what my life would have been if – if you'd made a thorough job of writing off your car.'

'You're a real one for self-examination, aren't you, love?' she said gently. 'But I don't think, do you, that this is quite the right day.'

Ruefully, he shook his head. 'I am getting used to the idea, though. It was just . . . Margaret might have told me. I thought we could say anything to each other. It definitely wasn't that I'd hoped we'd ever . . . Lord knows, I'm not exactly a catch now.'

Irene privately disagreed. But she must shelve that aspect. 'Self-pity doesn't help,' she told him briskly.

Startled, he gave her a look. 'We'll take it that we both know that really. But, for the record, Margaret'd had me believing she was eager to work with me again.'

'I gathered she was the person you'd telephoned. When you're ready, we'll find someone else.'

126

That didn't go down too well. But he made an effort. And he surprised her by reaching for her hand.

'How do I make up to you for this lousy day?'

'You begin by being sensible and eating something.'

'A cup of tea first, I'm dying of thirst. And bring a cup for yourself. Your vast knowledge of medicine must confirm that I shan't pass out yet for lack of nourishment.'

She insisted that they had their pot of tea in the kitchen while she prepared soup and sandwiches which he attacked enthusiastically. It was long past midnight, but Irene didn't care. Back in his room she began remaking the bed.

From the chair, Richard watched her intently. In the artificial light her face resembled carved marble, but warmer. Worn loose, her pale hair swung forward as she shook up the pillows and smoothed the wrinkled sheets, her slender hands strong as well as deft. He smiled. 'Know something? You look domesticated tonight.'

'So I don't as a rule?'

He laughed, shaking his head. 'Very rarely. You're too much the professional for anything so mundane.' For anything ordinary.

Absurdly, Irene felt hurt. 'That sounds cold . . . '

Richard smiled again. 'Rather intimidating at times, as well!'

'I'm sorry,' she said stiffly, unable to laugh with him.

He remained amused. He'd surprised her with the remark. He loved surprising her. All too often it was the only way to glimpse what she really felt. Even today, he couldn't be sorry that she wanted him to notice more than the professional façade.

'That wasn't supposed to be the image,' Irene persisted. 'What then?'

'Just – a friend, to make life easier.'

'You're that all right.'

It was too ready to be anything but the truth. Irene couldn't control her smile. Nor could she totally contain her feelings. Impulsively, she hurried to kneel before the chair, gazing up at him. 'Oh, Rich!'

All laughter fled from his eyes. Long before his quiet voice began, she knew what he was going to tell her.

'Only two people ever called me that, Daphne and . . . '

'I can guess.' She sighed. 'So, there'll be reminders, there always are. But that's one mistake I shan't make twice.'

Richard was shaking his head, though. His hand rested on her hair. 'Times change – happen we do as well. We'll keep it to two people now, shall we?' He paused. 'I've never been the sort to encourage familiarity, Irene. Maybe that's the reason I create hell when someone just goes, without a word.'

'Aye, well – she underestimated you. She wasn't to know you could take it. I daresay you're tougher now than ever in the past.'

His long fingers plunged deep into her hair, caressing the back of her head, while he gazed into her blue eyes. 'You reckon?'

'You'd face anything squarely, as you have this illness. You'll see – you'll come out on top.'

'With a lot of pushing from you.'

'You'll get that, and no mistake.' She got to her feet. 'Time you were back in bed.'

'Must I?'

Laughing, she indicated the clock. Richard was surprised. 'Is it really? Then I mustn't have you stay up a minute longer.'

'It's not that. Broken nights were an occupational hazard. But I am supposed to be keeping an eye on you.'

'And keeping me happy?' The hint of fun in his dark eyes increased Irene's longing for them to be free to just enjoy life together.

'Didn't know anyone could tonight.'

'I'll give you a fair crack at it. And you could start by ensuring I have a breath of air. Where's that stick I should be using?'

Taking her arm as well, Richard limped towards the french windows. He stood there, breathing deeply. The warm night felt as reassuring as her nearness, and as quieting. 'Fancy a walk along the terrace?'

'You're impossible!'

'Only since you started me doing impossible things.'

They reached the far wall and Richard leaned against the cold stone, studying her face in the light from his room. Finally, looking very serious, he spoke: 'I must be the ungrateful bastard of all time! You've given me over a year of patient devotion . . .'

'For which I'm well paid.'

Slowly, he shook his head. 'Money never bought that. Devotion, care, kindness – and all you get is a fit of the sulks when things go wrong.' He found her hand. 'Forgive me, and go on forgiving me, until I learn I am lucky. I do believe that really, you know. I might have been dead – twice, with today.' He swallowed. 'But I'm thankful I'm not. And very glad I didn't endure this day alone.'

'Come on, time we went indoors.'

'Not yet. Even – even when I refused to acknowledge you, I knew you were there and . . . well, you know it helped.' He kissed her then, tenderly. 'I may not be the one whose kisses'll turn your head, Irene, but you're too good to go without affection.'

Like this, he could turn her entire being to turmoil. Her eyes misted. She thought Richard hadn't noticed, until they were in his room and she was securing the french windows and closing the curtains.

'Shouldn't I have done that?'

Irene pretended not to understand.

'I spotted the emotion.'

She smiled. 'It wasn't that at all.'

'What then?'

Richard would pursue things best left unsaid. And the joy of feeling his lips on hers had reminded her of what Giles had assumed. Whatever she felt for Richard Hughes, she was discovering it was deeper and more enduring than any emotion she'd ever experienced.

She grinned. 'You, you dope. I could get quite fond of you, in an odd sort of way.'

'A love-hate relationship?'

'I've only hated you the once – when you told me a few home truths, and I soon forgave you.'

'That's a relief!' He smiled. 'I feel great now, could talk for hours.'

Irene groaned, and Richard laughed again, affectionately. 'Fair enough – you run off upstairs, you've earned a break. I've had today's ration of your time.'

But she was much too interested to leave. 'What is it, Rich?'

'Oh – night thoughts. Life and what it means to me. You – and how you fit into my scheme of things.'

That was unexpected. And although Irene wasn't entirely happy about the prospect of merely having to fit into his scheme, she hadn't imagined she'd figured very large in his thoughts today. She might be recognizing her own commitment to him but that hadn't assured her of her significance in his plans.

'Get into bed then, I'll hear you out.' As she went to the bedside chair, she was quelling sudden irrational excitement. But if Richard needed her at all she must let that content her. She mustn't even think of how much she really wished to mean to him.

Irene had reckoned without Richard's overactive mind. An hour later, still talking, he had barely touched on his deepest feelings. She smothered a yawn; worry had taken its toll. Yet while he wished to talk to her, she wouldn't go up to her own room.

'Come here,' he suggested. 'You'll be safe enough. I couldn't try anything, if I would, remember. Curl up under the eiderdown.'

Irene was astonished, didn't know what to do. It made sense, she longed to rest her head somewhere, but . . . She trapped another yawn.

Richard grinned. 'You might just as well.'

She rose and moved her chair, giving herself time to think. It couldn't hurt. She was wearing a housecoat, but only because she'd slipped off her dress, otherwise she was fully clothed. But the longer she considered the more doubts she unearthed.

Richard seemed amused. She could see why, but couldn't share the joke. She went slowly to the bed, he moved over and raised the eiderdown for her. And he turned off the light. Irene was very glad; her cheeks were burning. It was stupid, she was behaving like some naive virgin. And she had no right to. That stung like a blow in the face, and was the real source of her discomfort. There was something so . . . well-disciplined about Richard, she'd have given anything to know she'd always matched that.

'You look very appealing, Irene – like a wide-eyed innocent child.'

'You know damned well I'm not!' She was thankful, nevertheless, that this was what he thought. She'd been afraid just now that he might believe her capable of jumping into bed with any man. After all, he knew about John.

Richard adjusted his position and drew her head towards his good shoulder. 'You are to me, innocent as the day you walked through that door. I was wrong about the professional manner – it goes missing now and again. Your eyes gave you away that first day. Too full of concern, and fear for how you'd cope.'

She'd been idiotic to worry that being this close to Richard could be anything but a comfort. Did this feel *too* right, though, wasn't it all too easy? She'd needed reassurance that she had a place at North Fell, but she'd have to curb fantasies now – about really belonging.

Richard seemed to have forgotten that he wished to talk.

'Well then,' she prompted him, 'tell me what you want from life.'

She felt, rather than heard, his chuckle. 'All this has cut me down to size. I don't hope to move mountains any longer. Just to make myself useful.'

This was so like her own original ambition. And Richard's most urgent need was an occupation. 'Good idea. I suggest you start on Monday.'

'Monday? This Monday?' He sounded incredulous.

'Why not?'

'Thought we'd agreed I'd achieve walking properly first?'

131

She sensed his reluctance to take action after being so long immobilized. 'You don't keep your brains in your feet.'

'But . . .'

Irene giggled. 'A real one for making excuses to yourself, aren't you?' It was meant to goad him and did.

'It was you who said I ought to wait.'

'Changed my mind, that's another woman's privilege.'

For a long time Richard was silent, thinking. Irene guessed the reason behind certain misgivings. 'Ay, love – it would be all right, physically. I wouldn't take chances with your health.'

'Thought reader! I was wondering how I'd face another stroke, couldn't haul myself out of this again.'

'You won't have to. And you're not the only one who couldn't do this twice. I'd have run out of tactics to keep you going!'

They both laughed, then Irene continued, quietly. 'I'll watch you like the proverbial hawk, Richard – no overwork, no strain. All my medical know-how is at your disposal. I'll make damned sure it's put to good use.'

Giles *wasn't* wrong, she thought; she was confident she could take care of Richard. Giles had known she would do so. For as long as she was permitted.

Richard's lips brushed her ear, surprising her again. 'Then we'll make a start. In fact, I've been asked advice on a conveyancing problem – an old client. He'll be only too happy . . .' His voice dropped. '. . . and so will I. Get the grey matter stirring again.'

The detailed outline of how he visualized the practicalities showed how much thought he'd already given to working again, and delighted Irene. He elaborated on the ways in which he expected her to contribute to their routine then, when he at last stopped for breath, she laughed a little.

'I think that gives some indication of your thoughts, if we dispose of the rest I might be allowed to retire for the night!'

'You can go now, nobody's stopping . . .'

She smiled into the darkness. 'I was only teasing.'

'Can't remember anything else.' His tone had changed abruptly. He couldn't really forget the news he'd learned a few hours ago. There was no region of his life that Margaret hadn't touched.

'Life – and what it means to you,' Irene prompted, then wished she hadn't.

When Richard eventually spoke again, it was with a sigh. 'Work, that's all there is. And even that . . . ' His voice trailed off dismally.

'What?'

'Doesn't matter.' He sounded choked.

'Rich . . . ?'

'It's only – Margaret did say she'd look forward to sharing what she called "our extra dimension" again.'

Irene quelled her own sigh. Richard seemed to have had a very special relationship with this woman. And now it was up to *her* to convince him that he must accept a different future. God knew, she understood how hard that was. *And how necessary.*

Before she could do anything, however, Richard was speaking again. 'Both in the same boat, aren't we?'

'Shall we start rowing in the same direction?' Irene said lightly.

He squeezed her shoulders. 'From tomorrow.'

She touched his cheek with her lips. And then swung her legs off the bed. 'I'll let you sleep. Shall I bring your tablets and a drink?'

He didn't reply.

'Richard?'

'Stay . . . '

'All night?'

'Why not?'

'Why?'

Irene heard his rueful snort. 'You've a remarkable facility with awkward questions. As an insulation, I guess, against my thoughts.'

It was so noisy he couldn't even think. Norman had been back in the mill for over a week, and nothing was as he

133

remembered. None of 'em seemed right sure what was going on; not Jack Dewhurst, the mill owner, nor their foreman, Bert Kettlewell, and certainly not the weavers and the rest of the overlookers.

Norman hadn't reckoned with it taking time to get back into full production of Dewhurst's usual good-quality cotton. He hadn't been there through the war when they'd been producing tents and overalls, and anything else the government ordered. And he hadn't realized what poorquality weft they'd have to put up with now the war was over.

'Is it 'cos the yarn's so bad that t'looms are making such a racket?' he'd asked on his second day here.

Bert had stared at him, then grinned. 'Nay, Norman lad, it's nowt of the sort! It's no worse nor it were afore. It's you that's altered, can't you tell? You've been away too long, it's bound to feel strange.'

'You can't deny this is poor stuff, though,' Norman persisted, tugging at damaged threads that were caught up in the loom. 'Where it'd break once in the old days it breaks twenty times now.' And more often than not it jammed the whole lot, especially since the warp threads could snap just as easily as the weft.

'Afraid it's all we've got,' Bert responded, turning away. 'Do the best you can.'

I allus do, thought Norman. 'Look at yon . . .' he persisted, pointing across the aisle to a second loom that was stopped, awaiting his attention. 'That bloody shuttle's gone all haywire, made a right mess, it has.'

And both these looms were Lily Atkinson's, he felt that sorry they were standing idle. All the weavers were on piece work, and he'd soon found out Lily had a hard time of it, trying to help out at home financially. She'd started at Dewhurst's in the war, managing to avoid being sent away to work because of the number of kids her mother had to cope with.

She'd confided to Norman today that things weren't going to be much easier now her father was home. 'Can't blame him, I suppose, he's had to do without long enough, though it were t'same sometimes after he'd been on leave. But he should have been more careful – my mam's forty-seven, what a time of life to have another bairn on the way!'

It had taken him a minute or two to understand; he wasn't used to young ladies being so forthright, especially about their parents. But then he'd felt immediate sympathy for Lily and the prospect of having to supplement the family income to help provide for another youngster. She was too young and pretty to be compelled to struggle. He'd like to see her grey eyes glint with mischief, and to stop her thrusting her hands through that bonny dark hair as if she was distracted.

He smiled at her now, as she glanced sideways at him from one loom that was running properly. 'Happen it won't be long afore I've got this one going again,' he mouthed so that she could lip-read amid the clattering.

Nodding, Lily beamed back. 'Thanks, Norman, you're a good 'un.'

He was good an' all, to her. She knew already that he favoured her, and hoped the other weavers hadn't noticed. She supposed really she ought to remind him he had to be fair. None of them wanted their looms out of action. Still, she did need the brass.

Norman would like to ask her out. He'd heard she was good at tennis, and he used to play a fair game before he joined up. Or there was always the pictures. Happen that'd be the best. He was finding manual work hard again, could do with a sit-down when he finished at half past five. He ought really to wait while he'd caught up on some sleep, though. He'd gone on his own to the Regal t'other night, and had missed half of the big picture with falling asleep. But the trouble was he'd never relished waiting.

'Are you doing anything on Saturday?' he inquired as he eventually set the shuttle in motion again.

Lily grinned. 'Aye – afraid so. My mam and dad are off to see Grandma. She's not so well, you know, and she lives just outside Morecambe. I'll be looking after the little 'uns.'

'Oh, I see.'

'You could come round, if you like. Listen to t'wireless or summat – I shall have got the kids to bed by half past seven.'

'All right then, thanks. Where do you live?'

'In Hanson Lane,' Lily said, and told him the number. 'It's above a shop, a bit further down than Hesselden's Gents' Outfitters.'

'I'll look forward to that.'

As Saturday approached, though, Norman's feelings grew mixed. He wasn't used to just sitting on his own, talking with a lass. In the RAF he'd mostly met girls at the camp dances, or with a crowd of other chaps when they'd descended on a neighbouring pub. Even dates to visit the cinema had generally involved him in a foursome.

Norman needn't have worried. He arrived late, mainly because he'd been so uneasy and his pace had slowed considerably as he walked down Parkinson Lane and then along Francis Street. Lily had been watching out for him; as soon as he rang the bell beside the door she came running down the narrow steps.

'Ay, I'm glad to see you!' she exclaimed. 'I were beginning to think you must have forgotten.'

'No, sorry I'm late,' he began.

Lily grinned. 'Doesn't matter, now you're here. But I haven't been able to get our Herbert to settle, you'll have to put up with him for a bit.'

Herbert, who looked all of two years old in washed-out pyjamas that failed to meet at the waist, was standing on the arm of an easy chair, fiddling with the knobs of the wireless set. He turned and glanced towards them as they entered, beaming as the speaker emitted a selection of high-pitched shrieks and whistles.

'Songs!' he announced.

'What have I told you,' his sister snapped, striding across and tapping him on a seat well padded with nappy. 'You're not to touch that, and you're not to go climbing! Else you'll fall on your head, and be dafter than you are already.'

'Not daft,' Herbert protested.

136

'Trouble is, he isn't,' Lily assured Norman quietly as she indicated a chair. 'His mind's that active, we always have trouble getting him to sleep.'

'You'll have tried reading him a story, I suppose?'

'You haven't seen their bedroom. There's four of 'em, in it – Beth's three year old, and the eldest in there is Sammy, he's just started school. If you make a sound, there'll be one or t'other on 'em determined to get up.'

'Down here then?'

Lily's laugh was rueful. 'I can tell you're not used to dealing with kids. Nay, I'm not starting that, the little beggar would soon learn he'd rather sit down here listening to stories than trying to get to sleep.'

While they were talking Herbert had wriggled free of her grasp and was exploring the contents of the coal bucket.

'I say . . . ' Norman began, pointing towards the hearth.

'Oh, look at you now!' Lily seized the youngster, skilfully trapping both his black wrists in one hand before he could either apply them to his face or wipe them down his pyjamas.

She hustled him towards the tiny sink beyond the open door of a cupboard and swiftly cleaned him up.

'It's bed for you now, my lad, you'd best get used to the idea.'

After Lily had whisked her brother upstairs, Norman glanced around the room, and wondered how so many bodies fitted in there. It couldn't be more than twelve feet by twelve, and a scrubbed wooden table filled the centre with several straight-backed chairs as well as the two armchairs. There were cupboards to either side of the fireplace, the one containing the sink also accommodating a tiny gas ring.

'Not so big, is it?'

He was embarrassed because Lily had returned so softly that she'd caught him staring, but she only laughed.

'Nay, don't feel awkward, love,' she said. 'We're quite proud of how we manage here.'

'How many of you are there?'

'With my mum and dad, nine. I've two sisters a few years younger nor me, they share my room. Don't look so worried, we're the happiest folk in Hanson Lane.'

Lily certainly seemed cheerful enough tonight. Smiling to herself and shaking her head, she re-tuned the wireless set. 'My dad would give our Herbert a good hiding, if he knew. There's no brass left over for luxuries like this set. If owt happened to it, we'd have to do without. I hope you like a drop of nice music?'

'Anything,' said Norman, 'so long as it's not too loud.'

'You don't like noise, do you?' Lily observed, having located a channel with a dance band.

Norman shrugged. 'You mean in t'mill. It's just – well, seems a lot worse nor when I went away.'

'You'll get used to it. Took me a while.'

'Aye, but I'd worked there before, you know. Keep wondering if it's me – the way I've been.' Without intending anything of the kind, Norman began telling her about being shot down and escaping through France. And then he couldn't stop himself talking about collapsing, and how afraid he'd been that it was his heart.

'Ay, dear. What a fright you must have had.'

'I had an' all. And since then – even though it turned out it was all due to my thyroid and I was given tablets, I don't seem quite the same, somehow.'

'You seem right enough to me.'

Norman grinned. 'Happen so, but I can't tolerate as much, not a racket going on, or owt that's agitating. I have to say summat.'

Lily had a pleasant laugh, it sounded delighted as well as sympathetic.

'There's nowt wrong wi' that. I like a man that can stand up for himself.'

'I'm just afraid I'll start getting cantankerous.'

'I'll soon tell you when you are!'

Norman liked the implication that they would be spending more time in each other's company. And not only at the mill. Lily was an attractive lass with her dark hair which gleamed with golden lights in the glow from the

138

fire. Her grey eyes looked kind, and often sparkled with amusement. She dressed nicely, an' all – even though the maroon two-piece she had on wasn't new, it was well pressed and didn't smell.

'Will you come to t'pictures with me some time?' he asked, needing reassurance already that he hadn't been wrong in thinking they were getting on together.

'I'd like that, thanks. I don't get out so much, except to the tennis club. Do you play, Norman?'

He told her how he used to before the war. 'I don't know if I'd be any good now, though.'

'There's one way to find out. You'd probably need a bit of practice.'

The thought of practising with Lily appealed to him. He could imagine her in a light dress, dashing about the court. She had long slender arms, he could picture her having a wizard serve.

'Happen we'd better not risk it,' he said ruefully. 'I'm not sure I'd take to having you beat me!'

'Oh, I'd let you win once or twice,' Lily began.

'Nay, I'll not have that!' snapped Norman. 'Nobody patronizes me.'

'Hey – it was only for summat to say,' Lily responded quickly. 'Don't get on your high horse.'

'Sorry, love, sorry.'

'You will be an' all, if you keep standing on your dignity. There's no need with me, Norman. I allus take folk as I find them. And you're not so bad. For a fella.'

He recognized that as praise, and laughed. Suddenly, he felt more at ease than he had for months. He wanted to hang on to this relationship, though he wasn't certain yet how that might be achieved. How his mates in the RAF would have laughed. Out in a crowd, he'd tended to be one of those who led any high jinks. And look how many years he'd resisted the idea of getting serious about any lass.

'What are you thinking?' asked Lily quietly.

'Mostly about the RAF.'

'You miss it, don't you?'

'I was in for five years.'

'How old are you then now?'

'Twenty-seven.'

'I'm twenty-nine,' Lily admitted, and wondered if that would finish it all before it got properly started.

Norman was surprised, and by his own reaction. Her being that bit older increased the longing to give her a break by getting her away from her folk. And not a short break either. He'd never felt like this about anybody before. And yet he hardly knew her.

'We've had enough about our family, tell me about yours,' Lily suggested. 'Your father's a doctor, isn't he?'

He smiled to himself, pleased that she'd taken the trouble to find that out.

'Oh, all t'other lasses had summat to say about you, when they knew you were coming back,' she exclaimed, flattening the satisfaction by revealing that the information had come to her unsought. But Lily was smiling, anyway, and delighted him with a wink. 'Them that had worked wi' you afore seemed to think you'd liven the place up a bit.'

'And I haven't, have I?'

'Not so's you'd notice. I don't believe they had you weighed up quite right. You're not one for asserting yourself afore you've found your feet, are you?'

'Am I not?'

'Go on – you know yourself pretty well. And you're not all that keen on t'mill, not these days, are you? Second best, is it?'

Norman nodded, and soon he was revealing his old longing to be a civilian pilot. 'I'm determined to put that behind me, but it'll take a while. Dad doesn't help, he can't dismiss his hopes for me.'

'He wanted you to continue flying as well then?'

'Dad wants me to do owt but work down yonder, thinks I ought to better myself.'

'And what does your mother say?'

'Ay, she allus wants what'll keep my father happy.'

'Do you have any brothers or sisters, Norman?'

140

'Two sisters – one of 'em is married with a baby, the other works away. Not so far away now, t'other side of Skipton.'

'Lucky her – it's lovely out that way, I believe.'

For once, Norman refrained from saying why their Irene was anything but lucky. Strangely, though, he felt Lily would have understood.

She made supper when it got to ten o'clock and Norman left before eleven. They had done nothing in particular all evening, and yet he walked back towards Parkinson Lane feeling elated. In another few weeks when their Mavis came back to pick up the rest of her things before settling in London, the family were planning a bit of a do. He was determined that, if he had owt to do with it, Lily would be there.

141

9

The sun, streaming in through long curtains, was making an unfamiliar pattern on her pillow. Irene glanced across the room, wondered why she was here.

She became aware of Richard smiling at her, and smiled back.

'I must be unique,' he said. 'The one man you can sleep with – and sleep all the time.'

His harsh tone made Irene cringe. She went to draw back the curtains. 'Does that worry you?' she asked, staring hard at the garden. 'Not about me – in general.'

He was a very long time answering, and then she had to turn to catch what he said.

'Every man, surely, prefers to know he is a man.'

'It's not impossible, given time.'

'Be realistic, Irene.'

'I've told you before – your only real debility's impatience!'

She crossed towards the door, but stopped when she reached it. If he needed to know, there wasn't really much to lose by revealing the one thing that she'd intended keeping to herself.

'And,' she added quietly, 'from what I recall before falling asleep, you generate the appropriate responses.'

Irene left him hurriedly, before his startled expression made her smile. She took a leisurely, very thoughtful, bath before dressing slowly and going down to breakfast. She was thankful that Sunday was normally one day when Daphne slept late. She couldn't bear anyone intruding, not yet. She might be amused by Richard's evident amazement, but she'd only told him the truth. And she herself was a little taken aback. Even though she'd acknowledged weeks ago that he was attractive. Happen she'd somehow imagined she was immune, it was easy to visualize their relationship without any sexual involvement.

Today, she was relieved to keep it like that. She might have fantasized about living here with a child of her own, but that had been just a dream. Reality was knowing that, in every other way, Richard had allowed her far closer than she'd ever expected, and that gave her a lot of joy. She was glad he'd never become more demanding; nothing would be permitted to threaten this hard-won affinity.

Popping the weekly bacon ration into the pan, she heard voices across the hall, then Daphne came into the kitchen.

Her lovely green eyes were glistening. 'So – he's back in the land of living. Thanks to you.' She crossed quickly and gave Irene's shoulders a squeeze.

Irene was holding her breath, wondering what else Daphne knew. She couldn't think Daphne would approve of her spending the night with Richard, however innocuously. But her next words were reassuring.

'You are a love, aren't you! Rich told me how you let him talk everything out last night, then he was able to sleep.'

So that was all. Irene nodded, then smiled over her shoulder as Richard's sister moved away. Daphne was looking uneasy, though, while she found herself a cup and saucer and reached for the teapot.

'Irene – I . . . er, owe you an apology.'

That made her turn her back on the cooker. 'You do?'

Daphne was frowning as she stirred her tea, and then she met Irene's gaze. 'I was a long time making you welcome here, wasn't I? That was rotten, especially when your being here allowed me to work again. It . . . well, don't be embarrassed, but it was because I knew.'

'Knew?' Irene asked, and gradually realized what it would be.

'Who you were – that you'd . . . '

' . . . Been struck off?' Irene couldn't help smiling. It seemed less important now, yet had nearly cost her her life.

'I remembered your name, recognized you from the papers. We seem to be a family for learning things we'd rather not know, don't we! I was so bored I nearly read the print off everything.' Daphne swallowed. 'I was afraid you were keeping the truth from Rich, that you were using him.'

Irene grinned. 'I was – all of that. But he does know, guessed most of it before I'd been here very long. He would! I was alarmed at the time, but I've been thankful since. I've felt so . . . free. And as for using Richard – well, I believe I'm some use *to* him, so I hope that squares it.'

Daphne smiled. 'I'm sure it does, Irene. Well, I'm glad that's off my chest. It's always made me feel uncomfortable.'

Irene smiled back, her blue eyes lighting. 'I think that squares it between us two, as well, don't you?'

Now that the two of them had established a good rapport, she half wanted to stay and talk, but the tea was growing cold. Leaving Daphne in charge of the bacon, she hurried towards Richard's room.

He was sitting in a chair, looking more pensive than she liked. Margaret, again! she thought, and when he began talking she sensed he'd have to work at sorting his emotions before interring them.

'We always spoke the same language, you know. Sometimes we'd sit in the office for hours after the others had left – just talking. I thought that was one thing that could still be the same.' He had aimed towards that image, as towards a signpost barely visible through fog. But there had been more. He'd been going to show Margaret how he'd survived the worst – that all the things they'd held about single-mindedness, and determination, were true.

'She can't be the only person tuned in to your wavelength.'

'Logical, I know. Unfortunately, these days, I've precious little left over from the effort of existing.' And, he added silently, I don't make the same mistake a second time. However much I need you.

144

God, what a task, thought Irene, I've got to *make* him look forward to a life without that woman! But he wasn't ready yet to stiffen himself to cope unaided. 'Time you off-loaded a bit of the weight.'

'On to you?' He was surprised she was suggesting that. He'd noticed how irritated she was when he mentioned Margaret again.

'I wasn't suggesting anyone else,' said Irene, handing him a cup.

'I hate using people.'

'I've gathered that, Richard.'

'If only I could explain. She was my sort, took life seriously. We both read all kinds of things – Gide, Dostoevsky . . .'

'And I'm only illiterate!'

'Irene?' But he should understand her reaction. He was still ramming Margaret down her throat, making her feel inadequate.

'Don't mind me, get on with it.'

He wanted to undo the hurt he'd caused. 'I know you're doing all you can. It's just – things would have been so different, if only . . .'

'And that's it, isn't it? Those two words should be banned from the English language. As of now, we're banning them here. The sentiments they generate are utterly pointless. And if I was your doctor I'd warn you this negative attitude is the swiftest means of ensuring a setback.'

Richard's dark eyebrows soared.

'Yes, I'm being cruel,' Irene continued. 'But I bet you know this already at heart – until you accept that you won't be sharing anything with Margaret again, you won't be up to working.'

'You know it all, don't you?' he snapped.

Irene shook her head. 'If I know anything, it wasn't learned easily.'

'Experience?' He sighed. 'True, I suppose. I wasn't thinking. But, Irene, how can I put this . . . work alone will never be enough.'

145

She smiled to herself. 'I don't believe it's meant to be, not for any of us. Although I'd have thought that happen it'd have given you sufficient to occupy yourself, at least until the office is operational.'

'Okay. It was only – letting go can't happen overnight. The friendship we had went, for want of a better word, right to the soul.'

'You don't have to call it a day because you can't talk out all the philosophizing with the person you'd choose.'

'And because I'm no longer flattered by believing *I* was the one who'd aroused her interest in all these different authors, in these fascinating subjects.'

'Oh, aye? I didn't know you saw yourself as a mentor.'

'Do you permit me no vanity?' Richard asked, a smile in his voice at last.

'It'll not do you any harm – seems to be freely admitted.'

'Well, if blocking out a whole area of life proves difficult, I can attempt to look ahead instead – realistically. *How* exactly, though, Irene? You must know . . .'

'Determination, not much else. Willing yourself not to think too deeply about the past.'

'So we try, okay. Concentrate on work, leave the rest.'

'Not quite, Richard. I'm not well read, if I wasn't studying medical tomes it had to be escapist stuff.'

'Understood. I don't expect you to . . .'

'But I expect something of you. Exercise that keen mind – the truth you unearthed must, as least, tell you to go on using it.'

'To what purpose?' But as he asked the question he recollected how she'd admitted when she first arrived here that her life was in a mess.

'In all that reading, didn't you come across anything to help me?'

'Oh, Irene – can't even remember what I did read.' He couldn't close the door on her, yet he literally was too shattered to think.

She smiled to herself. 'You will, when you're not as tired. You'll say to yourself, "That's what I'll give that silly woman to read." '

'Not silly.'

Still smiling, Irene continued, ' . . . put a bit of sense into that thick skull of hers.'

'That's not how I think of you.'

'Oh, compliments, compliments!'

Later that same day Irene found him in his room again, leaning against a chair, over by the bookshelves. Smiling, he swung round and handed her a thick volume.

'That might help.'

She smiled up at him. 'Thanks. I'll come to you for help with all t'long words.'

'You won't need to. But I might be flattered if you do.'

Richard didn't refer to that night again until she went into his room early on the Monday morning.

'I missed you last night – it was rather quiet, and very lonely!'

Irene laughed, loving the fun glowing in his dark eyes. 'You needn't think that's becoming a habit, my lad!'

'I see – a treat, for high days and holidays?'

'You're getting no such promises.'

They began that day to sort out the room Richard had chosen for his office. Previously his study, it already contained many of his legal books. They measured up the available space then began ordering army-surplus desks and filing cabinets, as eagerly as if they were from the most elegant prewar suppliers.

As they organized everything the weeks flew by. Richard attended to the conveyancing job he'd mentioned and, once they found people were glad he was reopening his practice, they started seeking staff.

They advertised for a typist and Anita Robins, an attractive blond in her twenties and with a ready smile, was taken on. What Richard really needed, though, was a solicitor's clerk.

And then one morning when Irene answered the door-bell, a man of around twenty-eight was on the steps. He asked after Richard. Evidently, he had been in New Zealand since the end of the war, and hadn't learned of Richard's illness until his return.

Irene took him through, noted the mutual delight produced by their reunion, then went to make coffee. She took in the steaming cups, intending to leave the men to talk, but Richard introduced David Beck to her, then insisted she join them.

David was bringing Richard up to date. 'So, I've called to see if you know of any vacancies. Still want to live somewhere around Skipton. Of course, I didn't know you'd been out of touch.'

'I don't believe it!' Richard exclaimed, then just as quickly his smile faded. 'But you wouldn't consider it, anyway. It'd be too dull, too quiet. You want to be right in Skipton itself, or maybe Ilkley, not in a remote house out here.'

'Are you offering me a job?'

'I'd plead with you to take it, David, if I didn't think that'd be unfair.'

'Unfair – how?'

'We're a bit off the beaten track, aren't we? There are hardly any houses really close – a few cottages here and there, well spaced out.'

'Suits us.'

'Us?' Richard raised an eyebrow.

'Haven't had chance to tell you. Got myself married – just before the voyage home.' David smiled engagingly, his hazel eyes alight. 'So, we might enjoy the quiet, if we find a decent little house somewhere round about.'

Irene grinned. 'This is one spot where you might manage that in time. Have you heard about the housing shortage? Can't get anywhere in the towns for love nor money.'

'Is that a deal then?' David persisted. 'We're living with my mum at present in Gargrave, that's handy enough by motorbike.'

'Fair enough, but – ' Frowning, Richard hesitated. 'If the number of clients builds up the way it promises, you might discover you need broad shoulders. You see, this young lady . . .' He glanced towards Irene, smiled briefly, '. . . insists I don't overdo things.'

David grinned, indicating his ample frame. Irene was warming to him, had hoped immediately that he would join Richard. 'You load it all on me,' he was saying. 'I'm following in your footsteps. The navy gave me time to think. Who'd remain a solicitor's clerk for ever? I'm studying again, need any experience you'd throw my way.'

Irene left them to discuss details of salary and how soon David would begin work, and afterwards remarked on how fortunate they were.

'I can't really believe it,' Richard confessed. 'It certainly appears that we were destined to have just the assistance I require.'

'David seems a lovely chap, I'm delighted he's joining you.'

'Us,' he corrected her. 'Joining us. This isn't my practice, it'll belong to all the people who'll make it work, the whole team. Though most of all to you and me. And you don't need me to elaborate on the reasons.'

Daphne came in while they were sitting talking, and grasped Irene's shoulder. 'Glad to hear you saying that, Rich. And I couldn't be more pleased that you're up to working again. Thanks to Irene.'

As their plans gradually materialized, Irene grew contented. Both David and Anita were pleasant folk to have around, and hard workers as well. Now that many of Richard's old clients were coming back to him together with new ones, he was transformed. Watching him, she often caught herself smiling. He radiated such vitality that even she soon ceased to notice the limp and that weak right hand. With his expression constantly so alert and interested he'd become so animated that she couldn't keep her eyes off him.

She was guarding his health – surreptitiously, for confidence in his own ability to endure a working routine was essential. But she ensured some relaxation during evenings and weekends.

When she saw that the new film of *Great Expectations* was showing locally, she asked if Richard wanted to see it.

He didn't hesitate. He was no longer daunted by the number of steps he might have to negotiate.

'Why not? And we'll go into Skipton early, have a look around then a spot of tea somewhere.'

Although all cafes and restaurants still were restricted to serving inexpensive simple fare, they enjoyed lingering while there was tea remaining in the pot.

'I've always loved Skipton,' Richard confided. 'Ever since I was a lad and used to look for bargains on the toy stall at the market.'

'Didn't know you'd needed to watch the pennies,' Irene teased. 'Thought your family'd always had plenty of brass.'

He chuckled. 'Nay lass, don't forget I am Yorkshire!'

'You've never sounded it before.'

'Have you heard yourself? Or some of the time – I have to admit I've noticed how the native vernacular resurrects after a visit to your family.'

Raising a fair eyebrow, Irene smiled back at him. 'I must have mislaid the accent when I was in London, I suppose.'

'And during your training. As I did, at university. When you're with educated people who aren't from your own region you tend, if unconsciously, to conform.'

Irene laughed. 'There was one girl, at medical school, used to embarrass me no end. She was always picking me up on the way I pronounced my vowels.'

'Sounds obnoxious to me.'

'Happen she was. For a long time she made me so conscious of the fact that I didn't speak properly that I hardly said anything at all.'

Richard frowned, but Irene shook her head at him.

'The inhibition didn't last too long, I think!'

'Nevertheless – people shouldn't be expected to adapt. Individuality should always be prized.'

Irene nodded. 'I like that idea, though I don't reckon I could have put it as well as you.'

Briefly, at the cinema pay desk, Irene felt awkward when Richard insisted on getting their tickets. 'But coming here was my suggestion,' she protested.

He only laughed. 'You've just told me you know I'm not short of brass.'

They were settled in their seats when the advertisements ended and the newsreel began. Although there was word from Nuremberg that the war crimes tribunal would shortly begin to deliver its judgement, they were cheered by other signs that prewar interests and values were flourishing again. In Cannes the Film Festival postponed from 1939 had opened, King George II of Greece had returned to Athens from exile, and football was drawing crowds of fans to the first few matches of the Saturday League which had been restored.

After the B movie, a short documentary on the birdlife of a remote Scottish island made their mood relaxed. Irene soon wondered if she'd succumbed too thoroughly to its influence. The beginning of *Great Expectations* was such a contrast and, being so atmospheric, gripped her. When the convict startled Pip in the graveyard, she flinched and struggled to contain a cry.

In the darkness beside her Richard smiled, and then he took her hand. His fingers were warm, their grasp very firm. Briefly, emotion choked her as she recognized the change from how lifeless they had felt, how cold, and only just over a year ago. But the film was too enthralling to dwell for more than a few seconds on anything else, though it didn't prevent her from remaining aware of his hand on hers.

'I hope you enjoyed that as much as I did,' she exclaimed, after they had stood for the National Anthem.

Richard grinned. 'I did indeed – even if I didn't react quite so forcefully.'

'You're lucky I managed not to scream!'

'I wouldn't have disowned you,' he assured her, still smiling. 'I'm only glad when something penetrates the professionalism.'

'On about that again, are we?' she groaned. And then grew silent, smiling to herself, remembering his holding her hand. If she'd needed confirmation that he didn't only consider her usefulness to him, she'd had the evidence tonight.

The interior of the car felt cold, and Irene realized that it wouldn't be long before autumn was followed by winter, bringing icy winds and snow to these Yorkshire fells.

'If we're planning any more outings, we'd better not delay too long in case we're snowbound,' she remarked.

'There's one thing I hope to arrange,' Richard began. 'Now that more business is coming our way, and you and the other two are proving so invaluable, I mean us to celebrate.' Although there were restrictions still on eating out, he'd one hotel in mind where the catering was such that even limited fare could seem attractive.

'What a lovely idea – will that be soon?'

'As soon as we can get it organized.' Going out today had not only proved how much he could tolerate, but had convinced him that this idea he'd had must become reality.

By the time of that celebration Richard's practice had grown even busier. As well as conveyancing for people who wanted to invest in property after returning to civilian life, there was the legal advice being sought by men who were eager to set up in business again.

'It's a good job you decided earlier on having this night out,' Irene exclaimed when they were ready to leave North Fell House. 'Or you might have considered we couldn't make time for it!'

Smiling, Richard shook his head. Nothing would have prevented his doing this for them.

They were a small party, but in excellent spirits as they met up in the hotel overlooking the river.

Irene was wearing a simple black dress, preserved from before the war, but perfectly cut with a softly draped bodice. She'd always admitted secretly that she felt it was flattering. She had caught her pale hair into a neat coil at the back of her head but then, wondering if the style were too severe, had teased out soft, curling tendrils. They seemed to accentuate her high cheekbones and the brilliance of her eyes.

Daphne, at her brother's side, was glowing in an elegant dress the green of her eyes. And Richard himself, in a dark suit with a white shirt complementing the tan he'd acquired, looked magnificent.

David Beck, his satisfaction evident, was introducing his wife, Clare, to everyone. She was a charming girl, not especially glamorous, but bubbling over with a young bride's joy – and enchanting them all with her New Zealand accent. Anita was the only person who appeared a little subdued; she had come alone because her husband was away on a business trip. Although thoroughly integrated by now into their office life, here she appeared rather ill at ease.

'You've managed to find a dress that exactly matches your hair,' Irene complimented her as they assembled near the bar. 'It's most effective.'

Anita smiled. 'Thank you. Jeff chose it – just for the reason you noticed. He let me have some of his coupons towards it, an' all. Thought I'd put it on tonight – boost my morale a bit. I hate going anywhere on my own. When you've been married a while, you get that used to being one of a couple.'

Irene nodded her understanding.

Anita smiled again. 'For anybody else but Mr Hughes, I'd have got out of coming, but somehow I couldn't. He's a bit of a special boss, isn't he?'

Irene nodded again. 'You've found that out already then?'

'Did you work for him before? You seem to know him better than the rest of us.'

'No, David did – briefly, before he joined up. I just came on the scene while Richard was ill.'

'Oh?' Anita was puzzled. 'What did you do?'

Irene grinned. 'Not so much . . .'

'Irene, don't lie!' It was Daphne, coming between them. A hand on each of their shoulders, she smiled at Anita. 'Irene, here, is the reason you have a job. Without her, Richard would still be immobilized on his back, unable to speak . . .'

Anita stared hard towards her boss, taking in the animation with which he was laughing and talking with David and Clare. Her grey eyes misted.

Irene turned to Daphne. 'Nay, but you're embarrassing us,' she said, though she smiled nevertheless, glad to be appreciated.

'It's incredible,' Anita exclaimed, her voice hushed. 'I knew, of course, that he'd been very poorly, but I never suspected it was owt as serious as that.'

'It's a miracle,' said Daphne quietly. 'Thank God Irene came when she did.' And her gaze held Irene's steady blue eyes.

The meal was excellent despite government restrictions, and it was served with a good balance between attentiveness and being left to relax. Irene was seated to Richard's right, his sister facing her and telling her about previous visits here. Richard was exuberant, entertaining them all with anecdotes from his early experiences in the courtroom and other, more extravagent, yarns of his university days.

Irene couldn't give much attention to anybody else. The amusement glinting so frequently in his glance was devastatingly attractive, a powerful magnet. When, as they so often did, those dark eyes sought hers she found breathing difficult. Thinking ruefully that she'd have welcomed feeling easier, so that she might perhaps have sparkled a bit, she could only be glad of the rest of them round the table who kept the conversation brisk and lively.

When the meal finally ended, Richard suggested that they adjourn to North Fell House. After welcoming everyone in through the beautiful pale green hall, Richard asked Irene to help him distribute drinks while Daphne assembled a collection of popular records, calling to Irene to inquire if she had any favourites.

As soon as the music began Clare tried to get David to jive with her. He protested he'd eaten too much for being so energetic, so Clare drew Anita to her feet. Presently, the rhythm changed to a slower number, David claimed his wife and they began to dance, their arms locked about each other. Irene smiled as she watched, happy for them, yet rather envying their uncomplicated love for each other.

Suddenly, she felt a touch on her shoulder. Richard was smiling down at her. 'You're rather quiet tonight, my dear.'

'Just happy, very happy.'

He grinned. 'I'm about to ruin all that.' He glanced towards Clare and David. 'I want to try that. You're the only one who understands my limitations.'

She rose eagerly. And smiled into his eyes. 'The way you look tonight, Rich, I'm not going to believe limitations exist.'

He laughed. 'You're always flattering me! What're you after?'

As he held her to him, she gazed upwards again. 'This?'

'And so am I.' The lightness had gone from his tone, replaced by a slight huskiness. 'You say you're happy, what do you think I am? And you've given me this, all of it.'

'No, love, I haven't – you've worked for it yourself.'

He shook his head. 'You told me once I've a talent for self-examination. I know the truth. But we won't argue, not tonight.' She felt his lips against her hair, his arm tightened about her.

'Know something?' he murmured. 'While we were out I was so utterly pleased with life I wanted to hang on to everyone, prolonging the occasion far into the night. Yet now, suddenly, I'd like to send them all away and just have you, and the excuse for holding you this way.'

'You can't dismiss them yet,' Irene began, and paused. 'You feel you need an excuse then?'

Richard smiled rather wryly, his dark eyes glinting. 'I'm not certain. Not entirely sure where I am with you, yet.'

That's mutual, Irene thought, but wasn't prepared either to laugh about it, or to reveal that the uncertainty mattered. She was happy just relaxing against him, noticing as they danced that his excellent rhythm compensated for the limp.

'How am I doing?' he inquired presently, with a concern that went straight to her heart.

'Ay, Richard love, you're wonderful.'

'Steady now,' he said quietly, 'isn't that just a bit excessive?' But then he tilted her chin, and saw the tears glistening in her blue eyes.

155

'Better not,' he cautioned her. 'I just might join you.'

His arm tightened again, drawing her so near that she could feel his heart beating at her breast, his breath a gentle stirring of her hair.

'Let's lose ourselves somewhere,' he suggested in a whisper. 'Go and make coffee or something.'

Daphne had beaten them to the kitchen, already had the coffee pot filled, and was setting out cups. In the doorway, Richard turned to Irene and smiled ruefully.

'You should be with your guests,' his sister reproved. 'I don't know what you're thinking of, wandering off. Did you suppose I wouldn't organize coffee?'

'I didn't know how soon, did I?' He was trying to keep a straight face.

'I guess not. Actually, David and Clare don't wish to be too late, I rather suspect dancing put other ideas into their heads. And they're giving Anita a lift.'

'Want any help, Daphne?' Irene asked.

'No, thanks, it's all but ready. Do you two want coffee as well?'

'Not for me,' Richard replied. 'I'm having more wine.'

Daphne frowned. 'Are you certain you should?'

'To hell with that!' he retorted. 'I've kept to wine, and I've only had a couple of glasses so far.'

Daphne glanced anxiously towards Irene.

She laughed. 'Let him please himself, he'll be all right. It is his night, after all.'

In the hall, on the way to the sitting room, Richard took her by the wrist.

'If it is my night, there's one thing I must be granted . . .' He drew her into his arms. But even as his head lowered and Irene closed her eyes anticipating his kiss, somebody spoke.

'Irene, where's . . . ? Oh – sorry.'

It was Anita. Turning, Irene was compelled to smile.

'I am sorry,' Anita repeated, acutely embarrassed. Irene glanced up at Richard. He winked.

'What did you want, Anita?' Irene was still smiling.

'I only wondered where Daphne was.'

As Irene was telling her, Daphne appeared, taking coffee through to the others.

'Are you having coffee, Irene?' Richard asked, opening another bottle of wine.

'I don't think so, it might keep me awake for the rest of the night.'

'Join me with a glass of this?'

'Fine, thanks.' She had drunk very little while they were out, aware that she would be driving home.

His glance lingered with hers as he handed over the glass. And then slowly, appreciatively, his brown eyes approved her simple gown, her exquisite hair, and the curve of her breasts at the low neckline.

'Let's sit.' They went to the pale sofa.

Richard began talking with David and Clare, asking more about New Zealand, yet all the while his arm rested across Irene's shoulders, and his long fingers stirred affectionately. Their touch was sufficiently sensual to send urgent pulsings through her veins. Yet it was much more a reminder that seemed to say 'It's you I'm thinking of.'

As they closed the door after seeing off their guests, Daphne yawned a couple of times. She smiled at them both, then kissed each in turn. Her magnificent eyes gleamed when she looked at Irene.

'You said this was Richard's night. I'm not at all certain this wasn't really all in your honour.'

'No, please . . . ' Irene was overwhelmed with emotion again.

Richard took over, slipping an arm about her waist, smiling first at her and then at Daphne.

'Perceptive as always, young sister! You also know me well enough to understand I don't make pretty speeches. But this is true, Irene. I hope you've taken a long, hard look at me tonight. My joy must have been self-evident, and far more eloquent than I'll ever be.'

He hugged her then, fiercely. As Daphne walked away and up the stairs he led the way back into the sitting room.

Struggling for a bit of composure, Irene began collecting up empty glasses and cups.

'No.' Half smiling, he checked her. 'For God's sake, do you always have to be so practical!'

Slightly bewildered, she watched as he crossed to the record player. The tune he chose was a jive that had had feet tapping ever since it was introduced over here by the Yanks.

He extended a hand towards her.

'Richard Hughes, how much have you been drinking?'

'Don't you start. I've a sister to nag me, that is *not* your role. Now come on – maybe this won't be very proficient, but I have to try. Now the others have left.'

Smiling again, her heart in her eyes, Irene went to him. The jive would have won no medals, but her spirits soared with the comparison between Richard now and as she'd first seen him.

'There are times, you know,' she exclaimed breathlessly, 'when I believe you're a little crazy.'

He laughed. 'There are times when crazy is precisely the way I want to be. Happen it's something I missed out, the first time around. I plan on making up for that.'

They were both laughing by the time the track ended. Irene was about to flop into a chair, but Richard shook his head, keeping a hold on her as he returned to the gramophone. The melody he chose was much slower and, almost as an afterthought, he turned down the lights.

'I've never said you're beautiful, Irene,' he murmured as he held her close. 'Even now, no words do justice to how you look, nor to what I am feeling.' He stopped their slow progression around the room and simply held her, close against his heart.

Irene realized that she had never felt so happy in her life before, and never more deeply moved. And nor had she ever felt so secure, so well protected – not feelings that she'd believed she wanted.

She glanced up and in his eyes was a gleam of moisture to match the tears in her own. She hugged him to her. Richard's kisses started on her hair, moved to her closed eyelids. And then his lips found hers, lingering there as though he as well would have nothing separate them, and could not have enough of this total ecstasy.

10

It was only afterwards that Irene's euphoria began to dampen. She'd been too elated at the time to worry about the way their relationship was developing. But she was too much of a realist to refuse now to consider the misgivings as soon as they arose. Hadn't she been *surprised* as much as delighted when Richard appeared to reciprocate all that she was feeling? Within a day she was beginning to realize that he could merely be falling for the person who'd helped in the healing process.

There was nothing wrong with expressing gratitude, but she didn't want to suspect there mightn't be much more than that behind his sudden demonstration of affection. And their kisses were causing a bit of a stir. Anita was teasing her one day in the office, and Irene wasn't sorry when she was interrupted by a phone call from Norman.

He laughingly reassured Irene when she inquired if something was wrong. 'On the contrary. I'm feeling champion, these days. I've just got a bit of news that I'd like you to keep to yourself.'

'Have you, by Jove? Let's be knowing then . . . '

'I take it you will be going to that do Mum's putting on for our Mavis and Ralph?'

'I suppose so – haven't heard exactly when it is yet.'

'You mustn't even think of giving it a miss. Mavis'd be that disappointed, and I'm sure Ralph would.'

'Didn't know you were all that pally with him . . . '

'That's just where you're wrong. Mind you, I'll admit it did seem a bit unlikely once. Any road, he's been in touch wi' me a couple of times, talking over how I've found adjusting to leaving the forces.'

'Is that what you rang to tell me?'

'No – just that I'm hoping to have a lass with me – Lily. And if you're there I know it'll be all right. But don't hang on at home, will you? If they say owt, act as if you know nowt about her.'

Reflecting on Norman's news gave her a break in considering her own situation. And there wasn't much time for that, they were busier than ever now, too busy to pay much attention to anything else. Richard was teaching her a great deal about a solicitor's routine. And, rather to Irene's surprise, she was finding everything interesting.

She was particularly fascinated by the intricacies of drawing up wills, perhaps because even the legal language failed to conceal the human emotions they represented. Seemingly ordinary folk revealed themselves as vindictive; cutting out some relative, or diminishing their bequests to demonstrate in an ultimate blow that old animosities exacted their price. And then there were others, of course, who looked as though they hadn't a farthing to their name, yet sacrificed to endow their offspring with more money than they'd ever use.

Strangely, it was the day she was confronted with the depressing aspect of wills when Irene began to feel most at home with her job.

Richard had returned to the office before the rest of them, cutting short his lunch for a telephoned appointment. Presently, he emerged.

'I need your help with this, Irene. I've got a Mrs Simmonds here. She's old, bewildered, and distressed. Her husband died yesterday. I need to do some phoning on her behalf, she'll only become more worked up if that's in her hearing. The old man's will was among those left with a fellow solicitor when I believed I'd never practise again.'

'And you'd rather Mrs Simmonds wasn't on her own too long.'

'That's right. She ought to have had somebody accompany her, but they have no family.'

The elderly lady had left her chair, and was hovering uncertainly midway between Richard's desk and the door.

'Hallo,' said Irene gently. 'I'm Mr Hughes' assistant. We were wondering if you might like a cup of tea while you're waiting.'

The wrinkles multiplied in a forehead narrowed by the black felt hat from the cloche era. 'Ay, love – thank you, but do you mind if I don't? This lot's fair upset my insides, I can't stop going.'

'But you will sit down again, won't you?'

Mrs Simmonds seemed to sway on her feet, and looked as though she'd lost two stone since she'd last worn the good black coat. Irene went to put an arm round her shoulders, and led her back to the seat.

'I've never been soft like this before, it were allus me that kept going, no matter what,' Mrs Simmonds announced anxiously.

'I'm sure. And now you shouldn't be letting that bother you. Folk understand, know you've had a nasty shock.' Irene leaned against the desk, took a thin-skinned hand in her own.

'My Jack went that quick, you see. One minute he were penning the sheep, t'next he'd fallen forward over t'edge of the gate. I knew summat was wrong straight off. I were there, you see, saw it all.'

'How dreadful for you.'

'It were that! I'd only gone to call him for his dinner. It weren't like him not to think on, and you can't shout him across yon fields. Hard of hearing he is – was.'

'Well, at least he can't have had to endure a lot of pain, if he went that quickly, Mrs Simmonds.'

'That's what I hope – it's bad enough that he had to pass on, without . . . ' She stopped speaking, shook her head.

'Haven't you got anybody who'd help you with the arrangements?' Irene felt like accompanying her to the funeral parlour or wherever.

'No, there's nob'dy. We never had any childer, and all Jack's folk went long since. But I've got it all seen to by now.'

'You're a real brick, Mrs Simmonds.'

'Nay, I'm not. Let him down, I did.'

'I'm sure you didn't,' Irene began.

The interruption was firm, despite the old lady's quivering chin. 'I did an' all. He were depending on me, weren't he, to do summat. And I were that gob-smacked I couldn't do owt but stand and gawp.'

'Steady, Mrs Simmonds, all right . . .'

She was weeping now, copiously. 'Other folk might have known what to do – summat that'd have saved him.'

'And they might not. And any road, it mightn't have been best for *him* to have been saved, not if he'd always be an invalid at after.'

'Do you think – do you think he could have been?'

'Very possibly. I don't suppose he'd have liked that very much.'

'Jack'd have hated it! He were allus miserable if he got a bit of a cold.'

'There you are then.'

'If only I could stop seeing his face the way it was, all a funny colour, and his eyes gone – vacant. And I couldn't fetch him back.'

When Richard returned to the office Mrs Simmonds was drying her eyes. The thin old frame was steadier now. Some of the tension was drained. She wasn't yet equal to accepting what had happened, but was past being rigid with the need to fight its being true.

Irene was surprisingly calm, rewarded by knowing that she'd been some use. And in a way which employed the skills developed over the years helping patients compelled to face bereavement.

She couldn't credit the unfortunate coincidence later that day when another client was confronting a similar loss – and a more untimely one.

Irene admitted a local businessman whom she knew slightly and, thinking that he looked strained, showed him straight into the office.

'Good afternoon, Mr Mason,' Richard began, then saw how troubled his client's eyes were. And how his normal ebullience was drained.

'I don't know if you can help,' Barry Mason began, flopping on to a chair as though someone had removed the bones and sinew from his legs. 'She hadn't made a will, not with anybody. She was so young.'

'Not . . . ?'

'Bessie, aye. She went, last night. Just like that.'

'Oh, I am sorry, deeply sorry.' Richard hadn't socialized with the Masons, but he knew they were a devoted couple.

'It was her asthma. She'd had it all her life, it often caught up with her. But I never dreamed it could finish her like that.'

'It's certainly possible for folk with it to live to a good age.'

'If I'd been in, I could have done something. But I was at the Lit and Phil – Bessie never minded me going.' Suddenly, he gulped.

'A pot of tea perhaps?' Richard suggested to Irene and escorted Barry Mason away from David and Anita and towards the sitting room.

Their client was still in no state to attempt to drink tea by the time Irene took in a tray. Richard was looking covertly at his watch.

He drew her aside into the hall. 'Can you cope? I'm overdue at the station. One of my regulars who's always getting himself arrested for driving irregularities. I've to be there while the police charge him.'

'Sure – okay. I'll see Mr Mason's all right.'

'As soon as he gets himself in control a bit, take down any particulars. He might need help with claiming insurances, that sort of thing. And if she truly hasn't left a will, do assure him that I'll do whatever I can to see him through sorting her affairs.'

When Irene returned to Mr Mason he seemed to have regained control.

'Sorry,' he said awkwardly.

'There's no need, I'm used to this. And other folk who've gone through sudden loss will tell you you've got to go easy on yourself.'

He gave her a surprised look. 'Because the doctor's said there was nothing I could have done to save her, you mean?'

'Partly. But more that it's normal to have your composure shattered by shock. There'll be times when you don't feel like work or anything else, and others when you can't contain all that sorrow. You'll need to remember then that most people have experienced grief.'

'Don't think I've broken down since I was a nipper.'

'It's better for you than fighting it now, will prepare you *in time* for picking up the pieces.'

Afterwards, when Richard returned from the police station, he was feeling relieved by having obtained bail for his client there.

'How did you cope? Gruelling for you, having to deal with two bereavements in one day.'

'I managed. The details are on your desk. I said you'd ring him. I'm only thankful experience has provided clues to what was needed.'

'Thanks, anyway. It's not all gloom here, you know. You'll enjoy your involvement in conveyancing,' Richard told her. 'There's a lot of satisfaction in helping people acquire the home they've set their hearts on.'

As yet, though, even out in the country like this, the housing shortage made life difficult. The first few places available at the end of the war had sold, and not nearly enough were being built.

Business transactions were less easy for Irene to understand, but she was resolved to master some of the details of company law. And applying herself to the way that firms were run gave her fresh insight into Richard's practice. She had never thought she had much of a head for the business world, but discovering that her common sense made a good foundation encouraged her to build up her knowledge.

'Your comprehension's quite thorough,' Richard complimented her one afternoon, but such reassurance was rare, and she noticed that with the others also he only occasionally offered any praise. But then, he was exerting a lot of effort just to keep going, and to ensure they had more work coming their way.

In many ways, Richard was standing up to being in the office far better than she had expected, although he did tend to neglect relaxation. If he listened without her prompting to the *Brains Trust* on the wireless, or to another favourite, *Transatlantic Quiz*, that seemed to be as much. Irene suspected that he regarded the past months as written off; in order to compensate he wouldn't let go too often.

She tried to get him to accompany her to Halifax for the family gathering being arranged for Mavis who was coming to the West Riding to collect the last of her belongings.

Richard frowned. He suddenly felt perplexed. A part of him – the part that yearned to belong with her – was saying 'Yes', being delighted to be asked. But the old torment rose to quell enthusiasm before he dared give it rein. Where was the fairness in tying Irene to him? He had proved how readily he'd grown fond of her, he'd never condemn her to a share of his uncertain future.

Smiling, he shook his head. 'No – really. It's most kind of you to ask. But I think this is one occasion when your family don't need intruders.'

'But you wouldn't . . . ' Irene began.

She was interrupted, swiftly. Somehow, he had to free her. 'You need to get away from me, once in a while, to adjust your outlook.'

Smarting under what she saw as Richard's warning to keep off, she concealed her disturbance. She would just have to forget him for a few hours, and make sure she enjoyed seeing all her folk again.

Irene arrived on the Saturday afternoon and was shaken to hear her parents arguing as soon as she opened the front door. And although she read in their sharpness their common dread of losing Mavis and young Heather, she longed to shout them down. She felt like asking if they couldn't have tried to create a happier atmosphere.

165

Disciplining the urge, she hurried through to join them in the kitchen, inquiring what was wrong as she removed her coat.

'Nowt,' Elsie replied, and contradicted herself by elaborating.

'It's your father getting on at me again. I wonder why it's always my fault!'

Donald Hainsworth cast his gaze heavenwards before turning aside to greet Irene. 'See you in a minute,' he muttered, and strode through into the hall.

They could hear him running upstairs, then slamming drawers in the master bedroom.

Irene noticed tears in her mother's brown eyes, and put an arm round her bony shoulders. 'What's up, Mum?'

'I got them a card, if I hadn't done I could understand him. To wish them a happy life in their new home. I were going to give it her tonight.'

'And so you can, surely.'

'Aye, but that's not good enough now, is it? Not for your Dad. Just because *their* card came first post this morning.'

'From Ralph's parents?'

Elsie nodded. 'And now he's got me thinking like him – that our Mavis'll believe we don't care or summat.'

'What – when you're laying on a spread for them?'

Her mother sniffed. 'My custard tarts have gone wrong, an' all. The pastry's risen up from the base, a right mess they are. And all them precious eggs wasted . . .'

Irene controlled her grin. 'Knowing you, there'll be that much more besides, no one'll miss your custards.'

'They won't miss 'em, that's true – they'll be there to get eaten. We haven't brass to throw stuff away, not like some folk.'

So, her mother was feeling the inequality between their family and the Parkins. Irene gave her a hug, and was thankful when she received a watery smile.

'Any road – how are you, Irene love? I see you've come on your own, after all.'

166

'Yes. Happen Richard thought a lot of company might be too much for him.' She didn't know whether she was relieved he hadn't found her mum and dad scrapping, or disappointed that they wouldn't yet have the satisfaction of recognizing her friendship with such a personable man. Still, if he'd been in his present frame of mind, proving his detachment, his being here mightn't have been much of an asset.

'Where is our Mavis?'

'Bathing young Heather. Ralph's up there, an' all. Whatever else, he's taken a real shine to that child. Can't seem to get enough of her.'

'Good. I am glad.'

'Aye, he's framing far better than ever I expected as a father. And a husband. Not that I agree wi' all his ideas, mind.'

'Oh . . . ?' But Elsie Hainsworth didn't need any prompting.

'Keeping her up, they are, tonight. They tried to get her to sleep longer after dinner, to make up for it, but it's still not right. The bairn's too little to be kept awake that long, and with so many folk here.'

'Who's coming then, as well as family?'

'There's a weaver from the mill, for a start. Our Norman's just gone to fetch her. It'll be t'first time we've set eyes on her, so don't ask me what she's like. Lily, her name is.'

'I didn't know he was courting.'

'You're not the only one! I asked him if he'd known her before the war, like, but he weren't for telling. Seems to me, Norman's getting secretive.'

'Happen he – well, got used to going his own way while he was joined up.'

'I daresay, but we're here now, aren't we? He knows we care.'

'And how is he, these days?'

'Up and down, cantankerous at times.' Elsie sighed, picturing the to-do they'd had over this lass coming, and them knowing nowt about her.

167

They'd just finished tea last Sunday and Elsie was feeling contented, there weren't that many mealtimes when Donald got to sit down with them and no patients interrupting. Mavis and the bairn would be home at the end of the week and, this far away from all that baking, Elsie was simply relishing the prospect of having them here again. 'Ay, it will be grand to see our little Heather, I'll bet we shall see a difference in her, after all this time.'

'I've been thinking,' said Norman, 'about the do – there's a lass I want to ask. I take it that'll be all right?'

'Aye, lad, of course,' his father said, grinning.

'Now, hold on a minute,' Elsie began, alarmed by the prospect of another of her family starting courting. 'Who is this girl?'

'One of t'weavers down at Dewhurst's.'

'You hadn't told us owt about going out with anybody.'

Norman's smile faded. Sometimes, he felt proper smothered. 'I'm not a bit of a kid, didn't know I was supposed to report everything.'

'Watch it, lad,' Donald said just as brusquely. 'That's no way to talk to your mother.'

'I'm sorry, but it's how I feel. And I'm nearly thirty, I can handle my own life.'

'You'll keep a civil tongue in your head, though,' his father continued, 'while you live in this house.'

'All I asked in t'first place was if Lily could come here. If she won't be welcome, we can forget it.'

'When have I ever failed to welcome any of your friends?' Elsie demanded. 'You've all three on you allus been free to bring folk in.'

But Norman was annoyed, could feel his pulse rate speeding up. Even though he knew full well that it wasn't serious heart trouble, he still had to remind himself that he could cope with this reaction. When it happened at the mill he generally quietened down by sort of withdrawing into himself until he'd regained control. At home, they'd soon start asking what he'd turned so quiet about.

'I know that, Mum. We've always all got on champion. Happen that's why I'm so set on bringing Lily here.'

168

'We haven't said no, have we?' his mother responded, still a little sharply. She'd been afraid for a minute that Norman was going to announce that he was the next that'd be getting wed. 'As far as I'm concerned, you can bring this Lily. But I'd have liked to have known of her existence a bit before she came here.'

Norman had had the sense not to struggle for anything more gracious. He knew his mother well enough, and that she'd take anybody to her heart so long as they weren't snobbish or patronizing.

'I shall be very interested to see what the lass is like,' Elsie remarked now to Irene, and glanced at the clock. 'And if I don't get a move on I shan't have changed into my best frock when they arrive.'

'Is there anything you want doing?' Irene inquired.

Her mother surprised her by grinning. 'Aye, if you can wave a magic wand, and get your father and me agreeing again!'

When Elsie arrived upstairs in their bedroom, however, Donald was already contrite.

'Come here, love,' he said, his arms extended for her. 'We're both a bit on edge, aren't we? Not liking to admit how much we'd prefer to hang on to our Mavis.'

'Careful, Don,' she whispered against his chest. 'They're only in the next room, getting ready.'

He smiled conspiratorially. 'And we mustn't spoil their happiness.'

'It could have been a lot worse,' Elsie acknowledged. 'I was that afraid for a long time that Ralph wouldn't settle to being married.'

Norman and Lily arrived while Irene was the only one downstairs.

'Mum and Dad won't be a minute,' she said after Norman had introduced them.

'I gather you don't live round here nowadays,' Lily began, as Irene took her coat.

'That's right. I'm in a lovely spot, just the other side of Skipton. The scenery's smashing; mind you, the fells are a bit daunting in bad weather.'

'I'll bet!' exclaimed Lily, although she'd only a vague recollection of the countryside out that way. 'And what's your job then?'

'Oh – sort of personal assistant, to a solicitor.'

'Sounds very important. Bet you're good at it, you talk nice, don't you?'

Irene smiled.

Norman was grinning. 'Our Irene always has,' he began, then clammed up when he felt her warning look.

Mavis came running down the stairs, with Ralph behind her and Heather in his arms. They were closely followed by Elsie and Donald.

'You must be Lily,' Mavis said, beaming, and began showing off her husband and baby amid excited introductions.

Mavis was glad Norman had brought this lass today. Although she appreciated what Mum and Dad were doing, putting on a spread for them, she'd have preferred it if they hadn't arranged anything. She could have done without so much emphasis on her moving away.

Living in a London flat with Ralph was wonderful, especially seeing him with their Heather. She'd never imagined he'd become so besotted with a bairn. But it was still a long way from home, and there was nothing definite yet about when he would be giving up the army. The married life she'd pictured, with a smaller edition of this house and near enough to visit Mum and Dad, seemed to be a long time coming.

'Well, there's no sense in us all standing around in the hall,' said Elsie, eventually. 'Come on through into the living room.'

Irene glanced around the familiar room, smiling to herself as she noticed how clean looking everything was. She could see their mother had been sponging the arms of the moquette chairs and sofa. They were a lightish grey and often seemed grubby. The worn carpet was brighter as well, she could imagine that would have been treated with damp tea leaves before a thorough vacuuming. Her mother's mother had always sworn by tea leaves for bringing up a carpet like new.

170

'What're you thinking?' her father asked, just behind her.

She smiled. 'That it's grand to be here, I suppose. Good that there isn't so much that changes.'

Donald nodded. He had given Mavis and Ralph that card while they were upstairs and he was wondering by now why it had seemed to matter that the Parkins had got in first. At least, they weren't able to come today. Because of another engagement, they'd said. He didn't know if he believed that or not, and nor did he care.

They were joined a few minutes later by Dorothy and Ted Bradshaw. Dorothy was a godmother to Mavis, it wouldn't have been right to leave them out.

Irene tensed as soon as she heard their voices, but steeled herself to stick a smile on her lips and go into the hall to greet them.

'You're looking tired, Irene,' Dorothy remarked after they had shaken hands. 'Is learning a new job proving a bit much for you?'

Irene willed the smile not to wane. 'It's demanding, certainly, familiarizing myself with a whole new world. But it's very stimulating.'

Ted Bradshaw was grinning. 'And in such lovely country. You ought to be looking in good form – 'twere a lot better for me nor living round here.'

'And how is the back, these days?'

'Not so bad, thanks. It's my knees now keep playing up.'

Elsie sniffed, and turned to Dorothy. 'Your Ted doesn't improve with keeping, does he? I bet he doesn't spend half as much time considering how you're feeling.'

Dorothy smiled nervously. 'Well, no – but then I'm usually all right, aren't I?'

Irene was beginning to wonder if her parents' disagreement had made her mother so abrasive. Normally, she'd do anything rather than let Dorothy see her impatience towards Ted. But their neighbour seemed unperturbed, though she did stick up for her husband.

'Ted's very good, you know, in lots of ways,' she said firmly. 'And he can be extremely generous.'

Ted's generosity became evident a few moments later. 'This is from Dorothy and me,' he announced and handed Mavis a heavy parcel.

'Thank you very much, Uncle Ted – and you as well, Auntie,' she responded swiftly and went over to Ralph so that they could unwrap the gift together. 'Oh, I say – how beautiful!' she exclaimed.

The box contained a canteen of silver cutlery.

'That really is very fine,' said Ralph. 'Thank you, indeed, both of you.'

Donald beamed and grasped his friend by the shoulder. 'Nice gesture, Ted. I know they'll always treasure that.'

Some while later when Irene was in the kitchen, busy with the kettle, Lily came to join her.

'Can I have a word with you?'

Irene smiled. 'Aye, love, of course. What is it?'

'I just – well, feel that embarrassed. I didn't know, you see – I haven't bought 'em owt.'

'And nor have I! All the family gave them stuff when they got married, naturally. I must admit I never thought of bringing owt today.'

'Yes, but – I mean, I wasn't there then, was I?'

'But Norman was. He gave them a handsome present, a wireless set.'

'Oh . . . ' Lily still was frowning.

'Our Mavis won't care, honest. She's taken to you already, any road, I can tell. You just forget everything and enjoy yourself. Besides, it's Norman you're here to please, and you've only to look at him to know how well you're doing that.'

Most of them had accepted Lily at once, she was so unaffected. And when Heather began grizzling and Lily rushed across the room and quietened her, Elsie started having fewer doubts concerning her son's young lady. While Ralph gave Norman an approving thumbs up.

Donald Hainsworth had a few reservations about her. The lass was all right: as a patient, she'd have seemed pleasant enough, cheerful. But he'd be a touch uneasy if Norman settled down with her. He had aspirations for his son. Even if he'd been compelled to shelve the hopes he'd had of Norman piloting civil aircraft, he still longed for him to better himself. And Lily might be too easily contented.

Now that Mavis had seen how keen on babies Lily was, she was glad to let her help with Heather. And Ralph was happy to include Lily while he was talking to Norman, drawing her into their yarns about life in the forces, yet showing he understood how different life was for somebody like her who'd never left civvy street.

Lily began to let her hair down. She couldn't remember such a good party, it was a relief not having to keep an eye on all her brothers and sisters. 'I've right enjoyed it, thank you ever so much,' she said before Norman set out with her to walk her home.

By Sunday morning when she also was leaving, Irene was feeling just as pleased; and especially since Ralph was looking after Heather to free Mavis for going to say farewell to some of her old friends.

'She loved working in that factory, you know,' he remarked to Irene, confirming that he'd far more understanding of his wife than any of them had supposed.

'Aye, I think she did,' Irene agreed. Mavis might have grumbled about the dirt and the long hours, but being among other girls committed to seeing a hard job through had given her a good experience of comradeship.

Later, as the bus approached the fells with twilight darkening them, Irene began to feel uneasy, wondering if she was losing the comradeship which *she* had felt was so intrinsic a part of her life at North Fell House. She was still trying not to dwell on the emotions Richard had aroused by his refusal to accompany her home.

She was welcomed warmly enough, nevertheless; he came out into the hall, and asked immediately how the weekend had gone.

'Daphne's not back from Peggy's, so I waited supper. I hope you can manage to eat something despite all your feasting!'

She hadn't felt hungry, but was sufficiently pleased to try and tackle whatever was offered. And Richard had assembled a creditable salad to complement cold meats. He had, in truth, been thankful to do anything that alleviated his obsession with the hands of the clock which had been behaving very sluggishly.

'What're you reading this time?' she inquired, noticing his book open on the occasional table.

'Dostoevsky, and finding it just as satisfying the second time around.'

He had taken to rereading many of the volumes on his shelves. This was, in the main, a result of introducing Irene to some of them. Being able to arouse her interest in reading pleased him far more than his pretended amusement often conveyed.

After the interlude in Halifax Irene soon discovered that their existence at North Fell remained substantially unchanged. Whatever Rich had intended by his refusal to go away with her, he seemed to treat her no differently from before. Their life could be very satisfying. And she admitted freely to herself that she wasn't sorry to do without the stresses generated by the physical relationship she'd had with John. She and Rich had several shared interests, these days, as well as their determination to build up his solicitor's practice.

There came a night, though, when she felt restless, her mind was too active for sleep. She had been reading, finishing a book by Thomas Mann. As she reached the last page, still much too alert, she decided to go and make a nightcap.

On the way to the kitchen, she spotted a sliver of light beneath Richard's door and knocked, intending to return the book, and offer him a hot drink.

He was sitting up in bed and, as it happened, reading something by the same author. Hot drinks forgotten, they began discussing Thomas Mann and before they knew it the hall clock was striking one.

Irene jumped up. 'Sorry, Rich, I'm keeping you awake. I'd better go.'

'You needn't . . .'

'This isn't either a high day or a holiday!'

Richard laughed. 'You wouldn't promise me anything about them, anyway.'

Irene felt torn, warmed by the knowledge that he wanted her here, and yet . . . She glanced towards the door.

He spoke again. 'You'd better turn the key in that, if you decide to stay. We were careless before, others mightn't understand.'

You've soon forgotten I haven't a reputation worth protecting, she thought, and wondered if that would always hurt. Why, these days, did it seem to have been an *affair*, rather than the love she'd believed it to be? Here, though, she was being offered the closeness which she had feared might be denied her. Slowly, she crossed to lock the door. But still she felt rather uncertain about her decision. Switching off every light except the bedside one, she went to him. And even then she almost changed her mind. She was wearing only a nightgown beneath her thin dressing gown.

The click of the bedside light going out startled her.

'Come along.' Richard's voice was gentle, as if he sensed that she felt ridiculously awkward. For weeks now she had been longing to feel his arms about her again, and now, quite suddenly, she was being offered more. She wished she could stop her emotions gyrating.

As before, Irene noticed how warm he was, became aware that this time he certainly hadn't just shifted the eiderdown aside. Even remaining thankful for the darkness, she caught herself wondering if that had been accidental or by intent.

And privately she smiled. She shouldn't be caring, but who was to know? And who was to know either that elation seemed to be overpowering her other feelings? What an idiot she was – how could she have forgotten that, with Richard, she could experience this delightful, innocent, bliss?

When he suddenly laughed she realized he'd said something and she hadn't even heard.

'Well, are you keen on Thomas Mann?' he repeated. "I gathered you were.'

'Oh – yes.'

'You don't sound very sure.' Richard was still amused.

'I was just thinking about something else.'

'Indeed?'

She wasn't going to be prompted by that! But they were talking quietly and easily enough, and then his arm came round her shoulders.

'I can't keep on saying it, Irene, and anyway it keeps getting crowded out. But I am eternally grateful. There's all your practical help, but mostly keeping an eye on me health-wise. I had such a bad scare, I thought I'd never cease worrying about the risk of another stroke. Thanks to you, I'm learning to.'

Before she could say anything, he was continuing: 'Life's great again now – and I never dreamed it could be.'

'Oh, Rich,' she began, again he interrupted.

'You're filling the gap in my life, always around in the office and outside it.' He paused. 'And this . . .'

Irene swallowed. It was very good to be appreciated. 'I have tried to be some use. In the beginning, to help compensate for the wrong I did living with John. I so nearly ruined their marriage.'

'And what of marriage yourself – do you hope for that one day?' It was something he had to face, there was no way he would go on for ever blindly assuming she would always be here.

His taut-voiced question shook Irene. She had deliberately chosen not to dwell too long or too deeply on her sister's happiness, nor on the prospect of Norman being the next to get wed.

'There's still a lot to learn about working in a solicitor's office, isn't there? I'm content here.'

His kiss was tender, and on her lips. 'You'll have to stay here then, won't you?'

'Like this?' she teased, suddenly feeling mischievous.

Richard chuckled. 'It wasn't precisely what I meant, but I'm the last to discourage you!'

Irene awakened during the night, wondered briefly where she was, then smiled when she heard Richard's even breathing beside her head. But she lay sleepless for some long while. When she'd stayed the night here before she'd been aware of wanting Rich. Tonight, she could hardly ignore the pulsing deep within her body. It was becoming an intrinsic part of all she felt for him. But she couldn't regret any of her feelings. And if this need must remain suppressed that could do no harm. Harm, hurt, came in going after what you wanted, not in learning to be content because you valued being with someone.

Mavis had adapted to living in London far better than Ralph had hoped. And she was always so unfailingly cheerful and loving that he continued to relish coming home to her.

Their flat was meagre, by his standards, the top storey of a semi-detached Victorian house. It hadn't endeared itself to him by having been so evidently the servants' quarters in better days when the family could afford staff. They also were obliged to share the bathroom on the floor below with Mrs Needler, the widowed owner of the property.

Mavis seemed not to mind that they were given a timetable for bathing, and that they were requested not to make any noise if they had occasion to get up early. And popping Heather into the sink in the narrow kitchen for her bath was just a bit of fun. Not that Ralph objected to that – he could watch quite comfortably from one of the straightbacked wooden chairs.

'You've certainly taken to her!' Mavis exclaimed one evening when, not for the first time, her husband took the towel-shrouded baby from her arms. 'Just make sure she's properly dry, that's all. And I'll go get her nightdress.'

Heather's clothes were warming in front of the gas fire. The flat often felt damp; Mavis wasn't going to have their bairn come to any harm.

Returning to the kitchen, she paused just short of the connecting doorway. Ralph was dancing Heather on his knee, laughing as she kicked chubby legs and giggled.

'Ay, that's a fair treat, seeing you like that! You're that good with her, you make me think sometimes you could do without me.'

'Not really,' Ralph responded, over his shoulder. 'I don't mind admitting, though, that I've surprised myself.'

'Here . . .' She handed him the tiny vest and winceyette nightgown.

Just for a moment, Ralph hesitated. He'd never before tried encouraging those restless arms and flailing fists into a garment. But then he decided to have a go. Heather was so deliciously fragrant, fresh from her bath, and her skin so warm and soft.

Still watching, Mavis leaned against the door jamb. He had such elegant hands, yet the long fingers were strong as well. Noticing how tenderly he took the bairn's wrist as he coaxed her hand through a sleeve scarcely wider than his finger, she experienced an intense longing to feel his hands on her.

'You're framing all right,' she told him. 'We'll soon have her in her cot.' And let's hope she settles quickly.

As usual, they went together into their one bedroom, and while Ralph crossed to draw the curtains Mavis laid Heather down. At the foot of the cot was an old teddy, once Ralph's and now one of the baby's favourite possessions. When he came to stand beside her, he made as if to pick up the toy, but Mavis checked him with a hand on his sleeve.

'Not tonight, don't get her all excited with playing. Let's see if she'll go straight to sleep.'

Back in the living room, Mavis crossed immediately to the faded moquette chesterfield, hauled it closer to the fire.

'Come on, love, eh?'

Ralph smiled, came slowly towards her, taking off his uniform jacket then discarding it on a nearby chair. His wife had kicked off the old shoes she wore as slippers, was stretching out so luxuriously the sofa might have been of finely upholstered velvet.

'Oh, I forgot,' Mavis said, 'pass us a cushion, will you. Don't want that broken spring boring into my bum.'

He tossed the cushion lightly on to her full breasts then followed it down, pushing it aside so that as he lowered himself on to her he felt how firm she was, pressing at his chest.

'Hang on a sec,' Mavis protested. 'I haven't got that cushion right . . . '

'There's no need.'

His mouth covered hers as he twisted his entire body, hauling her with him until he was supine on the battered sofa, and she a delightful pressure against him.

At first, Mavis was rather bewildered. She was accustomed to having Ralph on top of her, enjoyed the symbolized mastery of her almost as much as she relished his lovemaking. But now he was beginning to move beneath her, stirring until she could no longer remain still. The frock she had on fastened all down the front, Ralph began loosening the top buttons.

His hand tested the soft skin just inside her bra, making her long to have him touch her everywhere. His mouth was devouring hers again, his tongue darting over her teeth, lingering with her own tongue.

'You'll have to ease up a bit,' he said, gasping in air.

She felt him tugging the rest of her buttons free, whisking her dress aside, then he started on his own buttons.

Mavis giggled. 'You'll not get your trousers off like that.'

Ralph didn't intend to.

She could feel him through his pants, straining against her. The only answer she knew was to thrust herself closer.

'You're gorgeous,' he sighed, and began kissing her once more, feverishly.

He was caressing her now, increasing her desire so intensely that she moaned.

'Soon, my darling, soon,' he murmured.

She felt the elastic biting into her hips as he eased her knickers away. And then she was leaning into the warmth and the strength of him, urging him to fulfil her.

And now they lay skin to skin, awareness nearing its crescendo, need so fierce that anticipation was pain as well as ecstasy.

'I want you so much,' Mavis cried breathlessly.

Ralph smiled against her lips. 'You know what to do.'

Taking him into her incited her to stir more urgently, to will him with the whole of her being to find all he needed there. Together, they demanded and they gave, surrendering self and discovering joy had new horizons.

Sated, they slept, in blissful disregard of their uncomfortable positions. When they wakened it was three hours later, and the room was stifling in the heat from the gas fire. And both were so stiff that moving was near impossible.

Ralph laughed. 'You're the one that'll have to shift first!'

'I know. Just wait a tick – I ache all over.'

'What about me, I'm suffocating as well as squashed.'

'Your idea, remember!' she reminded him, gradually easing herself up and then off the sofa on to legs that seemed to have their own will.

'I'm not complaining,' said Ralph, beaming at her in the firelight.

He'd never been happier than with his bright little wife who'd given him such a delightful daughter.

When he slowly got to his feet, he went to her, drew her against him again.

'Don't ever change,' he said huskily into her hair. 'Let's always be fun together as well as loving. You've shown me how to just let go of everything except us.'

11

Norman was furious, couldn't remember ever being so blazing mad. He'd contained his annoyance while they were in the weaving shed. He didn't trust his own tongue enough to let rip with Lily looking on, he'd not have her doubting that he was in command of himself.

Here, though, in the foreman's office it was different, he'd have right done by him. And soon, an' all – he'd had a bellyful of waiting and wondering.

'What's up wi' you, lad?' Bert Kettlewell began. 'I could see back yonder that you were fair seething.'

'I'm not a lad now,' Norman corrected him sharply.

Bert grinned. 'Aye, I know. And you know, as well, that it's nobbut my way of talking. But we haven't come in 'ere to discuss way I speak, I am sure.'

'Quite the opposite, in fact,' Norman snapped. 'It's *not* being talked to, *not* being kept in the picture, that I object to.'

'I don't follow,' Bert began, removing the cloth cap he wore in the mill as well as outdoors, and scratching his greasy bald head.

'It's about them new looms we're thinking on getting – I've heard tell they're to be foreign – Swiss, or summat.'

'And what if they are . . . ?'

'What's wrong wi' British made suddenly? What have we been fighting over, if it weren't for t'good of this country? And didn't nobody think to ask them that's got to keep 'em running what's going to be t'most suitable here!'

'You'd better ask Mr Dewhurst that, lad. It weren't me that had any say in what sort of looms we'll be getting. Any road, I'm not so sure owt's decided yet.'

'I'll ask him all right. I'm not scared on his sort, dictators or not. They haven't the decency to keep t'workers informed.'

'Here now – Norman, steady on. Think what you're about. Don't go queering t'pitch for thyself, just by being hasty. It's allus boss's right to make decisions, after all.'

'I've had plenty of time for thinking, Bert. More than I liked. And if he's going to take the huff, too bad.' There were times when Norman wouldn't be entirely sorry to be shot of this place. If all that noise weren't bad enough, there was them looms allus breaking down, and the poor yarn they had to contend with. And now this – the management going in for new machinery that nobody knew a thing about.

Being obliged to wait a few days before Jack Dewhurst would see him had done nothing to sweeten Norman's mood. Even with Lily he'd been so on edge that the poor lass had been convinced she'd done something to upset him. He'd had to explain all the way up from the town last night after the pictures, and still he hadn't totally reassured her that it was trouble here that was bothering him.

'They're not doing right by any on us,' he'd told her.

Now it was his chance to make Mr Dewhurst see how inconsiderate he was being to all the workforce.

'Kettlewell informs me you have certain misgivings about our proposed new machinery,' Jack Dewhurst began, leaning back in his leather-upholstered chair.

'Aye, I'm afraid so, Mr Dewhurst. It's like this, you see . . .' Norman went on to reiterate the feelings he'd expressed to their foreman. The stern eyes regarding him so narrowly grew inscrutable. In an effort to win some understanding, Norman smiled slightly. 'Well, that's how I feel, Mr Dewhurst. Like I said, we're the ones that'll have to keep t'looms running. These days, when I see summat that I think is wrong, I can't bottle it up. Not anyhow.'

Jack Dewhurst nodded. He'd liked young Hainsworth before the war. Now, he was less certain. Kettlewell seemed to think he might develop into a troublemaker. He'd proved he wasn't afraid of speaking up.

Again, Jack Dewhurst inclined his head. Then he faced Norman and gestured towards the door. 'Leave it with me. I – want to make a few inquiries.' Such inquiries, however, would not concern alternatives to the looms he planned to obtain, but Hainsworth's background. He needed to know the strength of the opposition – if the chap was involved in a union or anything of that sort.

Convinced that he'd impressed his boss, Norman cheered up at once. He took Lily dancing that weekend, and considered the one and sixpence for each ticket well spent. She was a lovely lass, there was nothing more exciting than holding her close to him for hour after hour.

'I didn't think it'd be so crowded,' Lily exclaimed while she sipped the port and lemon he'd bought her during the interval.

'It's a good night out, that's why it's so popular.' And he'd nowt to grumble about. If it had been less crowded, his lack of skill with fancy steps might have been more evident, and they'd not have been pressed so near to each other that desire kept surging through him.

'This is a real treat for me,' she confided, beaming. 'I don't come into town dancing, as a rule. If I manage to get to a dance run by Park Congregational it's as much.'

Norman could believe that. The more he got to know about Lily Atkinson, the less he thought of her folk. Her mum and dad seemed to keep her short of brass as well as expecting her help with the kids. Still, he was doing his best to give her a bit of fun, and if he had owt to do with it he'd soon be seeing even more of her.

'We can come here every week, since you like dancing so much,' he promised.

Her frown disappointed him. 'Ay, love – I wish I could. But it's my mam, you see. She's getting near her time now, I'll have to stop at home more.'

'What about your sisters, the ones nearer your age, couldn't they do more?' he asked sharply. It wasn't right that Lily should always be the one at everyone's beck and call.

Lily grinned. 'You don't know what they're like – my mother says she wouldn't trust 'em an inch.'

'Time they were learnt to be more responsible then, if only for their own good.' And it was high time Lily had some freedom to be herself.

Norman didn't pursue the matter, he'd no intention of ruining the rest of the evening by dwelling on Lily's family. But when he led her on to the floor for the quick-step which began the second session of dances, his arm tightened around her. She was too good a lass to be put upon, and he was the one who was going to look after that for her.

He felt so protective towards Lily it dulled the longing she'd aroused earlier. Although not consciously considering it, he was growing aware that these feelings would one day combine, and would be the best thing that could happen. For both of them.

They seemed so close, even without speaking, maybe especially while they were silent. Side by side they strode over the ewe-cropped turf, well-matched in pace, despite the stick that Richard still used. His glance went frequently to the fells ahead, strayed occasionally when some bird darted from a tree.

Now and then, he glanced sideways at her, and smiled. His dark eyes warmed her, as they did so often. In the office, for instance, where they'd all grown so busy there was little time for conversation. And their wordless communication somehow conveyed far more. Irene would sense his steady gaze on her and, meeting it, would experience the pull of a force far stronger than mere attraction. Thrilling to the sensation of being drawn to him, loving its headiness, she'd hardly be able to think. Today, she wondered if Richard could remain unconscious of the power in each look he gave her.

Out here, well wrapped against the keen winds of late autumn, she felt content, secure in the assurance that she was needed. This had been brought home to her only this morning.

Health-wise, Richard continued to improve. He could get around the house and garden without the stick that he only tolerated. But what cheered him most was the increasing use in his right hand. He exercised it a great deal, determined to get back to normal, and she gave regular massage.

'You're so patient,' he'd remarked today, the hand between hers.

'And aren't you? Despite what *I* say to the contrary,' she'd responded lightly.

'It's enforced on me. But not on you. Yet you still stick this out, even when I've had you hard at it in the office all week.'

'You make it sound like very hard work.' She longed to be free to say more, to convince him of how deeply committed she'd become. Only his evident reservations prevented her.

'And isn't it hard?' he'd asked.

'No. There isn't a day when I don't learn something new, about some aspect of law or just concerning the people you help. Then away from the office there's always so much to think about.'

'Wasn't there with John?'

The question had jolted her. John hadn't been mentioned for a long time. What had been going on behind Richard's composure? 'Why bring him up?'

He hadn't replied. Happen an answer hadn't been necessary.

'Rich, you and I share so much. You have every bit of me that's worth anything.'

And now they shared the impressive sweep of fells, the afternoon sky splashed with red and orange which gradually was replacing a brilliant blue-green. Ever-changing clouds reared from behind distant crags to roam before the wind, their charcoal and purple etched with gold by the sun which they were crushing.

Together, they paused to watch the sun sinking, lost in its own dazzle, beyond the farthest moor.

'We'll have to turn soon,' said Richard regretfully. 'Looks like there's a storm brewing.'

'Even snow,' Irene laughed, shivering slightly as the grass about them, flattened by the wind, deepened towards emerald, and limestone screes developed a strange luminosity.

'You cold?' he inquired anxiously, yearning for a life where he might gather her to him and give no thought to consequence.

Smiling, she shook her head. 'You should know by now that clambering over your hills soon warms me up!'

He grinned. 'And you a Yorkshire lass? I felt sure there were hills in Halifax.'

'Aye, there are, an' all!' she exclaimed. 'But none of them stretch as far as this, and they're not so rugged to the feet.'

'And nor are they as beautiful.'

'I'll grant you that, Richard. I sometimes ache to stay out here, even when the alternative's returning to your lovely home.'

She was learning to know the curve of every valley, the shading of the grass on each slope of the fells, the streams and the tarn, birds and where they nested. In all seasons now, she had savoured the view upwards from North Fell House, and had gazed from above to where it lay in perfect tranquillity.

And yet, perversely, it was of John that Irene dreamed that night, maybe because of his being mentioned. The dream was vivid, bringing alive that brief period when they'd lived together. She awakened trembling, feeling his arms about her still, the pressure of his body, kisses searing her lips. Too agitated to sleep, she lay there, feeling isolated by memories . . . of having John walk away from their relationship and, worse, of being confronted by the General Medical Council. She longed to turn to Richard, then told herself he would be sleeping, and she'd no right to assume he would automatically offer the comfort that she needed.

Switching on the light, she glanced towards the clock; five past two. The night stretched before her, lifetime long. But she would read, get through to the morning that way. Looking around for her book, she recalled leaving it in the sitting room. Wearily, she shrugged on her dressing gown.

As before, a light showed beneath Richard's door, drawing her towards it. But she hesitated in the hall. And yet she'd be able to sleep, if only she could just talk to him.

Irene knocked quietly in case he'd fallen asleep with the light on.

Richard called, 'Come in.'

He was reading in bed, and raised an eyebrow inquiringly.

She forced a smile. 'Looks as though you're wide awake an' all.'

'Something of the sort. What is it, Irene?'

'I just wanted to talk, can't sleep – I had this dream.'

Looking at him, she realized how badly she needed to be here with him, how she ached to rest her tense head against his shoulder, to feel his arm around her, to have him listen.

Richard half closed the book, but kept a finger in the pages. He might have been asserting she must be brief. Irene felt wounded.

'Sit down.' He nodded towards the chair.

Irene stared at the bed. 'Not . . . ?'

He frowned. 'I'm sorry, no.'

She couldn't have felt more cut if he'd slapped her. On top of everything resurrected by that dream, it was more than she could take. But she'd not show that. She ran out and along to the kitchen and shut the door behind her. She sat at the pine table and stared unblinkingly into space, willing self-control. But the concern was so one-sided. Like most things here. She had learned to accept that everything was geared to Richard's career, had tried to adapt to working only as one of his team. But it was in their personal life that there were more flaws, because he made all the rules. And couldn't realize when she needed him. Would he never understand her?

She didn't hear Richard come in and jumped when he touched her shoulder. 'Irene . . . ' She tried to shrug away his hand, but he wasn't put off that easily.

Dragging over a chair, he sat beside her. 'I was afraid I'd find this. Irene, I'm sorry – I hope you'll understand when I explain.'

'There's nothing to explain. It's just different when it isn't you that wants something.'

She turned slightly, and was astonished when she detected a hint of amusement behind his obvious concern.

'Will you listen?' Richard persisted.

Irene nodded.

'I nearly told you at the time . . . ' He paused, then continued: 'When you last stayed in my room, I – had a disturbed night.'

'Okay, so you prefer to sleep, we'll forget it. But there wasn't much evidence that you were sleeping just now.'

'Exactly. Now, let me finish.' His dark eyes were laughing, infuriating her, how could he actually be amused by her distress?

'On that occasion,' Richard went on quite evenly, 'you were having such a devastating effect that I couldn't relax.'

Irene stared at him.

He nodded. 'So you see, I wasn't sorry about it, on the contrary. Ought to have told you, but . . . it might have proved embarrassing.'

She began smiling as well. 'I think somebody who's been a GP has a smattering of knowledge on the facts of life.'

'Doubtless. *You* would have known which words to choose – I found that rather daunting.'

'I never thought it'd be that.' She felt relieved already. And also, on his behalf, anything but sorry.

Richard crossed the kitchen and put on milk to warm. 'I don't imagine you did. After all, the recovery was rather sudden.' He adjusted the gas then turned to look at her. 'You understand now?'

Irene nodded and he returned to the task. While he was setting a steaming cup before her and sitting down, he spoke again.

'I won't play with fire, as they say, with you. I'm too fond of you.'

'But . . . ?' It was a wonder she hadn't echoed 'fond'!
He'd confused her so often.

'Margaret? That seems a long time ago now. There are
stronger ties.' Still smiling, he prompted her. 'I'm ready
to listen. What's upset you?'

Irene shook her head. 'Doesn't matter now.' This was
hardly the moment. 'Anyway, glad to hear you're returning
to normal.'

He suggested they found somewhere more comfortable, and she followed him into the sitting room. He
checked her as she headed for one of the armchairs,
and with a grin indicated the sofa. 'I dare trust myself
this far!'

Responding to his light approach, Irene was unwinding
rapidly, beginning to think again. 'Thank you, Rich,' she
said presently.

'Whatever for?'

'After the affair I'd had with John, some folk might have
taken advantage, assuming I was fair game.' If *he* ever had,
that would have ruined everything. Would have been far
worse than coldness.

'What I feel for you is infinitely deeper than sex. You
can't have forgotten the state I was in when you arrived
here. And the intervening time hasn't all been hard slog.'
He turned to her, his smile encouraging. 'So, let's give a
bit in return. What is bothering you, love?'

Irene sighed, wishing to keep her life with John where
it belonged – in the past. Especially since being reassured
that Richard cared.

'Well?' He was determined to have the truth.

'Just a silly dream, about John. Goodness knows why, I
haven't really thought about him for ages.'

'And you wakened missing him? Just symbolic of the
need for contact with other people. I used to consider
myself more independent than most, but it was there – in
some form. I suppose Margaret used to satisfy that need.
Not physically, we never . . . ' He sounded rather prim as
his voice trailed off.

'But this was physical, very.'

Richard laughed. 'Don't be scandalized by your dreams. They're beyond your control. And probably far more usual than you think.'

'But I am scandalized. And by what I did.'

'High time you forgave yourself all that. It's how we learn, by acknowledging mistakes, regretting them.'

'That doesn't stop me feeling bad now.'

'For the occasional sexy dream? Oh, come on, Irene – who doesn't have? I'm beginning to believe that, for a doctor, you're remarkably naive.'

'It's all right for you to talk!'

'You've forgotten that I was awake as well, reading to try and keep my mind off – ' He paused, a smile tugging at his mouth. 'Off a certain young lady who then presented herself beside my bed.'

Gently, he tilted her chin until she met his now-serious eyes. She's still scared, he thought tenderly, scared of what her own feelings might do. 'I can't always discipline my thoughts, Irene. But the rest will remain under strict control. *Not* because I don't wish to make love with you, but because it could destroy this wonderful friendship of ours.'

She could hardly believe they were speaking so openly, but was very thankful, and happier because of Richard's care of her. As they finished their hot drinks she realized she was feeling ready for sleep, she would rest now, reassured about their relationship.

Richard stood up, extended a hand to her. When she was on her feet he gazed into her eyes for a long moment, then drew her to him.

'I'm always here,' he told her quietly. 'We both know I'm not a hundred per cent fit. But, within those limits, I'm yours, Irene.'

'You shouldn't say that. You shouldn't make commitments you could later regret.' He might one day need the full, sexual relationship which he wasn't going to permit with her. 'Supposing you meet somebody you want to marry?'

'That won't happen,' he said very quickly.

They seemed closer after their straightforward talk, yet still there were few opportunities for Irene to show him any affection. And now he'd done more than remind her that she couldn't exist in a vacuum, he'd proved to her that what she felt for him was love.

Irene's working days had become frenetic. She had discovered an aptitude for figures and Richard was exploiting that by making her responsible for all invoicing. Busy though she was, she was glad to be used to the full. One day she was totalling a long column when the telephone began ringing insistently at the other side of the office. David was in court and Anita making another pot of the coffee that sustained them. They were into 1947 and high winds and surrounding snow were proving how cold and draughty North Fell House could be.

Close to the shrilling instrument, Richard answered it. Irene saw him frown on learning who was calling. He beckoned her with a terse 'For you', and strode out of the room.

She was puzzled. She rarely had private calls; almost all her time was devoted to Richard and the practice, wasn't it? She had no friends now who weren't friends of his.

Irene immediately recognized the voice, and felt quite ill. 'Oh, no! John, this really is too bad of you!'

'Wait till you've heard me out,' he began agitatedly.

'I've a good mind to slam this phone down. How on earth did you get this number?'

'From someone at your home, your brother?'

'But how . . . ?' And then she remembered. John knew her father was a doctor, there wasn't another Dr Hainsworth anywhere near Halifax.

'I was desperate, Irene. I've got to see you.'

'That's out of the question. I'm not coming.'

'I'll come to you. I'm in Skipton.'

'Keep away from here,' she said firmly.

'I need your help. I've got to talk to you.'

'No, no. It's over and done with, I'm not raking that up again.'

'I'm not asking you to.' He sounded weary, and *strange*. 'I'm in a bad way, Irene.'

'What's wrong?' she asked anxiously. Wishing to avoid John was a different matter from being unconcerned if he was ill.

'I won't beat about the bush with you. It's the Dexedrine – and Benzedrine. Can't seem to stop needing them.'

'You idiot! Why in the world did you start?'

'Mostly to keep awake, towards the end of the war. Pilots took them, didn't they. *I* was sleeping at odd hours, as well, with Vera being on such peculiar shifts in the Land Army.'

'You don't expect me to pick up the pieces, I hope.' Not when he was admitting it was through engineering his married life that he'd become addicted. 'Get your wife to see you through it.'

'She won't. Went back to her mother when I lost the job.'

'Lost? You hadn't . . . ?'

'Where else do you think I got them?'

'God, what a mess! Look – John, go to your own doctor, tell him all this – everything about it, he'll help.'

'He's washed his hands of me.'

'No doctor would do that.'

Evidently, his had. Irene seemed to have no control over the voice agreeing to meet him in Skipton the following Saturday afternoon. As she replaced the receiver she was feeling appallingly sick.

Richard came back into the office, and glared at her, but he saved what he had to say until the others had left that evening.

'Something wrong?' he inquired, avoiding her eyes.

She had intended confiding to him her horror of meeting John, and how she couldn't help going. A part of her would remain a doctor, always. But Richard's abrasive tone revealed ill-disguised annoyance, and wariness that seemed to be waiting for her to confirm his suspicions about this John whom she was seeing. While she herself didn't fully understand why she was going, how could

192

she expect Richard to? She simply shook her head. 'No, nothing.'

Being so busy in the office meant that Saturday approached all too swiftly through days when Irene's mind was only partially alert to details of house purchases and wills, clients' accounts and arrangements for Richard to represent someone in court.

During the morning she sensed her lack of concentration was justifying Richard's reproachful looks, but she was even more troubled when it was time to leave.

The bus was late due to the continuing heavy snow and John was waiting already near the entrance to Skipton castle.

Irene was devastated by shock. Thin, unkempt, broad shoulders hunched, his eyes confirming all that he had told her, he seemed repulsive. She ought to have turned away. She wanted anything rather than acknowledging this individual standing amid the greying snow of the town. But her medical training, yet again, was on his side.

'John,' she exclaimed, shaking her head, appalled.

She followed him away from the main shopping street which, even in winter, was crowded. They spent the afternoon in a cafe so seedy that Irene would have doubted she'd find such a place in Skipton. They drank endless cups of stale tea, with a waitress glancing suspiciously at them. It was sordid, and embarrassing. That wouldn't have mattered if she hadn't been afraid it all was pointless.

John had begun telling her again how it had all started. But she soon checked him, she could do without a résumé of how he'd contrived time with Vera. All that counted was convincing him of the dangers of experimenting with drugs whose effects weren't yet fully understood. And of how vital it was to find a cure.

But John had tried every remedy – except perhaps the extreme effort of will which might save him. While he was still employed he'd badgered the chief pharmacist for some means of getting him off the drugs. By the sound of it, this chap in charge had believed he was paring down John's dosage, weakening his dependence. That was before they'd done their year-end stock taking, and found deficiencies in both Dexedrine and Benzedrine.

'They wouldn't even consider that it might have been somebody else,' he said indignantly.

'And was it?'

John sighed, shook his head. 'Maybe not. Though I didn't think I'd had that many.'

'What's all this about your GP then – he surely wouldn't abandon you?'

'He simply doesn't understand me at all.'

'I can well believe it! I certainly don't. Not why you began taking the things, nor what's preventing you being firm with yourself till you give them up. You had it all made, John – your wife, and a fine son.'

'Don't remind me. Didn't I tell you Vera's taken the boy to her mother's?'

'So, go back to your doctor.'

'Can't – told him to go to blazes.'

'Find another then.'

'You're the only one I have any faith in. You'll pull me through.'

'Like hell I will!' she shouted, oblivious of interested folk at surrounding tables. 'I've got a job that I love, with a man who's worth ten of you. Because he's fought back from problems far worse than any you've ever faced.'

John shook his head. 'Couldn't be worse. What do you think it did to me when you and I split up? Why do you imagine I was in need of some kind of prop . . .'

She stood up. 'Don't blame me for your instability. You weren't a child when you started the relationship, nor when *you* ended it. I'm going.'

John followed her to the door, and then he checked. 'Hang on a minute.' He disappeared towards the cloakroom.

Out on the pavement, holding her head down against driving snow, Irene struggled with the temptation to make straight for home. She wanted nothing further with this wretched man who, even now, could be shovelling down more tablets. But she would try – just once more – to make him take responsibility for his own life, for having it cured.

'John, you've got to take yourself in hand,' she told him. 'You can do it, and only you. Happen it was necessary, in wartime, for folk to take something that'd keep them alert till all hours. That's never been really necessary for you, and it certainly isn't now.'

'I want nothing more than to be done with all this, but I've got nothing now, don't you see, no job to cling to – no one. But if you were with me, keeping an eye . . .'

'That's blackmail,' she interrupted.

John grinned.

'Well, it is simply *not on*,' Irene said, and turned away from him. When she'd crossed the road towards her bus stop, something made her look back. John was getting into the old MG that she recalled only too well. She couldn't let him drive, not in this state, in all this snow which was freezing hard as it fell. He'd kill either himself or some innocent person.

She ran back, opened the driver's door. 'Move over. And stay sufficiently *compos mentis* to tell me where you're staying.'

It was a miserable journey. Irene refused to speak, nothing was going to influence him today. She closed her mind to everything but keeping the car on the snow-packed road, and her ears to all but his directions.

Irene had always liked the pleasant market town of Skipton, today when she found herself outside a dingy hotel crammed in between warehouses, she felt revolted. The windows were filthy, the doors had peeling paint. She loathed John for sinking to this. And the only way he'd change would be by being compelled to face up to what he was doing to himself. As she switched off the ignition, she turned to him.

'It's your life, John, you'll improve it or not, but it'll be without me. Go back to your doctor, apologize, he'll listen. You almost ruined my life once, you won't touch it now. Straighten yourself out, get Vera and the child back. You can if you want to. Try ringing me again, and I shan't speak to you.'

She got out of the car and, avoiding a patch of vomit on the step, entered the hotel. She asked for the landlord, and handed him John's keys.

'He's outside, in no fit state to drive. I'd like you to hold those until morning.'

John was where she'd left him. Woodenly, she walked past his car, and along the narrow street, in what she hoped she recalled correctly as the general direction of the town centre.

'Has Irene gone off to Halifax, did she say she wouldn't be in for dinner?' Daphne's green eyes were faintly puzzled as she glanced across the table.

Richard shook his head.

His sister persisted. 'It's hardly fit to go as far as the end of the lane, never mind any distance. And it's not like her not to say.'

Silently, Richard willed her to shut up.

'She goes out so rarely on her own, seems very strange without her, doesn't it.'

'There's no reason she should wish to spend seven days of every week in our company,' he observed.

'No, but . . . I rather gathered by now that that *was* what she wanted to do.' She smiled. 'You're very fond of her, aren't you?'

Fond? What sort of a word was that for everything he felt for Irene? The classic understatement of all time. And more.

'Where has she gone? Do you really not know, Rich?'

'To meet an old friend,' he said very quickly.

Daphne was watching his eyes. She hadn't seen her brother disturbed like this in months. He knew more than he was telling, that was obvious; and what he knew he did not like. He could be jealous, she supposed, although she felt sure he had no cause. Unless . . . all at once, she had a dreadful thought.

'It's not – is it the man she once lived with?'

Richard was staring down at his plate. When he faced her again his dark eyes were forbidding.

'Hardly our concern, is it? Irene is a free agent.'

'I thought she was over him.'

'Has she said so?' The rapid question was off his tongue before he could check it. He'd not had the slightest intention of revealing the need for assurance.

Daphne shook her head. 'The subject's never arisen.'

'But you know – about her and John. How much more do you know?'

'About her being struck off, you mean?'

Richard frowned. 'I can't think she told you.'

'Didn't have to. When you were really ill, old love, I read the lot, devoured every newspaper. I knew when she came here.'

His frown deepened. 'Lord, that would make her feel good! It was the very thing Irene was desperate to avoid.'

'You don't think I greeted her with it?'

'No – no, I don't imagine you did.'

'I'll admit that, for a time, it did colour my attitude.'

'Let's get one thing straight,' he interrupted fiercely. 'As far as I am concerned, Irene is and always will be a very fine doctor. You know what I owe her – more than I like, perhaps. You will not criticize her in my hearing ever again.'

'I wasn't doing, Richard. In fact, ages ago I admitted to her what I knew – *and* how good she's always been for you. These days, she and I understand one another.'

Richard didn't say any more. As soon as they finished eating he went to his room. Daphne was listening to a play on the wireless. Normally, he might have enjoyed it. Tonight, he wanted to get away.

A book was open on his lap when Daphne looked in to say good night. He hadn't read one word. Pretending he wasn't perturbed was as hopeless as concealing his emotions from her perceptive eyes during an entire evening. He was thankful that she was going to bed. Except that it did underline how late it was, and that Irene still hadn't returned.

Once, while he could hear the news distantly on the sitting room wireless, the telephone had rung. Breathing suspended, he'd waited for Daphne to tell him Irene had called. There had been no message. His depression had deepened.

Time and again, he'd silently repeated what he'd said to his sister: Irene is a free agent. Each time it bit that fraction sharper, and he steeled himself against the pain.

No matter how long she had lived here in his home, lavishing on him undeniable devotion, sharing the most intimate moments of his soul, she was no more his than on the day she had walked anxiously through that door. And she could not be.

Would he never be satisfied – that life was so enriched by working again in the job that he loved? And with her to assist. This was the very first time that she had gone off to meet anyone else. Couldn't he get the whole business into perspective?

But why did it have to be *him*? The faceless man for whom Irene had cared far more than for her career. The man for whose child she had wept. How could he believe now that she'd meant what she was saying when she'd declared that affair finished.

The clock chimed another hour. Grimly, Richard sighed. Why wasn't she home? What was she doing? He gritted his teeth, willing the question unformed, willing imagination inert. Ever since lunchtime, he had forced himself *not* to even wonder where she might be, much less what she might be doing.

And now he was too exhausted to quell his meandering thoughts, or to make memory selective. So many occasions which, in context, had even seemed amusing, now appeared to threaten.

That dream she'd confessed – of wanting John. Not long ago. Had she found today how readily feelings, once considered dead, might be aroused? She was a warm and affectionate woman, why hadn't he contemplated earlier what the past several months must have been doing to her? Was it so great a surprise if, now, all her generous emotions sought release? With someone who didn't hesitate about showing his need of her.

He felt certain John didn't live anywhere in the vicinity; he would be staying in some hotel. And where more private than an anonymous hotel room for a couple to become reacquainted.

The suspicion acknowledged, desire flared through him. Richard closed his eyes. Not again, not now, when the need to sublimate could no longer express thankfulness, or love. So many times, over the months, he had denied the life surging within him, even feeling glad that he possessed sufficient restraint. This, as well as the desire itself, was proof he was alive, a man again. Because of her. It was a kind of joy to know this secret force, and to compel its acquiescence. Even the discomfort had been willingly endured; a token of all that he would endure, for her. For love.

Richard swallowed, gripping the chair arm as the pulsing grew more forceful. For the hundredth time, he re-examined the situation. But he had been taught well to analyse – was not mistaken in his conclusions.

He wanted and needed Irene more deeply and passionately than he'd thought possible. He yearned to make her his, irrevocably. But what could he give? There might be joy – he liked to believe there would have been, in the moments while she learned and received full evidence of his love. But along with himself he would give insecurity, potential heartache, permanent anxiety. And this he could not do, to her.

His need asserted itself again, demanding a satisfaction which he feared would never be his. Slowly, he rose, poured whisky into a tumbler. Solemnly, he regarded the golden liquid. He'd taken only wine on that one occasion when they'd all gone out for a meal. The first alcohol since the stroke. And that had made him feel quite heady. It hadn't mattered then, it mattered less tonight. He didn't care very much that Giles Holroyd had advised that he'd be better not drinking. He'd always been abstemious, all he wanted now was enough to dull this persistent ache into submission.

Richard sipped, reflecting, returned to the chair. And he sighed. He had not been wrong – there was no way that he might justify committing Irene to him. No way to hold her close, always, as he held her in his heart. No way either to assuage this massive urgency.

He could never tie her to his precarious health. And nor could *he* dismiss it. The only way he could give was by withholding. And he would give her the one thing he could – freedom to live her own life.

12

There was nobody at the bus stop when Irene had trudged back to the centre of Skipton. In fact, there were only three people in sight now, young fellows pelting each other with snowballs as they dodged in and out of alleyways between shops.

The blizzard had intensified, if anything, plastering a layer of snow all over the collar and down the front of her thick coat. Her umbrella frequently grew heavy with accumulated flakes, making her wrist ache until she attempted to shake them off. She'd never been as cold, her feet felt leaden.

After glancing repeatedly at her watch she began to suspect that the buses had stopped running. When she eventually crossed the road to a hotel and inquired, the barman nodded.

'We've just had the news on, you'll none get a bus tonight out of Skipton, not in any direction.'

'That's what I was afraid of. Could you ring for a taxi for me, please, I'll pay for the call.'

Five telephone calls later, the barman came to her, shaking his head. 'Nothing doing, I'm afraid, love. There's nobody'll turn out in this. Have you far to go?'

Irene told him. 'It's not that far, really. Within walking distance.'

'On a night like this? Nay, love, you want to stay put. We can offer you a room.'

But staying here wouldn't be any good. She was aching to be with Richard, to tell him about her terrible day. She longed to have him sympathize while she talked it out, as they had talked so much. It was only today that she'd begun to understand quite how deeply she depended on

Rich; sometimes simply to listen, mostly just to be there, caring.

Shuddering in the night air, she strode along the icy pavements, past all the shops which looked glum behind their blinds. At least walking restored a little circulation to her numbed feet and legs, might bring them back to life by the time she arrived home.

The last few houses and shops of Skipton centre came into sight through the slanting flakes, and were passed. And now she must take care. The road surface where ice had compacted was like a bottle. With visibility this poor, she mustn't risk falling – the driver of any car wouldn't have a hope of seeing her on the ground. Her coat was covered by now, as white as her surroundings.

Keeping well in to the side of the road, stumbling over obstacles concealed in the snow, Irene slithered and staggered along. Whenever a vehicle approached she leaped for the verge, and felt another cold trickle soaking into her stockings when she went in over the tops of her wellington boots. Progress was appallingly slow, and not aided by a head muzzy from lack of a good meal. Somehow, though, she had got to keep going until she reached North Fell House.

To take her mind off her distressing meeting with John, she planned what she would eat when she arrived – while she told Richard how awful it had been. And how she'd realized that she had needed none of this to convince her that she'd been cured of John for many a month.

She was wheezing with exertion when she struggled up the lane and glimpsed the trees surrounding the house. Yet her features, rigid though they were with cold, formed a slight smile. How solid it was, how welcoming. One gate had been left ajar, otherwise she'd not have shifted them against a drift of at least four feet. But she saw a light in the hall, another shone from Richard's room to the left. They gave her a burst of speed, and she floundered, trying to run up the drive towards the front steps. Carefully, slowly placing her feet on one step after the other, she felt in her pocket for her key.

She flung open the door, paused only to stamp her boots on the mat, then closed it behind her and leaned against the wood.

She gazed around the pale green walls which seemed even more attractive than ever, she'd never felt more thankful to be here.

Richard's door opened. 'Have a good time then?' He wasn't smiling and his voice was brittle.

Too breathless to speak, Irene shook her head.

'You must have had, you're late enough.' As well as snow-covered, she was dishevelled, her beautiful hair tangled beneath the headscarf she was removing. Was she so totally unashamed of the association that she'd not think to conceal its effects? Or was she simply telling him, wordlessly, that she still loved John?

Irene was upset by his disapproving frown, and far too exhausted to explain anything coherently. She'd been hurt in the past when others condemned her for what she'd done. She couldn't take Richard's criticism, especially unjustified.

Miserably, she swallowed. 'Have you looked out tonight? If you're questioning the time I've come in, there is good reason.'

'I'm sure,' he retorted sharply. And reminded himself to level his tone. 'You're free to choose your friends, Irene, and what you do.'

Now his voice was low it seemed all the more perturbing to her. 'Richard, I want to tell you about it . . .' she began earnestly.

Briefly, he noticed the anguish in her eyes, and longed to hold her. But the whisky had been a mistake. It had liberated desire, increasing the urge to pull her against his hard body. He forced his arms rigidly to his sides. The drink had also slackened the discipline over his tongue. He couldn't continue lying about his emotions; he'd either blurt out his love, or curse her soundly for sleeping with someone else.

'Richard, listen . . .'

He froze. He could not bear to know anything about the hours she'd spent with that man. Dread tightened his throat. 'No, Irene, I don't care . . .' He choked. ' . . . to hear about it,' didn't come out. He turned abruptly. Tears welled in his eyes. Before he made a complete fool of himself he'd closed and locked his door.

Shattered, Irene was shuddering. 'I don't care . . .' echoed round the empty hall. 'No,' she murmured despairingly. The entire day had been like the proverbial nightmare, but this – *could not be happening*. It wasn't possible. Not Richard who was always, unfailingly, fair. Tears coursing down her face, she stumbled towards the stairs.

Although she'd hardly slept at all, Irene got up early, desperate to talk to Richard. There must have been some mistake. She couldn't really believe that he didn't care what had happened yesterday to distress her. She slipped on her dressing gown, went to make a pot of tea, then knocked on his door.

'Oh, it's you,' he observed, his eyes narrowing, but he let her in. 'Thanks' he said for the tea, and 'All right' when asked how he was.

Irene sighed and, sitting down, began sipping from her cup. She'd never felt more upset. Seeing John again, and in such a state, had brought back all the hurt of being forbidden to attempt curing people. Just as it had resurrected all the wretched despair which had nearly ended her life. She felt too choked to tell Richard. If only he'd meet her halfway. But his closed expression told her there wasn't much hope of that. Inside her constricted chest her heart felt sore. She couldn't endure this strain though. 'Richard, about yesterday . . .'

'Let's leave it. None of my business,' he said tersely. He'd been shaken when she'd come to his room, trapping him with this awful truth which he had no wish to face. Later, bit by bit, he would come to accept it; he'd have to. But not today, after a night struggling to stifle this longing for her, while each time his eyelids lowered he'd seen again that strange wildness in her eyes, her disordered hair.

Irene gnawed her lip. She was so shattered she felt ill. She gulped down more tea, and tried once again.

'I only saw John, you know, because he needs medical help.'

'Then leave him to the professionals.' Just get him out of your life, out of *ours*.

If he'd been aiming to hurt her, Richard couldn't have found a better weapon. Her hand shook, rattling the cup in its saucer as she placed them on the tray.

He glanced up at the sound, but didn't say anything. If she genuinely meant to let John's doctor take charge now, she'd have said.

Almost at a run, Irene went out and along to the kitchen. She clattered down the tray, then hurried upstairs to her room. She still couldn't credit that Rich was capable of being so uncaring.

Standing at the window, she stared out. She'd never seen such snow. It had ceased falling, but the quantity surrounding the house was staggering. The boundary wall had disappeared beneath drifts, and some of the shrubs were concealed also, as were her own footprints.

Eventually, Irene bathed and dressed; feeling no better, she went back downstairs. She helped Daphne with meals, but with Sunday newspapers kept back by the snow, had nothing else to distract her. During the afternoon, she and Richard happened to be alone in the sitting room. She tried again to get him to listen.

As soon as she began speaking he pointedly picked up a book. 'Let's think about something else, shall we?'

Irene wondered briefly what he would do if she snatched the book from him and compelled him to hear her out. But she knew he was quite likely to stride out of the room. He'd shattered her pride already with his remark about leaving John to the professionals, she wouldn't risk receiving another blow. She was so disappointed in Rich – she had been convinced until yesterday that he trusted her. That he wouldn't even have contemplated the possibility of her going back to John. And now she was so upset she was behaving quite out of character, had nearly divulged John's problems, as no doctor would.

During the following week the atmosphere between them remained as frigid as the world outdoors. And the efforts made by David and Anita to reach North Fell House through massive drifts had generated something of the wartime spirit. This contrasted acutely with the patent mistrust between herself and Richard. Each time the others glanced her way Irene felt they were condemning her for disturbing the boss who always commanded their affection as well as respect. She could hardly explain that *he* was the one who appeared intent on distressing her.

The weather was so bad that Richard had offered both David and Anita rooms in the house to save them the journey through such deep snow. Both had declined with thanks, determined not to be kept from their respective partners. Fortunately, they lived in the same direction and travelled together. But each day when they arrived they carried fresh news of houses and farms cut off with snow up to the bedroom windows, and of sheep and other animals lost. Numerous motor vehicles were abandoned, and trains on the Settle to Carlisle railway had ceased any attempt to keep running.

On the Friday afternoon of the following week the telephone rang, and even as Richard answered it Irene felt her heart plummeting. He laid the receiver on the desk with a curt 'Your boyfriend' and went out, slamming the door.

Irene couldn't have been more determined that she wouldn't see John again. But he sounded far worse with the fortnight that had elapsed – scarcely coherent. Even while she was telling him that she would *not* go there, she was picturing the journey as far as that dreadful hotel in the back streets of Skipton.

'Get yourself out of there,' she told him firmly. 'Report to the nearest hospital. And for God's sake tell them what you're on.'

'Can't – not on my own. Irene, you've got to help me.'

She hitched a lift on a milk wagon from roughly halfway into Skipton. But when they set her down, the snow that had spilled over the tops of her wellingtons as she left North Fell had turned her feet as cold as the surrounding drifts. At least, in the town, some of the roads had been cleared slightly, she could walk along without floundering through the thickest stuff. The hotel, though, looked no more inviting than it had previously. And the landlord glowered as she brought in a sprinkling of snow along with the blast of chill air.

Initially she refused when he offered to show her up to John's room, but he seemed to know how difficult it would be to get him to comply with her insistence that he should come downstairs.

The room was indescribably untidy, and smelled foul. She tried not to look as she rushed to open the window. It had jammed. Her fruitless rattling increased John's agitated breathing.

Half dressed, he lay on top of the covers, unshaven, unwashed, and moaning. He appeared oblivious to the cold. His eyes weren't closed, yet he seemed unable to focus. Instinctively, Irene went to check his heart rate. His pulse was hammering at nearly twice the normal rate, his entire body was tremoring. On the bed was a tablet bottle, its cap on the bedside table, and her feet crunched on scattered tablets. Before she finished reading the label he was convulsing.

Irene daren't leave him. She shouted down the stairs for them to telephone for an ambulance. When it made its way there at last, she accompanied John to hospital. He was just about conscious, but would be incapable of giving an account of what had happened. And she was snared – by her concern for any sick person, by her still-present urge to heal, to relieve suffering.

Irene told the hospital what kind of tablets John had taken, and remained while they began treating his overdose and cleaning him up.

'I'm afraid I have to go now,' she told the ward sister firmly once she'd been assured that John would recover provided he accepted that he must keep off the drugs. Some extra sense must have warned him that she was going.

'Irene . . . ' he called hoarsely, from behind the curtains drawn round the bed.

'You can't just leave,' the sister said.

Wearily Irene shook her head. Clad in hospital pyjamas and no longer shaking, John looked better already, well enough to be left in their care. And she had to ensure that he stopped depending upon her.

'This can't go on, you know that,' she told him, from the foot of the bed. 'You're wrecking your health, as well as your career. And it's up to you to halt that. I can't do it for you. You're the only one who can fight this. You've got to stiffen yourself against shovelling down tablets . . . '

'Okay,' he interrupted. 'If I have help, Irene, your help.'

She couldn't believe him. Her being there now was doing no good at all. He was coming up with all the old arguments that he'd dragged before her last time. And she couldn't be with him every minute of the day, a watchdog, even if she wanted to. Swiftly, she turned away, thrust aside the screening curtains, and began running.

In the corridor, she felt someone take her arm. It was the sister. A young houseman, grave-faced, caught up with them.

'Do you know what you're doing?' he demanded. 'That chap needs somebody to see him through. He's been on that stuff too long, he's going to have a devil of a job doing without it.'

Irene swallowed, close to tears. 'He has a wife. Get her, *please*. I've told you all I can.'

Freeing herself wasn't that simple. Back at North Fell House, she couldn't dismiss John from her mind. Seeing him so badly affected by the drugs had brought home how serious the outcome might be. Both Benzedrine and Dexedrine may have been in use for a time, but who fully understood yet what the consequences of their abuse might be? And she was given too much time for thinking. Richard's determination to limit their contact outside business hours left her alone too long.

On the following Wednesday the hospital rang. John was responding, but was suffering withdrawal symptoms. They had contacted Vera, she had said the snow made getting there impossible. John needed just one person to show concern for him, wouldn't Irene reconsider?

That evening she went to Richard. Briefly and unemotionally, she brought him up to date, and tried to express the aversion she felt for visiting John. To explain that she'd had too many years of conditioning to be able to keep away.

'*Only* because you still feel like any doctor about someone in his state?' he asked, trying to quell the realization that by refusing to listen earlier he'd denied himself access to a truth which was more palatable than his own suppositions.

'Of course. I want you to understand that. I can't even like him any longer. But he is sick.'

'And you don't have it in you to turn your back on that. Lord knows, I should be able to grasp that you live to try and cure folk! And you're going again, you say?'

'One last time – and I mean last. He is beginning to respond. And once the snow clears his wife can get there. It'll be up to her then, and the doctors.'

Richard nodded, he smiled though his dark eyes didn't light. 'It sounds as though you've done all you could to help him recover.'

Irene visited John that last time. And she made it clear that she would not return. If she had to fight with every scrap of will, she would conquer the part of her that was trained to care about making folk better. If it wasn't too late already, she must salvage something of the relationship with Richard which still seemed strained.

'I'm getting serious about you. I hope you know that, lass.'

Norman had spent a miserable fortnight without Lily. Her mother had slipped on their icy step and broken her ankle, and had kept Lily away from the mill to look after the new baby and the other little ones. It was only now that one of her sisters had agreed to stop at home that he was even seeing Lily at work.

He'd visited the house in Hanson Lane one Saturday afternoon, but had found that Lily had been sent down to the bottom market to shop, and he hadn't been invited in.

'I want to give you a better life, a different carry-on,' he continued, when Lily's only answer was a smile.

'Ay, I wish many a time that you could,' she admitted, taking his arm as they tried to make their way over compacted snow that had frozen solid time and again on all the pavements. She was used to being expected to look after the kids, but not seeing Norman had shown her how she relied on him now: for the only pleasure that alleviated hard graft. 'Where would we live, though? If we did get married.'

'I've thought of that,' he said, and explained the idea he was considering. 'It wouldn't be ideal, but it would give us a bit of a start. We could begin getting stuff together, and happen by then there'd be some sort of housing available.'

Lily took to his idea, far more readily than he had dared to hope. It would be an adventure, she said. And one that she relished, if the glow in her lovely grey eyes was any indication.

'Do you want me to ask your Dad if he'll let us get married?' Norman inquired the next time they were out together.

Lily shook her head. 'Better not. There's no need, is there, I'm long past twenty-one.'

'Aye, but – I want to do everything right.'

'He'll only find all sorts of reasons for opposing the idea. It's best if we make arrangements, then tell folk.'

'They're not going to want you getting wed, are they?' said Norman gravely.

'I don't suppose so, no.'

'*You're* sure though, aren't you, love?'

'Course I am. Nay, lad, don't you know by now I'm potty about you! We'll go and see the minister tomorrow night, if you like, that's how certain I am.'

210

Norman hadn't thought about where the actual ceremony would be, nor about who they'd invite. 'I daresay my mum'll put on a bit of a spread for us at after,' he began.

Although she was smiling, Lily shook her head. 'No, love. I'd rather she didn't. It's up to my side to provide that, you know. I've been thinking we'd be able to have the Sunday school. And the caretaker's wife is good at laying on sandwiches, and sausage rolls and homemade buns.'

'All right, I'll leave that to you. But think on – if it's costing more than you can manage, let me know. I wonder if our Mavis and her husband will be able to make it from London.'

'And there's your other sister, the one that lives Skipton way.'

'Irene, aye. Happen she'd like to bring that chap she works for.'

Once they had seen the minister and arranged the wedding for the first Saturday in April, the initial excitement seemed to wane. Norman would have preferred it to be sooner than that, but he was too much of a realist to think they could just walk straight into any kind of accommodation.

He hadn't told either of his parents more than that he and Lily were planning to get married. He didn't relish his mother's probable reaction to where they intended living, and spent a lot of time fielding her suggestions that he and Lily should have one of their rooms.

'Makes more sense than you paying out rent to other folk, and this house has allus seemed to have too many bedrooms, with having to be big enough to allow your father space downstairs for his surgery.'

Lily hadn't told her family much either, and they hadn't wanted to know. Her mother's disappointment that she was losing her eldest daughter had only momentarily been displaced – by dread that Lily might be in the family way.

'There's nowt like that,' she was assured very smartly. 'But it is time I had a home of my own, and Norman's that good to me.'

Mr and Mrs Atkinson, satisfied they weren't to be disgraced, still asked relatively few questions, and conveyed the impression that they'd have nothing to do with their daughter's desertion of them.

'I don't know what I'm going to wear,' Lily confided to her fiancé one evening. They were sitting in the pavilion in People's Park. Still surrounded by a good depth of snow, it was dreadfully cold. But now they were saving hard they only went to the pictures once a fortnight, and after they'd both been on their feet in the weaving shed all day they were more than ready for a sit-down.

'How do you mean, you don't know? Aren't you having a white frock?'

'Don't see how I'll have enough coupons, love. Not for a long one.'

'I'll ask at home if you like, or talk to our Irene, somebody might have a few to spare.'

'No. No, thanks – I'd rather you didn't.' The truth was Lily was as short of money as clothing coupons, but she'd not let on about that to Norman, else he'd be insisting he helped out. She felt bad enough as it was, not having much bottom drawer stuff to bring with her, never mind letting him clothe her an' all.

'I was wondering about a costume, that might come in at after,' she added eventually, gazing towards the marble statue of Frank Crossley. A member of the well-known Halifax family, he'd been responsible for providing the park. I bet he didn't have trouble deciding if he could be dressed nice, she thought, or if looking right would stop him putting on a bit of a wedding breakfast.

'That could be in white, couldn't it?' suggested Norman, still wishing to see her as the traditional bride.

Lily's grin was rueful. 'I can see me wearing that later on, I must say! There'd be smuts all over it, first time I walked into Halifax.' But happen she could dye the costume when the actual wedding was over. And an idea was forming as to how she'd get hold of a good length of cloth without laying out too much brass.

She approached Bert Kettlewell as soon as she was back at work after the weekend. The ends of pieces and sometimes those that had a few flaws were offered cheap to the workers. And if you were lucky, without sacrificing coupons. By the end of that week, Lily had a couple of lengths of cloth, both woven in the same yarn; it'd only take a bit of scheming to cut out her costume without having any seams where they shouldn't be.

Lily'd always been handy with her needle. Her mother had once worked as a machinist at Sheldrake's and had taught her eldest most of what she knew.

When she began sewing Lily felt the first gnawing disappointment. The cloth was a good cotton, the best Dewhurst's produced. But it was far stronger and stiffer than any used for clothing. No matter how she tried, Lily couldn't get it to hang right. By the time she had it all tacked together and tried it on she could have wept. Both the skirt and the jacket with its nipped-in waist stuck out around her, they might have been constructed in cardboard.

I've made a right mess of this, she thought, I'd have looked better in owt I've got in my wardrobe! But she'd not waste good material, she'd bought it for her wedding day, and that was when it would be worn. She washed it carefully several times, and still it was rigid. Maybe at after, when it was dyed, it'd lose some of that stiffness.

Norman didn't see too much amiss with his bride's outfit. As he glanced back down the aisle towards her, he was only aware that she seemed to glow all light against the dark interior. And he was a bit distracted himself, none too comfortable. Mum had tackled that demob suit months ago, taking it up and in, but until today he'd resisted her assertion that it was perfectly all right now. Only the knowledge that he didn't possess another suit had got him into it. He wasn't lashing out on owt else new, and he could hardly be wed in a sports coat and flannels. Even if this didn't feel like a proper church.

Built for the Crossley family, Park Congregational was as different from his own St Paul's church as any consecrated building could be. Typically Nonconformist, it seemed dominated by the organ and the pulpit; lacking anything that Norman would call an altar, it had failed to provide him with a focal point. Until Lily appeared.

Now she was advancing towards him he felt his face relaxing into a smile. He'd put up with anything: she was here, as radiant as any man could hope his bride might be. She'd had her hair done, and it framed her face, but most of all it gleamed, dark but shining with golden threads as the light reflected from its strands.

Norman cleared his throat, stepped forward as she approached, and was filled with the longing to savour every moment of the ceremony. It passed in a rush, nevertheless, and in a conglomeration of impressions. As they began making their vows he grew conscious of Lily's father, slightly behind them and to their left, forcefully blowing his nose. For the first time, he felt sympathy for this older man whom he hardly knew. And then there was the faintest sigh as their union was blessed. He recognized that as their Irene's, and wished he could give her a future to extinguish past upheavals. But all these sentiments vanished at once, with the intrusion of an unmistakable sound of trickling.

He willed himself not to turn round. The minister was addressing them, he had to concentrate. Whichever of Lily's young sibling attendants was having this misfortune, there was nowt he could do.

Beside him, his bride stiffened, and then her shoulders quivered and he recognized contained laughter.

'Did you hear that?' she hissed later as they processed towards the Registrar who had to be present because this wasn't the Established Church.

'Aye, I did an' all.'

'It'll be our Herbert. Mam refused to put a nappy on him, but he still wets when he gets excited.'

'Never mind. It hasn't spoilt owt.'

'Except the chapel floor! We'll have to offer to pay for extra cleaning.'

Impulsively, Norman leaned sideways and kissed her. 'I do love you! Even now, you can't stop being practical.'

Lily and he needed to summon all their practicality to face their families when the service and the buffet meal that followed were over. For so long now, they had kept their counsel about their first home, fending off any inquiries with firm assertions that they wanted it to be a surprise.

'Ready?' he asked her, his pulse racing, while Lily was packing the remainder of the cake into a large carton.

'Aye,' she said, and grinned. She was that happy, she no longer had any misgivings about showing anyone where they were going to live.

Because of the reception being in the Sunday school next door to the church, the cars he'd hired had been standing idle in Francis Street. The mate who was his best man called them into service again now to ferry his family and hers down through the town centre to the outskirts of Halifax. The drivers halted where he'd already instructed them. Heads high, arm in arm and their pace lively, he and Lily led the way through tall grass and a mass of weeds.

'Wait till you see inside,' he told his parents briskly, before either of them could speak. He'd heard his mother's gasp, and could imagine Dad was too flabbergasted to say owt.

They'd done the best they could with the exterior of the Nissen hut in the weeks since Norman had been tipped off that they were all right for squatting in – just while folk got on their feet and a few pieces of furniture together. They offered privacy which was all he cared about, and Lily had insisted it would be a bit of fun staying here till they managed to find a house.

'You're having us on, of course,' Donald Hainsworth said at last, standing to Lily's right, precisely where the rust on the corrugated iron was at its worst.

'A good joke,' Ralph echoed, glad of the hope that Norman, who'd become a chum, was teasing. 'Now show us where your place really is.'

But Norman was inserting his key in the padlock that secured the door. 'Just a minute,' he said, swung Lily into his arms, and carried her inside. 'Come on in then . . .'

Lily's parents said so little that he might have believed they had been told already, if she herself hadn't been giggling last night over the surprise they'd get. 'Not that I care,' she'd said. 'Whatever anybody says, we shall be on our own, with nobody to interfere.'

His own folk compensated for Lily's mum and dad withholding whatever they might be thinking.

'I know you're used to living in places like this,' Mavis began. 'But have you thought how different it's going to be for Lily?'

''Course, I've thought. Do you really believe we haven't given this a lot of consideration!' The pulse which had been rising with excitement was accelerating alarmingly now, with annoyance. 'I'll look after Lily, don't you fret – and a damned sight better nor lots of husbands do! You'll see – we'll be out of here before so long, in a house full o' nice things.'

'Ay, I do hope so,' Lily's mother murmured. She was emerging at last from being mortified about their Herbert's little accident.

Lily was smiling at her. 'Getting married is an adventure, isn't it, this just makes it even more so. And it really is very . . .' Briefly, she paused, seeking the right word.

'Civilized,' Irene continued for her. 'I can see you've put in a lot of hard work, the pair of you. Do you mind if we look round?'

'It's what we've brought you all here for,' her brother said, but quite sharply. He wasn't certain Irene had no trace of sarcasm in her voice. He hadn't expected Mum and Dad to approve, and he hadn't cared too much what Mavis or her husband thought; but Irene was one on her own. She'd either tell him he ought to be ashamed of himself, or . . .

'You've got a nice clean sink, any road,' she told Lily swiftly. 'And them cupboards look as if they'll hold a good lot.'

'We brought them with us,' her new sister-in-law announced, crossing the echoing boards to her side. 'They're free-standing, so's they'll go in our kitchen when we get one. We're calling the next section the living room, though all we've got so far is that table and a couple of chairs. My grandma's promised me a rocker, though, soon as we can get it brought over.'

'And the far end's your bedroom.'

'That's right, Irene. But come and have a proper look. We thought we'd curtain it off, cos it gets a bit draughty.'

'I'm sure. One big room like this'll take a bit of heating.'

'We've a good stove, though. One we can move about, so long as we're careful. Norman says it's like they had in the RAF.'

'Same as everything else here!' Elsie Hainsworth snapped. 'Norman, how could you? Didn't you think before you decided to move in? It isn't fair on Lily, you know, bringing her to this sort of place. It's bound to be damp, and just look at that wilderness out there, you'll get all sorts of creatures coming in.'

'That's hardly the point, is it?' her husband put in. 'This is no sort of a beginning. Nay, lad – we haven't brought you up to this.'

'I didn't expect you to be glad, Father. But it is only for a start, as I keep saying. If you lived in the real world, you'd know we're far from being the only ones driven to squatting.'

His father had recoiled at 'real world' and momentarily was silenced. Mavis took the opportunity to offer further observations.

'I just hope you see to it that there's no bairn before you get out of 'ere. I wouldn't let our Heather spend more than an hour in this place.'

Heather, however, was relishing the sound given off by the wooden floor, alternating an energetic stomping with racing around.

'Just look at her,' Irene remarked to Lily as they came back towards the others. 'She's not concerned for any refinements.'

217

'And nor am I,' Lily asserted seriously. 'I've wanted your Norman since I first got to know him, and I know he'll do right by me.'

'Happen so,' her father said at last. He'd been too disturbed to know what to say for the best, especially with Norman's folk being educated people. Even at the reception, he'd kept very quiet, frightened of putting his foot in it.

'At least Norman's found them a home, and we all know there's a housing shortage,' his wife added, and bit her lip. They couldn't have accommodated them down Hanson Lane, the kids were allus falling over each other, as it was. And their Lily had said Norman wouldn't entertain living with his folk.

'Well, I offered you a room, and that offer still stands,' Elsie reminded her son. She couldn't bear to leave him in this place.

'Thanks, but we shan't be needing it.'

'Just think on – there's only one way you can go from here, and that's up,' his father said tersely. 'Come on, Elsie, it's time we were getting home.'

'But I was going to give you all a cup of tea,' Lily protested, noticing that her own family, including the strangely subdued children, were moving towards the door.

Ralph was there already, waiting with scarcely concealed exasperation while Mavis collared their daughter.

'I'd stay gladly, but I've got to get back to North Fell tonight,' Irene told them. She'd not been sure Richard believed it was Halifax she was coming to, she wouldn't risk a night away. He still hadn't unfrozen towards her, their only discussions since all the trouble had centred on work, or the weather. And even snow that had wrecked every transport system, icebergs off the coast of Norfolk, and the subsequent extensive flooding weren't quite so extraordinary that they would cause all other conversation to cease.

Irene gave first Lily and then Norman a hug. 'I know you'll be happy,' she said quietly. 'Take no notice of them.'

Norman grinned. 'Don't worry, I've asserted myself, haven't I?'

He was disappointed, nonetheless, that Lily's folk hadn't had one good word to say. They'd got some furniture already, hadn't they? And he wasn't afraid of the work which would provide everything else they would need.

'I thought your mum and dad let us off quite lightly,' said Lily, as they watched from the door while their families made their way across the overgrown parade ground.

Her husband grunted. 'Only because I held my tongue. I'm sick to death with 'em trotting out how they would have given us a home. They don't know me at all if they can't get it into their heads that I don't want owt giving!'

Her eyes sparkling, Lily giggled. 'Don't . . . ?' she asked mischievously. 'And there was I thinking there was summat you'd been after for a long time.'

His face relaxed into a smile. 'Aye, well – that's different, isn't it. You belong to me now.'

Slowly, gently, he began leading up to proving the statement. Drawing her against him, he felt how stiff the material of her costume was, could believe it crackled.

'You haven't starched this, have you?'

Lily's smile was rueful. 'This is just how it come off t'loom. Except that I did try washing it, to soften it up. It didn't.'

'Can't get near you.' He'd anticipated she would feel all yielding, not as if she was wearing armour.

'I'll just go take it off.'

'Good idea.'

Her wedge-heeled sandals clattering, she headed towards the other end of the hut, and through the curtain. When she seemed to be taking a long time, Norman followed to investigate.

Lily was sitting at the card table where he'd set up his shaving mirror. She was brushing out her hair.

Seeing him, she rose, turned to face him.

She was wearing a skimpy nightgown which, except for trailing on the floor, resembled a petticoat. Lily had chosen rayon locknit because it was supposed to look alluring. The thing clung over her breasts and hips, but they were so small that it also emphasized every one of her ribs.

'Come here, love,' he said, and gathered her to him.

She raised her face for his kisses, wound her arms around him, pressing close.

Norman kissed her eyelids and her hair, then her cheek and finally her glossy mouth.

'Like the taste?' she teased. She'd treated herself to a Tangee Natural lipstick.

'Aye, aye,' he responded hastily. But she'd never been one for making herself up before. Combined with the strange garment she was wearing, it increased the unfamiliarity. Anxiety gnawed into him, and he felt his heartbeat quicken again, but for all the wrong reasons.

He'd be hard put to it to explain, but Lily now was agitating him almost as much as his parents had done. He'd thought she was just going to put a different frock on. So they could sit and have a talk. After the way nearly everybody had reacted to this place, he needed reassuring that they hadn't been wrong to move in here. There was only Irene who'd had anything good to say.

Slowly, he turned and walked away. He was thoroughly disappointed in Ralph. Hadn't he believed they'd developed quite a feeling of camaraderie, an understanding of the difficulties of returning to civilian life? Until today, when Ralph had reverted to being the brother-in-law who always seemed better off than other folk. It was Mum and Dad's words that had smarted most, though, making it sound as if he was condemning Lily to misery here.

'You could try smiling,' she suggested gently, coming to sit near to where he'd settled at the table. 'They'll get over it. Specially when they see how happy we are together here.'

'You don't blame me, love, do you? For wanting to get wed afore we'd found a house?'

''Course I don't. You shouldn't take your responsibilities so seriously. Not today, any road. We've done our best to do it proper and give 'em all a good day. But it's to live

220

as *we* want that we've come here, it's no use letting their opinions haunt us.'

Haunted, though, was precisely how Norman felt, as if the place had recorded every disapproving word, and their shocked expressions.

Lily made a pot of tea, and he began to feel better while they were drinking it. There was a feather cake, as well, which she'd baked in between preparations for their wedding.

'You're making this into a real home,' he said warmly, taking off the dark brown jacket. 'You'll just have to keep reminding me not to let what other folk think spoil things.'

'There won't be much time for dwelling on anybody else, will there, not with us both working full time.'

'No, I suppose not.'

'Won't it be nice, though, having each other for company going to the mill?'

Norman smiled. She was a game one, no mistake. Other lasses might have been moaning about having to travel so far.

He felt overwhelmed with the longing to hug her, to go on holding her to him to show how glad he was that she was the one he'd married.

'Be with you in a minute,' he said, heading for the door.

The lavatories and washing facilities were in a block, shared by the other folk using the former army camp. They would smell in hot weather. For the first time, he cursed his brainwave of squatting here. He'd have been glad today to have their own bathroom.

When he got back to the Nissen hut Lily was standing against the curtain of their bedroom, looking like a tall young girl who'd shot up and overgrown her strength. In what felt like two or three strides he was across to her side, and drawing her close, holding her there.

'I'll look after you, love.'

'I know you will, Norman.'

Responding to her kisses was natural enough; it seemed all right when Lily began unbuttoning his shirt. Her slender hands edged around him to his back, and he felt

221

good, needed. But that was all. He couldn't remain un-moved by his bride's wish to belong with him, but nor could he detect the return of his own strangely absent desire.

There was too much going on in his mind, snatches of their wedding kept parading by, but mostly it was the disastrous visit here by both their families.

Later, lying beside her, he realized how hot he felt, and how cold the bed was. A pulse was drumming in the ear pressed into the pillow. His dratted thyroid was playing up again, with all the tension of the ceremony and the trauma here at after. He hadn't taken his tablets, couldn't even be certain where they were.

'Isn't this lovely,' Lily exclaimed. 'Right away from everybody, just you and me.'

Has she always talked in clichés, he wondered. Or is it just because she's needing reassurance? Her folk had hardly said a word here, even her brothers and sisters had stood there, riveted to the floor near the entrance.

He drew her to him, affectionately, holding her in his arms and pressing his lips into her shining hair. She'd looked that fragile and pathetic standing there in that cheap nightie, he wanted to hug her to death!

Against him, Lily stirred. Norman willed himself to forget feeling sympathetic, to share her eagerness; to forget everyone's disapproval. But even with her silky-textured nightgown smooth against his limbs all he felt was drained, dead.

13

All the way back to Skipton in the bus Irene stared through the window beside her, scarcely seeing anything of the hills or the valleys crammed with factories. Even when she arrived and walked around, killing time before the next bus out towards North Fell, she found she was looking in the direction of the castle, yet not even noticing this building which had always interested her. All she could really see was that pathetic Nissen hut, its curved corrugated iron whitewashed on the inside in an attempt to make it more homely.

She'd liked Lily from the start; today she felt massive admiration for her. Their Norman had a bride to be proud of, she'd shown 'em all that she could make anywhere into a home. And be content there, for as long as it took to find a better place.

To Irene, it seemed that her new sister-in-law had dismissed any doubts she might have entertained far swifter than Norman himself. But then, all the Hainsworth family were accustomed to heeding both parents, even if they eventually refused to concur with the opinions thrust upon them.

By the time she was walking the last few yards to the house, Irene was feeling overwhelmed by the pluck those two had shown. What guts it must have taken, not only to set up home there, but to let everyone see how they were prepared to live simply in order to be together.

'How was the wedding?' Richard asked when she went into the sittingroom. Irene was looking so grave he was forced to overcome their strained relations and inquire.

'Very nice, thanks.'

'But . . . ?'

She went to the sofa, and glanced across towards his chair. 'Ay, I don't know. It's been a funny day. Our Norman hadn't let on where he'd found for them to live. After the reception, he took us to see. Oh, Richard, it's a Nissen hut, on a deserted army camp.'

'Squatting, you mean?' He sounded dismayed.

'Bit different to this, isn't it! I never thought . . . I mean, our Norman's not earning a bad wage. Then there was his gratuity.'

'How's his bride taking to the thought of living there?'

'Well, that's what flabbergasts me – she's not complaining. Do you know, she even seems proud of the place.'

'Good for them! Still – one hates to think of people existing like that, especially when he's back from serving in the forces.' Richard paused for a minute, thinking. 'You can tell him from me that if he's in need of a loan, he can come to me. On a businesslike basis, naturally, though I'd charge very little by way of interest.'

'That's ever so kind, Rich. I really appreciate the offer. Trouble is, I don't know that our Norman would.'

'No, well – up to him. See what you think.'

'I'm not saying he wouldn't be grateful. But he is very independent. He jumped down Mother's throat more nor once, because she kept saying there was a room they could have.'

Richard grinned, and nodded. 'But this wouldn't be anything more than a financial arrangement. He wouldn't be obliged to family.'

'I know. Ay, it is good of you! I'll see how they get on, put it to them if they're desperate to get out. Only, of course, they'd have to find a house an' all. There's hardly any being built round there yet that aren't for t'council.'

'And they wouldn't qualify?'

'I doubt it. Even families with bairns are having to go on a waiting list, I believe. I know my father keeps giving folk letters to say they need better housing on medical grounds.'

'What must it have been like, during the past few months with so much snow around . . . !'

'It was nearly up to the top of the gas lamps at Wainstalls and other outlying districts, I gather.'

'Heavens! And we thought it was cold enough in here.'

She watched him as he glanced slowly around the elegant room, reflecting in turn on the pale suite upholstered in luxurious cloth, the fitted carpet only a shade or two deeper, the white marble fireplace. He's not blasé like some well-off folk, she thought, I don't believe he ever has been. It's possible to want nice things, and to get them, without losing a true sense of their significance.

No matter what the past few weeks had been like, they hadn't dispersed her admiration for Richard, nor her love. All at once, she felt choked by the long misunderstanding straining their relationship.

'It's good to talk again,' he announced suddenly. 'To hear where you've been, how things have gone.'

She read something in his dark eyes which suggested he had, indeed, feared she was going elsewhere today.

Before she could say anything, however, Rich was speaking again. 'Sorry I've misjudged you, Irene. Don't know how I could have been so stupid.'

Relief mingled with her emotion, and she lightened her tone in case she let go and wept. 'And I don't know why you've been so concerned.'

'Don't you?' He met her glance, briefly, then looked away. 'You weren't jealous?'

'What do you think?'

Certainly, jealous was the way that he had behaved. And he'd told her in the past that he cared deeply about her. She'd wasted too much time letting the strain between them keep them apart. 'There never was any cause for you to be jealous, Richard. There never will be.'

He still continued looking into space. And then when he did face her she hated the sadness in his eyes.

'Feeling like this isn't the end of the world, Rich.'

'Isn't it?'

He crossed swiftly to stand by the window, his back to her. Irene followed and laid a hand on his arm. 'Richard, look at me.'

As soon as he turned she wished he hadn't. She couldn't bear the hopelessness in his expression. Then suddenly he slid an arm around her, drawing her fiercely to him. They clung together in a kiss which finally convinced her that he certainly did need her completely.

Equally abruptly, Richard let her go. 'If I knew I'd ever be a hundred per cent fit . . . ' he began, stopped, and sighed. Where was his resolution? Hadn't he struggled all along not to tie her to him?

'That doesn't matter, Rich.'

'It does to me.' He grasped her by the shoulders, gazing solemnly into her blue eyes. 'You need a whole person. But I'd have given anything to take care of you.'

'No. Listen – you're the person I've grown so fond of that no other considerations count. For your sake, I hope you'll improve further. For my own though, I only want us to be together.'

But even this made no substantial difference. And whilst she understood his dread of another stroke, she was convinced he'd be far better if he ceased letting that past illness inhibit him. Shaken by her own feelings, Irene soon began to hate being unable to commit herself completely to him. She had known for a long time that she was fond of Richard, had suspected that she loved him, she was discovering now just how deeply in love she was.

'I love you, don't I, you know that, Ralph. I'll be all right, once we get back there.'

Mavis had been anything but happy, though, about returning to Halifax so soon. Even when Ralph reminded her about seeing Norman and Lily again. She'd only just settled in London, hadn't she? And she *had* settled here – had taken to folk far better than she'd expected.

The news that her husband was leaving the army had come so suddenly. Ralph had simply walked in at the end of last week and stood in the living room of their little flat, telling her that his days in uniform were all but ended. Mavis had wondered why he hadn't known earlier. In fact, he must have known – he wasn't merely a bit of a private, there'd have been discussions about his future. During the past day or two she'd learned that he'd already fixed up when he'd start working with his father, who'd left the army for the family works.

'And they have an eye on a house which sounds suitable for us,' he'd added.

'Good,' she'd said, forcing herself to smile. But she'd wanted to be the first to see their new home, if they had to have one. *This* was home to her, the one place where she'd felt she was doing things right. When she'd lived in Halifax there'd always been Mum there, taking her over, insisting that everything was done in the way it had been for donkeys' years, to *her* liking.

Ever since Ralph first mentioned returning to Yorkshire, she'd been itching to say she hoped they'd live some little way from both sets of parents. But it sounded so awful she hadn't ventured to put that sentiment into words. And she'd never heard of the road where these houses were being built.

'Where exactly is it?' she asked him now, deciding that she might as well show a bit more interest. They had to go where his work was.

'Up Warley somewhere, I think it's off Edgeholme Lane.'

That meant nothing to her. She'd been to Warley, naturally, but only on the bus so's she could have a bit of a walk away from the smoke of the town.

'Is it far from the mill then?' she asked, trying to be diplomatic. She knew his father lived within half a mile of the blanket works.

Ralph grinned. 'It'll not take me long in the car.'

The prospect of having a car made Mavis's new life appear brighter. When he continued that they'd be nicely placed for taking a ride farther out into the country at weekends, and to the seaside, she cheered up even more.

'Our Heather'll like that.' And happen with a car her old friends would see that she'd done nicely for herself – even if their stay in London hadn't lasted so long.

When Ralph chose the car, a beautiful black and grey Morris Ten, it wasn't so difficult to fall in with his

227

insistence that she should spend most of her days in sorting their possessions and packing. Luckily, Heather seemed to think it was all a game, and except for delaying Mavis while she pried into cases and exclaimed over rediscovered toys, she was content to remain indoors.

Mavis had explained to her daughter that they would soon be living near Halifax again, not so far from Grandma and Grandad Hainsworth, but the toddler's grasp of distance and places wasn't strong enough for that to mean very much. What she did understand, though, was that her daddy was pleased they were going there, and Mummy was beginning to talk about living in a new house as if it would be a treat.

'I think there'll be a garden – you'll be able to play out.'

Here in London, and living in a flat, she'd been obliged to confine Heather's expeditions to visits to the local shops or walking in the park.

'You won't forget Edward, will you, Mummy?'

'Of course I won't. He'll be in your little bed every night, just like here.' Edward, the elderly bear inherited from Ralph, had never had his dignity reduced by being called Teddy, but that didn't mean there were any reservations about Heather's affection for him.

'And we'll see if Father Christmas can bring you a doll's pram for your Bunty the next time he comes.' It would certainly be a relief to have somewhere for the child to play in safety. It would be good, an' all, to see her own mum and dad occasionally.

What Mavis hadn't reckoned with was staying at the imposing house owned by Ralph's parents until the one they were buying was ready for occupation. From the day that he drew up there after briefly explaining that he'd made the arrangement, Mavis began to wonder if she'd ever really understand her husband. It wasn't that Mr and Mrs Parkin were unduly difficult, they couldn't help being overwhelming.

'If I'd known our own place weren't going to be ready yet, I'd have stopped in London till it were,' she soon confided to Elsie.

But her mother couldn't see that Mavis had any problems. 'You want to count yourself lucky, young lady. Just look at your brother . . . !'

She and Dad had visited Norman and Lily again last week. She'd tried to make the idea of their having a room in the family home more attractive to the young couple. And Donald had said what he felt. 'You're our only son, we'd like to think of you in somewhere better.'

Norman had taken that the wrong way. Noticing him all rigid and pale, she'd continued gently: 'You can't live like this, lad.'

'We *are* living here,' he'd asserted, his voice that cold it had struck right through her like the wind during all them blizzards.

Lily, bless her, had tried to smooth things over, reasserting that she was quite happy in the Nissen hut. As if anybody could be!

'Ralph's mum and dad are only doing what they can for you,' she told Mavis now. 'Just think on and be agreeable about it. I didn't bring you up to be ungrateful, did I now?'

Her younger daughter knew that well enough. But the knowledge only made her uncomfortable in her old home, and her visits there which had been growing frequent soon dwindled. She had asked Ralph to teach her to drive the car, but he'd said he hadn't time. Instead, she often filled her afternoons by taking Heather on the bus to Warley, then walking uphill to stand outside their new home, searching the exterior for signs that it was a bit nearer completion.

At least, it was a nice-looking little house, she had something to look forward to now, providing that living with her in-laws didn't drive her crackers first.

Irene spent a long weekend in Halifax, catching up on news of Mavis's move from London and getting to know young Heather all over again. She also called on Lily and Norman.

Somehow, although they had added various pieces of furniture, the place looked more bleak than it had during her first visit. For a hot summer's day, it was windy, and dust blew in clouds from end to end of the former army camp. She had caught Lily with a long brush in her hand, sweeping a wide arc just inside the entrance to their hut, but by the time Irene was leaving she was crunching over another layer of the fine-grained sand that blew under the ill-fitting door.

She'd been wondering if they were any nearer getting a better place, but had willed herself not to inquire. Her admiration for their acceptance of the life here had strengthened, if anything. She wasn't going to say one word that might destroy their contentment.

On the way back to Parkinson Lane, though, she felt heartbroken for them. And yet their marriage seemed stronger rather than weaker as a result. She oughtn't to feel sorry for anybody who had the guts to survive in their circumstances.

'They certainly appear to be all right there,' she said, mainly for her mother's benefit, that evening.

Elsie sniffed. 'I'm saying nowt. Every time I open my mouth in front of our Norman, these days, I say summat I regret.'

'He has had a packet, love,' her husband reminded her gently. 'What with the way they're behaving towards him at the mill.'

'How do you mean?' Irene asked. 'What's up there?'

'He hasn't told you then?' Elsie raised a greying eyebrow and sighed. 'He were that blazing mad, he came here rather than going straight home. Don't think he wanted Lily to see him letting off steam.'

'She wasn't at Dewhurst's at the time then?'

'Nay, I think our Norman had stopped behind at after, to see the boss like,' Donald explained.

They had only learned what their son had chosen to tell them: the full effect it had had upon him was even worse. It had all begun earlier that week, when the rumour started going round the weaving shed that they were finally getting the new looms which had been planned since the war ended. The story Norman heard, though, had made him furious.

The new machinery was on order now, from a place in Switzerland. He'd been riled ages ago when he discovered that they could be buying stuff from abroad but what he heard now made him more angry than ever.

Evidently, the manufacturers advised that somebody should go over there for a week or two, to familiarize himself with the complexity of the looms and to learn how to maintain them. The first Norman heard of this was one of the younger overlookers, Desmond Batley, crowing to a bunch of weavers that he was the one Jack Dewhurst had chosen.

At finishing time Norman went striding towards Bert Kettlewell, and demanded of the foreman what Dewhurst thought he was doing.

'I know only what I've been told, Norman lad,' Bert had replied cautiously. He'd been primed to expect a reaction.

'Then it's him I'm going to see.' Norman strode on again, no less aggressively, until he came to Jack Dewhurst's office.

'Can I have word with you?'

There was more demand than request in his tone, and although the boss had been ready for him, he was irritated by the absence of any 'please', much less any indication of deference.

'Aye, go on, Hainsworth . . . '

'You must know what it's about . . . '

'I can guess. It isn't often that we do something as radical as investing in new looms.'

'Well, it isn't what I was on about afore – though I don't think much of supporting a load of foreigners when we could have bought British stuff. No – it's how you're choosing to send young Batley out there. I'd like to know the reason!'

Jack Dewhurst smiled blandly. 'It's simple enough, Hainsworth. You've answered yourself now, in a manner of speaking.'

'Nay, I haven't.' Norman felt bewildered, not something he relished. 'Don't know what you're talking about.'

'Your attitude, that's what. Look, lad – I know you had a bad time, in the war. But that's over and done with. Yet you still go shooting your mouth off, yelling afore you're hurt.'

'Before? Of course I'm hurt! What do you expect? I were an overlooker here long afore Desmond Batley thought of working. If anybody should be going tripping off, it ought to be me. Fair's fair.'

'I'm sorry, but that's the way it is. We need somebody over in Switzerland that'll pick up all they've got to teach him. I'll not send a chap who can't be relied on to simmer down if the least little thing upsets him. It's got to be somebody who'll keep a cool head and give all his attention to learning.'

The confrontation had continued for the best part of half an hour, and all similar in content. By the time Norman declared that he might as well be getting home, he was convinced that he'd been done a serious injustice. And Jack Dewhurst was convinced afresh that his assessment of his loom overlookers had been accurate.

'He as good as told me I were unreliable, I shan't forget that,' he'd asserted to his parents.

No, love, Elsie had thought. And you're the only one *that* is going to harm.

'I hope you still keep those tablets by you,' his father had said as he saw him to the door.

'I wouldn't need them if it weren't for folk like them down yonder,' Norman had snapped. But all the way home he had wondered if Jack Dewhurst was right, and if he'd never really be fit again. Would never feel he was the equal of any man; and more capable than most. He'd been respected in the RAF for his expertise, which had won him responsibility – aye, even for men's lives. Down there, amid that confounded clattering from the looms, all his skills were disregarded.

'Happen they'll get somewhere better to live in before long,' Irene suggested now to their mother. 'That might stop him feeling he's in a situation that he can't improve.'

'And what about your situation?' Elsie asked, finally voicing another matter which had troubled her for long enough. 'You don't seem as content as you were at first at that there North Fell.'

Irene could have done without the question. And didn't know how she might answer it. How could she be content while her relationship with Richard remained so unsatisfactory? It seemed so long ago now since the days when she'd simply been glad to avoid another complex association. She sometimes caught herself in a silent reminder that she'd never intended being so *daft* that she fell in love again.

It seemed no consolation now that she understood most of the reasoning behind Richard's assertion that he'd never marry. All she knew was that being unable to express her affection for him – to say nothing of her need – was growing increasingly difficult. And while she felt driven by the urge to love him she was acutely aware that Richard was free, as she was, to be loved. How would she continue to hold back for ever from loving him completely?

In the office, the volume of work (which had already doubled again and again) was still increasing. Naturally, Richard was elated by this resurge of success. Time was passing even more swiftly, and it was with a kind of shock that Irene noticed how hot the weather was becoming. The trees were in full leaf once more, and sheep were grazing over higher ground on the fells. She noticed that Rich seemed to tire more easily in the heat, and tried to persuade him to ensure more relaxation; but he merely smiled slightly and said nothing. She wondered if he didn't realize he was confirming her supposition that he was keeping busy as one means of avoiding any deepening of their relationship.

One Sunday when Daphne was lunching with Peggy and her husband, Irene was delighted to see Shaun O'Connor come strolling through the garden towards the kitchen where she was making a pot of tea. They hardly ever saw Shaun, these days, a fact which she'd regretted since he'd always seemed so amiable.

'Are you and Rich doing anything today?' he asked, his blue eyes gleaming like a small boy's in anticipation of a treat. 'I've been trying to ring you, but there's a fault on our line.'

'Nothing much,' she replied. 'Have you something in mind?'

Shaun grinned. 'Certainly have! I've been asked to house-sit, for some friends who live quite near here and are on holiday. They've said I'm welcome to use their pool. Swimming around on my own's rather boring, but I thought you two might like to join me.'

When Richard was asked, he looked rather anxious. Irene smiled. 'Swimming's marvellous exercise. What are you waiting for?'

Although he still appeared to have reservations, he agreed to go. As Irene looked for her costume and a towel she stifled an inward groan; she suspected his misgivings didn't really concern his health.

The pool was large for a private one. There was plenty of room for three to swim without getting in each other's way, and Irene paused more than once, noticing how strongly Richard was swimming, and with considerable energy.

When they eventually emerged from the water they lingered for about an hour, chatting with Shaun on the sun-warmed terrace. Irene had thought for ages how fit Richard was looking. He had spent a lot of time gardening at North Fell, while his lean body acquired a tan, enhancing his dark hair and eyes. By the time they set out to walk home she was glad to be alone with him again. And privately admitted that he'd been justified in supposing himself safer fully clothed!

He had tugged on the shorts he'd been wearing earlier that day, but carried his sports shirt. As they waved goodbye to Shaun from the gate of his friends' property, Irene felt a bare arm go about her shoulders. Through the thin blue dress she'd slipped on after swimming, his touch sent delight shimmering over and within her body. She checked an instinctive smile.

The way back to the house was along a meandering path that hugged the contour of the hill and at intervals was tree-shaded, so that they moved in and out of shadow.

Alongside a private garden, the trees were conifers, their scent heady in the day's heat. Irene wondered briefly if it could be intoxicating, but suspected the man beside her was responsible for her accelerating pulse and the sudden unevenness of her breathing.

Back at the house, he suggested a cold drink and stood, leaning against the kitchen door frame while she found tall glasses. Irene grew acutely conscious of the silent, empty house, and of the masculinity of this man whom she loved so unreservedly.

'Do you want this in the garden or indoors?' she inquired, and noticed how her own voice betrayed her edginess.

'Anywhere. Doesn't matter.'

Richard, too, sounded tense. She compelled her gaze to keep away from him. It wouldn't take much to make her reveal what she was feeling. And she had sensed all along that giving way to their emotions could well make him believe they'd ruined their relationship.

'You look nice in that,' he remarked evenly, when they were in the sitting room, their armchairs either side of the open french windows.

Irene reached out and switched on the radio, saw Richard smile to himself, and was certain he'd guessed she needed a distraction.

He rested his head against the back of the chair, stretched out his long legs, appearing to relax. Yet she *knew* he was as taut as she was.

It wasn't until she was in the kitchen again, rinsing out the glasses, that he came to her. Less than a pace behind her, he spoke: 'Irene . . . '

She turned and his arms came around her. His mouth, hard and relentless, anchored on to hers. Irene clung to him, returning kiss for kiss, every nerve alive with need. The blood seemed to simmer in her veins, urging her to respond to the body pressing at her own, diminishing the power to move away.

Richard sighed abruptly, lowered his arms, stepped back from her. He swung on his heel, but as he reached the door Irene gathered her flailing wits and stopped him.

'You don't have to distance yourself, I don't need more than a hint. And besides we have so much, haven't we, without . . .' Determinedly, she swallowed. 'I've enjoyed today such a lot – our swim, walking home. There's a great deal of tranquillity, isn't there, just – well, generated by the countryside.'

Richard nodded, spoke with considerable effort. 'As Thoreau discovered. You've read him, of course?'

When she shook her head, he smiled. 'Then you shall. Come on – I'll find my copy of *Walden* while I have it in mind.'

The silence was there again, in his room, while they stood together before the bookshelves. The attraction had increased if anything, hauling her towards him.

'Here . . .' He handed her a thin volume, worn from frequent rereading.

'Thank you.' Glancing at it, Irene recognized that he was sharing with her an important influence in his life. 'You're very kind to me,' she began, and wished she could concentrate and say more.

'Kind!' Rich interrupted. 'God, how can I ever do enough? You're everything to me!'

He pulled her to him again, sharply, hugging her close while his lips savaged her own. She sensed him looking to the bed behind her; she loved him so much, how could she even contemplate protesting?

She lay there, imprisoned gladly, his kisses and his stirring body growing increasingly demanding.

His sigh was almost a moan. 'Oh, my love.' He slid a hand beneath her, drawing her even nearer. And then abruptly he moved right away, stepped back from the bed. 'That would spoil it all.'

'Are you sure?'

'Irene, for heaven's sake!'

She rose and walked slowly out of the room, so shaken by their passion that her legs were quaking. In the hall he caught her by the arm, forced her to face him. 'Wouldn't it?'

When she could not answer, Richard persisted. 'We don't have to live out our lives on the common denominator of sex.'

No, she thought, you're the person who thinks he's so immaculately self-disciplined! And always right to be so. *Was* he right? As she herself had said, they still shared a lot that was worth while. But what about *love*? It wasn't only sex that he intended denying.

On the following Wednesday, when Rich suggested driving out towards Skipton and stopping for a drink somewhere, Irene began to feel they might have found a workable way of life. They were both tired and, at present, she'd enjoy nothing more than a quiet evening with him.

The wayside pub was busy, they sat outdoors, listening to a nearby brook as it rushed over a tiny weir. The evening was cooling, though the air was still, and they sat on there, watching the sky darkening until, swathed in a fine mist, the summit of the fells disappeared.

It seemed for a while that her own ferment cooled, and vanished with them, and they drove back in a peace that was at one with the still countryside. Irene felt perfectly in tune with Richard, even though he'd apologized with a grin for not being exactly garrulous.

The surrounding darkness cocooned them, isolating them in the car from everything except each other. By the time they reached North Fell House Irene had become aware of his steady breathing beside her, every slight movement he made, the scent of him which combined the soap he always used with the freshness from sitting outdoors.

As Richard unlocked the front door, Daphne turned at the foot of the staircase. 'Had a good evening?' she asked.

'Fine, thanks,' he replied. 'How about joining us for a nightcap? Irene deserves one for being so abstemious because of driving.'

Daphne went through and drew the sitting room curtains across, turned on the standard lamp. The glow through its parchment shade was soft, leaving the room corners shadowy, creating a calm atmosphere.

'You both look contented,' she remarked as her brother went to pour drinks. 'Is the practice still growing?'

Richard groaned, but he was grinning. 'We went out with the idea of forgetting work!'

But Irene realized that Daphne rarely was included in conversations about their job. 'He's really built it up again tremendously well.'

'I'm very glad, you know,' said Daphne.

'I know.' Rich smiled down at her as he handed over her glass.

'Being able to work at something worth while matters a lot,' Daphne added and, briefly, her green eyes shadowed. But she smiled again. 'The way Rich has re-established himself is a tonic for anyone.'

Irene wanted to tell Daphne she hoped she would find more satisfying work, but she hesitated. Daphne always seemed so self-contained. Suddenly, though, she was revealing her feelings.

'I just wish I knew what I really wanted to do. There has to be more than the job I'm in at present. I've thought and thought, but it doesn't seem to be something I can generate myself.'

Not long afterwards she said she'd go up to bed. Impulsively, Irene rose and walked with her to the hall, squeezed her shoulders as they said good night. 'Happen you'll find something before long.'

Richard was behind her in the room, he pulled her to him, his lips claimed hers. She sensed the control in him, longed to make it snap, yearned to end this half-loving, this denial of feeling, this emptiness. They could be so happy here. She slid a hand to the back of his head, kissing him, trying to make him let go of all this tension. Running the tip of her tongue over his lips, she parted them.

Richard's arms tightened, his breathing quickened. His mouth began searching, exploring her face, her throat, the softness beneath the low neckline of her dress. Then almost roughly he pushed her away, said hastily: 'We'd better call it a day.'

'That's what you want, isn't it, to shrug me off as if I don't really exist? Because there might be a few problems.'

'This certainly makes an already difficult life even harder.'

He couldn't have hurt her more deeply if the observation had been calculated for that purpose. But what she really couldn't take was feeling that he didn't want or need her. 'Oh, why do I bother! If you cared anything for me, you couldn't just send me to my room.'

'If I didn't, I'd have had you months ago.'

He turned, and strode swiftly across the hall to his bedroom. There, he leaned against the door. God, if only he *did* care less, if only he weren't perpetually tortured by this prospect of making her his, and then as a consequence burdening her with his uncertainties.

'There's one thing is certain, Lily, I'm not going to let anyone at Dewhurst's provoke me again, not before we get a proper home.'

It was weeks since Norman had talked with his boss, but though he hated having young Batley go to Switzerland, he'd live with that. He was managing with fewer tablets, refusing to give in to agitation. Even though there was plenty to make him dissatisfied. Ironically, it wasn't their meagre first home that caused Norman the most disappointment, though conditions there might have been part of the problem. The real trouble was that he still hadn't made love to his wife.

Lily, bless her, couldn't have been more patient about it, just as she was patient about his job. As they arrived at the Nissen hut this evening, she only slid her arm out of his to find her key and unfasten the door. Then she drew him to her as she shut it behind them.

'We're home, Norman love, and you've given me such a happy place here, even if it isn't much to look at. Nobody'll spoil it for us.'

He'd never experienced so much affection, nor had he known anyone who had so little regard for material things. Lily was a marvellous homemaker, transformed this miserable hut with her sweeping and dusting, her good meals, her bright presence. And she hadn't yet begun to talk about the furniture they really needed, or anything else that some women would have harped on about. He'd like to give her a treat. 'We could afford a Utility sideboard,' he told her, smiling. 'How about going into town to pick one on Sat'day afternoon?'

'That'd be nice. If you're sure we shan't be scun up, at after.'

'I've said we can afford. Just be glad newlyweds are allowed to buy furniture, you needn't be worrying your head about money.'

'I'm not,' said Lily, and grinned. 'The day I wed you, I stopped worrying about owt. So long as you're all right.'

But was he? Norman wondered for the hundredth time. There must be summat up when he'd not taken her yet. And he was getting scared now, afraid Lily wouldn't go on being content with kisses and cuddles.

'I'd better get on with our tea,' she said, gave him a final hug and headed towards the cooker. She still called their evening meal tea, although she always provided something hot.

'I'll lay the table for you in a minute,' Norman promised. He couldn't do enough to help, he was that thankful for the agreeable life Lily was creating here. If only that were sufficient . . .

While they were eating their sausages and mash, Norman was making a determined effort to forget the bother at work. With them both being employed at Dewhurst's Lily was all too conscious of it when they were there.

'How about going dancing at the weekend?' he suggested. 'We haven't been since we were married.' And happen it might resurrect the situation where he'd been desperate to do more than hold her tightly against the hardness of his body.

'I'd like that,' she responded quickly. But Norman didn't miss the slight reservation in her voice.

'Aye, we can afford that an' all,' he answered her unspoken question. 'We might as well enjoy the brass, if there's no pleasure earning it any more!'

The argument began after they'd finished the cup of tea which followed their jam roly-poly. And it was all over summat and nowt, just because he wanted to give a hand again as she did the washing up.

He couldn't help pointing out that she had no method. He watched her every time, siding the pots from the table and scattering them all over the wooden draining board, with no pretence at stacking them.

'I've told you before,' Lily said, 'I get it done, that's all that matters. When you've been brought up wi' that many dirty pots round you that you can't put a pin down, you get used to just plodding through 'em.'

'But there's nowhere to put the clean ones, like this, love.'

'Go and sit yourself down, I'm managing.'

Lily had filled the washing-up bowl from the kettle, and was working up a lather with the dishcloth and her tablet of Fairy soap when she noticed that she hadn't emptied the teapot. Looking about for somewhere to place the bowl while she got rid of the tea leaves, she rested it to one side overhanging the sink.

'Look what you're doing,' said Norman, but too late. The bowl toppled sideways into the sink, drenching the front of Lily's dress.

She burst out laughing as water began dripping from her saturated clothes on to her feet and the floor.

'You'd better get that frock off, it'll soak through to your skin,' he exclaimed.

Still laughing, Lily shook her head. 'Too late, any road, it has done!'

''Ere – leave me to see to that while you go and get changed,' Norman insisted, pushing her away from the sink.

Chuckling to herself, his wife hurried towards the bed-room area. Not that she'd any intention of letting him do all the washing-up. She'd just slip on some fresh under-wear and find another frock. There was one she'd taken off yesterday and put to one side ready for her washday, it would do till bedtime.

Norman had been meticulously stacking all the dishes in piles, every item graded according to size; and that was as far as he'd got when Lily returned.

He glanced in her direction, and felt a stab of pity. The amusement had evaporated, leaving her thin face serious, and shadows beneath her eyes revealed how the day standing at her looms always tired her. The frock was a washed-out cotton, not yet replaced because clothing coupons were scarce. Creased with being bundled up, it looked pathetic.

'Come here, love.' He wiped his hands on the tea towel, and outstretched his arms for her.

'I'm sorry,' he murmured, holding her to him. 'I'm always criticizing the way you wash up. And it's the only thing you don't do perfectly.'

'It's all right,' she said. 'It doesn't bother me.'

'But you cope so well, with the rationing, with this place . . .'

Suddenly overwhelmed with love, Norman held her even more tightly, kissing her mouth, feeling it yield. Concern for her welled up inside him, and with it the surge of desire that had been too long absent.

'Lily,' he gasped, pressing at her, his hands sliding down the back of her old cotton dress then anchoring her more closely to him.

She was kissing him back, exciting him as she had before they were married, increasing the urgency that was flaring anew. When he stirred, she echoed the movement, and he felt her slender fingers on his spine locking him to her. When they drew apart it was only to hasten, eyes blurred with passion, towards the bed.

He discarded his trousers hurriedly, anxious in case his need might wane. Then they were together, hugging and caressing as they had in the past, but with this fresh exhilaration. And now when he came close he could feel her responding again. After the first brief moment of tension he was aware of nothing except his own massive desire and her eagerness. As soon as he began pressing at her, he felt Lily drawing him into her until

242

they were fused. Never again would he dread what the future held, never be alone to face what life might do to him.

14

Mavis was as bright as her ice-blue rayon frock, sparkling with the thrill of it all. They were in their own house, at last, this party was to celebrate installing all their belongings. And now Ralph's mum and dad had gone home she could really enjoy herself.

'You are staying a bit longer, aren't you?' she insisted to her own parents, checking that Ralph was out of earshot. She wouldn't upset him for anything, especially when he'd given her such a lovely home. But she had taken care to choose a Friday evening, aware by now that her father-in-law liked an early night when it was work next morning.

Donald Hainsworth grinned. 'You'll have me late for surgery tomorrow!'

'Not if I know you,' Mavis protested. 'You've always been a bit of an owl, haven't you?'

'Wise, you mean?' he teased.

His daughter laughed. 'Nay, Dad – you'll not get me to admit to that! Though you are a love – both you and Mum are.' Her parents had been extremely generous, offering them all the bed linen they could spare and other items, mostly furniture.

'That three-piece looks grand in here,' Elsie exclaimed. 'A lot better than that Utility stuff that's all you can get nowadays.' Seeing it in Mavis's front room more than compensated for the barren appearance of their own sitting room now. And they hardly ever went in there, any road, not with no family at home.

'You're both welcome to come and use it here, you know,' Ralph assured them smoothly, arriving at his mother-in-law's side.

'So long as you ring us up first, just to make sure there's somebody in,' Mavis added swiftly. She was going to like having a telephone, even though it had been paid for by Ralph's father who'd insisted he must be able to contact his son at home.

Mr and Mrs Parkin had also provided them with all their curtains and a larder full of tinned food and groceries. And no mention of any rationing or coupons. Mavis was afraid that they'd all been acquired on the black market, but what could she do about that? They meant well by it, and the curtains looked beautiful. She was just glad that it was *his* parents that might be up to something not quite above board.

Ralph was smiling at her now. 'I think we've set your Norman and Lily off,' he remarked. 'When I joined them just now I couldn't help hearing him talking of going to see the council about a house.'

'He's been already, several times,' Elsie asserted quickly. 'I gather that they're well up on the list by now.' Her reluctance to have her son occupying a council house was evaporating before Ralph's insinuation that Norman needed prompting to try and obtain a home.

'Aye, that's right,' Donald confirmed. 'There's a campaign on locally to get all squatters into better accommodation.'

'I should think so, as well.' Ralph was glad for Norman's sake.

Donald stared hard at him over the pipe he was lighting, shook the match till it was extinguished and tossed it into the fire. 'Norman did what he could at the time. It's given them a start, and they're no worse for the bit of hardship.' He'd never liked Ralph knowing Norman's first home upset him, he'd not have his son criticized now.

But Ralph was in no mood for distressing anyone. He'd have been better pleased if he'd been able to provide their own home and everything in it with no help from anyone. But though it was over two years since the end of the war, shortages still continued. And at least he and Mavis were on their own again, to look after Heather in their way. He wouldn't like to have to relive the past few weeks. His mother only did what she could for the best, but he'd never seen Mavis bristle so often and so much, because nothing she did ever seemed to be right. By contrast, his in-laws appeared a tolerant couple, more easy-going than he'd first supposed.

Both he and Mavis were quite sorry to see them leave that night, but Dr and Mrs Hainsworth were driving Norman and Lily out to the camp before heading towards Parkinson Lane.

'I wish our Irene had been here,' Mavis confessed, after their visitors had departed, and she and Ralph were going upstairs to look in on Heather.

'She said she was too busy to take the afternoon off to get here, didn't she?'

'Aye – if you ask me, she's doing far too much, it seems to be nowt but work for her, these days.'

Quietly, she opened the door of their daughter's bedroom, smiled down at the sleeping child whose curly head gleamed in the light flowing through from the landing.

'Look how well she's settled.'

Ralph nodded. 'Despite all the noise from downstairs. She's a good kiddy, darling.'

'I know. Most of the time. I certainly didn't think she'd take to having a room on her own this easily, and without a night-light.'

'Wonder if Norman and Lily will start a family, once they get a proper home.'

'I bet they'll have lots of kids, look how many her mother's had.' But as they went to their own room Mavis's thoughts returned to her sister. Sometimes, over the years, she and Irene had seemed close, at others they'd appeared to have nowt in common; yet she was troubled now by sensing persistently that Irene was anything but happy.

It was the little reminders that caught her unawares, rubbing in the unsatisfactory state of her own life. No matter how resolute Irene remained, she couldn't dispel her yearning for married life, with Richard.

She had been a coward over the housewarming, even though her brother-in-law had made a point of telephoning her at North Fell to try and talk her round. She'd liked Ralph more than ever in the past for his intervention.

'Mavis is pretending she's not concerned because you won't be with us, but I know differently. And I shall be sorry if you don't join us, we want to share our pleasure with the whole family.'

Their pleasure. That was just the trouble. She knew Ralph and Mavis, could picture how their delight in Heather would now be extended to encompass their home. Jealousy was an ugly emotion, she wasn't proud of its presence, but it was anguishing. When all she wanted was to belong in *her* own home, with Richard.

She had made him her excuse, emphasizing how busy they were in the office, which was true, and how he shouldn't have to bear additional work. 'I can't expect him to cover for me, not even for one afternoon.' But she had known in her heart that Rich would have been appalled to hear her. And the fact that his attitude was making her too disturbed to accept the invitation was no justification for her dissembling.

Richard seemed able to behave as though they had never shared any really close friendship, much less anything deeper. In the main, his conversation outside of the office was centred on national or international issues. This week his subject was the government's decision to suspend nationalization plans due to the economic crisis. Much as she appreciated that Britain's present situation was grave, her personal crisis prevented her feeling involved.

The news items *she* couldn't help noticing were connected with next month's wedding of Princess Elizabeth. Both press and radio seemed to report every detail, even how the Princess's trousseau was being curtailed in the interest of economy. Agreed, the royal engagement alleviated the general depression induced by cuts in already meagre rations, and exports that failed to equal our imports. But it felt as if everything was geared to reminding her how important marriage was. Sometimes, she longed to escape her own heart-rending trap.

It wasn't solely that she longed to get wed. If nothing else, the affair with John had shown her that she could be sufficiently unconventional to demonstrate her commitment without the benefit of the accepted legalities. Maybe half the trouble was that Richard also knew this – and seemed incapable of understanding that her love for *him* was far more overwhelming than anything she'd experienced previously. He knew also, as well as she did, that if they were to live together without marrying, his practice would suffer.

Irene wasn't certain she could do that to him. But then she could hardly think straight; her emotions were raw, savaged forever by his assertion that she was making a difficult life even harder. She couldn't believe any longer that anything he might say or do would eradicate those words. If she'd known where she wanted to go, or what to do with her life, she could have been out of here on the very next morning. But Richard, blast him, had given her a job that felt worth while, one that had almost compensated for losing her career.

Ahead of her loomed Christmas, another hurdle, a trial to endure. She suspected already that she wouldn't be spending it at North Fell House, wished with all her heart that there was somewhere where she might avoid some of the pain.

Norman was taking a few hours off work on the quiet, an arrangement which hadn't been easy, with his wife employed in the same weaving shed. He'd made the excuse that he had to have a check-up concerning the medication he was still receiving for thyroid trouble. He'd felt awful about the white lie, especially when Lily had got all upset, thinking he was worse again. He'd reassured her, indicating that they might be reducing his tablets. And it was all far better than building up her hopes only to have them deflated.

He'd heard the other night about the prefabs the council were offering. He'd been in the toilet block on the camp while a couple of the chaps were talking. There'd been prefabricated houses available round Halifax previously, ever since the factories once turning out aircraft had gone over to producing them. These were the first he'd got wind of before they all were allocated.

'How many did you hear they've got?' he'd asked, trying not to get excited too soon.

'They reckon about a dozen, nowhere near enough. Me and Ted, here, is going to get down to the office first thing, long afore they open. It's t'only way we'll stand any sort of a chance.'

And so now here Norman was, shivering in the still-dark November morning, stamping his feet to try and keep a bit of circulation in them, wishing he still had his air-force gloves. They had been past further darning, chucked out after that last atrocious winter. And what with getting married and setting up there'd been no brass to spare for luxuries. Lily had promised to knit him another pair, but there was never enough time, and she was always worn out with standing all day at her looms.

If only he could get this little house, she'd not seem nearly so tired. He knew his Lily, she'd be that enthusiastic it'd put new life into her. He'd not be sorry either to get out of that Nissen hut. Even these days, he still often felt as if he were still in the RAF. He might have overcome the inhibitions that had caused, wreaking havoc with his sex life, but there were occasions now when he wakened wondering if that was a plane landing, if his pals had made it back from across the Channel.

There were less than a dozen folk in front of him in the queue. He kept counting, assuring himself that waiting here long before daylight might prove worth while. But there was no knowing how them in charge worked out priorities. There'd be others that had kiddies – them two from the camp, for instance. And what if some had parents depending on them for a home, an' all . . . ?

Torturing himself was no good, he kept asserting silently. He could only wait and see, and wish he was better at doing nowt. And wish an' all that it was a coat warmer!

He'd been glad the morning was dry, but it wasn't half parky.

Norman had yearned for the minute when they'd unlock the doors. When it came, he felt the familiar surge of agitation that had recurred so frequently ever since he'd bailed out over France. Happen he ought to have been seeing somebody about his treatment . . . but happen today he'd have the sort of news that'd set him up for good – so's he'd never need to worry about owt again.

The men in front of him had been talking among themselves, making him feel as if he was one on his own, there without a pal. The two from the camp were just a bit ahead of him, they'd nodded to him but were too far away for a chat. Now everybody fell silent; some awed by the officials responsible for their future, all conscious of the significance of the decisions that would be made.

The chap behind the desk had a voice that carried and, despite his smile, a manner that asserted he was in full command. Norman had known superior officers very like him, and had felt less uneasy in their presence. This fellow seemed to speak evenly enough, yet was very firm in refusing the first two that asked to be considered. Norman's heart sank, as he wondered if he had a hope of being given a home. But then the next three or four came away grinning from their conversations, carried forms for completion over to a table ready with pens and a bottle of Stephens' blue-black ink. The next chap walked away forlornly, pulling his greasy cloth cap down over his head, looking down at the shabby lace-up boots trudging towards the door.

The two men Norman knew were lucky, both giving him the thumbs up as they went to fill in their forms – and filling him with envy. He'd never ask for another thing from life, if only he could get Lily one of these houses.

His turn came, and he stood before the desk, willing himself not to ruin his chances by saying too much. Not that he needed to say more than who he was, anyhow – they already had the list of applicants for housing. Would be fully aware of who was entitled. And who was not.

'This is your lucky day, Mr Hainsworth. We only had seven houses available, you're the seventh.'

'By gum, is that all? I were told there were a dozen going.'

'Told? Not by us, I'm sure,' the man said evenly, but his voice was nearly lost in the exclamation just behind Norman.

'Oh, God – no! *Not again!*'

Norman looked round. The chap was appallingly thin; if anybody opened a window he'd keel over in the draught. He looked as if he'd been in Belsen, or a prisoner of the Japanese. Worst of all, though, his pale eyes had filled; tears he was too weak to contain began coursing down lined cheeks. Norman turned back to the desk.

'Are you certain this is t'only house you've got left? I really did hear there were more . . .'

'Rumours circulate, I know.' The comment was smooth, icily final.

He swallowed. 'Then you'd best let yon chap behind me have it. I reckon I can hang on a bit longer.'

'Are you sure?' The clerk was astounded. Everybody who came here was desperate for somewhere to live.

'Aye – go on.' He felt a thin hand reach out from behind him and grasp his shoulder. The poor fellow was too overcome to murmur more than an unsteady 'Thank you'.

Suddenly, all Norman wanted was to get away. But the chap in charge detained him, managed a slight smile. 'If you have a number where we could ring you, perhaps? Somebody might give backword.'

He'd believe that could happen the day he saw pigs soaring over this town hall! Still, he had to try and make up for what he'd done. He gave the works number, and his father's just in case old Dewhurst turned funny about him taking private calls.

Norman felt sick as he slowly walked away along Princess Street towards the town centre. This had been a right revelation. It mightn't have been so bad if he hadn't been led to suppose that more prefabs were available. It was that pathetic, having to stand in line all this time,

251

and for nowt. He could only be glad that he was strong enough to hold on to a bit of dignity. How on earth he'd steel himself to go through all that again, he didn't know. It was like being forced to beg for somewhere decent to live.

He was too het up to get on a bus and go straight to the mill. And, besides, having made Lily think he had to see the consultant about his tablets, he'd have to keep away long enough for that to seem convincing. Increasing his pace, he strode through Corn Market, then along Southgate next, scarcely thinking at all now, waiting for his feelings to settle down.

He was striding out even more quickly by the time he reached Skircoat Road. The day was still cold, despite the sun gleaming thinly through the mill smoke, but he was beginning to take some pleasure in his surroundings. There were lots of lovely houses on here, far bigger than he'd ever aspire to but grand to look at, and there were more still as he turned up Free School Lane. When he reached Savile Park – The Moor to local people – he was feeling a lot better, and even smiled to himself.

Henry Savile, who had offered this green open space to the town council for a nominal sum of £100, would have approved. He'd wanted folk to have somewhere for recreation, and had been keen to reduce the effect that smoke was having on the inhabitants of Halifax. Today, Norman strode on across the stretch of grass, and then past several houses that looked to him like mansions, towards Albert Promenade.

He'd hardly been here at all since the beginning of the war, yet this had always been his favourite spot, where he got recharged. He paused now, with huge rocks set below him and extending down into the woods. Ever since he was a little lad he'd felt this was truly a promenade. And better than the sea, for him, was the broad view of steep, wooded hillsides, the valley with canal, River Calder, roads and railway. Sowerby Bridge lay in the distance to his right and beyond that further slopes and the moors. This was *his* Yorkshire; with reminders of its vital industry, but

252

the freedom as well to walk these hills and breathe good country air.

And somehow the expanse of the vista, and maybe even the height of the nearby folly, Wainhouse Tower, widened his eyes so that he no longer felt depressed about not having that house. They were young enough, weren't they, both him and Lily. There'd be other chances, and next time he knew what to expect. Thank goodness he'd had the wit not to raise her hopes for nothing. And now he'd better be thinking up answers to her questions about where she'd thought he was going.

Two days later when Jack Dewhurst's secretary came seeking him to say he was wanted in the office, Norman felt sickened. His boss must have found out he hadn't been to the hospital, and now he was in trouble. The secretary was such an officious old bag that he would never dream of asking her what was wrong. He'd sooner suffer all the way through the weaving shed to see Jack Dewhurst.

Arriving to find the office empty, Norman glanced towards the woman who was following him in. She gestured towards the telephone. 'It's for you,' she announced, and sniffed disapprovingly.

'Oh, thanks,' he said. 'Sorry you've had the trouble,' he added, hoping she would go away.

He could feel her staring while he said his name into the mouthpiece.

'Ah – Mr Hainsworth. You were here the other morning inquiring about prefabricated houses.'

'Yes . . . ' he began, and was interrupted.

'If you're still interested, one of the prospective tenants has given backword. Seems he wasn't quite truthful about his situation – he isn't married yet, and his young lady has big ideas about the kind of home she expects. Provided you agree, we'll hold this for you until you can call in to sign . . . '

'Agree?' Course I'll agree. Oh, thank you, thank you! I'll come in my dinner hour. That's so long as you're open then?'

253

He hadn't intended telling Lily until he had something in writing, but she'd seen him heading towards Dewhurst's office.

'Whatever's wrong?' she mouthed, over the racket made by the looms. Norman looked ever so flushed, and his eyes were glittering. She couldn't understand.

'Nothing's wrong,' she lip-read back. 'We've got a pre-fab, I've got to go and sign for it this dinnertime.'

'Ay, love, I am pleased!' She could have hugged him in front of the rest of the weavers, and the other overlookers. Instead, she had to be content with coming round her loom and giving his arm a squeeze. 'I'm that proud of you!' she shouted into his ear. 'And you didn't even let on that we might be getting one.'

For the rest of that day Lily sang as she worked, uncaring that her voice was completely drowned in the rattle of machinery. When Norman came back grinning after dashing into town at midday she felt as if she'd burst with having to wait till stopping time to hear all about it.

She was hanging around near the mill gates when Norman crossed the yard in a run.

'Where is it then, have they told you?'

'Out Illingworth way somewhere, it'll still be a fair distance to come to work . . .'

'That doesn't matter,' Lily cut in. Even if she'd had to walk both ways, nothing would have put her off having a proper home of their own. 'When can we go and see it?'

'Saturday afternoon, we shall have got the key by then.'

'Can't we go before – just to have a look?' She couldn't bear not seeing it until the end of the week.

'Nay, love – what's the point? It's pitch dark now, isn't it, wrong time of year for going to see anywhere of an evening.'

They went, nevertheless, even before having their meal. As Norman had supposed, the prefabs weren't all that far from the camp where they'd been squatting. There were twelve houses, arranged in two rows of six, facing each other across minute plots awaiting cultivation.

'Ay, they've got gardens, an' all!' exclaimed Lily, completely overwhelmed. 'Which one's ours?'

'That, I can't tell you, love. Looks like they haven't got numbers on them yet.'

They would have difficulty reading any numbers, anyway, the only illumination came from one gas lamp situated where their path led off from the lane where the bus stopped.

The rest of that week seemed to Lily to drag, even though the new looms from Switzerland were beginning to arrive, and Norman and the other overlookers became extremely busy. He and Desmond Batley were to unpack the new machines and install them in the area already prepared, while the rest of the men kept the original looms running.

'It's all happening at once, isn't it?' she said excitedly one night as they lay in bed listening to rain rattling on the iron of the Nissen hut.

'Aye, I just hope I can get out of working Saturday afternoon. Bert Kettlewell's been asking for volunteers.'

'But you'll not volunteer, will you – not when we've got to go to the house?'

'No, love, I don't suppose I will.' But he could have done without so much on his plate. Ever since Batley had come back from Switzerland he'd been clevering it over the rest of them. Norman didn't want to be pushed out. And then there was the money. Having lost that few hours the other day, he could have used the overtime.

When Saturday came, however, and he took Lily to the house that was to be theirs, he forgot everything except her delight. The minute he opened the door and she began to look around, she gasped in ecstasy.

'Just look at that kitchen – I've never seen owt so modern and compact.'

Norman smiled. Compact it certainly was, with all the units built around a tiny bit of floor space. The bathroom was minute as well, very different from his parents' with its big Victorian bath and elaborate washbasin and lavatory. But this was *theirs*, and none of the rooms would take much keeping warm in winter.

Lily soon began measuring up for curtains, planning where they would put each piece of furniture. 'Now we will enjoy saving up for other stuff that we need, it'll all be so worth while.'

They were able to move in the following weekend. As soon as they had arranged their bits of furniture and unpacked their belongings, they took it in turns to have a bath. They agreed afterwards, sitting over cups of cocoa, that they'd never relished a bath so much.

'We must have your mum and dad for tea next Sunday,' Lily announced. 'Mine can come the week after.' She would have to keep a sharp eye on the young ones, though, she wasn't going to have them messing about in here.

What Lily really fancied was having somebody to stay. She'd love to show them what a lovely life they were going to have here. 'Do you think your Irene would like to come for Christmas?' she asked Norman eventually.

'What for?'

Lily laughed. 'It'd be a change for her.'

'It would an' all!' From what he'd gathered about the house where she was living, it must be every bit as huge as any around Savile Park. And out in the country, as well. 'You can ask her, I suppose. But don't be disappointed if she says no.'

Lily's invitation startled her out of the rut of dejection into which she was withdrawing. The very surprise acted as a tonic. And it did give her a reason for getting away from North Fell. Ever since Richard had grown so intransigent about curbing their relationship, Irene had felt she was existing in limbo. So far as she knew, she still did her work as efficiently, and she certainly still ensured that Richard's health was safeguarded while he increased his workload. But there it ended, there was no pleasure any longer. There was no easing either of her love which was permitted no expression.

When Christmas came Irene was glad to be able to say that she was going to stay with her brother and his wife.

For the first time since meeting Richard, she had no reservations about leaving him where he was.

Lily had put a lot of effort into festive preparations. She had managed to buy some paper on the cheap, and had borrowed poster paints from her youngest sister. She had covered the table with a protective layer of newspaper, then sat there all one Saturday morning making coloured paper chains. Norman hadn't said anything when he walked in after working over.

Irene, however, exclaimed as soon as she came through the door. 'My, but haven't you got this looking bright!' She felt a lump rising in her throat, as she realized the decorations were homemade.

Lily grinned, and hugged her all the more enthusiastically. 'Give us your coat, then I'll show you round.'

The tour of the prefab was completed in less than five minutes, and left Irene scarcely able to swallow. There was so much love evident in the touches Lily had already added to their stark little home. The living room had an enormous bunch of everlasting flowers in a vase which she recognized as coming from Woolworths. The cheap dressing-table top was scarcely visible through its generous scattering of crocheted mats, and a strong smell of polish from the bathroom drew attention to the high gloss of the toilet seat. There were containers of potpourri in every room, and each chair had a cushion which, from the undisguised fading of the cloth, had been made out of something else. All the windows were hung with curtains made from blast-netting which had been soaked to remove the stiffening.

'You've soon made this into a real home, Lily.'

Her sister-in-law smiled. 'Well, I've been dying for a place like this for that long – don't seem able to stop myself doing more to it.'

They talked in the kitchen while Lily made a pot of tea. Evidently, Norman was working over. Installing the Swiss looms was taking longer than anyone had expected. But he'd put his mind to cooperating, she was proud of how hard he was working – for their future.

'In some ways, I'm not sorry I've been so busy with our house. I haven't had time to worry what it'll be like changing on to different looms, and I've been told I'm one of them that's going on 'em.'

'When will that be then?'

'Straight after Christmas, that's why Norman and the other overlookers are working on 'em now.'

'And what does he think about your home, now you're getting it organized?'

'He likes it, of course, not that he says much. I think it's the bathroom we both appreciate most. Silly really, when you think how little time you spend in there.'

When Norman finally arrived home and the holiday began, Irene was determined to give herself entirely to being with her family. Certainly, staying with Lily and Norman was more acceptable than with anyone else: they were both so besotted with their little house that they were fully occupied without inquiring into her relationships. And when they all had Christmas dinner at their old home in Parkinson Lane and spent Boxing Day with Mavis and Ralph, no one seemed to notice if Irene was rather quiet.

The trouble was within herself. She *hadn't* left Richard at North Fell House; no matter where she was, she couldn't dismiss him. Even the disparity between her brother's prefab and Richard's home seemed only to emphasize that she was a part of two worlds, yet unable to detach herself from his. While the family were all together, and young Heather was demanding attention, the rest of them were alternately laughing with her or disapproving of her overexcitement. Irene felt raw, hardly able to join in; would she never shrug off being oppressed by this longing for a child of her own?

The years were passing swiftly, soon three would have gone by since she'd left London. She didn't need to be a doctor to understand that at thirty-five she didn't have that many to spare if she wished to have a family. Would she eventually reconcile herself to having that desire unfulfilled? Or would she finally acknowledge that her job wasn't sufficient, and she'd have to get away from the man who ensured that she excluded all thought of other potential partners?

The day she returned to North Fell the air was crisp, but the winter sun was brilliant. All the way from Halifax to Skipton in the bus, Irene relished the scenery. Even the towns themselves were brighter; with Christmas Day on the Thursday, several mill owners had decided against working on the Saturday morning. And so there was, in the main, just the smoke from domestic fires drifting about the grey slate roofs. By the time she reached Skipton, she was feeling elated. Although there was quite a wait for her next bus, she didn't care.

Walking briskly, she hastened along the street which always looked rather bare when there was no market. And then she stood for several minutes before the castle, admiring the stout gatehouse and its flanking drum towers. She would love to have a good look round the inside, was it open to visitors? Maybe in the summer she and Richard could come and wander around here.

15

Before they were halfway through 1948 Irene was finally
becoming convinced that there would be no further outings with Richard, there was no real communication
between them any longer. If it wasn't work he was discussing, he still seemed interested in nothing but national
or international problems. Not that there was any shortage
of those.

All this trouble made Irene increasingly restless, would
there always be nothing but fratching? The assassination of
Gandhi was creating more contention between the Hindus
and Muslims whom he had struggled to unite. Communists
took over in Czechoslovakia; then relations between the
Allied powers were threatened when the Soviet delegation
walked out of talks on Berlin. The Arab quarter in Haifa
was attacked by Jews, and clashes continued in Palestine as
the date in May approached when British troops were
scheduled to withdraw.

The Second World War was long since over, yet she felt
as if there was little true peace anywhere. Now that they
themselves seemed to do nothing but argue about items
from the wireless or in the papers, these wider problems
were intensifying her need for a drastic alteration.

How ever had she once thought she was well attuned
with Richard? He was beginning to sound as if nobody
else could ever be right. 'I heartily disapprove!' he'd
announced as soon as the railways were nationalized at the
beginning of the new year. When lots of doctors threatened
to boycott the proposed National Health Service, he was
quick to support them. 'I should think so! The scheme's
got to be stopped before they become no more than paid
servants of bureaucracy.'

Irene hadn't cared what he thought about railways, but on this she couldn't agree, she had seen too many families, both in London and in her father's area, who were too poor to obtain the care they needed. Anything that gave everyone access to necessary medicines and operations was bound to be an improvement. She only wished that she had the chance of returning to her old career, she'd soon show how effectively the new Health Service could work.

'Personally, I can't wait to see it happen. There's too many folk are unequal with regard to wages, housing, their whole standard of living. I'm just glad that looking after their physical wellbeing is one way in which they'll be treated like everybody else.' She refrained from adding that he shouldn't talk – he was in a position to obtain whatever attention he'd ever needed.

Richard didn't say any more, but he looked surprised that her opinions were so strong, and that she was expressing them. That was when it struck her that she'd spent ages being made miserable by his ideas – as though, even to herself, her own were less important, and even when they concerned their relationship. Worst of all, she still suspected he wasn't being honest about his real feelings for her, that they *hadn't* diminished, but were being suppressed. She couldn't forget that he'd said she was making a difficult life even harder. But what did he believe he was doing now? He was certainly creating an intolerable situation. And she was beginning to realize that she would have to be the one who hardened herself to make changes.

The day the news broke of the first operations on human hearts, Irene knew she couldn't just continue marking time here. It was 10th June, and she had spent the previous weekend with her parents.

Her mother had been uncharacteristically depressed, made uneasy by her husband's health. 'Your dad's that short-tempered, Irene, I can't do owt right for him. And it's all because he's doing too much. Lord knows what's going to happen when that new scheme comes in. He says there's loads more paperwork.'

And that was something she could do. Even in an unofficial capacity, she could assist her father by filling in forms, maybe helping to set up a new system of patient records. It wouldn't be what she really wanted, but it was no use eating her heart out because she couldn't practise again. She would be in touch with medicine – and at this exciting time when research, and even experiments in the treatment of casualties from the last war, were accelerating progress.

Although her decision had really been forming over many months, Irene felt physically ill about leaving Richard. And on the evening when she'd steeled herself to tell him, she was compelled to wait because he and David were attending a meeting.

Far too disturbed to sit chatting with his sister, she went up to her room as soon as they'd eaten dinner. Slowly, she wandered around, running her hands affectionately over the familiar furniture, knowing this was close to being the last time. She drew the curtains across, she couldn't bear to look at her beloved view. The summer sun glowing over the fells contrasted starkly with her desolation. And finding some purpose in her life again felt as daunting as they could appear.

Around eleven o'clock, Irene heard Richard insert his key in the lock, calling good night to David who had driven him home. He smiled, guardedly, when she met him in the hall.

'Thought you'd have gone up ages ago.'

'Was that what you'd hoped?'

He frowned, puzzled. 'No. I merely supposed that after another heavy day you'd be glad of an early night.' That's what he'd have chosen, if that meeting hadn't been imperative. Although it had proved an antidote for all the pressures. After a change of company he felt totally different, able to live with any difficulties.

'Richard, I've got to talk to you.'

An eyebrow raised, he followed her into the sitting room, waited for her to sit. When she didn't do so, he straightened his shoulders, met her steely gaze.

He saw she was taking her time, struggling for words. Thinking to cut the confrontation short, he smiled. 'If it's about the salary increase that's long overdue, I have to admit I've been lax in not showing my appreciation earlier. I am going to make that up to you.'

'It's nothing like that.' She didn't want money from him, she never really had done. 'I – we wanted to be sure the practice was on its feet.' She swallowed. 'And now it is doing well, it's time I considered what I'm going to do with my life.'

Richard anticipated what was coming, and was appalled. Yet he could blame no one but himself, he'd have been a fool to imagine, these days, that she was finding life here congenial. Containing the love he felt was harder than he'd believed. Restraining his emotions was only possible by remaining brutally cold, keeping distance between them, protecting her from the shadow over his future. He had fought, hadn't he, against himself – to avoid making her feel committed.

'My father's not getting any younger,' Irene continued, falling back on well-worn phrases. 'He's already too busy, with this new scheme he'll be so overloaded he'll be heading for a breakdown. I can take on some of the drudgery – paperwork, that kind of thing.'

What could he say, for God's sake? Except the one thing he wouldn't – that he needed her, and not only to work. Eventually, he managed to speak. 'I think that's most likely the wisest course.'

Irene forbade herself to stare incredulously. Was he really able to face the prospect with this cool equanimity? If that was so, she certainly couldn't live here; her heart was being shattered.

'I'll work whatever notice you wish,' she said, equally steadily, willing back tears. 'A month perhaps.'

'No. No, that won't be necessary. I think a clean break, don't you?' he added, unable to contemplate surviving more than a week.

On that last morning Daphne was in the kitchen when Irene went down. Although she had to pause for a moment in the doorway, steadying herself, she was glad Richard's sister was there. Irene felt her green eyes scrutinizing her, heard her sigh.

'You're going ahead with it then – you are leaving?'

'Afraid so, I . . . I'm sorry.'

Daphne shook her head. 'So am I, but I can't entirely blame you.'

Irene gave her a look. How much had Daphne gathered, over all these months, about their relationship, or the absence of one?

'It isn't because you're eager to work with your father, is it?'

Irene didn't reply, but Daphne needed no telling. 'You're in love, aren't you? And he's his usual, old-fashioned self. Unmarried, he wouldn't sleep with you, it's not something we were brought up to do. And he thinks his health precludes taking a wife, responsibility . . .'

'He hasn't said . . . ?' Irene interrupted.

'I've seen for ages what he feels for you, he can't conceal it. He's a fool, Irene – a dear, obstinate fool. I'd so hoped that you'd find some way, work something out.' Swallowing, she shook her head.

After a minute or more Daphne spoke again, concernedly. '*Are* you going to your parents?'

'For a while, yes.'

'Make sure you leave their address with him, please.'

'Oh, no.' She'd got up this early, determined on not seeing Rich. The last day or two had been dreadful. Telling him in the first place had been traumatic enough, but she had steeled herself to do so. She couldn't take any more.

'I'm off now, anyway, Daphne,' she announced hastily after a pause. 'I know you'll take care of him. As much as he'll permit.' And when I can not.

'You must at least have a cup of tea.'

'No, thanks.' One mouthful would choke her.

'Oh, Irene – we owe you so much, this should never have happened. It needn't have.'

'If we were two different people. But we aren't. We have to live with facts.'

264

Daphne glanced towards Irene's suitcase in the hall. 'Have you ordered a taxi?'

'No, I'll be all right on the bus.'

'Let me drive you into Skipton.'

'Thanks for the offer, but there's no need.' She hugged Daphne, turned away as she said goodbye.

She glanced briefly towards Richard's room. There was no sun at all, yet the elegant hall seemed bright. She'd always loved the contrast of pale green walls and dark old furniture. Loved this home.

It was starting to rain, the thin, hill-country drizzle which saturated far more swiftly than ever you expected. Most of the nearby fell was obliterated by dank cloud, and the visible part was dismal with flattened grass, and no sheep in sight.

Irene reached the bus stop and waited alone. She was half glad, the other half longing for someone to talk to, anything to blot out thinking, until the bus arrived.

A vehicle was approaching, slowing for the bend. Sensing it was too light for the bus, she didn't even glance up. The driver sounded his horn to attract her attention. It was Giles Holroyd.

'Going on holiday?' He opened the car door. 'You'd better get in, can't stand around in this stuff.'

Irene couldn't refuse. But Richard's doctor was the last person she wanted to see.

'Surprised Daphne didn't offer to run you into Skipton. I take it that is where you're starting off from?'

'Thanks, yes. She did offer, I just didn't want to bother her.'

She sensed Giles staring curiously at her. He narrowly avoided scraping a parked car.

'Well, you've earned a break. This is the first time you've taken more than the odd day or two off.'

'Yes,' said Irene dully, wishing already that she'd declined the ride. The doctor's remarks seemed probing. If he asked her directly, she wouldn't lie. But she couldn't get through another explanation. Each time she thought about what she was doing the pain of coming away from

Richard intensified. All she wanted was to be left alone, to weep.

They were nearing the town. She couldn't hold on to her composure as far as her bus. 'You can drop me here, if you like,' she said hurriedly.

'You're very edgy, Irene. I thought you and your boss got on very amicably?'

Irene couldn't speak.

'*Is* it a holiday?' Giles persisted.

'Why? Are you going to tell me off for deserting?'

'No. You might not be the one I'd rebuke – if that was what I intended. But I ought to know if my patient is likely to be disturbed.'

'And what do I say to that? That he won't be, because he's not even expecting me to work any notice. He's the one who suggested I clear out now.'

'Doubtless because he's already thought long and hard, and has failed to come up with an acceptable alternative. Pity we lose the impetuosity of the young when we mature.'

Despite her emotions, Irene was forced to smile. 'Are you advocating what I think you are?'

'You're consenting adults, aren't you? Both free, each greatly attached to the other; no one on this earth would blame you for sealing in the accustomed way the commitment that's already there.'

'Everyone seems to know as much of what Richard and I feel for each other as we do ourselves.'

'More, probably, in his case. You should have got yourself pregnant, Irene. He'd have married you instantly. In your situation, it'd have been justified.'

'There are certain prerequisites of pregnancy.'

'Dear me, he has been circumspect. Still, happen that's no bad thing. Your absence should plague him all the more.'

As he slowed the car, Irene raised a puzzled eyebrow.

'Haven't *you* wondered what it'd be like with him?' he asked her.

And that's why things have gone so badly wrong, she thought, getting out of the car, and thanking him as she

266

took her suitcase. Suddenly, she couldn't bear any more. She recalled the day when Giles had met her off the train from London. And it seemed now that leaving was inevitable, an inexorable conclusion decreed from the beginning. Yet still she felt sharply aware that she was being forced into behaviour that was contrary to all her nature.

Giles called to her as she hastened away. 'Just one thing more, Irene. Remember always – you cured him.'

Crying openly on a bus was something she'd never done in her life before. Today, she was no longer capable of stemming emotion. She could only be thankful that she had a good few miles in which to pull herself together. And that once she reached Halifax her father would surely keep her busy.

'All right, Norman love, I'll try to ease up a bit now. But you know how there's never enough time for everything.'

Lily had started a baby not long after settling into the prefab, and Norman was concerned because she still wore herself out with meticulous housework as well as spending all those hours on her feet in the mill.

'You'll just have to let things go a bit, the place is that tiny it shouldn't take all this keeping tidy.'

'But I like doing it, I've allus wanted my own home.'

'I know, love, I know.' There wasn't much he could do to help out here, either. Since they'd got the new looms running, old Dewhurst kept insisting that they increased their output. Instead of disposing of some of the old machines, as originally intended, he was hanging on to every one of them. Naturally, he expected them all kept running, and no extra men taken on.

Norman had never really settled completely at the mill since being demobbed. The noise still bothered him at times, it was a dirty job, and often physically hard. If he'd been happier about how he got on with Jack Dewhurst and with the other overlookers, he'd have put up with all the rest; as things were, he longed to get out.

And all at once he'd been presented with an idea of how he might be taken on in work that he'd love to do. It had been on the news that the Russians were blockading Berlin, folk were liable to starve. Only now an airlift was being organized. They were wanting men to pilot as many planes as there were available. Surely, they wouldn't be as particular as in wartime about you being on top form, they wouldn't investigate every bit of an ailment you might have had?

Norman found out the address of one of the places where the airlift was being organized, and wrote to the man in charge. He outlined his war service, listing the types of aircraft he had flown, they'd be eager to get men with his experience. He didn't tell Lily, there was no point in her being disturbed until he knew one way or the other.

He'd confided in their foreman, Bert Kettlewell, though – he'd always respected Bert, and didn't want him to be hard put to it to find another overlooker if he got taken on as a pilot. What Norman hadn't even remembered was that Bert's cousin was one of the weavers who was pally with Lily.

The evening she hardly spoke all the way home in the bus, he wondered what was wrong. As soon as they were inside their own front door tears poured down her cheeks.

'You might have told me, Norman. How could you think of trying to get set on as a pilot again, and not hang on about it to me!'

He put an arm round her, then drew her against him. 'I was only trying to spare you getting upset, specially wi' you being the way you are. Where was the sense in going through all this, if they were going to turn me down, any road?'

'I just hope they do, anyway – turn you down. I don't want you flying off at all hours, risking your neck.'

'Folk are starving, love, we can't just stand by.'

He made it sound as if she didn't care. Did he think she was incapable of feeling for folk who'd gone through so much in the war, and now couldn't have a decent meal? No matter who they were.

'It doesn't have to be you. There must be hundreds of men that were trained to fly.'

'Aye – and some on 'em haven't been stopped from piloting for airlines.'

'I never stopped you.' But she'd never really taken in before how much his heart was set on flying.

'I know, love. It were having to rely on these damned tablets that did that.'

Lily felt utterly confounded, as shaken by learning what he really wished to do with his life as by finding out he wanted to keep flying off to Germany now.

She gulped. 'How long would it last, this what-d'you-call-it – airlift? Would you be going over there a lot?'

'Don't know, depends how long the Russians keep up this blockade.' Seeing her wince, he smiled reassuringly. 'And we don't know yet that I'd even be taken on.'

They were not obliged to wait indefinitely with this uncertainty hanging over them. But despite Lily's undisguised relief, Norman was badly hit by the decision that he was still unfit for flying. They seemed particularly keen to sift out all folk who'd any history of ill health, and especially when that could involve reacting badly to stress.

'We appreciate your volunteering, sir,' he was told very smartly. 'But the conditions, in many cases, are as critical as during hostilities. We can't take additional risks.'

'I hope you're not suggesting I'm unreliable,' Norman began.

'Of course not, sir. It's simply that we have to ensure our pilots will withstand these, often quite gruelling, operations.'

The chap went on to explain that they didn't want anybody to be endangered. It made no difference to Norman whether it was his neck they were concerned about or their aircraft, he was sorely disappointed.

For about a fortnight afterwards he was subdued, but Lily was so thankful that he wouldn't be going away that she put up with his indifference towards her and everything else. And Norman gradually resolved to try and make life at the mill more acceptable.

He tackled Bert Kettlewell on the day that he explained that he wouldn't be leaving Dewhurst's. 'And since I'm bound to be stopping here, I want a different carry-on. You can tell Mr Dewhurst from me that I'm going to settle down and put my back into it. But I hope I'll be treated right. There ought to be no more giving preference to them that's not worked here as long as me.'

When the foreman passed on what Norman had said, Jack Dewhurst laughed. 'Hainsworth's a good overlooker, so long as he doesn't keep getting on his dignity. And he seems to be proving that whilst he can speak up, he doesn't go inciting others. You needn't say owt to him, but I shall hang on to him, he's a conscientious worker.'

Irene had been too upset about leaving Richard to even consider how she would be received at her old home. She certainly hadn't risked opposition, or cross-questioning, by letting them know what she intended. And she couldn't have visualized the scene awaiting her as she approached the house in Parkinson Lane.

Unable to find a taxi in the town centre, she had been obliged to catch a bus and walk uphill from the junction with Queens Road. Her suitcase seemed abominably heavy, and the handbag crammed with more personal items didn't feel much lighter. Suddenly, though, all discomfort was forgotten. Whatever could have happened to her father – hadn't he started surgery? People were queuing down the road and along the next street.

After hurrying the last few yards, she found the front door was open, and folk were clustered in the hall, overflowing from the waiting room. She realized then that she'd been too preoccupied to notice the impact the National Health Service was having. Here in Halifax, at least, there could be no doubting that it had caught on!

''Ere, what do you think you're doing?' a voice demanded, as she edged herself and her luggage past them. A pallid face framed with a turban concealing metal curlers levelled with her. 'You'll have to wait your turn.'

'Actually, I live here,' Irene stated. 'If you give me a chance, I'll maybe help to keep things moving.'

Hearing her daughter's voice, Elsie glanced towards her from the elderly man she was just conducting into the surgery. 'Well, I never!' she exclaimed, regardless of their audience. 'I hope you're not needing owt. You can see how things are.'

'Aye. Well, I thought I'd come to help,' said Irene dryly, too amazed to remain totally immersed in misery.

'You'd better get your things off then. When you're ready, you can relieve me directing traffic.'

The first time Irene showed a patient into his surgery, her father raised his eyebrows, then grinned. 'All hands on deck, eh?'

She nodded. 'Tell you later.'

Her mother had disappeared in the direction of the bathroom. When she returned she took Irene into the kitchen for a minute so that they could talk. 'This is by far the worst day we've had so far. Since the scheme came in, I've been trying to get some sort of system going, writing down names and addresses, things like that, while folk were waiting. I'm afraid today that's had to go by the board.'

'Is Dad just taking a note of each patient that comes in then?'

'Summat like that, aye.'

'Don't worry. I'll have a go at filling in details, if you can continue keeping them on the move. Where are the forms, Mum?'

It was hours later when the last patient had been seen. Shattered, his face grey with tiredness, Donald walked slowly out of his surgery.

'Hallo, love,' he said to Irene who was sitting at the hall table, sorting forms into alphabetical order. 'Thank God you came when you did.'

'Nice to be a bit of use.' The grimness behind her attempt at a smile revealed how unwanted she'd been feeling elsewhere.

Her father squeezed her shoulders, kissed the side of her cheek.

'I only hope you're not off back tonight or tomorrow.'

271

'As a matter of fact, I'm not going back at all.'

He looked so shaken by her announcement that she was forced to grin. 'You'd better go and have a wash or something, Mum's started cooking. We'll have a talk at after.'

Her parents' obvious exhaustion prevented her going into any detail when explaining why she had left her job. Over the past few years since returning from London, she had recognized that they still had as much concern for all their family as ever they'd had while the three of them were living at home. And they had enough pressure just now without anxiety about her personal life.

'I suppose it was that I'd come to feel I wasn't really needed by Richard any longer,' she said. And willed her eyes to remain dry. 'I thought I might be able to give a hand here for a bit, if only till you've got all your records organized. Must admit I hadn't realized that the new Health Service had begun yet.'

'It was last Monday – July fifth.'

Irene felt her mother giving her a look. It wasn't the sort of thing that she'd normally have missed.

'*Are* the forms for each patient the bulk of what you've got to get up to date, Dad?' she inquired. She was better keeping off the matter that had brought her home to Halifax.

'I'll show you tomorrow.'

She could see he'd had enough for now. 'But today's Saturday. You haven't got another surgery later on?'

'Aye – unfortunately, only way I can cope. It's the ones during the day that seem to be worst, though. Folk have been saving up all their requests for eye tests and for every kind of bandage and dressing imaginable, to say nothing of illnesses that have had to be managed without treatment while that had to be paid for.'

After a sigh, Donald shook his head, smiled and continued. 'Don't get me wrong – it's a grand idea, no mistake. All t'district nurses are highly delighted, they can give folk whatever's required, now they've got endless supplies of cotton wool, ointments, slings and the like. And I've always

272

maintained everybody should be entitled to hospital treatment when it's needed.'

'You'll allus get some folk who take advantage, that's the only trouble,' her mother put in. 'Some women are after wigs on the National Health, you know. As well as new teeth and glasses.'

'It'll settle down, with time,' her husband acknowledged. 'Meanwhile, it certainly won't hurt to have another pair of hands. I'll pay you, of course, goes without saying.'

Irene ensured that most of what she earned there was ploughed back in board-money which she insisted on giving her mother. She hadn't come here looking to earn, but seeking a respite while she recovered and found herself a new direction. Her father's attempt at a filing system had suffered under the sheer volume of work. The partial records which he and her mother had begun were often incomplete. On many an evening, she sat with him in the surgery, going through the new files and cross-checking with his original cards for every patient.

'It's nearly like the way I once hoped we'd be,' he said one night, as they tidied away, leaving everything neat for the following day.

Except that I'm only permitted to take the boring routine off your shoulders, she thought. I'm not allowed to really get near folk, to become involved in their problems. She swallowed, smiled – and wondered if her parents could see how wooden this smile was that she plastered so regularly on to her face.

'I'm sorry,' her father said now. 'Tact never was my strong point, was it? You've been hurt, I know, by what happened.' Fractionally, he paused. 'And since then . . . ?'

'If I have, I don't want to talk about it. All right, Dad?'

'All right, love.'

Forgetting was impossible, she was finding, as she'd suspected it would be. But she was getting through first one day and then the next, keeping busy. For the present, that would have to do. Later on it wouldn't be sufficient, but she couldn't yet tackle the future which must be planned to ensure some kind of satisfaction.

Seeing Norman and Lily from time to time and, less frequently, Mavis and Ralph, provided interludes in work, but served also to remind her how reluctant she was to spend the rest of her life alone. And the worst of it was that, having grown to love Richard, she couldn't believe that anyone else would be more than second best.

Heather was growing into a lovely little girl, and old enough now to remember her Aunt Irene from previous visits. An affectionate child, she often clambered on to her lap, giving her a hug before launching into excited chatter about what she'd been doing.

'She's a right old-fashioned 'un, is our Heather,' Mavis remarked one Sunday afternoon. 'She'd as soon sit and talk to you as play with any of her toys.'

'I wonder who she gets that from,' said Irene wryly. Most of her childhood memories were of her small sister holding forth until she gained all the limelight.

'From her daddy, I suppose,' Mavis answered unblinkingly. 'Ralph's a good talker.'

Whichever of them had bestowed this tendency, Irene loved their daughter, which only made her present unfulfilling state all the harder. And not only was she unable to prevent Richard from remaining as much a part of her as her own skin, intuition kept insisting that this separation was such a *waste*. Because he could have been just as happy as she would to have a family.

And now her sister-in-law was expecting, and talking of nothing else but how wonderful it would be when the baby arrived. Irene was very fond of Lily, but found it difficult to endure with a smile and avoid revealing her own yearning. Eventually, she began to believe Lily and Norman must think her particularly odd because of spending so much of the time at their house in silence. How could she change that, though, when she'd do anything rather than ram her own oversensitivity into the open?

Gradually, the initial rush of people wishing to make full use of the Health Service was dwindling. She was helping her father now by doing a lot of the work involved in arranging admissions to hospital or writing letters requesting appointments with consultants. Because she was familiar with medical terms, Donald often needed only to outline the patient's symptoms and supply her with names, and she would soon have something on his desk awaiting signature.

Donald was less exhausted now, better able to cope with days which still were busy without being quite so daunting.

'Another few weeks and we'll have this routine mastered,' he told her one Friday morning, when he discovered he was actually looking forward to opening up for patients, as he had in the past.

Irene hadn't needed telling. Now he'd aired the sentiment, she was compelled to acknowledge that she was feeling superfluous again. And, here, there was no escaping the constant reminders that she'd have sacrificed a very great deal to be able to practise again. If she was going to find any sort of inner peace, she would have to get right away.

16

Irene left Halifax on a brilliantly sunny day when even the centre of town appeared less smoky, but as her heels echoed across the boards of the station entrance she felt utterly subdued. Continuing over the wooden bridge towards her platform, she struggled against the urge to turn back.

But what was the point in stopping here? It hadn't worked, had it — not to any degree that might have convinced her that she'd ever be happy in her old home. Her stay there had served — to give her father assistance while that was necessary, and for herself to begin making a life without Richard.

As the train steamed south she wondered ruefully if she had chosen London for the very reason that she'd originally selected North Fell House. Privately, she wasn't above admitting that she felt she was running away again. But, whilst being well aware that she wasn't the only one to blame for the circumstances, she was also conscious that this was the point where she would cease trying to escape. Whatever she found in London, it must be something to give purpose to her life, something to restore satisfaction.

The carriage wheels drummed over the tracks, pulsing through her, all too reminiscent of that evening when the sound had hammered in the fact that she'd been deprived of her career. Grimly, she closed her eyes, clamped her lips together, refusing to give way to anguish. But feeling raw like this, how could she look forward? That other, dreadful, day she had been so certain that she had no future. Had wanted none. Since then she'd learned to love again, to love as she never had in the past. Now that was denied her. But she hadn't been the one, or certainly not the *only* one, who'd discarded the life she'd had with Rich, the life she might have had. And now she wanted no other.

London no longer looked the same. Some areas of war damage were already being rebuilt. Others were levelled; only by wiping out old homes, shops, factories could reconstruction begin. Leaving Kings Cross, Irene stared about her, towards concrete offices incongruous amid streets of Victorian houses which had been repaired and refurbished.

Unready for the next stage, she'd ignored the queue for taxis, but now one slowed beside her as she walked pensively along.

'Where to, dear?'

Bewildered, she let him take her case then clambered into the back. She must have appeared to be signalling him to stop.

'Where to?' he repeated, less gently.

She gave him an address.

Again, the place looked unfamiliar, smaller, coming here was a mistake. She paid the driver, took up her suitcase but only to set it down again on the pavement.

The paint on its windows and doors had been renewed, in crimson that clashed with the gentle terracotta of the brickwork. The name on the plaque seemed unfamiliar, making her dig back into memory, for some recollection of the man who'd taken over from her. Was he Indian, Pakistani? The brass plate was tarnished, scratched by badly removed graffiti.

The curtains at the window were immaculately clean, but garish, pink with an unfortunate stripe of gold Lurex. It all looked wrong, though not as wrong as she felt.

Yet suddenly she was aware of laughter, of people conversing quite cheerfully beyond those tawdry curtains. The present occupant must have rearranged things, replacing her surgery with the waiting room. Judging from the sounds, he kept his patients happy. Whatever she felt, neither he nor they would care. She didn't belong.

'It is! Irene – are you all right?'

A hand touched her elbow, she was turned to face the man who'd hurried around the corner and all but cannoned into her. She met a pair of brown eyes, gazing concernedly from beneath dark eyebrows now scattered with grey. Briefly, the eyes reminded her of Richard and she gulped. Because, yet again, nothing was right. Everything was far from right.

'Martin, I'm – sorry.'

'For what, giving me a surprise? You've done that, all right. You're the last person I expected.' He glanced towards the intersection with a tree-lined avenue. 'Are you coming in for tea?'

Irene tried to smile. 'Thank you, I'd . . . like to.'

His swift invitation immediately made her feel accepted. Somehow, she sensed that she need offer no explanation unless she wished. Martin seized her suitcase, and she noticed he was already carrying an enormous shopping bag stuffed to the top with groceries. Did he no longer have a housekeeper?

'You look as if you're busy.'

He grinned. 'You might say that. Mrs Rigby's rheumatism is becoming more of a problem. Today, she can barely hobble round the kitchen. I'm afraid she really ought to be replaced but . . . ' He sighed. 'She has no one now, her remaining brother died a few months ago.'

'So you keep her on, do the work yourself.' It was just like him. 'I'd forgotten how good you were, Martin.'

He laughed. 'That's an odd compliment!' But they were several yards along the avenue now and his amusement was slaughtered by her expression.

Irene attempted to contain her sigh, drew in a long breath, willing her emotions under control. Martin had appeared so suddenly beside her that she'd had no time for steeling herself to look at her old home. She wasn't prepared for this desolation. A quick glance revealed the house no longer stood empty, but it did seem terribly

278

neglected. She had known the people to whom she had sold had soon put the place up for sale again, when they emigrated, but . . .

'Squatters, initially, I'm afraid,' he explained, while she walked past the gateway, keeping her gaze straight ahead. 'Then the new owners didn't do much better. Divided it into flats, none of the tenants stay long. Don't like to see it like this.'

'Nor I.' Her voice was husky.

At the vicarage front door, he put down her case and felt in his pockets, fruitlessly. 'Afraid it means going in through the kitchen, forgotten my key.'

The kitchen looked more old-fashioned than Irene remembered, she couldn't help noticing it was far less tidy, and the old range needed black-leading. But the welcome in the elderly housekeeper's smile was as warm as ever, and pleased surprise lent a sparkle to fading blue eyes.

'Dr Hainsworth! Well, I don't know . . . !' Mrs Rigby struggled awkwardly to her feet from the table where she was sitting to peel potatoes.

Irene hurried across to meet her, felt her fingers being squeezed between both misshapen hands. Her smile dwindling, Mrs Rigby was gazing up into her face. 'You don't look very well, dear – have you been ill?'

'No, Mrs Rigby, just tired out. It seemed a long journey.'

'You've just come all the way from Yorkshire? Then you'd better sit down. I've got the kettle on.'

'Go through to the living room, Irene, will you?' Martin suggested. 'You know where it is. Be with you in a second.'

'You'll go now, sir,' his housekeeper reproved. 'Leaving an old friend on her own like that when she's only just arrived? The very idea! Just put that bag on the side there, I'll see to everything in time.'

'Thanks, Mrs Rigby.' Martin smiled at Irene, and led the way along the hall which always appeared rather gloomy with its sensible brown paint and well-worn carpet.

'Taking a break in your old territory then?' he inquired as she sat in one of the elderly hide armchairs.

Irene didn't reply at once. It would be so easy to imply that she was having a holiday. Yet she couldn't insult Martin with anything short of the truth. She would have to divulge as much as she could bear to recount.

She shook her head. 'I've left North Fell House.'

'Oh.' Sheer astonishment drained him of the ability to respond with any degree of sense or tact. From Irene's infrequent letters and from Giles, he had formed a picture of her living there permanently; a part of the household, if not fully of Richard's life. He had supposed that she and this greatly recovered solicitor would spend the rest of their lives together.

'Time to move on, eh?' he said eventually, trying to lighten his tone, and to discipline the urge to scrutinize her face for answers.

'Yes.' Irene looked down at her hands. They were stirring ceaselessly in her lap. She stilled them, gripping one with the other until her knuckles gleamed.

'Well, from what Giles said, you certainly achieved all you set out to – and far more. He's told me how well Richard's practice is doing now, how fit he is . . . '

Irene nodded. Then she stared hard at the ceiling. She couldn't look at Martin, had to keep her face averted, concealing the gloss of tears. If only Mrs Rigby would come in with tea, if only Martin would change the subject . . .

'And you found satisfaction in your work there. I'm so very glad, Irene.'

Her gasp emerged as a choking sob, too despairing to be contained. Abruptly, she sprang to her feet and hurried across the room to gaze out of the window. It was the worst move she could have made. She'd forgotten that this side overlooked the garden of her old home, and beyond it the house. The grass was nearly a foot high, thick with weeds. Overgrown roses tangled with the honey-suckle; the clematis that she had nurtured was hanging off the wall. So – not everyone cared about gardens, lots of Londoners travelled some distance to work, returned exhausted.

She thought of the immaculate garden at North Fell, of that very first time that she'd taken Richard out there. And of how, subsequently, he had gradually taken more and more interest in what was going on. This spring, as in the one previous, he'd filled the place with catalogues of seeds, bulbs, plants. It had come to symbolize his belief in the future. A future she would never share.

A tear splashed on to her hand, and then another; surreptitiously, she wiped them away.

'I daresay the new people there are working on the interior. Maybe when that's done they'll start on the garden,' Martin began gently.

He was just behind her. She was glad to feel his hands firm on her shoulders. Wearily, she leaned against him.

'I didn't think you'd still be this upset, about the house. Thought you were over all that by now.'

'I was – am. It's not that, not really.' Though it didn't make her feel any the better.

Before either of them could speak again, Mrs Rigby came in with tea. She stayed to pour while Martin passed Irene her cup and saucer and then some cake. She was thankful the housekeeper's presence prevented his delving further. If she even tried to speak of leaving Richard and what it was doing to her she would break down entirely.

Somehow, while Mrs Rigby was there Irene contributed a few words to the general conversation. Martin talked about old friends of hers; the housekeeper, of several neighbours. Someone had acquired a puppy who was causing havoc among the feline populace. Someone else had given birth, the old man in the end house had died, partly as a result of injuries received in an air raid which Irene vividly recalled. Yet these current events seemed totally remote from her, as unreal as if they concerned characters in a story. But listening to it all was infinitely preferable to dwelling on her thoughts.

281

After Mrs Rigby had taken the tray out, Irene felt Martin's brown gaze resting on her. He was frowning.

'Where are you staying?'

'I . . .' His question caught her without a ready answer, proved how detached she was from reality.

'Here?' He was smiling. 'You can, you know. There's more than enough space! And we always keep one room aired, in readiness for visiting clergy.'

'It's very good of you, Martin. I'm extremely grateful. But . . .'

Frowning again, he raised an eyebrow. 'Next door? Is seeing it so very painful?'

She shook her head. 'Only a bit now. I – just intended finding a hotel.'

'To be miserable in private.'

Startled, she looked at him. His eyes were very like Richard's and equally inescapable. She shrugged. 'You're as astute as always, aren't you? But I'm not ready to talk about it, Martin. All right?'

'And you will stay.'

'For a night or so. Thanks.'

'We shall make use of you, don't worry. Mrs Rigby freely admits she isn't coping fully. And I – ' He grinned. 'I'm not the best-organized person in the world. It's more than that, though. So often, Irene, I long to be treated as someone other than the local parson. There are times when this collar makes for a certain – isolation. You always have been just the girl next door.'

'Girl?' Despite her emotions, she was forced to smile. 'Not ancient crone?'

'Not even today!'

'Bloomin' heck, not in a parson's house!' Mavis exclaimed. Elsie had shown her Irene's letter before they sat down to tea.

Ralph grinned as he crossed towards the table. 'Didn't know Irene went in for religion.'

His wife laughed. 'Me neither! If carrying on wi' that married chap were owt to go by, she were never that way inclined.'

'What's carrying on?' Heather asked, as her grandfather helped her up on to a chair. She had continued to pursue her appetite for new words and expressions, not always to the delight of her parents.

'Now look what you've started,' Elsie reproved, giving her daughter a warning glance.

Mavis only chuckled. 'Nay, I wasn't the one, you brought the subject up.'

'Your mother only wanted to keep you up to date,' said Ralph.

'I know, silly. It were just a bit of fun, any road.'

'But what is carrying on?' Heather persisted.

'It can be what you're doing now,' Donald told her as he took the chair at the head of the table. 'And you'll have to learn, love, that there's times when grown-ups don't answer every question.'

'Why not?'

They all groaned, but their smiles were genial. Heather had remained a delightful child, despite receiving a lot of attention. So much so that Mavis and Ralph were hoping that she would have a brother or sister before another year was out. The only condition that Mavis made was that by the time both kiddies were at school she should seek part-time employment.

Ralph had agreed, if not wholeheartedly for he didn't want folk to get the idea that he couldn't support them. But Mavis was too bright to readily resign herself to staying at home for ever, and was also too restless to be satisfied without a job.

'I could go back to the library in Boots,' she had said. 'They take some part-timers. I allus liked it there, even though it was a bit more inhibited than when I were on munitions.'

'I certainly wouldn't wish you to do factory work again,' he'd said very quickly.

'The money'd be better,' Mavis had pointed out. She had been teasing, though, wanting to see him rise.

'You can get that idea out of your head. Nothing would induce me to allow it.'

Mavis hadn't been sorry to have him so adamant. Ralph putting his foot down always made her feel secure, protected. She herself might be assertive at times, over what she wore, and over the way she was bringing up Heather; but there was this underlying insecurity.

It had begun in the war. Daft really, when there'd been so little enemy action over Halifax. But she always had possessed an energetic imagination. She'd spent many an hour planning what she'd have to save if there was a bad air raid. In those days, she'd been proud of her appearance, there were lots of clothes she'd not part with, especially frocks she wore for going dancing, and some lovely shoes. She'd also collected a lot of make-up since her first experiments with Pond's Vanishing Cream. She'd have to remember her curling tongs they were old when Mum had passed them on to her, but after she shoved them in the fire to heat they always quickly revived her hairstyle. And there were her books. Having been a librarian, Mavis had been used to borrowing rather than buying. Maybe this was the reason that the few books she owned were treasured.

Even the titles which she had long outgrown had remained a part of her. She had loved the Romany books, especially after actually seeing him out with Raq, and learning that he lived locally. There were Angela Brazil stories and classics like *Little Women* and *A Tale of Two Cities*, Shakespeare's plays, volumes of poetry . . . Their common link had been romance, of one sort or another: the triumph of hopes and dreams, won through some extraordinary feat of persistence.

Mavis herself would have difficulty recalling now the hours that she had lain awake, planning how she must collect together her most valued possessions in the event of severe bombing. The effect had remained, nevertheless, to make her glad she needn't take sole responsibility for her future.

Ralph was good to her, proving how wrong everybody had been in the early days of their marriage when they'd been concerned in case he didn't settle down properly.

He'd also adapted to civilian life – far better than even Mavis had hoped he might. Perhaps because they'd both been used to the same kind of routine in the army, he and his father seemed to get on well together in the business. And once supplies of wool were obtained more easily, they would be greatly increasing production. As Ralph was always saying, these days, there'd be plenty of folk seeking new blankets.

'Do you know if Irene intends staying permanently in London?' he asked his father-in-law now.

Donald sighed. 'I'm afraid I haven't the foggiest. I only know I was sorry to see her go. She'd been invaluable to me. I shan't forget.'

Elsie smiled at her husband, nodded her agreement. From the minute that Irene had arrived, she'd taken a lot of weight off her father's shoulders, and the strain out of his eyes. All the same, Elsie had begun to suspect long before her daughter left that she was finding working on the periphery of medicine too tantalizing to be endured.

'We'll let you know, of course, when she sends a more permanent address,' she told them, but she was looking at Mavis rather than Ralph.

He had inquired because, until Irene departed so hurriedly, he'd been thinking of offering her a job in the office. A mill like theirs, which was intent on expanding, could use somebody who'd had experience in a solicitor's. They didn't believe in throwing good money away, and might have saved a substantial amount in fees if they'd been able to call on Irene's expertise whilst using her to cope with some of the paperwork which he'd come to see as tiresome.

'Happen Lily'll be wanting a lighter job once the baby's here and old enough to be left with a minder or somebody,' suggested Mavis.

Ralph disciplined an instinctive frown. He'd nothing against Lily, but she certainly wasn't the kind of young lady he was looking for. 'We shall need someone long before that,' he said dismissively, and wondered how his wife could possibly consider her sister-in-law might be of the slightest use to them.

'I shan't want you going out to work once the bairn's here, you know,' Norman was saying as they tackled the boiled ham and salad that was their Sunday tea. He'd been worried enough about how tired Lily always seemed during the first few months that they were married, never mind when she'd a youngster to look after an' all.

Lily smiled. 'So long as we're not going to be short of brass, I shan't be hankering to go back weaving.' She'd been older than lots of lasses when she got married, would relish devoting her time to caring for Norman and the baby. And she'd happen be able to give her mother more of a hand. Not that she'd mention that at home yet, her husband didn't trouble to conceal his opinion that her family had always put upon her.

'I've been working out a budget,' he continued seriously. 'We'll manage very well on what I'm getting. If we're careful, we'll even be able to get away for a bit of a holiday.'

'Ooh, love – are you sure?' Lily had never had more than a day at the seaside in her life, unless you counted visits to her grandmother in Morecambe, and with being responsible for younger brothers and sisters she'd hardly thought that was much of a change.

'Ever since Billy Butlin opened up another of his holiday camps at Filey, I've been hankering to go there. With a kiddie, a place like that'd be champion.'

'Happen your Mavis and Ralph would like to bring Heather an' all.'

'We'll have to see. I were thinking more of us getting away on our own, like.' Not for worlds would he have Lily suspect that Ralph would never agree to visiting Butlin's, much less with them. But he himself wasn't daft, he'd seen for a long time that his brother-in-law thought he was a cut above them.

'Mavis is ever so nice, isn't she? I've really got to like her. And she's that generous.' Mavis had recently passed on to her a pile of Heather's baby clothes, saying that even if they were to have another kiddie themselves there'd still be plenty of wear in them.

Despite this kindness, however, Lily herself was busy sewing and knitting for the expected infant. And she'd never been happier. They had such a lovely home, and she couldn't wish for a better husband.

Although he hoped one day to acquire a place that wasn't quite so cramped, the prefab also meant a lot to Norman. Since the day that he'd been turned down for the Berlin airlift he'd resolved to work conscientiously in his job and try to stop hankering for something better, but it was here with Lily where his heart was. Strangely it was being reminded about that bit of thyroid trouble that had made him think again. However could he have forgotten how afraid he'd been when he'd thought he had a bad heart. He'd put up with a lot (even at Dewhurst's) so long as he didn't end up like that friend of Irene's.

Lily was a splendid homemaker, and since they'd got away from squatting in that Nissen hut, they'd developed a satisfying love life. These days, of course, he was a bit wary, worried lest they might harm their expected child. But Lily had surprised him by being equally concerned that their intimacy should continue and by asking the doctor's advice. Although his own father was a doctor, Norman was afraid he'd not have brought himself to ask questions of that sort. But Lily had only laughed when he'd hinted at this, and had reminded him that in a family as big as hers there was no space left for embarrassment.

Norman had discovered that his wife possessed far more feeling for family than he himself. Even towards his own people, she was always the one who felt more responsible, and worried about giving offence. She'd told him off about today, because he'd turned down his mother's invitation to tea and he'd said that while she was still working at the mill Lily needed to rest as much as she could on Sundays.

287

'You're a love to me,' she had told him, 'but you can be a bit unkind to your mother.'

'She weren't bothered. There'll be enough of them, any road, once Heather gets going she'll keep them all occupied.'

When they'd finished the homemade feather cake which Lily had baked the previous day, Norman insisted that she sit in the rocking chair while he cleared the table and did the washing-up. She switched on the wireless, but couldn't find a programme that suited them both and turned it off again.

Lily had just started her second row of the matinée coat she was knitting when they jumped as somebody knocked loudly on the door. Their Cissie was standing on the path.

'It's our mam, can you come quick, Dad's sent me to fetch you. She's ever so poorly.'

'Aye, come on in. I'll just get my coat . . .'

'Coat?' Norman interrupted sharply. 'Where do you think you're going?' He nodded briefly to his sister-in-law.

'Hallo, Norman,' said Cissie, though her eyes were startled. She'd always thought their Lily's husband was quite gentlemanly.

'I'm only going to my mother's, Cis says she's poorly.'

'What with? Is it bad?'

'Bad enough. She can't keep owt down, she's been like it since yesterday.'

'I'd have thought one of you could cope,' Norman observed. 'You're nobbut a couple of years younger nor Lily. I don't see why she should have to turn out, not in her condition.'

Thrusting her arms into her coat, Lily was looking at the clock. 'If we hurry up, we'll just catch the bus you came on, on its way back into Halifax.'

'You're determined then,' said Norman. 'Well, think on you don't stop so long down yonder. It's work tomorrow, you need your rest.'

In the bus Lily questioned her sister about what was ailing their mother, and gathered that she wasn't the only one who was unwell.

'Our Herbert started last Thursday, and then the baby. Mam's the worst of the lot, though. We think it's gastric flu.'

Is that all, thought Lily, and began wishing that she'd inquired more closely before rushing out like this. Norman was right, their Cissie ought to be able to cope. And where was Millie? Asking elicited the information that she had gone out for tea.

The smell met her as soon as she set off up the narrow stairs. There could be no doubting that at least one person had been sick repeatedly.

'I didn't have time to clean up after her afore I set off to fetch you,' said Cissie forlornly.

Lily swallowed, trying to close her nostrils to the odour, and to compel her own stomach to settle. Their mam certainly looked ill, sitting hunched up in an armchair, in a stained nightdress with her winter coat clutched round her.

An enamel bucket contained the evidence of how sick she was, as did the dribble trailing from her pale lips.

'Ay, Mam – let's have a look at you,' Lily exclaimed, but as she crossed the room her insides rebelled. 'Oh, heck,' she muttered, and ran down the stairs again and round to the lavatory in the back yard. As she brought back her nice Sunday tea, she groaned ruefully. She couldn't do it. She'd have to tell their Cis what to do, and leave them to cope. This time, there was no way that she could stay and attend to everything. If she continued vomiting she might even harm the baby.

'I'm sorry,' she said, after forcing herself to return to the living-room.

'You're a lot of use,' her sister snapped.

'It's being the way I am, I suppose. You'll have to manage. You'd better start by giving Mam's face a sponge, then get rid of that lot. And wash your hands at after, before you spread this through all the family.' She turned to her mother. 'How are the little 'uns, are they still as bad?'

'No, love. Our Herbert's been playing out, and the baby's started taking milk again.'

289

Lily turned back to her sister. 'If Mam's no better by morning, think on you fetch the doctor.'

Their mother roused at that. 'Nay, we're not having him.'

'Fetch him,' Lily repeated. 'If you can't get him to come, let me know.'

On her way out she asked Cissie where their father was, and the other children.

'He cleared out, straight after tea, to the Raglan, I suppose.'

'And the kids?'

'Some tea party, or summat. Our Millie took them on her way out this aft. She should have brought 'em back by now.'

'Oh, well. They'll be out of your way while you're cleaning up.'

To her own astonishment, Lily felt no regret about leaving Cissie to cope. She wasn't so far short of thirty, after all. Just because there'd always been somebody else there to deal with things didn't have to mean that she was helpless.

By the time she was opening her own front door, she was totally recovered from the sickness, and smiling to herself.

'That was quick!' Norman exclaimed, and grinned. He'd been afraid she would go and offer to stay the night down Hanson Lane.

'Aye – I weren't a lot of good to 'em, I'm afraid. Soon as I smelled what it were like, that was it! I were sick an' all.'

'But you're all right now, love? Come and sit down, lass.'

Taking her coat off, Lily laughed. 'I'm fine now, thanks. It just turned my stomach. If I'd stopped there, they'd have been looking after me, an' all. And I don't reckon much to our Cissie's nursing.'

'How was your mother? What is wrong with her?'

'She's poorly, all right. Looks like gastric flu. And the bairns have had it, though they're getting better. I told

290

our Cis to get the doctor in if Mam's still as bad tomorrow.'

Lily began chuckling as she returned to her chair. 'Ay, I don't know – fancy me not being able to do owt! Seems as if it were meant to be, doesn't it, that they'll have to manage without me?'

'Pity you had to go all that way.'

'Oh, I'm not sorry. I showed willing, even our Cis can't hold that against me.'

Norman nodded. But he wasn't entirely satisfied. Although, as it had turned out, his wife hadn't been able to do anything for them he'd have been happier if she'd listened to him in the first place. He'd known all along, hadn't he, that he'd have to be firm if he was going to stop them relying on her whenever a problem arose. Lily still was looking quite peaky, if she'd been more herself he'd have said what he thought about her taking so little notice of him.

On the Monday evening, Lily startled him by announcing that she was going to call in on her family before she went home from work.

'Nay, love, don't. You're tired out.'

'I just want to see that Mam's no worse, or that she's had the doctor. I shan't stop more than a few minutes.'

'I'm coming with you then.'

Lily couldn't argue. But neither of them was pleased about the arrangement: Norman because all he wanted was to get home for a good hot tea, and Lily on account of her dread that he would say something she'd regret. He could be so outspoken when the mood took him.

With the exception of the two youngest children and Cissie who was getting them ready for bed, they were all sitting round the table. Even Mrs Atkinson was tucking in to the rabbit stew that made Norman's stomach rumble longingly.

'You're up and about then,' he remarked, quite sharply.

His mother-in-law nodded. 'Aye, lad – I'm a bit better today. Not that I stopped in bed afore, though.'

291

'Happen it'd have made more sense if you had done,' her husband said dourly. 'I only hope you haven't smickled me.'

'You'd have been showing signs by now, if she had,' Lily put in quickly.

Her father grunted. 'Not so sure about that.' From the speed with which he was clearing his plate, though, he appeared in good fettle.

'Did you have to have the doctor?' Lily asked.

Her mother shook her head, paused while she swallowed a mouthful of rabbit. 'No, I were coming round again afore we went to bed last night.'

'That's all right then. And none of the others have gone down with it?'

Even as she finished speaking, Lily sensed Norman's unspoken comment that the way they were all too evidently enjoying their food should be ample reassurance.

Cissie glanced across from towelling young Herbert's face, and addressed them for the first time since they'd arrived. 'I'm not feeling so well, but Mam's not up to doing so much yet.'

Lily gave her a look, was she putting it on? She didn't seem pale, nor particularly flushed. She sounded quite normal. But it wouldn't hurt her to call in here tomorrow, just in case. 'If you like, I'll . . .'

'No,' Norman contradicted firmly. He was staring towards Millie who seemed glued to her chair, with her knife and fork clamped to her fingers. 'There's always Millie, isn't there.' He steered Lily towards the door that led downstairs. 'We'll have to be going now, we've got to get our meal ready when we get home.'

'My mam still looked pale, and hasn't she gone thinner,' Lily remarked as they hurried into town to catch the bus.

'She'll pick up, now she's eating again.'

'You sound cross about it.'

'Nay, I'm not. I'm glad she's no worse. I just . . . well, they could have offered us a cup of tea.'

'I daresay they never thought.'

'Just so long as you understand you're no longer at their beck and call. I won't have it, love, not the way you are.'

Lily smiled. She wasn't sorry to have Norman sticking up for her. All the same, she wouldn't stop wanting to help out back there. They'd have to see about what went on in the future.

17

Irene was adapting, in some ways, to living in the shabby but homely vicarage. She was glad to be able to give Mrs Rigby a hand, and to sit with Martin, sometimes simply talking, rediscovering their old affinity.

There had never been time for long conversations in the past, but rather snatched moments of easy rapport as they met, greeted and parted. These days, they were becoming involved in deep discussions, especially when he tried out on her some aspect of a sermon he was preparing. There were occasions as well when an item in the news triggered them off. Today, they had been thrashing out the implications of the recently published Iron and Steel Bill with its threat to nationalize more than one hundred firms within the industry.

Irene was surprised that Martin supported the scheme, and he had laughed at her raised eyebrow.

'The Church isn't really the Tory Party at prayer, you know.'

She'd grinned. 'I'm not that naive! But I thought you'd be in favour of private enterprise.'

'Depends on the circumstances. At present, I happen to think some industries will be better served by cohesion — more of a concerted effort to ensure they pick up again.'

She hadn't argued with him on that, she'd been too certain in her own mind that she was right. And other lines of business were showing signs of recovery. The first full-scale motor show since the war had opened, with new models from both Morris and Austin, even if many of them were scheduled to help the export drive.

Good though it was to swap ideas with anyone who took life seriously, there were many times when Irene ached for the hours she had spent with Richard. From the first moments when he had used that alphabet, they had communicated so much. And she longed constantly, and quite desperately, to know how he was. The nights were worst of all, long restless nights when she lay awake, listening to the thrum of London traffic, yearning for the stillness of the Yorkshire countryside. Most of all, though, she needed the stillness of being with the man she loved.

A fierce unrelenting pain, this need of him never lessened. She could only subdue it if she succeeded in filling her entire being with other matters. Eventually, she explained to Martin that much as she appreciated living here, she had stayed on longer than ever she intended and must find some work to motivate her.

Martin smiled encouragingly. 'I don't want you to leave. But I agree this isn't particularly stimulating for you. Have you thought of applying to the General Medical Council to be reinstated?'

Irene had thought of this, but had needed someone else to believe they might restore her right to practise. She wrote off immediately, there was no sense in delaying, she'd have found for herself all kinds of reasons for supposing they wouldn't even consider her application.

Knowing how long most organizational bodies took over decisions, Irene was prepared for an extended wait. The reply came quite rapidly, and crushed every last hope. They wouldn't even contemplate a further hearing.

Martin was kindness personified during the next few days, but that wasn't enough. Irene needed to go home to Richard. To talk it all through with him, recovering the sweet reason they had found together. All at once her intuition grew very strong that everything she'd learned to believe with him *hadn't* vanished. If only she could see him, she'd be reassured that one could – one must – rise above a crisis by letting it happen, by surviving, not by struggling to fight a circumstance which one couldn't alter.

And then, only a day later, she saw the advertisement. She couldn't believe it was mere coincidence. This could install purpose in her life once more. A new laboratory for researching treatment for cancer was seeking staff, preferably with a medical background.

This was an application which didn't disappoint her. And her qualifications so impressed the people in charge that she was offered the position on the day that she was interviewed.

Learning of the job and securing it had happened so quickly that Irene could scarcely credit that it was settled on the morning she began working in the laboratory.

By the end of the first week it all seemed real enough. And, despite the purpose towards which everyone was working, each and every task that she had to carry out felt dreadfully mundane. Although she had hardly had time enough to think very deeply about her new job, she had visualized some element of excitement. Wasn't the whole team devoted to seeking a means of subduing one of the worst scourges to devastate civilized man?

She very soon discovered that, so far as she was concerned, each day comprised a succession of routine tests which had to be recorded meticulously. She repeatedly had to remind herself of the importance of all their minute detail. No matter how hard she tried, she was experiencing the gravest difficulty in remembering, for even a few hours, that whilst she was correlating these samples she was helping *people*. Somehow, she was incapable of connecting her tasks with her innate need to be of use to other folk.

'You're not happy, are you, Irene?' Martin observed one evening after she had spent the past six weeks compelling herself to work uncomplainingly.

'What makes you say that?' she asked defensively, ashamed of her inability to appreciate how worth while the job was.

'Since the first week you've hardly mentioned the laboratory at all. And your expression each time you set out and return is of stoic endurance. I keep looking for some spark of enthusiasm, but if it's there it's remarkably well concealed.'

'You're right, of course,' she admitted ruefully. 'Sadly, it's all a bit of an anticlimax. I know the work is vital, don't get me wrong, it simply doesn't appeal to me.'

'I'm sorry. Is it that your colleagues aren't congenial?'

'They're pleasant enough, though we have to concentrate too much for really getting to know each other. No, Martin, I'm afraid I'm the one at fault. I don't find working with samples, or keeping records, nearly so satisfying as . . .'

' . . . Having contact with people? I'm not surprised.'

'But I'd feel so guilty if I gave it up. This research is meant to be saving lives.'

'If your heart's not in it, somebody else might achieve more there. You could maybe work to far greater effect in a different line.'

'I can't keep changing jobs.'

'You haven't, have you. Your previous position was very definitely a continuation of your medical work. We all need to have someone depend on us, and that can be satisfied in various ways.' Suddenly, he was finding words impossible, looked down at his hands.

'I know. I often wish I was more like my sister, she's been that contented ever since she had their Heather.'

He glanced up. 'Ah. I've always thought you'd make a good mother.'

'You shouldn't have said that. I'm trying not to think . . .'

' . . . About having a family? Maybe such thoughts shouldn't be suppressed. They often occur for a purpose.'

'Like in the Prayer Book?'

'Linked with "the mutual society, help, and comfort, that the one ought to have of the other". Irene,' he continued, his voice very low, 'I haven't quite resigned myself to never rearing children. And we've always got on well together, haven't we? I've also concluded that I'm not nearly so successful here as I ought to be. I need someone at my side – a wife who'd be as supportive as I know you would.'

'*A wife*!' Irene was too astounded to contain her exclamation. Yet Martin was gazing towards her now, and was smiling.

'Is the idea that ludicrous?' he asked with no trace of resentment.

'I don't know, Martin. It's – startling, the last thing I expected you to suggest. If I knew you less well, I might ask if you were serious. But you're well grounded in what marriage is about. You wouldn't have put that forward without some thought.'

'True. I've done a great deal of thinking since you returned to London, Irene. Because I love having you here. I'm not saying I'm in love, in the romantic sense, but I do feel a very great affection for you. It could be sufficient, if you can reciprocate a little . . . '

'Oh, my dear. I don't know what on earth to say. You've always been good to me, and for me. Of course I'm fond of you. But . . . '

'Marriage is a big step? Especially when, because of my calling, it should be irrevocable.' He paused. 'You certainly don't have to decide tonight, nor for some while. Take as long as you need. I was afraid I would shake you. Now, I can see how greatly.'

'It's not only that.' Irene tried to smile but couldn't. 'There's a lot you'd need to understand, before we could come to any kind of agreement. Twice, Martin, I was sure I was in love. Twice, it hasn't worked out. Since you say you're *not* in love, it makes it easier for me to say likewise. And I'm not certain I would even contemplate a marriage based simply on affection and respect.'

'Even though you must know as well as I do that many fail because they lack those qualities? We could make it work. We might be blessed with children. In any case, you'd be given ample opportunity to fulfil your need to become involved with people.' He paused, shook his head. 'I must stop all this – I never meant to try persuasion.'

'And there's your parishioners – they wouldn't accept me, not after what I did.'

'I'd make sure they accepted you.'

'And prejudice your own relationship with them in the process? Martin, you mustn't.'

'You're assuming that we'd stay here. I often wonder if I've remained too long in one parish. A move would most likely do me the world of good.'

'Stop, stop!' Irene protested. 'This is all getting much too serious. Martin, promise me – you mustn't do anything, not about leaving, nor about talking to your parishioners. There are too many problems yet. Why, I'm not even sure I believe in what your work represents. You've only got to look around you: if God exists, he has a lot to answer for.'

'Your doubts aren't necessarily an insuperable barrier. You could still do an infinite amount of good alongside me.'

Irene swallowed before smiling across at him. She couldn't help feeling moved. 'Thank you, Martin – for thinking of me like this. And for making allowance for the shortcomings.'

'I only wish . . . well, that we'd met years ago, while we were both young enough to trust emotions a little more. I could readily believe that the desire you arouse, coupled with the friendship we have already, could prove a firm basis for something that would endure.'

Irene clamped her lips over the echo of the word desire. She couldn't have supposed that clergymen were immune? Why then should she be so astonished by what Martin had just declared?

He rose abruptly, as if reaching a decision. But as he walked towards her it was slowly enough to reveal uncertainty. His hand was cold on her arm, but there was nothing cool about the way he drew her to him.

'Start thinking differently about me, Irene. Forget I'm the local vicar, forget as well – if you can – that I've always been the neighbour who happened to be around.'

'I – I'd like to try, at least as far as that,' she murmured. 'As for the rest, I can see you might be better married. But I do have grave doubts about my suitability as your partner.'

'Will you let me attempt to convince you, though?'

Irene found she was nodding, without being at all sure of the reason. A part of her would like to marry Martin. Spending the rest of her life with him could be an agreeable prospect. But would that prove sufficient when she was not in love with him?

'And this . . . ?' he said huskily, his lips very close to her own.

He sounded quite vulnerable, reminding her of the rejection he risked. He was a dear, she couldn't hold him at arm's length.

As her arms went round him her lips found his, surely, in a kiss that began tentatively then somehow continued, expressing their deep friendship.

If only there was no one else, thought Irene, but she was forming wishes that had no connection with reality.

Living in Martin's home changed immediately; although there was never anything deeper than affection conveyed when they embraced. But he began making time to take her out. They went up to the West End for a show, or to eat at some restaurant where the cuisine was good enough to disguise the fact that food was still in short supply.

Declaring his wishes had given Martin fresh assertion. He often embarked on a discussion that made her think long and hard, and on some topic which she might otherwise have ignored.

'You're giving me a new lease of life,' she told him, one evening as they drove back to the vicarage after an orchestral concert. They had talked throughout both journeys, and during the interval, increasing their healthy respect for each other's, frequently divergent, opinions.

'Did you stagnate in the Yorkshire Dales then?' Martin inquired quite casually. 'I rather gathered from Giles that Richard Hughes possesses an extremely acute mind.'

Irene gulped silently, unable to reply. Martin's light words had undone any good generated during their evening. Just as she was beginning to feel he'd been right and they were both sufficiently mature to establish a good partnership, she was reminded of what her ideal marriage would have been.

'Giles assessed him pretty accurately,' she managed at last.

She was glad that Martin now understood a little more of what her feelings for Richard had been, but the knowledge didn't do much for their relationship. She sensed him trying all the harder, taking her out as much as possible, finding some time each day for them to be alone, and increasing the occasions when he took her in his arms.

It was being held close that Irene found hardest of all. Martin was an attractive man, but she wasn't able to respond in the way he needed. There was only one person to whom she felt committed, with anyone else there could be nothing more than friendship.

Before very long Irene decided she must be straightforward with Martin and explain her fear that marriage between them wouldn't work. But he was thoughtful and kind, much too kind for her to blurt out the truth without any consideration of what that would do to him. Once or twice she began her attempt at being honest with him, but the words never got said. She did, however, notice that he appeared aware of her growing reservations and had become less demonstrative.

One Saturday morning Irene was busy mending Martin's cassock. Mrs Rigby had been given a lift to the shops by the wife of one of their churchwardens, and Martin was writing his sermon. She wasn't surprised when he called to her as the doorbell rang.

'Be an angel and answer that, will you?'

She set aside her sewing and went out into the hall. The glass door panel revealed the outline of two figures.

'Yes?' Irene asked uninterestedly, opening the door. And then she saw their faces. Richard and Daphne.

'Rich!' She choked, couldn't say any more, and simply stared stupidly.

She jumped when Martin appeared by her shoulder. 'Well, ask them in – they've had a long journey.'

Irene flung the door wider, motioning them inside, but she was unable to speak. Martin took charge, collecting their coats, while she recovered sufficiently to murmur introductions. Martin offered coffee and headed towards the kitchen.

'How are you both?' she inquired, and asked about the journey, and if the weather had been worse than the dull, but dry, day in London. They sat in the front room, drinking coffee, and still saying very little. Irene was trembling inwardly and hoped that wasn't visible as well. She didn't trust her ability to cope with this. She had longed and prayed to see Richard again, now he was here she felt nowhere near ready.

As if at some prearranged signal, Martin and Daphne set down their cups and walked out of the room. Irene was sure now that all this had been organized, and purposely without her knowledge.

She had been watching Richard, noticing how haggard he looked, how on edge and uncomfortable. And so was she. She stood up, walked to the window, glanced out, then wandered around the room. She was picking things up, replacing them, terribly uncertain what to do.

Richard spoke first, his voice impersonal. 'I heard via Giles about your application to be reinstated. Sorry they refused.'

'Thanks. Happen I should have had more sense than to try.'

'Perhaps. But it did serve its purpose, confirmed where you'd moved to after leaving your father.'

'I'm – surprised you wanted to know.' It wasn't what she'd intended to say, but her tongue seemed beyond her control.

Richard snorted. 'So am I!' He didn't elaborate.

Irene was well aware that she was handling this badly, but she was too shaken to be able to discipline either her thoughts or her words. And, without warning, the thing that had hurt most of all tumbled out. 'After all, you'd said I made life even harder.'

He drew in a sharp breath, but although he looked whipped he merely shook his head ruefully. 'We're neither of us very good at this, are we? But I had to see you – once I knew you weren't with John.'

Irene's frown deepened. 'You didn't . . . you couldn't seriously think I'd go to him?'

'He did seem to need you, you do respond to that. And, frankly, there were other things I didn't seriously think you'd do. After you had left me, anything seemed possible.' Gravely, he shook his head. 'Forget I said that – I meant there to be no recriminations.'

Irene swallowed then suddenly extended her right hand towards him. 'Can we pretend you've just arrived? I could have been more welcoming. It is good to see you, Rich.'

'And you.' His voice was husky as he grasped her hand. He gazed deep into her eyes, and drew her close. He made no attempt to kiss her, he simply held her there, but as if he'd never let her go.

'I've brought no proposal of marriage,' he said at last, still hugging her. 'I've got to tell you that to avoid further misunderstandings. You know that's something I can't offer. I'll try to make you understand it almost breaks my heart.'

'Then why not . . . ?' she began, impulsively.

'Irene – not already! Can't you stop introducing arguments?'

'Sorry. Go on – what were you going to say?'

He surprised her by laughing a little, ruffling her hair affectionately. 'I'm no longer a hundred per cent sure. Sorting this out is going to take one hell of a time. You'll have to be patient with me.'

'We'd better sit down again.'

'In a minute.' He kissed her then, deeply and lingeringly. 'God, how I've missed you!' he exclaimed before leading her towards the sofa. 'I don't know where to begin,' he admitted. 'There's so much that I regretted not having the opportunity to say.'

'I just couldn't face that last morning.'

'And I should have seen long before then that I was being unrealistic about the physical side. Trouble is, I probably still am.'

'But you're here. I've never been more thankful to see anybody.'

He made a face. 'Startled, was how I'd have interpreted your expression.'

She laughed rather shakily, and Richard nodded approval. 'This is *us*, Irene. Beginning to discuss things rationally, with a bit of humour. This way, we might find a solution to a difficult situation.' Briefly, he paused. 'You see – I have changed, stopped kidding myself it'll be easy.'

'I'm not sure it's at all possible, Rich. I can't just drop everything. I have a responsible job.' Even if it isn't stimulating. And there was Martin to consider. His proposal.

Richard looked shaken, but he continued nevertheless. 'All the same, you have to know. I tried convincing myself it'd be okay, once accustomed to your – not being there. That failed. You know what I was like when Margaret married, this . . . .'

'But you loved her,' Irene began, and was interrupted fiercely.

'Love? That tiny emotion, grumbling away somewhere?' He'd learned since what love was, this exquisite agony of needing someone so much that he'd do almost anything. 'Irene, bear with me. There's been so little time since I learned you were here. Somehow, I've got to convince you it wouldn't all be problems and unhappiness if you came home with me.'

'With you?' She had sensed where this was leading, and now North Fell House with its surrounding slopes appeared on the screen of her mind. But she had said, hadn't she, there was her work here.

'Why else would I come? Irene my dear, I know I'm expecting a lot, that it wouldn't be ideal. But I loathe living without you.'

Her fingers felt for his, she swallowed hard. But before she could say anything Martin came into the room.

'Mrs Rigby says to tell you lunch is ready.'

Irene stared incredulously at the clock, unable to believe how time had passed.

Martin smiled. 'It's all right – you've the rest of the weekend, hasn't she, Richard?'

It seemed as though it was only mealtimes which interrupted their discussion of her possible return to Richard's home. But still Irene wouldn't commit herself again. Delighted though she was to see him, she couldn't help thinking she ought to have had longer in which to consider her future.

Just before midnight Richard stood up. 'Afraid I must get some sleep.'

She agreed rather anxiously. 'You didn't look well when you arrived. Are you all right, Richard?'

'Better than I was, now I've begun trying to convey what I feel. But you mustn't let this sway you. It has to be your choice, Irene. Take as long as you require, you don't have to decide this weekend.' He had been shaken by how settled she seemed here.

Irene was sitting dazedly by the living room fire when Martin came in with Daphne.

'Martin's been telling me about your job, Irene,' she said, her expression troubled. 'Sounds very worth while.'

'It is,' she said, exchanging a glance with Martin. 'I'm just not certain it's quite me.'

Daphne's green eyes brightened. 'Does that mean Richard stands a chance?'

Irene sighed. 'Don't know yet. But I'm glad you want me back at North Fell.'

Daphne came to Irene, gave her shoulders an affectionate squeeze then kissed her cheek as she said good night to them both.

Alone with Martin, Irene gave him a long, hard look. 'It's got to be said, love,' she began. 'And not only because Richard's arrived on the scene again.'

'About us?' He came to sit on the arm of the sofa to which she'd returned. 'You don't have to spell it out. Why do you think I made certain Giles Holroyd knew where you were?'

305

'Oh, Martin.'

'As soon as Richard came on the line, I knew that whatever hopes I might have had of marrying you, I could no longer hang on to them.'

'I'm sorry. But it'd be a lie, wouldn't it?'

'Having seen you and Richard together, yes.'

'But he's not proposing marriage.'

'Because of his health. So I gathered from Daphne.'

'We'd be living in the same house again, working closely together, relaxing . . . I'm not sure we'll always resist making love.'

'Do you expect me to throw up my hands, dismayed? Irene, I may be a parson, but I live in the same world, and the same century as everyone else.'

'You can't condone it?'

'It wouldn't be ideal. But, given the circumstances, understandable.'

'Always assuming that Richard would want that. I've a lurking suspicion that he might always fight his feelings.'

'Then I'm very sorry, for both of you.'

A few minutes later, in her own room, Irene realized she was surprised how unperturbed Martin seemed by her decision not to marry him. He'd said so little that she even wondered if he was somewhat relieved. Maybe he'd concluded long before all this that she was too given to dissatisfaction to make him a good partner.

She had expected not to sleep; indeed, she'd wanted to stay awake to savour Richard's coming here and to begin analysing her reactions to his ideas. But almost immediately after her head reached the pillow sleep overtook her.

Irene awakened early next morning, to the comforting realization that she and Richard were under the same roof again. Suddenly, though, this made examining her own conclusions dispassionately quite impossible. She reminded herself firmly that this was nonsense, that she must take time, assess the situation. She mustn't rush back to Yorkshire with him only to find she'd made another terrible mistake.

Being unable to endure their way of life before had been bad enough, opting out a second time would be far worse. She couldn't do that to Richard. And was pretty sure *she* couldn't take a further upheaval.

Going down to breakfast, things seemed no clearer. It had come to a head so suddenly, her brain couldn't instantly select the right course.

In the kitchen Mrs Rigby told her that Daphne had gone over to the church with Martin. Irene was going to inquire about Richard when he appeared in the doorway. Again, she felt stupidly tongue-tied, but Mrs Rigby sent them off towards the dining room.

Toying with her breakfast, Irene frequently caught herself gazing at Richard.

Appearing more relaxed than she was, he laughed at her scrutiny. 'Have I changed so vastly since we last had breakfast together?'

'I hope not,' she blurted. And blushed like a teenager.

'Promising – can't be all bad!'

'Oh, Rich!'

He smiled, reached for her hand. 'Whatever you decide, I'll always be glad we've had this. I so hated the knowledge that you were remembering me regretfully.'

'But I wasn't. God, no! Richard, surely you know I only came away because I'm too fond of you.'

By the end of the meal, however, they weren't much nearer a conclusion. Laughing and talking amicably, Martin and Daphne came in. It was when they had gone off again for the next service that Irene realized that, later that day, Daphne and Richard would set out for home. She felt suddenly cold and very empty.

'How long?' she began. 'How long before you have to leave?'

He shrugged. 'Depends on Daphne, she's the driver.' He grasped both her hands. 'Don't decide hurriedly, Irene, please. You could so easily be wrong.' His dark eyes sought hers earnestly. 'I'll come again, if necessary – don't make a mistake.'

'You mean opt out – say I'll stay away.'

'Either way. It could be just as disastrous together.'

'I know.'

'Let's get out – walk somewhere.'

They took the car. Irene intended driving to Hampstead Heath, but somehow missed a turning, and they were heading beyond that towards Hertfordshire. Eventually, she parked the car and they began strolling, still airing problems, but without reaching a conclusion.

Absorbed in their discussion and plagued by her own misgivings, she was oblivious to the direction they were taking. Richard had grown silent, was staring into the distance, frowning. Irene looked where he was looking, saw the A1, with cars rushing like so many ants – away from London. She glanced at the man beside her, sensed what he was thinking. Tears pricked at her eyes; she heard him sigh.

She touched his arm. 'Don't you dare leave me for long. Tell me we'll work something out, just as soon as I quit my job.'

'Are you sure?'

Irene nodded, willed her tears unshed.

Richard took her by the shoulders, gazing as if he would plumb through to her soul, then kissed her mouth hard. For some while he didn't speak, not even to say he was pleased or thankful. He simply kept an arm around her as they walked back to the car. As soon as they were inside he kissed her again, crushing her to him, but still he said nothing. She leaned her head against his shoulder.

'Thank you,' he whispered.

They sat like that for a time, still saying very little, just being together, occasionally exchanging a glance, smiling.

Lunchtime came and went unnoticed. Eventually, though, Irene suggested they ought to be heading back. 'They'll be wondering where we are.'

Richard laughed. 'Do you really think so? Won't they have guessed we're involved in something far more important than the next meal?'

Irene agreed, and he laughed again. 'And I rather suspect young Daphne's enjoying the change of company.'

'Martin?' Irene realized now that Richard's sister *had* gone off to church twice that morning. Having Martin himself go over there so frequently made you forget that not everyone attended every service.

Richard was grinning. 'I'll take your failing to notice as a compliment! I must have kept you pretty busy.' He glanced at his watch. 'Suppose you're right, we ought to get moving. Wonder if they'll have saved us anything to eat?'

'Are you hungry?'

He shook his head. 'Everything's so – nebulous.' He turned to face her again. 'I shan't believe I'm out of this wretched nightmare till I get you home to North Fell.'

He pulled her towards him, held her close, kissing her again and again. And then he chuckled ruefully. 'I was going to thrash this out with you, as well, *if* you gave me another chance. Intended asking if – if kissing you makes it intolerable that . . . ' He paused, suddenly dejected again. ' . . . That I'm the heel who starts you off along this road with no satisfactory conclusion.'

'Richard, don't. You're not.'

'Well, I can't, anyway. Offer to stop. I tried to frame the words, but couldn't say them. It's foreign to me. Where I love I have to give – even if that giving is only a token.'

And more than kissing? Irene wondered, but would not say it – just as she vowed she'd never mention marriage again. She leaned closer towards him. 'No matter what, Rich, I'll always love you.'

Richard limped quickly into the vicarage sitting room where Daphne and Martin were playing records. 'How long can we delay our departure, Daphne?'

She shrugged. 'Up to you. Only don't forget tomorrow's Monday.'

Irene turned to him. 'You ought to be on your way soon, you know. You've had an exhausting weekend, coming all this way. I'll pack in my job just as soon as I can now, it won't be long.'

With the prospect of leaving for Yorkshire herself in the near future, saying goodbye to Richard wasn't as traumatic as Irene had feared. In fact, by the time she was ready for setting out at the end of that week, she found leaving Martin quite painful. This was the second time she'd relied on him to see her through a bad period, and she couldn't forget that he'd cared enough to suggest that they marry.

On the station platform she hugged him, thanking him in words that seemed particularly inadequate, promising to keep in touch. 'This time you can dismiss my troubles, I shan't be reappearing here.' Unable to ignore the situation completely, she added: 'I hope I'm forgiven for declining your offer.'

'Of course, I understand,' Martin said, so quickly that she suspected he might indeed be relieved. And who could blame him, she'd arrived here in such a distraught state, she could hardly have done other than cast gloom over the entire house!

As the train drew out of Kings Cross and gathered speed through the grimy suburbs, she caught herself hoping that she and Richard would see Martin again. After all, it was through him that this had all begun, he seemed too important to be dismissed as a person she had once known.

18

Daphne and Richard were waiting in Skipton, both rushed
to hug her. For the present, Irene was far too happy to
recognize any of her doubts. Once in the car, she sat
forward in the seat, relishing every variation in her view
of the fells, the different shades of grass, limestone
rocks, the distant moorland. Sunlight glinted off the
stony brook, and seemed to fill her heart with joy to be
coming home.

And then there was North Fell House, solid and a little
imposing still, but blessedly familiar. She could feel Richard's brown eyes focused on her, and then his hand
warm as it grasped her own. If this is what home means,
she thought, I've never before fully understood.

'Welcome,' Richard breathed into her hair, as Daphne
negotiated the curve of the drive.

Irene turned to smile at him. 'I'm too full up to say so
much. Happen I will later on.'

They didn't have long to wait. As they went indoors
Daphne headed straight for the telephone. 'I don't know
what Martin said to you, but he made me promise I'd
confirm your safe arrival.'

Richard was smiling as Irene gazed affectionately around
the hall. Evening shadows were deepening about the sun
slanting through the windows to either side of the door,
throwing the dark furniture into sharper contrast with the
pale green walls that she'd always loved.

'I feel as though I'll have to go through every room to
prove all this is real!' Irene exclaimed.

'Try and defer it till we've had something to eat,'
Richard suggested.

'Haven't you had any dinner tonight?'

As Daphne replaced the telephone she exchanged an amused glance with her brother. '*I'm* certainly not hungry now,' she remarked, and left them to it.

'What are you cooking then?' Richard asked Irene.

When they reached the kitchen, he pushed the door to behind them. He took her in his arms, half laughing with relief. When he held her a little away from him, Irene saw his eyes were moist.

'I know,' he murmured. 'And I don't care who else knows. This is how much I love you. I'll never be able to thank you for coming home.'

Irene swallowed, determined not to go all emotional on him. But Richard sensed her mood, placed slender fingers at the back of her head and buried her face against him.

She was dry-eyed, nevertheless, when he tilted her chin and he nodded approvingly. And then he grinned. 'I really am famished, what shall we have?'

They fried bacon and eggs, laughing again with the sheer lightheartedness of being able to do so together.

'Promise me something . . . ' Richard began while they were eating.

Anything, Irene thought, but had suffered too much to be incautious enough to say it. 'What, Rich?'

'Don't ever do that again – making such a hasty decision to leave. Not without letting me remind you – us both – that nothing's worse than being apart. When I'm difficult, and I can be damned difficult, bear with me, Irene. Remind me, if necessary, of today. And of the hell that was the last few weeks.'

Solemnly, she nodded.

He surprised her then by adding: 'And believe me, this isn't the easy way out. It's taken a lot of soul-searching. To marry you would have been far easier.'

Richard had told her she needn't start work again immediately, although he'd admitted when visiting London that he hadn't even advertised her position. Irene didn't want time on her hands, though, and she needed to get over any possible awkwardness when she reappeared in the office. But Richard had evidently primed the other two, they accepted her return as easily as if she'd been on holiday.

Later that day when Richard was in court, Anita came and perched on her desk. 'Thank God you're back, he's been unbearable.'

They all laughed, freeing the atmosphere. After Anita had left for home David smiled across as he finished clearing his desk. 'I've known Richard for a long time; it's taken you to really touch him.'

'Surely there were others?'

'Margaret?'

'Did you know her, David?'

He nodded. 'She and Richard were very close – I thought. They'd plenty of common interests, and she was undeniably attractive. But there was none of this . . . devotion.' He paused. 'Quite honestly I didn't think we'd see you again. I'd gathered what his reasons were for not proposing. All very fine and noble, but generating an impossible situation. He must have been pretty desperate to persuade you to come back to face all that again.'

Irene gazed into space, fumbling as she replaced the cap on her fountain pen, then she smiled. 'He did put that across. And I didn't need much persuading.'

Within days she had picked up the routine in the office and had the bonus of feeling warmed each time she was reacquainted with clients. At last, she thought, recalling how she had hungered for contact with other folk all the time she was working on laboratory samples.

Only Richard himself seemed different, and his attitude towards her. She sensed change in his eyes seeking hers, even in his tone of voice. Evidently, her absence had brought recognition that she shouldn't be taken for granted. And there was no pretence now, no biting back of endearments in case they were misconstrued. Rich might have emphasized that they wouldn't marry, but in many ways he behaved like a loving husband. The only exception was his determination not to give in to their emotions and sleep with her. And otherwise he made Irene so happy that she felt she might shelve this eternal longing.

One night a week or so later they were sitting up talking when he rose and extended a hand. 'Come with me, something to show you.'

Puzzled, she followed Richard through the french windows and on to the terrace. The autumn air was cool, with a breeze whipping down off the fells, stirring his dark hair as he began speaking.

'This is the place, you know, where I started falling in love with you. The day I learned to stop fantasizing about a girl who'd once been important, to stop retiring into the past, and to acknowledge that everything that's good and worth while is here with me now.'

His kiss was gentle. 'Did that before, didn't I? Feeling unsure of you – more unsure of myself, but needing this contact, affection. And in that moment, reluctantly maybe, I began living again. Not existing, on a level plain, safe from disturbance, but reaching the depths and heights of living, and of loving.'

The words of every possible response seemed inadequate. Irene slid her arms about him beneath his jacket, holding him close, her head against his shoulder. Thanking God again that she had come home.

All Irene really wanted now she was back at North Fell House was to spend every moment she could with Richard, catching up on everything that she had missed about their relationship. But Daphne appeared exceptionally eager for her company, so much so that after the first few days she and Rich were rarely alone for long. And whilst she'd been away David and Clare had regularly invited him over for a meal of an evening, an arrangement which continued.

Irene had thanked them but declined when they extended the invite to her. She felt in her own heart that, however attached to each other they might be, they'd both be unwise to exclude everybody else. After Richard had gone out she nevertheless felt suddenly flat and irritated

314

with herself for not accompanying him. There might have been changes, but it was still Richard who did as he wished. She was the one who'd uprooted herself for him, yet here she was – isolated from any friends who could have prevented her relying totally on him.

That evening she and Daphne had dinner then washed the dishes together. Just as Irene was about to go upstairs and shampoo her hair, Daphne stopped her at the door.

'Irene, I'd like to talk, can you spare the time?'

She smiled, pleased to be reminded that Richard's sister had become so easy to get on with. 'Sure, go ahead.'

They hurried through to the sitting room. Daphne certainly appeared very eager to discuss whatever it was or confide.

'Better make yourself comfortable, Irene. I'm afraid this may take rather a long time, if you don't mind.'

She laughed. 'Between you and me, I was trying not to feel neglected. It's not good for either Richard or me to have no other friends. But I was wondering why most of mine are miles away.'

Daphne poured a couple of sherries before going to an armchair. She was quite some time sorting her words before she began speaking. 'When you came back, Irene, was it . . . is it permanently? I mean, you wouldn't leave Rich again, would you?'

'I'd try not to. I can't visualize any circumstances that might make me.'

'But then you couldn't before. And it must be difficult for you, even now, because he won't make any ultimate commitment.' When Irene made as though to speak, Daphne gestured her to wait. 'I need assurance from somebody and I know he'll only insist, as he always has, that I have my own life. But now it comes to the crunch I have to know that he would be all right.'

Irene contained her smile. It sounded as though she hadn't been wrong to be pleased that Daphne had seemed happy to attend church in London. Was she finally going off to the convent at Horbury?

'I daresay, Daphne, that I'll soon forget I've ever been away.'

'If not the reasons for going?'

'I am trying to put all the difficulties behind me. And I do think Rich and I have a better understanding, more realistic.'

This still didn't seem to make it exactly easy for his sister. She set her glass down on the coffee table, began pacing the room.

'You've known Martin for a long time, haven't you?' she asked.

Irene grinned, this wasn't quite what she'd anticipated. 'All the time I was a doctor in London. He's been a good friend to me.'

Daphne nodded. 'Are you surprised he wants to see me again – and frequently?'

'Well, in a way. But then again . . . ' Her voice trailed off, as she reflected that Daphne's churchgoing that weekend with Martin hadn't entirely resulted from a sudden return of her faith. 'I'm certainly very pleased, delighted for you both – hope it works out.'

'I know Rich will be pleased as well.'

'You've not told him yet?'

'He wouldn't like my checking on his future first, would he? It's become rather a habit, though, I'm afraid. And with Martin living so far away, I won't become involved unless I feel free to leave here.'

'You'd better let Rich in on your plans now, before I go and blurt them out!'

'I'll tell him tomorrow – tonight, if he's not late home.' Daphne returned to her chair, sipped the sherry before continuing. 'Martin's pretty wonderful, isn't he? So down to earth – about what he believes, about room for questioning. He's given me so much, Irene, already. Not only affection. I'd better start at the beginning . . . '

Irene braced herself to give no sign that she'd heard about Daphne's loss of faith, and the cause. As she listened, though, her emotions became involved, captured by certain phrases.

'... Even when Dad died suddenly and I was badly shaken, I told myself that this was to test my response, that I must go on. But after the stroke I couldn't bear seeing Rich like that, couldn't accept the injustice ... I couldn't pretend an allegiance that had vanished. It seemed for ages that, through something neither of us could help, Rich and I were adding to each other's misery.'

It felt like some long while before Daphne smiled again, straightened her shoulders. 'Anyway, that's all solved now. Thanks to your Martin.'

'*Your* Martin, perhaps?'

Daphne laughed. 'Well – it's early days, but we certainly hit it off. And you know, Irene, I never think of him without remembering that it was through you that we met. Keeps the four of us together very nicely, doesn't it?'

Irene smiled and nodded. Except that she and Richard were not completely committed in the way she suspected Martin and Daphne soon would be. Living with that was no easier now than she'd found it in the past. Still, she could be happy about Martin now, and thankful that Daphne and Richard hadn't delayed their journey to London. Martin might have entered into a loveless marriage. She shuddered.

Daphne frowned. 'Are you all right? You are pleased ... ?'

'As I said, couldn't hope more that it works out – and for Martin as much as you. I just still get scared when I think how terrible it would've been if you and Richard hadn't arrived at the vicarage that day.'

'And you didn't see what it had been like here!'

'I feel sure this is your chance of a new life, Daphne, one that will make up for everything that's happened before.'

'Gosh, I hope so. It's strange how things developed between us. Over the phone Martin had sounded a born organizer. I was rather taken aback to find him a bit impractical on the domestic front, though I adored the way he tries to look after Mrs Rigby. If he and I were to make

317

a go of it, I'd insist we should keep her on, she'd potter happily for the rest of her days.'

'That's good. She's been like a mother to him.'

Daphne chuckled as she refilled their glasses. 'Bet she's had to be. You should have seen him, Irene, while you and Rich were out. He was determined to relieve her of preparing lunch, yet half the time he seemed unfamiliar with his own kitchen.'

Irene nodded. 'Slightly the otherworldly clergyman, till you get down to matters which you expect to be insubstantial.'

'I know. He instantly sensed what was wrong. We hadn't been talking for more than half an hour, and I swear it wasn't on anything of any depth, when Martin turned to me. "God does know what he's doing, you know," he said – just like that.'

Thinking, she hesitated a moment then smiled. 'It panicked me a bit – as though he knew as much about me as I did, as if all my doubts were written across my face. "Take those two in there," he continued; "Coincidence couldn't have brought them together, either initially or now." He made me think, Irene, about things that go wrong – even things as bad as Richard's stroke. Martin suspects, and I'm beginning to believe him, that Rich could be happier now than he's ever been.'

'I doubt it. He led an active life, going wherever he wanted.'

'Alone.'

'What about Margaret?'

'I'd forgotten her. Just shows how unimportant she was. Rich and I have always been close, I'd have been more aware of her if she'd mattered that much to him. But the point is that it's what does happen that counts. Martin made it so clear. The things we can't anticipate or prevent. And what we do with them. What's past is past. No good thinking, what if I'd been a nun . . . I can forget all that. If I was asked, I'd concentrate on being a bloody good vicar's wife.' She laughed. 'Even if it took ages to start sounding like one!'

'So, you already think there might be a wedding?'

'I *hope*, but please don't say anything, not even to my dear brother. I'm to meet some of the flock, though, churchwardens and all that. Probably be ghastly, feeling on show. But at least with my father having been involved with religion, the language doesn't put me off, nor some of the pious folk you're confronted with. If I begin on the right foot, they might make allowance when I cram it into my mouth!'

'Except that you won't.'

'Don't lay all your money on it, Irene. Seriously though, I'd love to get a crack at something so worth while. Working with a man whose job I believe in – and I do mean believe.'

Irene was so happy to be back with Richard that shelving her misgivings about the limits of their relationship seemed bearable. Happen she'd attached too much importance to the incomplete nature of their life. Their days were full, and satisfying because she was not only helping Richard but proving useful to every client she met.

Because of being so occupied, and reluctant to share her leisure with anyone but him, she had put off returning to Halifax. When she finally made arrangements to spend a weekend there, they were into November, and the weather was dismal and wet. Richard had told her to use the car, and she'd been glad to accept. She had toyed with the idea of pressing him to accompany her, but had been surprised to find she preferred to keep this occasion to herself. Later perhaps, she would get him to come and meet her family; but for the present she needed one part of her life that was separate from him.

As soon as she drew up outside the house and saw her father's last few Saturday morning patients going up the steps, she was reminded of her previous stay here. She was better now, she knew at once, cured of the black despair and, even without marriage in prospect, felt assured that her life with Rich would endure.

319

Her mother called to her to come into the kitchen, and Irene smiled ruefully as she looked around after giving her a hug. 'It's only me,' she said. 'You're not feeding the Eighth Army!'

'Near enough, love, tomorrow! Our Mavis'll be here and Ralph and young Heather. Then there's Lily and Norman coming. He's got such an appetite, these days, thank goodness! And she's got to eat for the baby.'

Before the family gathering, though, was the quieter reunion with both parents. It was the letter that spoiled that, when Elsie remembered and retrieved it from behind the mantelpiece clock.

'This came for you t'other day. Didn't send it on, since I knew you were coming home.'

The strong handwriting on the envelope looked masculine, and seemed unfamiliar. When Irene took out the single sheet of notepaper she saw she ought to have recognized who it was from; as she read on, she realized he had changed as much as his writing.

Dear Irene,

I simply had to let you know that I have, at last, managed to kill the dependency. And to tell you how everlastingly grateful I am to you for forcing me to face how bad the situation was. Without you, I'd have continued getting worse and worse until there was either no hope, or no life!

I'm glad to say Vera came back to me once she could see I was serious about a cure. We're living in Leeds now and have had a second child, a girl. I got a job here in an independent chemist's as soon as I was fit. I risked telling my boss what had happened, and he's a lovely man who has made every effort to give me a chance to prove myself again.

I long to thank you properly for all you did, that's why I'm inviting you to meet me for a slap-up meal somewhere. Vera agrees this is something I must do.

320

Please ring me at this number, Irene. Now I'm living in Leeds it would be quite convenient. And I do so want to meet you again. My dear, please say you'll come – or let me drive over to some place of your choosing.

Yours,
John

Irene reached the end, growing increasingly aware of her own agitation. Her mother had gone out to the kitchen, and she wasn't sorry. She'd have hated to read this lot under anyone's concerned scrutiny.

She was thankful, naturally, that John was so much better. But she'd have been happier if she'd received the news through a third party. Even when he had the best of motives, John's persuasiveness still made her uncomfortable.

Her mother's brisk footsteps were approaching, and she herself was anchored beside the fireplace, gawping into the flames like somebody moonstruck. Hastily, she moved, and the envelope slid from her fingers, wafted on to the coals, and shrivelled beneath a sudden flare of yellow. The best place for the letter, an' all, she thought. But Elsie was in the doorway now, her eyes questioning.

Irene stuffed the letter into her handbag. 'It's something and nothing,' she said, 'just a few lines from an old friend.'

'Oh, aye.' Her mother's tone revealed disbelief.

There would be no explanation, that would have made the letter grow in significance. And, despite her own reaction to it, Irene was determined it must be forgotten. The first time she'd come back to Yorkshire she'd meant to put the past behind her. This time she was more certain than ever that she wasn't going to jeopardize this new life she was carving out with Richard. She was relieved on John's behalf, but there it ended, she didn't really want to even acknowledge his note.

She could sense her mother's continuing interest, that she was waiting to be told who the letter was from; they'd all grown up in a close-knit family where it was accepted that both parents liked to know all about their friends and acquaintances. Well, now Irene was sorry, but she was going to devote every scrap of attention to the future and that didn't allow for any digression.

'It's good to be back in Yorkshire,' she said firmly. 'I just want to concentrate on working with Richard again. We've got a great deal going for us, and giving my mind to that will be the best thing I've ever attempted.'

'I hope you're right, love. And I hope he appreciates how much you feel for him.'

Irene smiled. 'He came to London to make sure I went back to him, didn't I tell you?'

Elsie nodded. 'You did that, first time you rang after you'd got back to North Fell House. And has he said owt about – you know, getting married?'

'Plenty – and repeatedly, that it's not on, because of his precarious health.'

'*Is* it precarious now, Irene?' That was her father, as he strode into the room and bent to kiss her.

'Not really, or not as far as I can tell. But Rich had a nasty scare, doesn't want me to be burdened by his anxieties.'

'Doesn't he realize it'll take more than the absence of a wedding band to exclude you from them?' he asked.

She grinned. 'Happen not! Any road, that's the way it is. And I'm not going to let that spoil anything. Never mind me, though, how are you getting on, Dad? Got the National Health Service under control yet?'

'It's coming – or my bit of it is.'

'You're certainly looking less tired.'

'Thank goodness!' Elsie exclaimed.

It was Elsie herself, though, who seemed exhausted on the following day when all the family were there. Irene was glad to see that Mavis was quick to give a hand with tea, and Lily began the washing-up afterwards but then had to sit down again. She looked drained by the baby she was carrying.

'Are you all right, love?' Irene inquired just before Lily agreed to Norman's insistence that they mustn't be late getting home.

322

'Tired out, that's all. I never thought I'd be glad when I finished weaving, but I'm counting the days now.'

'Never mind, just take care, and don't keep on going out to work, think on. Not longer than you have to, there's more important things than having a bit of brass behind you. When your baby's here, though, you'll know how worth while all this has been.'

Lily smiled gratefully. It was good to have somebody understand. Norman's parents never said a lot, these days; their reluctance to interfere sometimes left her wondering if they cared. And her own family, when she saw them, implied that she was making a big fuss about expecting. But then, as Norman said, they were narked because she'd put her foot down regarding helping them out. And he himself was busier than ever at work, trying to get old Dewhurst to start a production drive. He'd been telling her the other day how sixty or more weaving mills over in Nelson had worked on one last summer. To help this country recover. Every mill had had its target, with posters, there'd even been a travelling exhibition of fabrics.

'How are your folk, Lily?' Irene asked.

Her sister-in-law grinned. 'I'd just been thinking about 'em. They're not so bad, thanks.'

'Apart from having to put up with me insisting that Lily doesn't wear herself out for them,' Norman said.

Irene was sorry they were leaving early, but couldn't help thinking it wouldn't hurt her mother to have fewer of them there. After they had waved Lily and Norman off at the door, she followed her into the kitchen.

'You're looking nearly as tired as Lily, do you know that?'

Elsie sighed, but then she smiled. 'I don't seem to sleep so well as I used to. Your dad says that's normal as you get older. But it's partly because I've allus got one ear cocked towards that blessed telephone. Or the doorbell. Some weeks, there's hardly a night goes by without somebody fetching him out of bed. All because it's dratted well free!'

'Oh, dear. Still, I suppose it's early days yet. Happen it'll quieten down a bit once folk get used to being able to call the doctor out without scrimping and saving to pay him.'

Elsie nodded. 'Aye. I know this is a good thing, don't get me wrong. It's just that it's come in at t'wrong time for us. We're getting past living such a hectic life.'

When they had finished tidying the kitchen and went through to the living room, Heather was dashing round the back of the settee, peeping around first one end then the other at her granddad. Each time that he obliged with appearing startled she shrieked with delight. Mavis and Ralph were laughing, oblivious to the disturbance Heather was creating.

'Come here, Heather,' said Irene. 'Let's find some paper and you can draw a house with me.'

She was pleased to discover that her niece was quite keen on making pictures, and for a child just turned three had a reasonable boredom threshold. Their drawing didn't interrupt family gossip, and lasted until Mavis announced it was time they were taking her home to bed.

A couple of hours later, as she drove through Skipton on the way back to North Fell, Irene realized that the day had again filled her with the old longing for children of her own. This time, however, there was a difference. The separation from Richard while she was in London had certainly taught her to sort a few priorities. Whatever the shortcomings of her future life, they could always be rationalized by comparison with the emptiness while they had been apart.

Irene was even resigned to her childlessness as she looked forward to Christmas which had tended to become the time of year when the longing was most persistent.

Because of the upheaval she had done no Christmas shopping, and was planning now to give the first Saturday in December to the task. She was delighted that Richard had decided to accompany her. In so many ways, they seemed like any other couple, happy to make plans together.

When that Saturday came, though, and she went into his room Richard cried off. He said he had a headache and was tired. Irene had been noticing how he hadn't entirely shaken off the exhaustion so apparent at the time she'd returned here. Although disappointed to be going out on her own, she agreed he should rest. And at least this would allow her opportunity to choose a gift for him.

'Anything I can get for you while I'm out?' she inquired. By next week, the shops would be busier, even more tiring.

'There are one or two items, if you don't mind.'

'Just jot them down, so I don't forget.' Searching her handbag, she found a sheet of paper, tore it in half, and put it on the bedside table.

Richard had made a list already, and handed it across. 'It's here – got this ready last night.'

'Fine then. I'll get what I can. I take it it's all right if I use your car?'

'Of course, you shouldn't need to ask. Take care, love.'

It was a cold but dry day and an early frost was disappearing as she drove down the dale towards Skipton. She'd decided that if she couldn't get everything there, she'd have time to go on elsewhere, maybe Ilkley.

She concentrated initially on the things on Richard's list, and already was beginning to feel happier. All the shops were festively decorated, even High Corn Mill in Chapel Street looked seasonally bright, making Irene wonder if there wasn't something she could purchase there.

Her family would be easiest to buy for, and she planned to choose things for them as quickly as possible, but all the while keeping her eyes open for suitable gifts for Martin and Daphne and, of course, for Richard.

She had saved quite a lot during her previous stay here and although some of that had been depleted while she was out of work in London, she wouldn't need to economize. The only problem would be finding shops that were well stocked. Clothing and many other items, including sweets, still were rationed. And although people were supposed to be producing more, there wasn't much evidence of a return to the wide choice of attractive goods available before the war.

She had decided on books for young Heather. Both Mavis and Ralph would appreciate something that encouraged her to be quiet, and neither of them appeared to have much idea themselves of how to keep her happy without her displaying all that natural exuberance.

Irene spent longer than she'd intended in the bookshop, she couldn't resist looking along the shelves, even when she'd chosen something suitable for her niece. But then she noticed a copy of *The Big Fisherman* by Lloyd C. Douglas, and remembered how she had been enthralled by *The Robe*, way back in 1943. She would get this as part of Richard's present, and perhaps a new recording of some favourite piece of music. Kathleen Ferrier had a remarkably fine voice.

Crossing near the town hall, she passed its arcaded front and eventually reached a fascinating shop with a window enticingly filled with hand-crafted articles. And there she saw the table lamps, their honey-pale shades beautifully made, their bases converted brass candlesticks. She hurried inside to buy the pair, already looking forward to giving one each to Martin and Daphne. And then she located a further set, red-shaded on burnished wood, which would help to brighten the room her parents had so depleted in helping furnish a home for Mavis and Ralph.

For the two of them, and also for Lily and Norman, she chose towels. Setting up house, in these days of shortages, meant that even with what they were given at their wedding, nobody ever had sufficient. And there was a special, large white soft towel for the coming infant. She would collect together baby powder, creams and a gentle soap, as well; Lily would be delighted.

Irene had eaten lunch in the cafe she recalled from that early meeting with Giles Holroyd, but otherwise the entire day had evaporated while she went from one shop to another. Emerging from the music shop, she noticed the sky, night-darkened, and releasing occasional flakes of snow which melted on to her face. Behind her, recorded carols from King's College, Cambridge brought close the truth of Christmas. Happy to be going home, she felt like joining in.

Glad to load all her purchases into the car, she stretched aching arms then got into the driving seat. As she started up and set out, she was humming one of the carols she'd heard, looking forward to a quiet evening with Richard.

Irene was singing under her breath when the cars ahead of her halted at an intersection to make way for a speeding ambulance. Trouble for somebody, she thought, and experienced as always the wish that she could still help such people.

'Now, less of that,' she said aloud in the cold of the car. More than ever since coming back to Rich, she was determined to ward off the might-have-beens. She was here in Yorkshire, so was he, and together they were leading a useful, as well as interesting life.

Driving the rest of the way up the increasingly narrow roads, she tried to picture what his expression would be on Christmas Day. She felt certain he would appreciate the book, and he always loved a good recording of classical music.

Irene grew puzzled as she approached the house. Not a single light was visible, yet this was almost the time when they normally had dinner. Slowing carefully for the thin snow covering on the curve of the drive, she told herself that Richard must be in one of the rooms to the rear. And his sister would be in the kitchen. At least, she'd have opportunity to get these parcels up to her room without too many inquisitive glances. After garaging the car, she decided that was what she must do first.

The hall felt cold, and she frowned and switched on the electric heater, but it wasn't until she was running downstairs again that Irene really noticed how singularly quiet the house was. She popped a head around the door of the kitchen, though since it was in darkness she wasn't surprised to find it empty. She shrugged; happen Daphne had gone over to Peggy's. It was unlike her, though, to fail to mention that she wouldn't be in that evening. Perhaps she had left a message with Richard. But where was he?

Beginning to feel uneasy, Irene knocked on the door of his room. There was no response, she hurried inside. The bed was unmade, but otherwise a quick glance revealed nothing unusual. She came out, stood frowning in the hall. She tried the office next, although no light shone from there either. It was exactly as they'd left it last evening.

19

It was the first time she'd been alone in the house, and she'd never been so aware of its size. With people in its rooms and everyday sounds coming from them, especially now the office was here, it had just seemed a large, but very lovely, home. Today, although its appearance was no different, it felt alarmingly big, impersonal. Irene called 'Daphne' and 'Richard'. The only response was a slight echo from the high ceiling above the staircase.

Worry was rising in her throat like a badly digested meal. She returned to Richard's room where she tried to ignore the empty bed. This time she noticed on the bedside table a glass containing half an inch of water. Beside it were the tablets he always carried, spilling from the box as if somebody had grabbed them hastily. Her heart thudding, she recalled the ambulance she'd seen on the road. 'Don't panic,' she said aloud, and strode towards the telephone.

Desperate to speak to somebody, she rang David and Clare. They'd neither heard from Richard all day nor seen him. She rang Peggy's number next, her husband told her Peggy was out. He was sure she knew nothing and hadn't seen Daphne for a while, certainly wasn't with her today.

Irene dialled Giles Holroyd's number, wondering despairingly what her next move would be if she got no joy from him. His wife answered, he was out on a call.

'Do you know where?'

'Sorry, I've no idea. It was an emergency, he just grabbed his bag and leapt into the car. But he normally phones me to let me know where he can be contacted, shall I . . . ?'

Irene interrupted Mrs Holroyd, thanking her but telling her not to bother. It was *now* that she needed him, wasn't it? Now that she was being driven beyond thinking straight.

Suddenly, she sat down on the telephone seat, her legs weak. She couldn't get that ambulance out of her mind, was so sure Richard had been inside it.

He'd looked rough ever since the day he'd turned up in London seeking her. Was she responsible? Hadn't she – the one person who was supposed to be looking after him – caused him the very strain which she knew full well he ought to avoid? And worse, only today, she'd gone shopping when she should have seen the danger signals, have stayed behind.

Irene forced herself to stop these fearful ramblings, and to set her mind on something constructive. She reached for the phone again. This time she got on to the hospital he'd once attended for physiotherapy. They hadn't had an admission in his name, but she gave details and the operator promised to ring back if there was any news.

She tried the Cottage Hospital next, but they'd admitted no one that day, and had no facilities for that kind of emergency. When she replaced the receiver she was breathing rapidly, shallowly, and swallowed, making herself steady up. She went through to the sitting room, found the brandy decanter and poured a generous tot into a glass and took one sip.

Unable to sit still, Irene returned to the hall, began pacing to and fro, wondering how in the world she could discover what was going on. She had snatched up the directory and begun going through for other hospitals when the telephone, shrieking at her elbow, shattered her.

For one moment she hesitated, looking at it, afraid of what it might bring, then she lifted the receiver. It was the hospital she'd spoken to earlier. The girl asked if Mr Hughes was a cardiac patient.

'Yes,' she said, and had to repeat the word. Her voice had been an inaudible whisper.

'Then he is here, was admitted fifteen minutes ago to the Intensive Care Unit.'

Irene gulped. 'How – how bad is he?'

330

'I'm sorry, I've no idea . . .'

'Thanks.' She replaced the receiver, and dashed out of the house, down the steps and around to the garage. Thank goodness she'd not had more than a sip or two of brandy, thank goodness the car was still warm and started instantly. But she had to summon immense effort of will to concentrate on the road instead of surrendering to the desperation tearing her inside out.

The snow was coming faster now, making the wipers sluggish, enforcing a moderate speed. She made herself accept the fact that the journey would take some time. And that her being there couldn't, in any case, help to save Richard. Through the town, traffic slowed to a crawl and she felt tears on her cheeks, brushed them away with the back of a hand. Once clear of the congestion, she began to imagine what might await her at the other end.

'Let him still be alive,' she prayed aloud. 'Let me see him again.' Only then she thought of what was so often the result of a succession of strokes; of people left to live out a crippled existence. And what this would do to Richard. She took a deep, sighing breath, but couldn't frame the words which she felt that she ought. 'Thy will be done,' she gabbled, 'Thy will be done.' Beyond tears now, she was dry-eyed, her throat aching with the struggle for composure.

She flung the car into a parking space not far from the hospital gates. But that meant she'd to walk, slithering repeatedly on the snow, up the seemingly endless path. Almost staggering, and gasping for breath, she reached the porters' lodge and rasped out her request for directions. A stitch in her side, she alternately walked and ran along a succession of corridors till she located Intensive Care. There was a box-like entrance, with wards behind swing doors on three sides. On one of the four chairs sat Daphne, her green eyes staring with anxiety, her face contrasting chalkily with her black hair.

'Thank God!' Daphne exclaimed as she saw Irene.

'Is he . . . ?' she demanded urgently, searching Daphne's face for some clue.

'I don't know — they won't tell me anything.' Daphne's lip trembled and her eyes filled with tears. 'I seem to have been here ages, and they just keep me waiting, without any proper news. People keep going in and coming out — Giles is in an office with someone now, the specialist, I think.'

'So Giles is here.'

'Oh, yes. He's been very good.'

'And Richard — is he conscious?'

'He was when we got him here, I've not been told otherwise.'

'That's something, any road. A good sign if he didn't pass out. What happened?'

'He complained of a headache and a pain in his chest, just before lunch, apparently it had bothered him since first thing. He said he felt sick, wouldn't eat anything. For long enough, he wouldn't hear of my ringing the doctor, told me off for fussing. In the end, though, I decided I wasn't going to be responsible for not calling Giles in.'

'Thank God you did. It was the only way.'

'But supposing it wasn't in time? If you'd been there you'd have known what to do.'

'Oh, don't — for heaven's sake! All the way over, I've cursed myself for going out, but I honestly never suspected anything serious might be wrong.'

'I know you didn't.'

The office door opened, there was a murmur of voices and Giles Holroyd emerged. He nodded briefly to Irene.

'How bad is it?' she inquired.

'You can see him.'

She and Daphne both moved towards the ward entrance.

'Only one of you,' Giles told them.

The two women looked at each other. Daphne nodded, motioned Irene ahead.

A hand on the door, she glanced back at their doctor. 'How is he, though?'

Giles shrugged. 'We're not sure yet,' he replied, pushing the door open for her.

Irene crossed to the bed where Richard was lying, propped against pillows, his face drawn, lips blue-tinged.

'You said this wouldn't happen,' he spat at her through clenched teeth, gesturing with both hands as though to keep her off. 'I was relying on your word.'

He wasn't connected to any of the machinery that would assist with breathing or regulate heart rate. Irene realized simultaneously that he didn't appear to have suffered another stroke and that he was utterly vexed with her. Breath caught in her throat in a choking sob, she was forced to turn away. She put both hands to her face as tears spilled between her fingers, and ran from the room.

Seeing the state she was in, Daphne dashed to her side. 'Is he . . . worse?'

Irene shook her head. 'No, take no notice. He's better than I expected. It's just – me, I'm upset, that's all.'

Together, they went back to the chairs. As Irene calmed slightly she began telling Daphne what she'd observed in the few seconds she'd been with Richard. After five minutes or so Giles joined them and announced that there wasn't much more they could do there that night.

'He's in good hands – will have every possible care, I suggest you go home now.'

They both protested, but he shook his head. 'They've sedated him. They don't believe it's another stroke – but we shan't know how he really is till we've got through the next three weeks.'

To both of them that stretched ahead like three years.

'But I've hung around all this time,' Daphne said. 'I have to see him first.'

Giles was looking straight at Irene. 'They might consent, when he's more calm.' He drew her towards the door, out of Daphne's hearing. 'I'm sorry, but I have to forbid you to go in there again. His blood pressure soared, you know that can be fatal.'

Irene bit her lip, closed her eyes.

'I am sorry, you know,' Giles went on, his voice gentle. 'I think he's being unreasonable. You and I understand nobody on this earth could have been positive this upset wouldn't occur – and I think Richard's always known it as well.'

She sighed. 'But what can I do?'

'Go and get some sleep.'

'As if I could!'

Giles smiled ruefully. 'I know. Just hang on while I let somebody know that Daphne's staying. Then I'll give you something to make sure you do sleep.'

As they left the hospital and reached his car, Giles told her to get inside for a minute. He wanted to talk.

'It's all my fault,' Irene began.

The doctor shook his head. 'You're wrong about that. We knew this could be on the cards if he got into a state, but because we got him here when we did there's every chance there'll be no real harm done.'

She wasn't reassured, she could only think of how guilty she felt for not being there. 'I should have been at home . . .'

'You're allowed some time off. You weren't to know Richard would pick today for a bit of a turn.'

'How bad is it? I'd better know . . .' But she was dreading the reply, thinking of all the months of fighting to restore use to Richard's limbs. Could he, could *she*, face that again?

'As you discovered, there's no loss of speech, there's no paralysis either . . .'

Irene heard her own gasp of relief.

' . . . So far,' Giles added. 'The next two or three days will be crucial, as you know. If there's no brain haemorrhage, he should be no worse. He's had a bad scare, we all have – I'm sorry he appears to be taking it out on you. I thought – hoped he'd react very differently on seeing you.'

'So did I,' she said emphatically. And she couldn't rid herself of the feeling that there had to be some further reason for Richard's attitude towards her.

'I know it makes it harder for you, Irene, loving him as you do.'

'Sounds as though that's common knowledge! I suppose you think it's all very romantic.'

'I know damned well it's not.' Giles paused. 'Some long while ago now Richard came to me for advice. I told him to go ahead, marry you, be happy.'

'And . . . ?'

'He said he'd think about it, but he couldn't disguise his own misgivings. And he asked a great many, very searching questions.'

'Like how long would he live, and if this did happen how much use would he be – to me?'

'Along those lines, yes.'

'And you told him the truth?'

'Shouldn't I have done?'

Irene sighed. 'Rich isn't a man you lie to, is he? And if he has the guts to face his future, I've got to live with mine.'

Before Giles gave her something to help her sleep, he suggested she might try again tomorrow and see if Richard was over this present mood. But she didn't need telling that she would have to be patient until he wanted to see her.

As soon as she arrived back at North Fell House, Irene took the tablets. Nothing else would get her through that night.

Around seven the next morning, she awakened with a heavy feeling that grew more terrible as she recalled details of the previous day. Seeing the parcels she'd bought, still where she'd abandoned them on a chair, tears pricked at her eyes. Refusing to dwell on anything, she pulled on a dressing gown and went to telephone the hospital.

'No change,' was the terse report, and she sighed grimly as she went to have a bath. Eventually, she made herself swallow down toast and coffee before setting out to see if Richard wished to see her.

Overnight the snow had turned to a steady drizzle which hung steamily in the air, seeping into the car, and drifting in misty clouds on the top of the fells.

The rain was heavier when she reached the car park, by the time she arrived at the hospital entrance she could feel her hair in rats' tails around her face. Impatiently, she pushed it away from her forehead as she hurried towards Intensive Care.

Daphne was looking much brighter, they'd found her a bed and she'd managed a few hours' sleep.

'What's he like this morning?' Irene inquired immediately.

She smiled. 'Well, I've just seen him. Only for five minutes. But he'll be all right, Irene, I'm sure of it. God, though, he did give me a fright yesterday!'

'Me too,' said Irene grimly.

'I thought you'd be coming, that's why I hung on – to ride back with you.'

'Aren't you staying then?'

'There's no point. Visiting's strictly rationed – he's had his quota for today.'

'You mean they won't let me in?' She felt as though the floor was giving way beneath her. She'd been counting on the way visiting hours were often relaxed in an intensive care unit. But that was if the people coming in would be good for the patient. Irene soon learned that the sister in charge didn't consider that *she* was in that category.

That wretched Sunday seemed horribly unreal, the haze it developed was only relieved when Giles Holroyd called to give a run-down on Richard's prognosis. Thankfully, he was far better than they had feared, but must continue to have complete rest for some time. And that included no kind of disturbance.

'Do you think I ought to keep away?' Irene asked, willing him to say otherwise.

Giles studied her hard, for a long while. 'Could you?'

Her laugh was harsh, empty. 'If I have to. For a few days, at least. There'll be things to see to, any road, in the office.' But would even that help? 'This is bloody hard!'

He nodded. 'I wouldn't have asked it of you.'

She walked with him to the door. 'Well, give him my love. Tell – tell him he's only to ask, and I'll come.'

But somehow she knew that before that happened she would have to get to the bottom of what was really disturbing Richard.

And, although sustained by the satisfactory reports conveyed by both Giles and Daphne, Irene found by the end of the week that staying away had grown harder. She had sent in flowers, but they had evoked only an all-too-polite relayed word of thanks. She was eating little, and sleeping purely under the sedation that Giles had supplied, and that didn't help her capacity for work.

It was the Saturday afternoon, and Daphne had talked her into visiting Richard. By the time she reached the small ward to which he'd been transferred from Intensive Care, her legs were shaking.

Looking astonished, Richard took a deep breath when she walked in.

'How are you?' she asked straight away, and felt pleased and relieved because his colour was much more normal.

'Improving, thank you – so they tell me.' His voice was cool, almost distant, and he didn't invite her to sit.

Irene stood there, feeling awkward, wondering if this really was the man she was in love with. 'How much longer will you be in here?'

'They don't know.'

'I'm sure it won't be long – Giles says you're no worse.'

'If you can believe it – if you can believe anything anybody says.'

Suddenly, she knew he wasn't only speaking about the shock of discovering he could become ill again. 'What's brought this on?'

'Do you really not understand?' He sighed. 'Despite the fact that you came back, I'm still not really sure where I stand with you, never quite sure you're not going to go off again to him!'

'I beg your pardon?'

Richard leaned sideways, opened his locker, and slid a scrap of paper from inside a book then tossed it towards her.

Irene picked it up off the bed. It was the last few lines torn from a letter. Remembering giving him something to write on a week ago, she reluctantly turned it over.

Please ring me at this number, Irene. Now I'm living in Leeds it would be quite convenient. And I do so want to meet you again. My dear, please say you'll come – or let me drive over to some place of your choosing.

Yours,
John

'Did you phone him?' Richard asked tersely.

Irene searched through her handbag, and eventually handed across the rest of the letter. 'Only to say I'm glad he's over the addiction. I've no intention whatever of seeing him again.'

Richard read the first part of the letter. Finding only John's assertion that he finally was off the drugs, he gave it back to her.

Irene tore up both halves and tossed them into the waste bin. 'You have no need to be like this about anyone, you're the one I love.'

He reached for her hand. 'I'm sorry for seeming to mistrust you. It's this situation – our not being married. And that's my fault.'

'Or circumstances. You needn't blame yourself. I couldn't feel more committed to you, Richard. And I am thankful that John can't even arouse my professional concern any longer.'

'Things seemed so bleak that day, I hated not being up to going out with you. And I'll admit I was scared by feeling rough. Then finding that note confronted me with not being the only man who'd wanted you.'

As his grasp on her hand tightened, Irene sat on the edge of the bed. 'I hope you've seen now that you can put all this behind you, and concentrate on getting better.'

She herself was improving by the moment after being relieved of the distress of Richard's refusal to see her. And this reminder of how much he wanted her would keep her going until he came home. Meanwhile there'd be daily visits, no more anguish generated by being kept away.

Familiar voices made them turn. They both smiled immediately, seeing not only Daphne but Martin walking towards them down the ward.

'How are you?' Martin inquired, shaking Richard's hand.

'Isn't this marvellous!' Daphne exclaimed and while the men were talking began explaining how Martin had decided to dash to Yorkshire. 'I didn't need proof of how lovely he is, but this has clinched it.'

Because of Martin's collar, no one objected to three of them round the bed, and the afternoon grew lively. When visiting ended Daphne and Martin waited in the corridor while Irene kissed Richard goodbye.

They were standing very close there, oblivious to visitors and nurses, failing to see Irene's approach, absorbed in each other.

Back at the house she'd never seen anyone more obviously in love. Daphne wanted to cook Martin a meal, but he insisted on joining her in the kitchen. When nothing got done, Irene took over cooking. Sitting at the dining table, she smiled to herself while they exchanged glances and teasing remarks, like lovers half their age.

After they had eaten, the pair insisted on doing the washing-up – a task which appeared to take an inordinate length of time. When they joined Irene in the sitting room, Daphne's cheeks were brighter than the rose-hued candles on the marble fireplace, and her dark hair was abnormally ruffled.

'You've a lovely home, darling,' Martin remarked, glancing around him. 'You're going to find mine very different.'

Irene contained a smile. So – matters were swiftly being sorted.

But Daphne was laughing. 'Wrong – *you're* going to find your home very different! You'll not recognize it once I get to work.'

'Steady on a minute – my name isn't Hughes. I'm an impecunious parson, don't forget.' But his smile belied any concern that Daphne might have grave trouble adjusting.

She herself was laughing again. 'Don't forget I'm a Yorkshire lass – it's bred in me to be careful with t'brass, even if Rich and I haven't needed to. I'll still transform that place of yours.'

'As you've transformed me,' he observed, and rather seriously.

'Have I?' She turned and included Irene. 'Have I, Irene?'

'Well, I've never seen Martin this happy. And I'll tell you something else – I'll be glad when Rich knows how *you* are now. He missed the best bits, while you were in that hospital corridor. He couldn't see the doctors and nurses doing a detour around the pair of you. Nor the porter who let a trolley, complete with patient, go coursing off because he was that fascinated with what was going on!'

'Irene, don't exaggerate!' Daphne exclaimed.

'Perhaps I was, a little. But it's great seeing you like this, don't change, either of you, will you?'

'We can't now,' Martin told her, beaming. 'This is the way we'll always be. Daphne's agreed to getting engaged at Christmas.'

'I hate leaving you on your own,' Daphne said early on the morning of Christmas Eve as she was getting ready to leave for London.

'You're not to give me a thought,' Irene assured her, smiling. 'I'm quite old enough to look after myself.'

'You know what I mean. And since the day after Christmas Day's a Sunday and Martin's tied up again he wants me to stay into next week.'

'And so you must! I shall spend my days tripping back and forth to hospital, I'll have no time to do more than snatch a meal in between.'

Although they were busy in the office, with Richard out of action for those few weeks, the three of them succeeded in getting things straight by mid-afternoon so that David and Anita could leave early.

Irene was finishing tidying her own desk when the telephone rang. Afraid that it was a last-minute client, she only reluctantly lifted the receiver. 'Yes?' she demanded quite tersely, without her normal query as to how she could help.

'You've to come and get me – if you'll have me; they're sick of me here!'

'Richard! Oh, that's wonderful. I'm so pleased!'

'What time then?' he asked eagerly.

'Just as soon as I can get there.'

'Drive carefully, mind.'

Irene sat for a moment, gazing at the telephone. 'Thank God,' she murmured, then rushed to get a coat.

On the way out, she bumped into Mrs O'Connor, and told her that Richard was being discharged. 'You can lay on all your splendid fare, after all, can't you?' Ever since Daphne had started going out to work again Mrs O'Connor's role had extended to become more that of a housekeeper than a cleaning lady.

Now, though, her homely features clouded. 'Ay, dear – what a to-do! And I've arranged for my brother to come and stop wi' us. He were widowed last back-end, and him and our Shaun get on right well.'

Irene smiled. 'That's fine with me, Mrs O'Connor, just carry on as you've arranged. Actually, I shall quite enjoy playing house.'

'Well, there's plenty of stuff in, any road. I've seen to that. And I'll get something going now for tonight for you both.'

Richard was waiting with everything to hand when Irene arrived. He quickly went round the ward thanking everyone before they drove off.

'I can see I shall soon be telling you off for fussing,' he remarked, but with a smile, as she insisted on giving him a car rug.

'It's jolly cold in here,' she said. 'You'll be glad of that.'

Richard wasted no time before going indoors once she had drawn up at North Fell House. 'Good to be back,' he exclaimed, gazing around.

'I hope you still think so tomorrow,' she said. 'Neither Mrs O'Connor nor I anticipated it being a proper Christmas, don't know what I'll rustle up for dinner!'

He grinned. 'I don't care. This is all I need.' He turned aside to greet the housekeeper who was waiting with her coat on to see him before going off to her own home.

'By, but you're looking champion, Mr Hughes! I can tell you're a lot better, thank goodness.'

Richard paused to thank her and chat, and Irene realized that she tended to take Mrs O'Connor very much for granted. But happen that fact was, in a way, a tribute to the woman's efficiency.

Despite their delight that Richard was home, the atmosphere between them once they were alone wasn't entirely easy. Once or twice, Irene almost wished Daphne was there to fill these alarming gaps that kept appearing in their conversation. During the evening, sitting together after they had eaten and she'd cleared away, she began wondering if their relationship had been damaged by the recent distress.

The telephone rang, and she found Daphne on the line.

'Just to tell you I've got a lovely engagement ring now – and so you don't feel too alone and left out of things. How's Rich?'

'You'd better ask him.' Irene laughed at Daphne's exclamation. 'Yes, great, isn't it!'

She handed Richard the receiver and walked away, leaving him to talk privately with his sister.

He seemed more at ease afterwards. She asked him what had changed.

'Your voice was a relief – when you told Daphne I was here. I knew then you were glad to have me here.'

Irene frowned. 'But, love, surely you never doubted that?'

'Naturally. I wouldn't have welcomed anybody who'd behaved as abominably as I have with you.'

He was standing, looking anxious again. She went to him, but feeling uncertain what to say. Then suddenly she was hugging him, and their kisses began speaking for them.

The rest of the evening was relaxed, and even the pauses in conversation seemed companionable. A little after ten o'clock Irene asked if it wasn't time Richard was heading for bed.

'Is there some hurry?' he inquired with a smile.

She explained that she'd intended going to church and wanted to see him settled first.

'I see.'

'What is it?' She could tell he had something on his mind.

'I'm going to be entirely selfish. Don't go, love, not tonight. I want you here with me, listening to the service on the wireless.'

'That'll suit me fine.'

When midnight came she'd persuaded him to stretch out on the sofa, and drew up a chair beside it.

Richard reached for her hand. 'I have a great many thanks to say, from a full heart. It's only now I understand why I was so bloody scared of losing my life. With you, it is infinitely precious.'

Irene awakened next morning as soon as the church bells started ringing. And had to curb the urge to run to Richard's room immediately and reassure herself that he really was home at last. Instead, she bathed and put on a new woollen dress which she'd bought in London. In concession to the New Look, it had a skirt which reached a good halfway down her shin, but it wasn't nearly so full as the more accentuated styles. The line was graceful, though, with the fullness draped towards her left hip and the bodice also crossing over in a beautifully cut swathe. The colour was an unusual one for her – a brown which fashion folk were calling 'snuff'. Today, with happiness warming her cheeks and restoring life to her blue eyes, the combination with her fair hair appeared to work.

Richard's eyes certainly told her that he approved. And as the day progressed it soon became evident that he also approved everything that she had done. He already knew and liked the author Lloyd C. Douglas; the record she'd chosen was played three times in all, leaving no doubt that it was appreciated. And even their meal, which was assembled around steak purchased by dint of hoarding rations, proved to be just as enjoyable as more traditional fare.

Irene's delight had been made complete by Richard's gift. Because of his being in hospital, she'd assumed he'd have done no shopping and she was expecting nothing. But once breakfast was finished and before she had handed over the things she had bought for him, he'd surprised her with a small package.

Opening up the box it contained, she'd gasped. Somewhere, amid all the rather indifferent jewellery available these days, he had found the most exquisite watch.

'Oh, how lovely, Rich! Thank you, thank you!'

And then he'd shown her the minute inscription engraved on the back: *Till the end of time* . . .

Trying to speak, she'd managed only something suspiciously like a sob. Richard had called her predictable, but he'd smiled appreciatively throughout the day when she gazed so frequently at the watch on her wrist.

Around ten o'clock that night they were sitting either side of the lovely pale marble fireplace, listening to a violin concerto. The flickering log fire alternately lit and shadowed Richard's smiling face. His eyes were closed but Irene was well aware that he wasn't sleeping.

'Know something?' she said. 'I could develop quite a liking for this.'

He looked at her and grinned. 'Well, excluding miracles, this is what I'd settle for, very happily. But *I've* grown accustomed to not being overactive.'

'You normally keep me busy enough the rest of the time to make this an agreeable antidote.'

'Ah – and that's one thing I meant to mention. Pleasant though it is to not have Daphne interrupting, we're going to miss her organizational skills around the house.'

'Are you suggesting I'm not up to that?'

Smiling, he shook his head. 'I'm sure you'd cope admirably. But I don't want you wearing yourself out with that as well as all you do in the office. I'm thinking of asking Mrs O'Connor to keep house for us, and if that's more than she wishes to take on we'll find another housekeeper.'

Although sorry in some ways that she wouldn't be looking after Rich and his home to quite the extent that she'd pictured, Irene thanked him and agreed. His consideration of her induced a lovely glow of contentment.

The rest of the Christmas holiday continued just as congenially, and when Richard said he was determined to start work immediately afterwards he appeared so well that Irene didn't attempt to deter him. Yet again, she was glad they were working side by side, and she could watch that he didn't become overtired.

As soon as Daphne returned from London, she began wedding preparations. She and Martin were marrying at the local church here in Yorkshire, and very shortly, for they must avoid a Lenten wedding which would hardly be appropriate for a clergyman. On Richard's insistence, several rooms at North Fell were being redecorated to make up for the years of wartime austerity and therefore almost up to the day itself they had workmen around the house.

It was dry, but crisp and frosty on that February morning, and the hazy sun finally shone and took a little of the chill out of the east wind.

Irene had invested in a new navy-blue winter coat, and was glad of its longer length and also that it was hugged to her by the closely fitting waist and had one of the new detachable shoulder capes. Even with a woollen ice-blue dress, which contrasted well with the navy, she was afraid the cold would penetrate before they had finished hanging around while photographs were taken.

It hadn't occurred to her that she would have any prominent part in the proceedings until Richard insisted that she must sit in the front pew. He, of course, was giving Daphne away and was determined that Irene must be there when he stepped back from his sister's side.

She had wondered what the various members of the Hughes family might make of that, but in the event she was too preoccupied to care.

The instant she saw how tall and commanding Richard looked as, with a barely perceptible limp, he escorted

Daphne towards Martin, Irene felt her eyes filling. She had warned him that she always cried at weddings, and when he smiled towards her as he came to her side he followed that with the offer of an immaculate white hand-kerchief.

She grinned, but couldn't disguise her emotion, and was forced to lift the navy veiling of her tiny ice-blue hat to dry away tears.

Daphne was wearing white velvet which fitted perfectly and made her seem even more beautiful than ever. Being this close, Irene had noticed the momentary gasp from across the aisle where Martin waited. There could be no doubting his admiration. Irene, for one, was delighted. Daphne was a lovely-looking woman who deserved to be appreciated for more than her affinity with Martin's cleri-cal vocation, genuine though that affinity was.

Much as Irene loved the ceremony, she hadn't been looking forward to the reception afterwards at North Fell House. She was well aware that families tended to specu-late on whose wedding might occur next, and wasn't re-lishing that prospect on Richard's behalf or her own.

For a while it seemed that she had worried needlessly. Most of the guests were friends rather than family, and they included David and Clare so she was happy to join them whilst Richard circulated. All at once, though, and from right across the sitting room she sensed him stiffen. A frown narrowed his eyes, and the ready smile which had remained with him all day swiftly disappeared.

Detaching herself from David and his wife, Irene headed across the room, determined on being to hand if Rich needed someone to alleviate tension.

He was speaking with a tall, austere lady whom Daphne had introduced as an aunt.

'Oh, no – I shan't marry. I'm afraid that's quite out of the question,' Richard was saying, his voice cold, as only he knew how to make it when irritated.

He turned from his aunt and strode away without even seeing Irene. But he had crossed to join Daphne's matron of honour, Peggy, and her husband, and soon was talking

346

affably with them. After so many months of growing accustomed to the situation, Irene herself wasn't greatly perturbed on her own account; but somehow she knew how deeply Richard had been disturbed.

There was little time that day, however, for anything but the excitement generated by the wedding. The hours seemed to race and suddenly it was late afternoon and Daphne and Martin were hugging them and saying goodbye.

'We'll always remember how you two brought us together,' said Martin. 'And we wouldn't dream of having distance keep us all apart for too long.'

'We shall expect you both to visit us in London, especially since theatres and other night spots are getting back to normal,' his bride added.

Richard laughed. 'Glad you realize I'll need some inducement to come and see you, young sister! I'm looking forward to freedom from your nagging.' He gave her another hug, nevertheless, and Irene heard Martin's murmured assurance that he'd take good care of Daphne.

It was almost seven o'clock when the last of the guests drove off and Richard put an arm round Irene's shoulders as they went back into the house.

Everything seemed very still after all the chatter. Mrs O'Connor, who had agreed to keep house but not to living in, had departed for her own home, with instructions to leave any clearing up for her to do tomorrow. But the caterers had left the place immaculate before finally driving away.

After changing into more comfortable clothes, they returned to the sitting room where Irene sighed luxuriously as she went to the sofa.

'It's been a lovely day, I couldn't have enjoyed it more.'

'Lucky you!' Richard exclaimed dourly, going to pour drinks. 'I'm having a good stiff whisky, what about you?'

'Nothing just now, thanks. And what did you mean, about today?'

He came to sit beside her. 'Always somebody to ruin an occasion, isn't there? Let's forget it, though.'

'No – tell me.' Not that she needed telling.

'One of the interfering aunts – what the hell is it to her if I remain single? Haven't they eyes to see the reason!'

'Don't let it get to you, Rich. It's not important . . .'

'Not important?' he interrupted. 'Christ, if that isn't, what is?'

'Richard, love, listen – we have a better relationship than lots of people, let that be sufficient. We don't need to have a piece of paper to confirm that we're committed to each other.'

20

On the following Monday when Irene awakened her throat was sore and her head was aching. Grimly, she smiled, thinking how she'd been worried in case Richard was affected by the wintry weather whilst standing around after the wedding, and she was the one who'd caught cold.

During the day it grew steadily worse so she had an early night, hoping to rid herself of the infection. It didn't work and nor did any of the remedies she tried throughout that week.

'You'd think I'd know how to dispose of a cold, after all my training, wouldn't you,' she exclaimed to Richard.

'If you knew an infallible cure, you'd be making far more than I'll ever pay you!'

He was, nevertheless, anxious about how pale and fatigued Irene seemed, and by the cough which grew deeper and more persistent as she tried to work on into a second week.

They had just finished their meal one evening when Giles Holroyd arrived. Irene gave Richard a look, but he was ready for her.

'I wasn't going to let you get worse and worse. If you can't look after yourself, I've got to do that for you.'

The doctor soon had her upstairs to her room and after he'd sounded her chest, he was frowning.

'I'm surprised at you – you should have recognized the symptoms.'

'Bronchitis?'

'So you did know. Why on earth didn't you treat yourself as you'd have advised anyone else? Well – no choice now. Into bed with you. I'll leave a prescription with Richard, he'll get it to the chemist first thing in the morning. And don't you dare get out of that bed till I say so. I'll be round some time tomorrow.'

Irene felt worse before she began improving – so ill that for days she was thankful just to lie there. Despite Giles Holroyd prescribing the new wonder drug penicillin, her cough was so deep seated that it didn't respond readily to treatment. Now she'd time to think, she realized that the stress before Christmas would have debilitated her sufficiently for the illness to take hold. And now both she and Rich were paying the price. Breathing hurt her and most nights became very difficult, whilst Richard was troubled by concern for her and tired by covering for her in the office.

'Are you delegating enough?' she asked one evening when he came to her room looking almost as bad as she was feeling. 'Can't the others do more?'

'They are doing, love. It's simply that there aren't enough pairs of hands around.'

All the time that she'd been laid low, Richard had been kindness itself, as had Mrs O'Connor, but as soon as she began feeling stronger Irene was yearning to be more active. And to get out.

For one thing, she ached to go to Halifax. Lily had given birth to a boy and Norman had sounded disappointed when he phoned with the news and Irene wasn't able to go over immediately to see the infant.

'I'll have to wait till I'm really over this,' Irene explained. 'The little lad will have some built-in protection against germs, but your Lily won't. And you know she's as thin as a bit of string at the best of times.'

Richard had heard her saying that. 'Have you seen yourself lately?' he asked when she'd replaced the receiver. 'This has really pulled you down. Just as soon as you're up to travelling, I'm taking you away from this wretched climate for a while. We're having a holiday.'

The end of March was the soonest they could manage to book a flight and accommodation. Richard had set his heart on going to southern Italy. 'I think they're over some of the ravages of war by now. And they aren't likely to

350

have hordes of tourists there, as they're now getting them in Switzerland.'

Irene didn't care where she went, so long as it was with Rich; even when she began feeling stronger she seemed to need to depend on him more than in the past. It wasn't a feeling she could wholeheartedly approve, for hadn't she always worked towards being self-sufficient, but Richard appeared happy with her greater reliance upon him. He did, however, tend to interfere once she was back to normal life and planning to go about more.

'Are you sure you ought to go so far?' he asked as soon as she said she was visiting Halifax to see her new nephew.

'Nay, it's no distance. And if you're that concerned you can come with me. Our Norman and his wife'd love to meet you.'

There was only a brief hesitation, and then Richard smiled. 'Why not? After all, it's high time I got to know your family. You've meant all the world to me for long enough!'

Irene was elated on the Sunday morning as she drove down the dale, through Skipton, and over the familiar route to Halifax. She had telephoned her mother, asking her to let Lily know when she saw her that she finally was up to accepting her invitation. And that she would have Richard with her.

Lily was looking well when she answered the door of the prefab, and she smiled as she shook Richard's hand while Irene introduced them.

'I'm right glad to meet you, at last. We were beginning to wonder what was up when we saw nowt of you. But come on in, both of you. Little Donald's been playing up, his dad's seeing to him.'

'Ay – hallo!' Norman exclaimed, over the top of the baby's head. 'Sorry, I can't get up, but his lordship's just beginning to calm down a bit, don't want to disturb him. So, you're Richard then – glad to meet you.'

Richard smiled back. 'And I'm pleased to meet the two of you – or three, I suppose . . .'

'Aye, our Donald will soon leave you in no doubt that he's here. Proper little boss he is – not that he's a bad youngster, sleeps at night, any road.'

'Has done from the start,' Lily concurred. 'It's just during the day that he likes to have something going on.'

'It's only the way young Heather was,' Irene began.

'Aye, Mavis were telling me that. I just hope he isn't quite as lively as Heather. She's a right little madam, these days, allus on the go. And I'm not as young as Mavis, remember, haven't that much energy.'

'You're looking well, though,' Irene remarked.

Lily nodded. 'I got over it better nor I expected. I was too eager to be up and doing, to give in to lying around for a fortnight at after. Mavis were very good, mind you, came over every day. And Heather, bless her, was fascinated with the baby.'

'You might say Lily looks well,' Norman interrupted. 'It's more nor I can say for you.'

Irene grinned. 'Yes, well – it's the first time I've had owt wrong with me since I came back up north, had to make sure I had my fair share of spoiling.'

'You didn't make a fuss of her, I hope?' Norman inquired of Richard. 'You don't want to give her a taste for it!'

Richard laughed. 'Oh, dear! And I've only recently gone and booked us a holiday abroad.'

Lily was surprised. 'I say, aren't we posh-off! But how nice it'll be, that'll build you up again, Irene love. Where're you going?'

Richard relaxed, and sitting back in the chair he'd been offered he outlined what he'd learned about Sorrento and the surrounding area. 'I only trust that there aren't too many reminders of the fighting out there. Monte Casino saw a lot of bloodshed.'

Norman nodded. 'I daresay the Italians will be wanting to get folk holidaying there now that package tours are becoming popular.'

For them that can afford them, thought Irene, and wondered if they shouldn't be playing down their trip abroad. But both Lily and Norman were so evidently well suited with their infant, she soon felt reassured that they envied no one.

After a while when Baby Donald was fast asleep, Norman carefully got to his feet and handed the infant to Irene. 'I'm going to show Richard round the garden. That's if you're interested . . .'

'I am and all.' But Irene noticed that Rich gave Baby Donald a pensive look before he followed Norman outside.

Lily smiled across at her sister-in-law. 'Your mum and dad are coming this aft – I had to ask 'em, your mother would have been ever so disappointed if she hadn't seen you. Especially when Richard were coming with you. He's lovely, isn't he, and doesn't he talk nice . . .'

Irene smiled. 'He's certainly been good to me these past few weeks while I've been under the weather.'

'I expect he'd be only too thankful to do summat in return, since you got him going after he were flat on his back so long.'

'How are Mum and Dad keeping? Any less tired than they both were just after the National Health started?'

'They're not so bad – leastways, your dad isn't. Not so sure about your mother.'

'I know. Their life seems to take more out of her, always at folk's beck and call, interrupted nights . . .' If *she'd* still been in medicine, she might have got him to ease up a bit by now. Shaking her head slightly to shrug away the thought, she looked across at Lily. 'I didn't know you'd decided to call the baby Donald.'

'We hadn't – I liked Stewart, but then it came to me all of a sudden. He is their first grandson, and your dad's a lovely man – I wish mine were half as thoughtful. So, Stewart's his second name, and I felt right champion telling 'em we'd picked Donald.'

Irene relaxed, chatting with Lily, feeling assured that Norman's wife was one person who'd always do right by her in-laws. By the time Richard and Norman came back indoors and they all sat down to Sunday dinner she was pounds better than when they'd set out.

And then during the afternoon her mother and father arrived, and took Richard to them so warmly that he might have been a member of the family newly restored to them.

'I shall feel a lot happier about our Irene now,' Elsie was soon telling him.

Richard grinned. 'Nay, Mrs Hainsworth, it's early days yet. You haven't been in my company half an hour!'

'I don't care, I can tell. And I can see, an' all, why she's stayed around at North Fell House so long.'

'And what's all this about taking Irene away to recuperate?' Donald put in, beaming. 'Just what she needs, by the look of her.'

Irene winced. 'Not you as well, Dad! Everybody's making me think I look terrible.'

'It's not terrible you look, you know,' Richard said much later, as they were driving home. 'Though you seem more fragile than I like, there's a different beauty in your eyes now, in your expression.' He'd noticed ever since he'd suggested their going away together, and believed that it had more than a little to do with his having proved the depth of his concern for her. 'I'm glad I've met some of your family,' he added, and hoped she wouldn't remind him that he'd denied himself that opportunity long ago. He wasn't ready to talk so much about today, he'd been staggered by his own emotions. He'd never had much contact with families before—with babies. Seeing that tiny boy had made him realize how good it must be to have a youngster whom you could help to develop in ways that fitted him for life.

'Aye, they're not so bad,' Irene said, smiling. Now that the round of introductions had begun she wasn't going to say anything to spoil things. Rich had fitted in better than she'd expected at Norman's, but she did wonder how he'd react when he came to meet their Mavis.

'Pity your sister wasn't there as well,' Richard remarked, and the coincidence nearly made her laugh.

'I think they'd been asked to a special do that Ralph's mother was putting on. There'd be no way Mavis could have wriggled out of that!'

'Like that, is it?'

'Very much so. I don't believe the way Mr and Mrs Parkin try to monopolize Mavis and Heather goes down too well with my parents. Mind you, in certain moods, our Mavis'll stand up to anybody.'

Before he was to see that for himself, however, Richard was delighted to be setting out for Italy. They flew to Naples, then made the short journey to Sorrento in the car which they had hired. Richard's only regret was that he'd done nothing yet about asking the consultant if he would be allowed to drive again. And although, following his illness last December, he'd agreed with Irene that waiting a while before seeking advice on that might result in a more satisfying answer, he didn't like watching her coping with driving on the right.

'I'm okay,' she assured him, 'just so long as you don't expect me to drive very fast.' And certainly many of the roads clung so precariously to the steep hillsides that no one ought to drive at speed along them.

When they arrived at their hotel a mile or so beyond Sorrento they both were pleasantly surprised. Clearly built since the end of the war, its interior was beautifully light and furnished to a standard of elegance that would be hard to find in the austerity still in force back home.

The owner laughed when complimented. 'Ah – so many of the things you see here were rescued from my family home which was badly damaged in the fighting. Mercifully, most of the curtains were too large for these windows, we were able to have them remade, cutting out parts that were ruined.'

'But they all look so new!' Irene exclaimed.

'We had refurbished the place in 1938. As you will comprehend, my wife she was desolate when our home was destroyed. But we are happy here now, the two of us, our family all survived. And now we have this new life, meeting people like yourselves.'

The agreeable surroundings and their host appeared to be equalled by the quality of the food and service there. That first night over dinner Irene tried to tell Richard how grateful she was.

He laughed. 'When I've been clever ensuring that I share every moment of your "cure"?'

Tired after their journey, they simply sat for a while afterwards, enjoying a leisurely drink in the lounge and gazing out over neighbouring orange groves towards the bay.

The following morning was far warmer than Irene had expected and they set out immediately after breakfast. They decided to leave the car, they would see much more on foot, and could turn back when tiredness dictated.

Vesuvius was very clear across the water of the bay which was enhanced by tiny boats dotted around as far as the horizon. As they walked downhill and turned a curve in the road, their view of Sorrento itself grew more distinct.

'You've certainly chosen a lovely spot,' said Irene, taking Richard's arm. 'I hope you're beginning to relax as much as I am.'

In the town they sat at a table in the square, sipping cappuccino and watching passers-by. Very few of the people in sight appeared to be visitors, and fewer still to be British. I could get a liking for this, Irene thought, and reflected that it was years since she'd taken a proper holiday.

They spent most of the afternoon wandering through the streets and gazing in shop windows, which seemed to have far more interesting goods than those back home. 'We did win the war, didn't we?' she said with a laugh. 'It looks as if we're slower to pick up afterwards.'

'You haven't seen some of the side streets in the poorer areas round Naples yet – I daresay you'd find slums that wrenched your heart. And there must be lots of places still crying out to be reconstructed.'

This wasn't the occasion, though, for finding scenes to awaken their concern. Richard was determined that everything must be geared to Irene's recuperation.

When the sun shone again next day they made the most of it by going swimming. After asking directions at the hotel they walked up the road for a short distance then turned off to their right down a sandy path. Lizards scooted away into the scrub surrounding trees, making them stand and stare before continuing down towards the cliffs. Their path emerged at a rocky shelf, several feet wide, ideal for sunbathing.

'At least, this early in the year, we shouldn't be in danger of sunstroke,' said Richard. 'I'm sure in the height of summer the heat will be intense.'

They stretched out on towels, absorbing the sun for an hour or so, then plunged into the crystal water. Icy, at first, it caught their breath, making them laugh rather ruefully, but they quickly grew accustomed to the temperature below the surface.

After swimming around for a while they turned over to float, gazing up at the cloudless azure sky. England and its north-country chill seemed a whole world away, making them both more carefree.

As they were leaving the water Irene's foot slipped on the uneven steps and she stumbled. Close behind, Richard swiftly steadied her, but somehow his touch on her arm was anything but stabilizing.

'Hang on,' he said, and put an arm around her waist.

Suddenly Irene was slithering down the rock, back into the sea, and into his arms. The water lapped about their shoulders and still he was holding her, more tightly now as their bodies met.

His kiss covered her mouth, instantly inviting, inciting her to acknowledge the pressure that his hips were exerting. Every part of her alive to him, Irene traced his lips with her tongue, felt the sharpness of his teeth.

'Lord, but you're gorgeous,' Richard sighed, his heartbeat quickening against her breast.

He was stirring against her, warm despite the cold water surrounding them, warmer than the sun. Irene moved with him, thrilling to his strength, yearning to be his.

He turned away at last, as she had known that he would, but once they had towelled themselves and stretched out on the ledge, he rolled towards her, and his mouth located hers. Irene drew him close, turned, and he came on top of her.

Her arms locked around him, holding him near. 'You see,' she murmured, 'I'm not afraid of anything.'

'Maybe you ought to be, of me.'

'We're not children, by any stretch of imagination; we know where to draw the line.'

'You make that sound very simple.'

She knew that it wasn't, but she also was abundantly aware that if she and Rich made love she'd have no regrets. Wanting him in this way had been, for such a very long time, just another facet of needing him. Their kisses grew fevered, deepening her longing, so that they failed to hear footsteps on the rough path until the group approaching were all but upon them. As their voices grew clearer through the trees, Richard moved away from her, got to his feet and went to stand a little way off, staring out to sea. Irene sensed that this would have happened even if no one had disturbed them.

The following day was cooler, though still sunny, and they drove along the cliff road to Amalfi, pausing repeatedly to admire the steep escarpments or tiny fishing communities far below in the coves along the picturesque shore. They ate lunch in Amalfi before visiting the cathedral and later sat with cool drinks at a promenade cafe. On the homeward run they stopped to explore the Emerald Grotto and returned, well pleased with their day, in time for a short rest before dinner.

Irene was feeling infinitely better, the last remnants of the cough had vanished, and all the anxieties of the previous year had dropped away. Richard, too, was benefiting from the absence of work and relishing the opportunity to see another country. They were alternating lazy, sunbathing days with excursions, and were both thrilled by Pompeii.

Neither Richard nor Irene was prepared for the extent of the ruined city, and together they marvelled at the detail of ancient life which had emerged from the lava. Irene particularly liked the bakery, complete with grindstones, and was entranced with the Casa dei Vettii and its many colourful murals. It was only when tiredness forced them to cease exploring the many roads, still scored by wheel tracks, that they reluctantly headed back to the hotel.

'We could come another day,' Richard suggested. He'd been too delighted by how they both had found Pompeii fascinating to resign himself to leaving any of it unseen.

Determined that nothing must spoil their holiday, Irene had insisted next morning that they should laze around until the evening. They had booked a table for dinner at a large hotel overhanging the sea.

She dressed carefully to go there, in a gown Richard had never seen, a subtle dusky pink. In the New Look style, it was wide skirted and reached almost to her ankles, the bodice was close fitting, with a sweetheart neckline.

Eventually, when they danced, she began to appreciate the full skirts as they stirred gracefully about her. Feeling more glamorous than usual seemed to induce a special awareness, of the music and inevitably of her partner.

Richard had been particularly attentive throughout, assisting with her chair each time they returned to the table, and when they danced holding her in a way that conveyed caring along with his pleasure. Irene had never loved an evening more, and was sorry when people began leaving.

When they finally went out to the car Richard drew her to him and kissed her lingeringly, in the shadows where nearby conifers assailed her nostrils while he disturbed all her senses.

Somewhere along the road he asked her to stop the car.

'What's wrong?' Irene asked, as she located a place to draw off the road.

'Nothing. Just this.' Taking her in his arms again, he covered her mouth with his, driving away her breath with a tongue that plunged between her teeth. Then all at once he drew away, sighed.

'What is it, Rich?'

'What do you think, loving you as I do, dancing with you all evening . . . '

After his voice trailed off, they each seemed isolated, aware of the sea dashing against the rocks far below them.

Inside the car, Irene listened to her watch ticking, Richard's breathing.

'I want you to need me – like that,' she said into the darkness.

'But I thought – you've seemed content recently, happy to remain as we are.'

'Nay, Richard! I've only tried to live with the way things were.'

'I've certainly had enough of this cold, calculated . . . torture,' he admitted. But that mustn't automatically mean that he would make love to her. He couldn't suddenly stifle all sense of responsibility.

Irene felt very thankful that Richard was beginning to understand how important their feelings were. She couldn't quite contain her soaring relief as she swiftly started up the car again. Only the thought of how startled he'd be prevented her singing.

Inside the hotel, at the door of her room, she handed him her key. 'I've loved you for so long, Richard. It's time you knew how much.'

Irene undressed, had a quick shower, and slipped into her nightgown. But it was beginning to look as if Rich had decided not to come. And though she sighed, she wasn't surprised. But she was sorry. Marriage would have been ideal, but she couldn't feel more committed to him, and they would have belonged together. Her only fear had been that he might think less of her afterwards, but she suspected all her other emotions would have outweighed that.

She found her book, began to read, or tried to. Time and again, she forced her attention back to the page, her clenched hand pressed at her lips. This hunger threatened to keep away sleep for ever.

Unable to ignore the longing that soared in every vein, Irene left the bed, walked towards the french windows and out on to the balcony. Across the bay, stark moonlight silhouetted Vesuvius against the sky. In a curve of hills, just to her right, Sorrento nestled. All the world seemed at peace, except for her corner of it. At times, since they'd arrived here, they'd been happier than ever, but would each day always end like this? Would they spend the rest of their lives tormented by this everlasting, unsatisfied yearning?

Silently, the door of her room opened. She sensed, rather than heard, Richard crossing the carpet towards her. As he joined her on the balcony he slid both arms around her from behind, buried his face in her pale hair. 'I had to come.'

He turned her in his arms so that their lips could meet. In kisses that seemed to draw her entire being up towards him. Clinging, near to frenzy, she felt him warm, hard, through the dressing gown he wore.

Rich took her with him back into the room, but left the curtains wide, and stood gazing at her moonlit form. And then his hands went to her nightgown, taking it from her with such haste that she shivered as its silk texture slithered away from her arms.

'You're very lovely, my darling.' His voice sounded strange, changed by emotion.

'I'm yours, Rich, have been for months.' Or was it years now?

He gathered her to him again, pressing at her spine, holding her against the need she created. As he stirred, so did she, echoing his urgency until they parted briefly, kissed yet again, and walked towards the bed.

Richard discarded dressing gown, pyjamas, as though they'd offended him, making her smile secretly before he came to join her. And then all his eagerness was in the strength of the arms pulling her towards him, and in the strength of his love, undisguised now against her.

How have we waited this long? she wondered.

'How could we delay?' he murmured.

And there were no words then, neither spoken nor framed in silence, only his closeness and his hands loving her as the prelude to the greater loving. He was more forceful than she'd believed possible, and more ardent. Irene blessed her own excitement for without it she'd have found Richard's urgent possession of her painful. Because she was ready, she

361

was aware only of the massive thrusting of his need, and of her own response, drawing him deep within her.

He said her name, and continued pressing, rhythmically, winning from her waves of delicious fervour. She was kissing him with all the passion of their stirring bodies; taking and giving, willing the ecstasy to endure yet seeking ultimate release.

When they finally grew still Rich exclaimed against her neck, 'God, but that was wonderful!'

He seemed to sleep then, but only for a time. After a while he began kissing her again, gently, almost tentatively. 'Was I selfish?' he inquired.

Irene smiled into his serious eyes. 'Was I? I couldn't get enough of you!'

He chuckled. 'I rather think you might! Before very long, if I'm not much mistaken.'

After making love a second time they slept, perfectly at peace, awakening only when the hotel staff were moving around in distant areas of the building next morning.

Richard looked serious now, making Irene wonder how much he was regretting. When he spoke, however, his words weren't at all regretful. 'You've made me so happy, Irene, because we belong together. Maybe we always have. Tell me, though – how deeply have you considered what it could be like if we were married?'

'Pretty marvellous, that's how I see it.'

'That isn't what I mean. Do you still believe my not being one hundred per cent fit makes no difference?'

Irene could have asserted that there'd been nothing last night to hint that he was anything but fine. She knew, though, that he required a solemn answer. 'Of course. If I thought it would work that way, I'd do everything in my power to convince you.'

'Have you faced the possibility of being widowed or, worse, tied to an invalid?'

Tears filling her eyes, she nodded. 'I've faced that – and know you've faced it for me . . . '

He raised an eyebrow. 'Giles?'

'Yes. When he believed I only wanted to opt out.'

'And what do you want, now?'

'To be with you, always, allowed to love you.'

He hugged her. 'I've so longed to give you something – myself, for all you've given me,' he said at last. 'It's been so hard holding anything back from you, my love.' He glanced at the clock. 'Let's get back.'

'Back?'

'To England, can't do anything here. If you agree, we could start packing now, I'll phone the airport.'

They left in a rush, as Richard suggested, and with only a hasty backward glance for Sorrento in its idyllic setting. All the way home he was busy with plans, checking now and again that Irene approved. By the time they touched down, she had agreed to his phoning Martin to inquire details of how you arranged a special licence. And to ask him if he could travel north with Daphne for another wedding, this time in Halifax.

'All this is incredible,' Richard had remarked as they flew over the English Channel and then the white cliffs. 'Lord, how I've changed! Used to think my horizons would always be those four walls.'

They stopped off in Halifax on Richard's suggestion. 'I know I don't have to ask your father's consent, but I do want them in the picture immediately, and to check that they can manage the date we have in mind.'

They had chosen the following Saturday week, neither of them wished to wait any longer than that, but they were trying to be sensible about arrangements which would have to be made. Irene wouldn't be wearing white, but planned on seeking a cream evening gown which could be some use afterwards. She was so thrilled that she was determined to have something more romantic than an afternoon dress or a costume. More than ever, she longed to look glamorous for Richard.

Her father had finished surgery when they arrived at the house in Parkinson Lane, and Mavis was there for the afternoon with Heather.

'What's up?' her mother asked Irene, coming out of the kitchen where she was finishing drying the lunchtime dishes. 'I thought you were in Italy. Weren't you enjoying yourselves?'

Irene all but choked. 'We were having a marvellous time, thanks.' Richard had insisted that he must announce their news, so she left it at that.

'What the heck's going on?' Mavis inquired, one eye on Heather who was running upstairs. After a hurried introduction to Richard, they had been turfed out of the room so that he could talk to her father.

'Richard wants a word with Dad, that's all. He's terribly old-fashioned, thinks he ought to ask for my hand or summat.'

'You're getting married at last!' her mother exclaimed, flinging the tea towel aside as she came to hug her. 'Ay, I'm that pleased, love!' .

'About time!' Mavis exclaimed, from the landing where she was retrieving her daughter. She descended in a rush, staggering slightly as Heather wriggled in her arms. As soon as she set the youngster on her feet, she embraced Irene. 'Seriously, old girl, I'm delighted. Can I be your matron of honour?'

Irene grinned. 'I suppose so – aye, of course! This has all happened so suddenly, we haven't got round to such things. I might be having Richard's sister an' all. Her husband's agreed to come up here and marry us. And I shall want Heather as my little bridesmaid.'

She began worrying in case Lily might feel left out if she wasn't asked to be an attendant as well, but she didn't want to overdo it, they weren't planning on a big wedding.

In the event, the service became much bigger than either Irene or Richard had anticipated. David, who was to be best man, had quietly informed all their regular clients of the time and place. When she entered St Paul's at her father's side, Irene was staggered.

'But I don't know anybody round here, these days,' she gasped. Beginning the walk through the rather stark church, she assumed that lots of folk had turned up to see their doctor's daughter married.

364

The ceremony was conducted by Martin with all the dignity and feeling that she could have wished. But it seemed only a short while before she and Richard were returning down the aisle. Irene was delighted that many of the smiling faces were from around North Fell.

'Just look how well-liked you are,' she whispered. And was glad to see how they had pleased him. Although she would long remember special moments − kneeling with Rich before the altar, the vows they had exchanged, his loving glance when placing on her finger the diamond eternity ring they'd chosen as a wedding band − she would treasure this as well. Rich needed this evidence of affection from his clients.

Greeting everyone outside the church ate into the time reserved for photographs, but Irene was determined no one who had travelled to Halifax for them should go away without knowing how much that was appreciated.

'If I'd have known, I'd have invited them all to the reception,' she told Richard in the car taking them to the White Swan hotel.

He grinned. 'Lucky for your father that you didn't know then!'

She smiled. 'I don't think he's hard put to it to pay for the reception, but I could have helped out, any road.'

Smiling back, he kissed her. 'You're a lovely woman, Irene.'

'Glad you've taken the plunge then?' she teased.

They both enjoyed the next few hours, relaxing completely with their families and friends. Richard's aunt, the one who only weeks ago had caused so much discomfort by pertinent questions, was quite elated.

'Proper foxed me, he did,' she confided to Irene, after giving them each a bristly kiss. 'I went away from our Daphne's wedding deeply upset because Richard thought he weren't up to getting wed. Or so he said. I can see now it were just to put me off the scent. And I couldn't be more thankful. I can see you're a sensible lass, you'll make sure he keeps as well as he's looking now.'

'You certainly don't seem to ail so much!' Irene exclaimed, much later in their room at the tiny hotel in Wharfedale where they were spending the night.

They had agreed mutually in the plane coming back to England that further lovemaking must wait until today. Having once made love, refraining had come all the harder, and neither of them was sorry that they'd planned to marry swiftly.

Richard had stopped her unpacking their overnight things, pulling her to him sharply, his kisses demanding but only half as urgent as the pressure of his hard body.

One hand traced the length of her spine while the other anchored her firmly against him. And as he stirred, she felt millions of tiny pulses answering within herself, willing her to respond, to go on responding for ever.

Her kisses grew more feverish, her sigh of passion incited his tongue to probe more deeply. And then they were on the bed, too hungry for each other to undress. Discarding the skirt of the suit she'd travelled in, Irene drew Richard to her. He'd unfastened his own buttons, contact with firm evidence of his love increased her own desire unbearably.

'Oh, Richard,' she gasped, and read amusement along with passion in his eyes before he bent his head to kiss her.

She had marvelled previously at the strength of his loving, today he seemed more forceful still, and yet more skilful. Despite the power of his need, he lingered, stirring within her, until her own yearning compelled him towards the long surge of delight that rippled repeatedly right through her being.

'I was such a fool not to marry you months ago, or even years,' he said at last.

Irene smiled. She had no worries now – and suspected that there'd be loving enough to compensate for any time of waiting.

21

Irene felt certain six weeks later that she was pregnant, and was delighted when her second visit to Giles Holroyd confirmed this. It was a Friday afternoon and she could hardly wait until Richard had finished in the office to tell him. He looked tired, though, as he often did at the end of the week, and somehow she kept the news to herself until he had relaxed during their evening meal.

They were having coffee in the sitting room while distant sounds of Mrs O'Connor clearing dishes into the kitchen made Irene reflect that, before long, she'd be even more thankful for help in the house. As Richard reached for a book, she took a deep breath. 'You haven't asked why I took this afternoon off . . .'

He shrugged. They'd agreed as soon as they married that Irene shouldn't work full time any longer. 'Shopping, I suppose.'

She shook her head. Richard didn't seem inclined towards guessing games, and she couldn't contain her excitement. 'I went to see Giles.'

'What's wrong, love?' He was frowning as he asked.

She smiled. 'Nothing. Darling, you're very naive if you can't begin to guess.'

'You mean . . . ?'

'Yes, I'm expecting.' But his frown didn't disappear. The smile she'd been anticipating didn't light his dark eyes.

'Oh.' Abruptly, Richard left his chair and went to stand gazing out over the twilit garden.

Irene slowly went to him, put a hand on his arm. 'You're not pleased.'

He sighed, said nothing. He'd known how much she had longed for a child. In normal circumstances, would have wanted nothing more than to ensure that her longing was granted swiftly.

'What is it, Rich?'

He was afraid all his misgivings would be in his eyes as he turned to her. How he wished he felt free to enjoy being as excited as she was. 'It'd be bad enough if you were left to cope on your own. But giving you the added responsibility of bringing up a child unaided . . .'

'You are being gloomy! You don't know that would happen.'

'Nor do you that it wouldn't.' He let her persuade him to sit down again, though he felt more like going off to think things through alone. Somehow, he must come to terms with having another person depend on him, a small person. But that would take time.

'I've been far too selfish, should have taken precautions.'

'No, Richard,' Irene contradicted. 'I wouldn't have agreed. I want this baby.'

'I know. You've had to wait too long already to become a mother.'

'Not just that. I want *this* child, darling, yours.'

Again, he heard his own sigh. An elbow on the chair arm, his chin on the hand, he stared into space, willed himself not to see Irene facing trouble. She wanted *his child*, for God's sake: if he'd only let it, this would become the most vital event of both their lives.

Irene came to sit on the arm of his chair. He began steeling himself not to draw her down on to his knee, not to hug her. He needed to think. He'd believed he was done with emotions that constantly battered each other. Would they never relent, must there always be this cloud over the things he'd love to have – this price that Irene might have to pay? He'd give anything to relinquish the perpetual need to protect her against his uncertain future.

'I'm sorry you're not pleased about this, Rich. I was thrilled. I – hoped you'd like a child.'

'Like? What's that got to do with it? Of course I'd like children, but the days are gone when I'd a right to whatever desire came into my mind. You can't have forgotten how things were at the end of last year?'

'You know I haven't – it's there, at the back of both our minds, always will be. Don't you see, it's partly because of that . . . '

'I don't see anything but you – with too much on your plate, if . . . '

'Darling, stop this,' she interrupted huskily, tears filling her eyes. 'I've faced all the possibilities, I've had to. It'd be bloody hard without you, but I am going to have something, some part of you. That would always keep me going, remind me how good we are together.'

At last, he smiled. 'Remind me of that, will you, when the worries return to come between me and the joy that children will bring.'

As her pregnancy progressed Irene realized that it might have been easier if she'd started the first baby before her mid-thirties. Although not greatly troubled by sickness, she did tire readily and suffered with ankles that were swollen and heavy.

'I don't want you to work much longer,' Richard told her. And Irene's agreement proved how drained she was feeling.

He did suggest one occasion, however, which pleased her tremendously. 'I've seen so little of your family with our marrying so quickly. I'd like to invite them all over here for a day, and it'd better be soon or you mightn't feel up to coping.'

They chose a Sunday in June and from the moment that she began telephoning to invite her folk, Irene felt elated. She recalled a time, only shortly after she'd first arrived at North Fell, when she had wished she could share her family with Richard. And now, just when his only sister had gone to live miles away, her original longing was coming to fruition.

The preparations seemed to fall into place quite easily. When she first had a chat with Mrs O'Connor she discovered that Richard had already suggested several of his favourite dishes as possibilities for lunch, and had indicated that tea might be taken in the garden if the day was warm.

'I haven't quite known what to say to you about him coming up wi' so many ideas,' the housekeeper admitted to Irene.

She simply laughed. It was so unlike Richard to wish to be involved in planning domestic details. 'He must have his way!' she exclaimed. 'And you're not to worry for a moment, Mrs O'Connor – select whatever you can manage most readily from his suggestions. So long as there's plenty to eat, and of your usual good cooking, neither our guests nor I will complain.'

On the day itself Irene was glad to leave all the catering to Mrs O'Connor and two of her nieces who had agreed to assist. Even when she awakened at seven, Irene noticed how hot it felt; by the time the first car with Ralph, Mavis, Norman, Lily and their children drew up, it had grown quite stifling.

'Isn't it a super day!' Mavis exclaimed. She had driven all the way and secretly had been suited to death because this was something neither Norman nor Lily could do. And she had passed Mum and Dad on the road just before they got to Skipton an' all. 'T'others are on their way,' she confided. 'We left 'em behind a good few miles back.'

Richard grinned. 'You're proud of yourself as a driver, aren't you, Mavis?' he remarked. 'And rightly so,' he added, in case she wasn't yet sure how to take everything he said.

She beamed up at him. 'I should think so, an' all. Look how long before me our Irene was driving. I had to do summat to catch up with her.'

Ralph was trying to restrain Heather by one arm to prevent her bounding off across the lawn. Grasping Richard's hand, he smiled. 'Nice to see you again, old chap. I gather from what Irene said over the phone that we'll maybe spend some time out of doors. It's to be hoped we do, if you value your home. Our Heather's been that excited all the way here she couldn't keep still. And I fear that she isn't going to improve . . . '

'That reminds me,' said his wife, glancing towards her sister. 'Where the lav, Irene love? She still wets when she gets worked up.'

'I'll show you, just hang on a tick.' Irene was taking Baby Donald so that Lily could more easily get out of the car. 'Come on in, all of you.'

'And how are you?' Mavis inquired as Heather skipped along at her side while they accompanied Irene up the steps and into the house. 'You're getting on a bit for a first, aren't you.'

'Thank you, Mavis,' said her sister dryly, but then she grinned. 'Aye, I have to agree, I am. And I do get pretty tired. But Richard's not going to allow me to work much longer. Though I have to confess I wonder how I'll fill my time then. There's a cloakroom along there,' she directed. 'We'll all be in the sitting room when you're ready.'

Irene turned then to usher in Ralph with Lily and Norman but again Richard was taking over and had them inside the room and occupying the chairs he'd indicated.

'Shall I take little Donald now?' Lily asked, recalling how soon she'd felt exhausted while she was carrying.

'No, he's fine just yet,' Irene responded, and wondered if her desire to hold on to the child was subconsciously connected with wishing Rich would accept the thought of their coming infant.

'So, you overtook Irene's parents then?' Richard remarked. He would be glad when they arrived. He felt he knew them rather better, and didn't have to make such a conscious effort to get along with them.

Ralph smiled. 'It's Mavis – she goes proper daft sometimes with that car. Not that her driving's unsafe, don't get me wrong. I'd soon tell her, I'd not have her endangering either herself or the kiddie. But she does love to show off.'

'And Dad's car's getting ancient now,' said Irene.

'I think he's past tearing along an' all,' Norman observed, with a grin. 'Specially when he isn't dashing off on an urgent call.'

Mavis appeared in the doorway and Heather launched herself past her, across the room, and on to her father's lap. Mavis groaned. 'I hope you're prepared. That you've shifted all your ornaments and anything else breakable out of reach of madam, here!'

'I certainly will do now,' her sister said, going to hand Baby Donald back to Lily.

'Here – give him here.' Norman took him instead. 'Lily had him flattening her lap all the way in the car, time I took over.'

Irene could see that her brother doted on his son, and was glad for them both. What a good marriage he and Lily were producing out of unprepossessing beginnings.

'How are you, Norman? These days, I never think to ask.'

'Very well, thanks, Irene. Haven't had to resort to tablets for ages. It's Lily keeps me on an even keel, and the little lad.'

'And how's work?'

He made a face. 'Not much different. They're talking now of getting more o' them new looms. Mind you, they run all right, we don't have many breakdowns with 'em. Happen old Dewhurst knew what he were doing, after all. Have to admit I'm allus eager to see production increased. The only trouble is he'll be reluctant to set on more folk to look after 'em.'

'I keep saying I'll have to go back weaving,' Lily began.

'And you know what I think to that idea,' her husband said firmly, though Irene could tell from Lily's dancing eyes that she'd only been teasing.

'You've got a beautiful place here,' Mavis said. 'I do like the colour of that hall.'

'So do I,' Irene agreed, 'I shall certainly protest if Rich ever wants the green of those walls changing.'

Her husband laughed, glancing first to Irene and then around all her family. 'You see how she's learning to dictate already. But maybe she's been weighing me up over the years.'

They heard a car in the drive and Irene, who had finished placing any precious items out of reach of tiny hands, went through with Richard towards the front door.

'You could have stayed where you were,' he said. 'I wanted to welcome them.'

She chuckled. 'And so you shall. But they are my mum and dad as well, you know!'

Richard grinned down at her as he opened the door. They went slowly down the steps and across to the car in time for Richard to open the passenger door.

'Thanks, love. Hallo, it's grand to see you again,' Elsie exclaimed as he helped her out of the car. 'I knew our Irene'd choose somebody with lovely manners. She always were very particular.'

Kissing her, Richard smiled again. 'Thank goodness you approve of me, so far! As you know, I've left it a bit late before being trained for any of this.'

'You'll do fine,' his mother-in-law confirmed, giving him a hug.

Irene and her father were standing side by side, too busy watching the encounter to greet each other. But then Richard hurried around the car bonnet to shake Donald's hand and Irene joined in asking how he was.

'Better ask your mother that one, she maintains I'm doing too much. I suspect the truth is that she feels like letting up herself. And that's not summat she'll ever do so long as I'm working.'

'Well, you were a bit slow off the mark today,' his wife put in.

'On the way here, you mean? Because our Mavis beat us to it! Much I care about that – if she wants to have that car guzzling down petrol that's her affair. Or Ralph's, he'll be the one as has the bills to pay.'

Irene was leading the way up to the front door, but Richard was content to linger, and she was glad to hear him checking that both her parents were really in good health. I'm pleased I married him, she thought again, he's going to be one of the best things that happened to our family. Norman was a good son, but he'd caused them anxiety in the past, they needed another man around who would be concerned for them. And she'd never been quite certain what her parents thought of Ralph.

Now that everyone was together there was no break in the conversation and Irene settled back into her chair, watching how Richard seemed to be integrating with them, arguing a point now and then with both Norman and Ralph, yet listening to their views. What amused her most was the way he was with Mavis.

Her sister had been obsessed with Ralph for so long that Irene had virtually forgotten what an overt flirt she was. And here she was now, fluttering her long eyelashes and widening those grey eyes at Rich while she gazed at him as if his word was law. And not just the product of a lawyer's clever tongue! There could be no doubting that he relished the admiration in her glance, which made Irene wonder if she'd have got him to the altar with a lot less hassle if she'd been more practised in the art of making sheep's eyes. Even Mavis's unpolished Yorkshire speech appeared to delight him, though Irene did detect an occasional amused glint in his dark eyes. But when Mavis finally said 'Ay, our Irene is lucky – you talk that posh!' Ralph decided his wife had been laying it on too thick.

'You're not supposed to make personal remarks,' he hissed.

It was too much for Irene, who went off to find Mrs O'Connor in order to have a good private smile without offending anyone.

'You're looking pleased with yourself, any road,' their housekeeper observed.

'We're certainly a mixed lot now,' she said. 'And no worse for it, don't get me wrong.'

'I'll bet it's doing Mr Hughes the power of good. Too quiet by half here, that's what it's allus been.'

'Well, you surely couldn't call it quiet today. But how's lunch coming along?'

'Give me ten minutes, will you? The table's been laid ages, so there's only the gravy to finish making and the

374

vegetables to dish up. I've got the girls doing that now, as you can see.'

Returning along the hall, Irene met Rich on his way to the dining room. 'Everything all right?' he asked. When she nodded he suggested she should remain with their guests. 'Somebody's got to entertain them, and I'm about to open up the wine. Thought we'd better offer white as well as red, not being quite sure of their tastes.'

Irene giggled. 'Don't know about Mavis and Ralph, since she's become better off, but I don't think even Mum and Dad often have wine with their Sunday dinner.'

'I don't suppose he'd drink a lot at any time, in case of being called out in an emergency. Anyway, it's nice to be able to provide whatever they might wish.'

'Aye, love, it is, you're looking after them proper champion. And there's one person who's very impressed already,' she teased.

'Your sister, you mean? She's definitely an appreciative young woman.' While Iris was out of the room Mavis had been ignoring Ralph's frown as she enthused on just about every item of her surroundings, climaxing with 'You have such lovely taste, Richard.'

High spirits predominated throughout the meal, leaving Irene wondering if she'd ever been uneasy about the way Rich might get on with her family. Afterwards, while they left Mrs O'Connor's nieces to clear away, Irene suggested everyone might wish to see the garden.

Feeling tired, she was happy to sit with her mother, and was glad when Lily came over to join them. Gradually, Ralph and Mavis appeared, followed by Norman and her father.

Looking rather anxious, Norman turned to Mavis. 'Your Heather's leading Richard a right dance. Keeps dashing off behind bushes and provoking him to catch her.'

'Aye, she has a lot of energy,' his sister said easily. 'She'll be ever so glad to have so much space to run about in.'

Shrieks could be heard from behind a row of screening conifers, and an occasional laugh from Rich. Wondering if she'd ever drop the habit of worrying in case he overdid things, Irene strolled away from the others until the pair were in sight.

Richard was haring across one corner of the lawn to where a bit of floral print frock betrayed Heather's hiding place. As he reached the laurel bush Heather giggled and he leaned down, picking her up and swirling her round before placing her on the ground beside his feet.

'Again, again, Uncle Rich,' she yelled and ran off in the opposite direction.

Once more he chased after her, and this time scooped her up to sit her astride a branch of the nearby tree. Steadying her with both hands he was saying, 'I've won now, you can't get away this time!' Watching, Irene could hardly tell which of them was enjoying the game more.

Suddenly, she thought of Rich as he'd been when she first brought him out into this garden, of the time before that when he'd remained incarcerated in his room. There seemed scarcely any resemblance between Richard then and this animated man, bounding around with her niece and brimming with vitality. And he loves kids, she realized, and felt the hairs at her nape tingling. She need not dwell for too long on his reluctance to allow himself to enjoy everything their life would offer.

For the rest of that day young Heather attached herself to her new uncle, and Irene noticed how that seemed to demolish any last traces of reserve between her folk and Richard. By the time they drove away that evening, they were all pressing them to visit Halifax frequently.

'And think on,' her mother told them, 'you can always stay a night or two, you might be glad of that, Irene, when you're nearer your time.'

As they returned indoors after waving them off, Richard turned to her. But before he could speak, Irene smiled up at him. 'Thanks a million!' she exclaimed. 'You were super, everybody loved you.'

He grinned, kissed her cheek. 'They're easy to like. We'll definitely have to see more of them.'

Some while later, as they went up to bed, he seemed pensive. 'When's that baby due?' he checked. 'We must make sure we have one of the cosier rooms ready as a nursery.'

By the time Irene was six months pregnant any occasional sickness that she'd experienced had abated. She felt enormous, though, and grew tired all too readily. Richard, however, was remarkably well and was, as she'd predicted, now bubbling over with enthusiasm for the coming infant. He astonished her, nevertheless, one day when they were looking around the room which would become the nursery.

'Let's do it ourselves,' he suggested, drawing her to his side. 'Decorate this room, it'd be such fun.'

Briefly, she thought of the hours he'd be busy instead of relaxing. But then she heard him groan, and knew he'd recognized her reservations. And here they were, expecting their first child, at an age when most folk take having a family for granted. She couldn't deny him anything involved in the experience.

'So long as you're prepared for me nagging you about resting as well – and if you feel too weary to finish the job, say so, for heaven's sake.'

The sheer joy in Richard's brown eyes when they were choosing wallpaper, paint and curtaining told her that agreeing had been the only possible course.

And she helped as well, trimming the edges off the wallpaper, then acting labourer to her ridiculously light-hearted husband. And when the room was decorated he looked on while she stowed away baby clothes which she had made or inherited from Lily. She began then to make the curtains.

It was a delicate, chintzy material with tiny flowers in autumnal shades. Rich had laughingly protested when she'd preferred a fabric smothered in pink roses. 'No son of mine's going to turn into a sissy through being surrounded by pretty-pretty things!'

'I promise I'll bear that in mind, if it's a boy.'

377

Rich had laughed again. 'It's not going to be, anyway, I've put in an order for a daughter.'

Irene was sitting at the machine, stitching away, one afternoon when she felt a twinge of pain. She dismissed it as cramp through sitting uncomfortably, it was difficult enough now to sit easily for long. She decided to wander upstairs to the nursery to have a look at the nearly completed curtains against the freshly papered walls.

Standing beside the window there, she felt another pain, and after a while a third. She began timing them, and acknowledged that her training had been asserting the real nature of their cause, despite her initial diagnosis of cramp. She'd brought enough babies into the world to have more than an idea of the symptoms. And she felt rather scared – this was only the seventh month.

She remained for a time, looking out over the garden, thinking, this is it, and remembering that Richard was in court that day. She wished to God he was in that office downstairs. And it was Mrs O'Connor's day off, she couldn't even turn to her for reassurance.

Methodically, she folded the curtains and popped them into a cupboard on top of a pile of nappies. The pains were well spaced, she'd have some long while to wait yet. The hospital, though, had been on at her about the risks involved in having a first baby at thirty-five, emphasizing that as soon as she suspected it was on its way she must be admitted.

She rang them from the hall, then tried to think what she might need to cram into her case. Unable to concentrate now, she shoved in a nightgown, washing things and a towel, and crossed towards the office door.

Anita came to her when she beckoned. 'I've got a feeling the baby's on its way,' Irene told her. 'Don't, whatever you do, disturb Richard in court. Even if I'm right, it's going to take ages. But if he's not back when you leave after work, phone him when you get home, will you? And tell him to have something to eat before he sets out for the hospital.'

Anita offered to come with her, but all Irene wanted was to make sure that Rich was kept in the picture. 'I'll be all right. I've ordered a taxi.' She didn't trust her own driving while she was in this condition.

By the time the taxi drew up at the hospital, she was having fierce, frequent pains – and wishing she hadn't stressed to Anita the lack of urgency. She wanted Richard there, couldn't bear the thought that he might not be contacted.

They examined her very swiftly, and hustled her straight towards the delivery room. Irene was puzzled, but heard one of the nurses whispering something about heartbeats. Her own pulse was strong enough, she'd noticed it pounding as her agitation increased: they didn't – surely, they didn't think something was wrong with her baby?

'What is it?' she asked, but they only trotted out instructions about breathing properly, about staying calm . . . As if she could. And they administered a pre-med; between that and the pains tearing her she couldn't form the words to ask, which made her feel even worse.

Irene awakened, sore and anxious, and was told that their daughter, whom they had decided to call Fiona, had been delivered by Caesarian section. She was just about hanging on to life, in an incubator. Although Irene had feared something like that, it took some facing. She desperately wanted Richard.

She was deeply ashamed later when she heard her own sobbing, but no one knew where he was. It was dark, the clock on the wall of her ward said four o'clock, which must mean early morning. And he hadn't arrived. Over and over again, she asked if they knew where he was, why he wasn't here, until they threatened to give her something to make her sleep if she didn't stop fretting.

Irene lay there, perspiring, a mass of pain, and watched the clock on the wall. Hour after hour the hands edged forwards, daylight began to show through the curtains, and still no Richard. She had stopped crying. She had to appear calm, they mustn't sedate her. She must stay awake to find out why – why he wasn't here with her.

379

When the day nurses came on duty, Irene decided the time had come for action. She couldn't go on lying there in that dreadful suspense. She called a nurse to her.

'Aren't you asleep yet? They said you ought to have a tablet . . .'

'No – no, don't give me anything. Just tell me – my husband, what's happened? You're keeping something from me, aren't you?'

Instinctively, the nurse frowned, shaking her head. And then she checked the reaction. 'Try not to worry, Mrs Hughes, you should be concentrating on getting your strength back. I'll just have a word with sister.'

She went out into the corridor, Irene could hear a distant murmured conversation, but not one word that might have identified what they were saying. It was the sister who came in afterwards. Standing beside the bed, she took Irene's hand, smoothed its dry skin. 'We didn't want to tell you till you were a bit stronger, love. We had a message while you were in theatre. I'm afraid your husband passed out at home, his doctor was called in. But he recovered consciousness, sends you all his love . . .'

They gave her an injection that knocked her out immediately. Hours later, when she surfaced again, the first thing she thought was about Richard being ill, that she didn't know how ill, and she'd got to find out. And then there was the baby, was she still holding on? How long had she herself been asleep, what had been happening? Was there anything else that they weren't telling her?

No one knew better than she did how doctors tend to tell their patients only what they believe they can cope with. How they keep back anything which might hinder their patient's progress. And Richard was ill . . .

Sister was no longer on duty, but Irene begged the staff nurse for a telephone.

'You're worrying about your husband, aren't you? And I'm sure you needn't.'

'You can't be sure, no one can. You don't know his history.'

The nurse was gazing at her, as if weighing her condition. 'I'll see what I can do about a phone.'

'Can you tell me if he is still at home, that he's not been taken into hospital?'

'So far as I know, he's just resting under the care of his own doctor. That he's been ordered bed rest.'

Until she could ring through to North Fell House, it seemed she would have to cling to that. And there were other questions, other anxieties, about Baby Fiona. She had been told the infant was extremely frail, would have to stay in the incubator for some time.

'Yes, but I want to see her. When can I?'

'Ay, love, that'll have to wait till you're starting to get over the Caesar – you're not up to being jolted along corridors in a wheelchair yet.'

They sedated her again, and even when she awakened Irene felt she was in a kind of torpor, unable to insist on seeing the baby or on anything. The round of being washed, examined and given unappetizing meals had begun, and seemed to drain the final dregs of her strength.

By the next day, however, they were able to confirm that someone had telephoned through from North Fell House, and Richard was still at home. They were saying he'd only fainted, that not having eaten all day had combined with the shock of her early admission to hospital. Irene wished she could believe that was all. But she herself was a bit stronger today, and insisted she was fit to be shown her child.

The nurse who assisted her into the wheelchair and then propelled her along the corridor was a Polish girl who spoke very little English, but her pale face was enhanced by a wide, sympathetic smile. 'She very small,' she kept repeating, clearly alarmed that Irene might be unprepared for how fragile the infant was.

And suddenly she was there, staring through the glass screen at the tiny morsel of humanity who had caused her so much pain, and Richard further anxiety. The nurse was still talking away, but if Irene had been able to understand the actual words their meaning still wouldn't really have

penetrated. She'd expected Fiona to be little, her birth
weight was about half the normal average, but she was
horrified by her colour. She had the dreadful blue tinge
which Irene had seen too often during her days as a doctor.
But while she watched, holding her breath, the baby
yawned, opened her eyes. They were too big for the tiny
face, but were that most beautiful shade of violet-blue
which she'd admired years ago in Heather's. And this was
the daughter Richard wanted. You've got to survive, Fiona,
she willed her. You've got to pull through.

Irene was overwhelmed by the powerful urge to hold
her, became obsessed with the thought that if she could
only hug the baby she might somehow transfer to her
enough strength to keep her alive. But all she could do
was sit slumped in that dratted wheelchair and ache,
physically – and mentally as well, because there was nothing she could do for her.

Strange fancies began plaguing her mind. This couldn't
really be happening, not her baby being so unhealthy on
top of hearing Richard was back in bed again. Maybe
they'd made a mistake, shown her somebody else's child.
And then the infant flung one scrawny arm sideways, as
if to show her the tag: *Baby Hughes*. The gorgeous eyes
opened once more, and somehow appeared darker. They
would turn brown, and wasn't there a marked resemblance
to Richard? *Oh, my little love . . .*

'You are distressing you,' the nurse declared. 'We go
now.'

'No, not yet.' Her own voice was hardly recognizable,
taut with emotion. God, but she'd never understood what
the precariousness of life did to people!

The nurse turned the chair, hurried her back to her own
ward.

If they hadn't let her phone home that day, she was
sure she'd have gone out of her mind. As it was, Richard
wasn't permitted to come to answer it, Giles had ordered
three days of complete rest. But she did get through to
the office and was assured by David that Richard wasn't
nearly so bad as they had feared. They were pretty sure

he'd suffered nothing worse than a blackout induced by anxiety.

Although relieved, Irene was also unsettled. She longed with all her heart to be at home. Unless she saw for herself how Rich was she wouldn't really believe it. The hospital, of course, wouldn't even discuss discharging her until she had fully recovered from the operation.

I'll just have to discipline myself to concentrating on keeping an eye on Fiona, she resolved. At least being taken to see the baby gave her days some point. And she was having visitors, her mother came over one afternoon, Mavis on the day following.

And then she glanced up from the *Daily Telegraph* one morning to see Giles Holroyd striding towards her bed.

'At last!' she exclaimed. 'Happen now I can get to the bottom of what's happened.'

But Giles didn't speak. The expected smile was absent from his face. He sat on the edge of the bed, reached for her hand as he cleared his throat.

'My dear, you've got to be very brave . . .'

22

'No.' The breath caught in her throat. It couldn't – *mustn't* be! Not Richard. Not that – she couldn't take it, not like this, nearly defeated already by pain and anxiety.

'No, no!' She heard herself screaming and couldn't check it. 'He's not – he can't be. I need him so much...' Sobbing now, she clung to Giles.

He was gripping her by the arms, all but shaking her, trying to make her heed him. But though his fingers were hurting he seemed a long way away, too far for her to reach through the bleakness that was the prospect of life without Richard.

'Irene, listen to me...'

She gave a shuddering sigh, and tried to quieten her sobs.

'Richard will be fine in another few days,' he told her steadily. 'We were only taking precautions.'

'He's not – he's not...?'

'He's very much alive, troubled by being unable to come to you. But, Irene, there is bad news, I'm afraid.'

'Go on...'

'I'm sorry, it's the baby. They can't do any more for her. She has nothing to fight with.'

She ought to have been more intensely distressed. Already, she sensed that she would yearn for this child throughout the rest of her own life. But she still had Rich, just now she couldn't feel anything beyond being so utterly thankful for that.

'I must go to her. Take me to her, please.'

When they reached the stark room Giles spoke with the nurse. Irene heard her: 'Does she know?' She didn't catch his reply, but was glad this was the cottage hospital where their own doctor was present. Fiona was no longer in the incubator. Only when Giles came to her again did she realize the significance of that. He told her gently.

'I'm very sorry, Irene, we're too late. While I came for you they were trying resuscitation – ' Gravely, he shook his head.

'I want to hold her.'

Giles placed Fiona in her arms, and walked away.

'Your father would have loved you,' she told the infant softly. She kissed the cool face, repeatedly, for Rich as well as herself. The tiny body seemed to be stiffening already beneath its enveloping blanket. Irene wished with all her heart that she knew nothing about the onslaught of death, that she hadn't any means of imagining what it would do to their baby. A part of her wanted to look beneath the blanket, to take into her heart a detailed picture of Fiona which would last for all time. Somehow, though, she knew that she must limit this experience or she'd crack. And she had to steady herself, and remain that way, to be ready to go home. But how she wished she could have seen her eyes again, how she had loved those eyes. She had waited so long to see this babe of hers.

She was hugging her to the soreness of her breasts when Giles eventually came back to them. 'This isn't good, not prolonging it like this,' he said gently. 'You'll have to steel yourself, my dear, to let her rest.'

One more kiss on an icy cheek, another on the top of her head. She felt downy hair beneath her lips and, looking, saw how dark the short fibres were. Richard's daughter. Irene wondered how she'd ever bear to tell him what she was like.

'She looks to be sleeping, at peace.' There was a catch in Giles Holroyd's voice, making Irene glance at him.

He looked old and worn, and she was sorry. He'd done so much for so long for Richard, seeing him through. And now it was beginning again, for her sake this time. Unless – she had been trained, all that time ago, trained to understand that death did occur, that it had to be faced. Giles would have to pass on the news about Fiona to

Richard, then he would be distressed, she couldn't give him the additional pain of her own heartache.

'You're right,' she said. 'You'd better take her now.' Time could do nothing for them, and she must get a grasp on her emotions.

'I'll be all right, you know,' she told Giles as they headed back to her ward. He would assure Rich of that. In private, she could cry her heart out, and all her regret about not getting there for the final goodbye which she knew couldn't really have helped Fiona. She'd be over the worst before they discharged her.

'You're young enough,' Giles reminded her before leaving. 'There'll be others.'

Irene shook her head. 'Never.'

'Tactless of me, I shouldn't have said that so soon. But there will, Irene, once you're stronger you'll . . . '

'No. Oh, no. It's not the dread of losing another baby. But you know what anxiety might do to Rich. I was beginning to forget how precarious our happiness is.'

After Giles had gone Irene sat beside her bed, thinking things through. She'd be years, if ever, before the image of her baby ceased to gnaw into her soul. But never again would she jeopardize Richard's life by longing for children. She was enough of a realist to know that, much as she doubted it right now, they could go back to the kind of life they enjoyed together. There was his work, she'd share it again, that could be immensely satisfying. They had other interests, books, music, they would walk again over the fells. She would ensure that he remained fit enough to cope with a full life. And now she must get better quickly so she could go home and begin on that.

Mrs O'Connor was on the steps, the front door open wide behind her, by the time the ambulance man helped Irene out on to the drive. Grimacing a little at the darts of pain from her inside, she walked slowly up the steps, as they turned the vehicle and drove off.

'Ay, bless you, Mrs Hughes, it's lovely to have you back.'

'Hallo, Mrs O'Connor. It's good to be home.' She prayed their housekeeper wouldn't mention Fiona. She felt emotional enough, didn't want to be in tears when she went in to Richard.

'Mr Hughes'll be that glad to have you back. He seems ever so well again now.'

'Where is he?'

'In the office, would you believe? I know – he's not supposed to go anywhere near. It's all right, he's not really working. I think he just couldn't keep away.'

Irene and Giles had decided to surprise Richard with her homecoming. Although he'd been up and about for days, he'd been advised by Giles to remain indoors. There was no physical reason. But since losing their baby the hospital had become associated with distress – *not* to be recommended as an aid to steady blood pressure.

Irene had grown resigned to not seeing him until she returned to North Fell House, and had wondered even if it might be better this way, allowing her time to begin to come to terms herself. Now, however, she couldn't wait a moment longer.

Hurrying much faster than she'd believed she could manage, she went towards the office door.

'Hallo everyone!' she said as soon as she saw them, and was pleased by how bright she made her voice.

'Darling!' Richard turned from David's desk, came at once to her side. 'No one said – I would have got a car to come and fetch you.'

'Wanted to surprise you.'

'You've certainly done that.' He was steering her away from the office towards his old room. Once alone there, he gathered her to him, kissing her lingeringly, then just holding her close.

'I'm so sorry,' he said at last, 'about Fiona, that you had to face all that alone.'

She wept at that, but it seemed not to matter. There was one thing, though, which must be said immediately. 'It's going to take some accepting.' She paused. 'But it could have been far worse.'

'Worse?' He held her a little away, his brown eyes bewildered as he searched her face.

'When Giles came to – to break it to me, I thought . . . Oh, God, I was so afraid it was you that I'd lost.'

Richard caught her to him again, let her cry while he stroked her hair, the nape of her neck.

Presently, Irene found a handkerchief, dried her eyes. 'I'm all right now. But how are you – really, I mean?'

'Feeling a fraud, only waiting for confirmation that I can go back to my usual working routine.'

'Oh, I am glad! This is just the tonic I need.'

Being together was what they both needed, but there was a certain restraint between them. On Irene's part, it was rooted in her determination not to tell Rich any detail about their baby's death. As she had suspected, Fiona's heart had failed, the post mortem had revealed a defect which, together with her being premature, had proved too much. When pressed, Giles had agreed that this wasn't the time for telling Richard.

And Rich, meanwhile, was uncomfortably aware that he'd been unable to provide Irene with support at the one time in her life when she'd been most in need. What was worse, he'd increased her burden by creating anxiety about himself. And somehow the fact that he'd merely passed out without being gravely ill made him feel worse still about the whole wretched business.

If only she'd talk to me about it, he thought, as days passed and she resolutely fielded all his efforts to share more fully the weight of bereavement. Even when they quietly left the tiny coffin in the fellside churchyard, there still seemed to be this barrier between him and whatever had occurred in that hospital.

But Richard had asked that he should see the baby before the coffin was sealed. No one had been able to disguise her colour, blue-tinged lips, and Giles had finally been compelled to face his questions.

'You told me her heart had failed, that she was too weak to survive,' he said grimly, drawing Giles aside when they arrived back at the house. 'Did you deliberately play down to me the extent of the heart problem?'

'Not really. It wasn't, after all, a defect which would necessarily prejudice the chances of a full-term infant.'

'And I was in no state for accepting unpleasant truths?'

Before Giles could reply to that they were joined by Mavis and Ralph who, together with all Irene's family, had come over to be with them. Realizing that this was no time to be digging out the truth, Rich let the matter rest, but it could not be forgotten.

Elsie and Donald Hainsworth were staying overnight. Initially Rich had been thankful, he knew Irene needed her own folk round her, and he wasn't sorry either to have them near. But now he was finding it difficult to think of anything but learning how badly affected his daughter's heart had been.

On the day after the funeral when his in-laws were lingering over breakfast, he followed Irene as she went up to their room. Quelling a sigh, he closed the door behind them.

'I don't want to upset you,' he began carefully. 'But there is something I have to know. About Fiona. How severe was her heart condition?'

When Irene hesitated, unsure how to reply, Richard sighed. 'I didn't get a straight answer from Giles either. Have you cooked this up between you?'

'Not really, it was only – well, you're weren't so good yourself and . . . '

She got no further. 'Just who is the man around here?' Richard shouted. 'Am I to be cushioned forever against everything!'

Turning swiftly, Irene winced. She was still sore, seemed today to be more conscious of the physical hurt. Happen because yesterday she'd resolved that she had to begin putting all other pain behind her.

'Oh, forget it,' said Richard. 'You're not up to this yet.'

'No, no – you're right. And I don't want this coming between us.'

'I saw Fiona, don't forget. The colour she was. But Giles fobbed me off, saying how weak she was.'

'Which was all too true. But though her heart was damaged, my darling, the flaw wasn't anything that could be traced back to you.'

It was all he needed to believe, but after days and days of being unable to learn the truth he couldn't trust what he was hearing. Irene read that in his eyes, tried again.

'It wasn't hereditary, Rich.'

'Then why keep quiet about it for so long?'

He took his anxiety away from her, out into the garden, walking swiftly, his shoes flattening the frosted grass.

His father-in-law watched from the dining room window, recognized trauma and went after him. Finding Richard staring woodenly over towards the snow-covered fells, he waited for a while before approaching.

He hadn't waited long enough for the tears to dry on Richard's cheeks. When he didn't move to dash them away, Donald recognized how deeply disturbed he was.

'Doctors!' Rich exclaimed grimly. 'Though since you're another of them I suppose I ought to bite my tongue. But Irene's holding out on me, I'm sure. "For my own good", no doubt, but I can't like her for it.'

'But you're all right, you don't have to go worrying. Only a bit of a scare, that was all you had.'

'I don't mean about myself.' Almost, he'd said 'don't *care*'. 'I want the truth about Fiona. How can I avoid thinking that she had this heart failure because of me?'

'By taking it from me that she didn't. It was a stroke you had, wasn't it. Haemorrhage into the tissue of the brain. The baby's problem was a hole in the heart. There's no connection whatever, Richard.'

'You're not . . . ?'

'Trying to protect you? Nay, I'm not. Why on earth should I? Irene's my eldest lass, remember. It's her I'm most concerned for, though I know I can rest easy in my mind that she'll be well looked after, once you've got this sorted out.'

'Thanks. Thanks.' Richard shook him by the hand, gripping fiercely. 'Sorry about the fuss. But I've had more than enough of being shielded.'

As the weather improved and trees filled with leaf and the garden with birdsong, Irene began to let go of the worst of her distress. Richard had agreed to her working with him again, and that helped a lot. They began going over to Halifax quite frequently at weekends, and also had other outings farther afield.

One Saturday early in September she came out of the kitchen as Richard was moving away from the telephone in the hall.

'Just had a word with Giles,' he told her, and waited for her to ask the reason.

'He must be pleased with you, surely?' Rich had been exceptionally well all summer.

'Don't know, didn't ask.' He put his arm around her shoulders and led her through to the sitting room. 'There are two of us, you know.' He motioned her to sit, but remained standing himself. 'I wanted to learn how soon you'd be fit, for starting another baby.'

Irene tried to check the shiver of apprehension. She glanced away, unable to meet his eyes. She thought of all those weary months of feeling unwell, of the anxiety over Fiona – the sickening loss, which even yet had scarcely eased. And she thought of the day that Richard simply hadn't arrived at the hospital, of the hours that seemed like months before she was told where he was. Rich might think he could endure all the worry again – if so, he was made of sterner stuff than ever she was.

Miserably, she shook her head. 'I – don't think so, Rich.'

His dark eyes were solemn when she finally met them. He sat on the chair arm, gently placed a hand at the back of her head so she continued looking at him. 'Please . . . '

Her eyes misted, she reached out and touched his hair. 'I wouldn't deny you anything else.'

'I know.' Presently, he sighed, moved away. 'Probably it's much too soon.'

They both knew that already it might not be soon enough. Irene couldn't bear to tell him that the time always would be wrong. And not because of any fear of losing another baby.

Although disturbed by her own refusal, Irene resolved that it shouldn't ruin their lives. There was their work, and they would continue to really use their leisure, ensuring that they enjoyed being together.

The following Christmas was the hardest time to bear, but she was aware by now of the strength of her own determination, and employed it to the full. Since they had the room they gathered all her family round them, and she schooled herself to discipline all emotions while she kept her nephew and niece amused. Mavis was pregnant again, and delighted; Irene willed herself to remember that she couldn't spend the rest of her life being oversensitive about every expectant mother.

After Christmas Daphne and Martin travelled north to be with them, and were so evidently happy with each other that Irene convinced herself that she and Rich needed nothing more.

The day he asked her again to bear his child all her composure was shattered. Grabbing her coat, she left him in the house, strode through the garden and headed for the fells. She followed a path they often walked together, felt the keen March breeze battering her face, gradually filling her lungs.

But the freshness and the sun seemed unable to get through to her. She felt so burdened with the heaviness in her heart. There was a new lamb bleating, and another, black-faced as their mothers, born tough to endure on these Yorkshire hills. Irene watched them for a moment, envying their placid acceptance of their circumstances. And then she walked on, climbing, gazing now and again towards the limestone crags, the snow lingering in their crevices.

In an unlikely bare-branched tree, birds were nest-building, chattering over their task, like housewives in a street. Farther away, their near neighbour whistled his dog, rounding up cattle for milking.

The way was steep, the grass slippery from earlier rain, and suddenly the fell was too daunting. She could no longer hurry. And she recognized then that she'd been running – running away. Standing quietly, she turned, looked again all around her. It still goes on, she thought. Until we try to stop it. Beyond the sheep, the trees, the farmer and his herd, was North Fell, its chimneys issuing smoke which soared and dispersed.

Time she got back. And told him her answer. It meant problems, struggling – against fear, risk, the danger of ending up alone. But the alternative was a kind of death, by avoiding life.

Mrs O'Connor was clattering around in the kitchen preparing a meal. Richard was in the office, the door ajar as he sorted through some papers. Tossing aside her coat, Irene ran upstairs.

Inhaling deeply, she opened the nursery door for the first time since it had happened. Somebody had taken down the cot, and put away all the baby things. She crossed to the cupboard and on top of the folded nappies were the curtains, as she had left them, unfinished.

She brushed a hand across her eyes, it was wet when she drew it away. 'You're an awful coward, Irene,' she said aloud, then ran downstairs with the curtains.

She was finishing the first hem when Richard walked in. She asked if he'd found what he was after in the office. While he was telling her he crossed to see what she was doing.

He ran the material through his fingers, the flowers fluttered as if in a breeze. Irene glanced up. He was almost smiling, had one eyebrow raised. She nodded, and he let the smile come.

She would remember that smile, cling to it, just in case . . .

After dinner that evening she went to pick up her sewing again, but Rich laid a hand on her arm, checking her. 'No more, not today.' He grinned. 'After all, nine months should give you time enough to finish them.'

She was surprised when he went to the cupboard for the chess set. Sitting opposite him, she watched while he laid out the pieces, his long fingers moving slowly yet precisely. She could tell he was thinking something through. The last pawn in place, he glanced across at her, smiled. 'You were the one who taught me that there has to be a time to let up – specially when problems have been faced.' Swivelling round the board, he said, 'You're white – first move's yours . . . '

Ruefully, Irene looked at him. 'Don't think I can give my mind to it.'

Richard laughed, startling her a bit. 'Nor I – never mind. Go on . . . '

He was the one who paused, though, after only half a dozen moves. Toying with her knight which he'd just captured, he spoke without looking up. 'Did I tell you I'm going to open up a second office in Skipton? I shall put David in charge of it, take on a youngster here – train him. It'll be great watching somebody develop over the years.' And would serve till their child was old enough to begin learning.